REDEMPTION LAKE

BY

Susan Clayton-Goldner

Tirgearr Publishing

Published by Tirgearr Publishing
Ireland
www.tirgearrpublishing.com

ISBN 978-1-910234-47-1

10 9 8 7 6 5 4 3 2 1

DEDICATION

This one is for you, David

ACKNOWLEDGEMENTS

It takes a village to write a novel. I'd like to thank my husband, Andreas, for his support and understanding of all the hours I spent in front of my computer; my children, Bonnie and David, for always believing in my dream; my family and friends; and especially Marjorie Reynolds, Martha Miller, Jane Sutherland, Susan Domingos, and the members of my Portland Critique Group for their endless readings and encouragement. In addition, I'd like to thank Jim Frey for showing me how to write a damn good novel and, as always, Tirgearr Publishing for taking a chance on me. Finally, a special thanks to Nichole Ferrari Hamm for my author photo.

"Man is not what he thinks he is—
he is what he hides."
- Andre Malraux

CHAPTER ONE

Tucson, Arizona – April 1989

More than anything, eighteen-year-old Matthew Garrison needed to believe in second chances. Trying to regain his composure, he paced the deck behind his best friend's house in Catalina, a small town in the Sonoran Desert about twelve miles north of Tucson. He needed someone to listen and tell him everything would be okay. The mauve cummerbund around his waist seemed to tighten.

The sun was setting and a sprinkling of rust, violet, and golden clouds gathered above the jagged peaks of the Catalina Mountains. A pale bruise-colored sky seeped through the Saguaros's giant arms. He wiped his palms on his pant legs. His starched tuxedo shirt made the back of his neck itch and he turned his head from one side to the other.

Through the sliding glass door, he saw Travis's mother standing in the middle of the kitchen, pivoting on her feet as if she were slow dancing. Crystal was a slender, curvy woman with big eyes, a small nose and full lips. She had a mass of curling blonde hair like her son. She wore her waitress uniform—a short denim skirt, red leather cowboy boots, a low-cut white blouse with a red bandanna tied round her neck. A bottle of beer swung like a pendulum between her thumb and forefinger.

He rapped on the glass, averting his gaze from the deep crevice between her full breasts.

She cocked her head as she opened the sliding glass door. Two black mascara streaks ran down her face.

1

"If it weren't for your outfit, I'd think you'd been to a funeral," he said. "Why are you so sad?"

She lowered her gaze for a moment. "Wait a minute. It's Saturday. Didn't your mother get married tonight at the fancy-pants Hacienda del Sol?" Picking up the edges of her skirt, she bent her knees in an exaggerated curtsy. A funny, subservient gesture that didn't match the sorrow on her face.

"Mom tied the knot. In spite of her dipshit son." He wondered if Crystal was sad because she hadn't been invited to the wedding— sad because she and Matt's mother were no longer friends.

He waited until her gaze met his. "Is Travis around?"

For a moment, she didn't respond. "Travis and Jennifer are dancing the night away. She turns into a pumpkin at midnight. Way I figure, Travis should be rolling in around 12:20."

Matt cuffed his forehead with the heel of his right hand. "The dance. I can't believe I forgot. Sorry to bother you, Mrs. Reynolds."

He turned to leave.

"I know your mother raised you to respect your elders, but I hate that Mrs. Reynolds crap."

Her words stopped him.

She threw her head back and laughed. "Call me Crystal. And by the way, you look downright gorgeous. Like Tom Cruise, except taller." Her gaze wandered over his tuxedo, then she lifted her hand, touched the front of his shirt and looked full into his face. "Gorgeous and tense as an Olympic sprinter before the gun goes off. I'm here for you, if you want to talk about it."

"I need to get going."

"Looks to me like you need a counselor." She handed him her beer and smiled. "Call me Dr. Phil."

It felt sort of weird to be drinking out of the same bottle as Crystal, but that didn't keep him from swilling what beer remained in one long swallow. When he stepped inside the kitchen, the air smelled like cigarette smoke.

She gently moved him aside so she could close the sliding glass door. "What's wrong, Mattie?"

Her use of the little boy name his mother used to call him

made his eyes water. He wiped his face with the back of his hand. He was both ashamed and really pissed off about the way he cried so easily. "I'm such a jerk." His voice sounded ragged. "I can't believe what I did." He paused, chased away the look of shock on his mother's face at the wedding. "I ruined the whole thing."

"You've come to the right place. I'm quite experienced at ruining things." She smiled at him then, a beautiful smile made with both her eyes and her mouth. It was a smile that came from her heart because she cared about him, and he knew it. A smile reminding him Crystal had always been an adult he could talk to.

Matt looked down at her cowboy boots and remembered the last time he'd seen Crystal and Travis together. They'd been fighting about her drinking and missing work. Travis had run out the back door and into the desert, Matt at his heels. "Sometimes I hate my life," Travis said. "Sometimes I wish my mother was friggin' dead."

It had surprised Matt, because Crystal and Travis's relationship had always amazed him. They were more like best friends than mother and son. They hung out together—at least, they used to before Travis met Jennifer.

Crystal had always accepted Travis. She never tried to change his internal landscape and make him into something he wasn't. Not that Travis needed remaking. He'd arrived on the planet with a little bit of everything—one of those rare kids; an honor student and a jock. Travis even tried out for Tony in *West Side Story*. With a little help from a black wig Crystal had slicked back and styled into a duck's ass, he got the part. Who knew the dude could sing?

"If Travis upset you, he didn't mean it."

"It's not Travis," she said, a slight tremble in her lower lip.

Matt didn't know what he'd do if she started to cry. "I should get going."

Crystal grabbed his arm and pulled him deeper into the kitchen.

"I don't want you to be late for work," he said.

She waitressed at The Silver Spur, a local steak house, and her slender arms were muscular from lifting trays of beer mugs. "I was supposed to work tonight, but I-I don't know, I just had to get out

3

of there. Gracie is covering for me." She tucked her hair behind her ears, exposing the gold cross earrings she always wore. "So how about a full bottle this time?"

He shook his head. "We'd better not."

With a nod, she gestured toward the kitchen table. "What's this *we* shit? I intend to have another beer and it looks like you could use one. Maybe a whole case." She headed to the refrigerator, a barely perceptible weave in her gait, grabbed two bottles of Pabst Blue Ribbon and glanced over at him. "You're almost as tall as your father. And you sound like him, too."

Matt slipped off his tuxedo jacket, draped it over the back of the chair and took a seat at the kitchen table. He unclipped his bow tie and cummerbund and stuffed them into the jacket pockets.

Crystal launched one of the beer bottles toward him, then flipped on the overhead fan. She settled, sideways, in the opposite chair. When she talked, her eyes sent out little sparks that made him feel like there was no one else in the world she'd rather be with.

"Now, what's this about you ruining the wedding?" She eased off the cap of her beer with a bottle opener that played the Arizona fight song. When Travis won a full-ride baseball scholarship, including a stipend to cover books and incidentals, the U of A recruiter had given Crystal and Travis shirts, hats, and jackets. She never wore any of them, but she sure loved that bottle opener.

Matt stared at the toes of his rented black shoes and thought about September—Travis going to the University of Arizona while Matt headed to either Iowa or Penn. How the two of them would be in different schools for the first time in their lives. How everything kept changing way too fast.

The refrigerator hummed steadily.

"It's okay, Matt. You can tell me."

"When Nate and Mom said their vows—tossing around the word 'forever' like it actually meant something—I kept thinking about my dad and the vows he and my mother made. And then I thought about Danni and how she broke us up for no good reason."

He hadn't meant for it to happen, but every dark aspect of his life had risen up at the wedding, demanding to be heard. There was no forever. Not for his parents. Not for him and Danni. Not for anyone.

Crystal sighed. "What did you do?"

"I kept hearing that word 'forever', and realizing it was meaningless crap. I didn't know I'd said 'bullshit' out loud until I saw the looks on their faces. My mom, who practically begged me to be part of the wedding, slapped me across the face and told me to leave." His mother had never once hit him before. Stunned, Matt had touched his cheek, felt the burn of her handprint rising. He looked around for an easy way out. Short of climbing over a six-foot stucco wall, there was none. He burst into tears, ran down the center aisle and outside, through the courtyard toward his car. The heat of a hundred disbelieving stares had followed him.

There was sadness in Crystal's eyes as she reached across the table to cover his hand with her own. Her fingernails were long, newly-manicured bright red, and her hand felt warm on top of his. "I'm sorry. I know what it feels like to put your foot in your mouth."

Matt said nothing. He wished he *had* put his foot in his mouth, or at least covered it with his hand to keep that horrible word inside.

"Tell me what happened with Danielle. I thought I'd be dancing at your wedding one of these days."

He shrugged, hesitated for a moment, then figured, what the hell. Crystal was the least judgmental person he'd ever known. "Her mother found this poem I'd written about how much I liked to touch her bare skin. She freaked out and told Danni to stop seeing me. Said she wouldn't have some sex-craved wannabe poet ruining her daughter's life."

Crystal removed her hand from his, raised her eyebrows and nodded, a slight smile on her face. "Personally, I have a soft spot for sex-craved poets." She lifted her beer bottle in a pretend toast.

He studied her wrist, small-boned and frail-looking. "After I screwed up the wedding, I stopped by Danni's house to talk, and found she'd hooked up with some football player from Tucson High." He couldn't believe how easily the words tumbled out of him. Usually when something bothered him, he'd write a poem that helped him understand what he felt. Poems he'd only shared with Danni and Travis.

"We've been together four years," he said. "I didn't think her mother…I thought we'd always—"

Crystal patted his hand. "I know exactly where you're coming from. Loving someone who breaks your heart hurts in ways you didn't know you could hurt."

"Who broke your heart?"

"My boyfriend of almost three years dumped me tonight." She stood, walked over to the refrigerator and grabbed two more beers. When she sat again, she pulled a cigarette from the pack on the table and put it in her mouth, but couldn't steady her hands enough to light it.

Matt struck a match and held it to the cigarette.

She drew in until it lit, then took a long draw and exhaled, the smoke rising above her in a thin white stream. She fluffed her hair with her fingertips, leaned forward and lowered her voice. "Let's go in the living room. These oak chairs are hard on the butt, even when you've got as much padding as I do." She patted the side of her slender hip.

In a different frame of mind, he would have given her the compliment she fished for and told her she looked great. But he remained silent. The beer slid, golden and cold, down his throat. He stood, pushed his chair under the table and followed her.

The night had grown cool, as the desert always did in late April, and she stoked the logs in the living room fireplace, flipped on the CD player, and they sat, side-by-side, on the sofa. She played love songs from the sixties, all of them slow.

For a while he closed his eyes and slumped back against the faded, red corduroy cushions—listening to the soft music and trying to lose himself.

When he finally opened his eyes, Crystal fixed him with a thoughtful and considering stare. "Come on. You can't fool me.

Something else is eating at you."

Ever since he was a little boy, he'd loved being around Crystal. She was as good at reading him as his mother had been. But unlike his mother, Karina, Crystal had no rules about eating only at the table, not jumping up and down on the beds, or having a pillow fight in the living room. Crystal hadn't cared if they wore their baseball caps through dinner or hadn't scrubbed every bit of dirt from under their fingernails. Remembering those childhood days, he felt a sudden loosening in his chest as if she had reached out and pulled a cord from somewhere deep inside him. "Last week, my father admitted he'd been lying to me. He did have an affair. The real reason my mother moved out." Matt ranted on about the way he'd defended his dad and chosen to live with him. About how much he'd hurt both his mom and younger sister.

Crystal listened but said nothing.

When they ran out of PBR, they started drinking bottles of Corona. And by the time he'd finished telling Crystal everything he needed to tell, he'd lost count of the number of beers he'd drunk and was crying again.

"If you stop expecting people to be perfect, you can start to love them for who they really are." She pulled him into her arms and rubbed his back. The wildflower smell of her perfume, as familiar as his own childhood, comforted him. "If you ask me, Matthew Garrison, you've got the world by its balls. You got accepted to all those good schools. Danielle's a fool not to see it."

Crystal let him go, slipped into the kitchen, and returned with more beer. She lit the candles on the coffee table.

Before he knew what happened, they were dancing to Bobby Vinton singing *Blue Velvet*, Crystal's warm cheek nestled in his neck. He felt the blades of her narrow shoulders, the thin cotton fabric over her breasts, the dot of each nipple as it pressed against his chest.

"You're a hell of a good dancer." She threw her head back and laughed. "Much better than the last time."

He thought about the way she'd taught him and Travis to slow dance, just in time for their sixth grade party. "I owe it all to you."

7

Matt laughed, too, a high-pitched, fake sound, then bent from the waist in an exaggerated bow. Though it wasn't even 9pm, he was dizzy from the beer, had never drunk so much before, and his head swirled, temples drumming to the slow and steady beat of the music. The candles seemed to float inside his eyelids like small full moons.

She undid the top two buttons of his shirt, then removed his cufflinks and studied them for a moment, flat silver squares with a raised initial 'M' in the center. "Travis got the plain ones. Your mother always did have a lot of class," she said, as she tucked them into his pocket and rolled up his sleeves. She ran her fingertips over his forearm to the small blue veins in the crook of his elbow. Then she unbuttoned the rest of his shirt, slipped it from his shoulders and dropped it onto the chair. It drifted down, draping itself over the arm of the scuffed, leather recliner like the wings of a huge white bird.

As if she pulled him by a string, he stepped forward, wrapped his arms around her and kissed her hard on the lips. He tasted the cigarettes and beer on her tongue, mixed with something minty like toothpaste. He dropped his hands to her waist, her body narrowing between his palms, like a slender and graceful vase. Blood pounded in his ears. This was his best friend's mother.

Stunned by his desire, the thought that he was doing something very wrong flickered for an instant before he pushed all thoughts aside. The scent of her perfume mingled with the beer and his dizziness, and when she took him by the hand and led him back to the sofa, he followed.

CHAPTER TWO

When it was over, the taut quivering strings inside Matt loosened. "I'm sorry," he slurred. "I never thought… well…I just never thought." Though he lay flat on his back, he felt as if he were on a yacht in the ocean, reeling from side to side. He tried to sit up, grabbed one of the cushions as the room spun in circles around him. Finally, he closed his eyes and lowered his head.

Crystal lifted his chin. "We both needed a little comfort tonight." She touched his cheek. "Nobody got hurt here."

He opened his eyes. "I…I…don't know. What about Travis?"

The look on her face went from tender to horrified. She leapt up from the sofa, then pulled on her blouse, carefully buttoning it all the way up. She slipped into her denim skirt, tugged at the hem as if trying to lengthen it. "I feel so ugly right now."

"You're not…you're not…" Though he hadn't intended to, he giggled, unable to make the word "ugly" come out of his mouth. He wanted to tell her all his and Travis's friends thought she was hot and totally funny. "You should…I mean you will probably… maybe…get married again." His tongue seemed to trip over his words.

She smiled sadly. "I can't see Travis with Baxter for his stepfather."

Thomas Baxter, an aging ex-boxer with a crush on Crystal, owned The Silver Spur and was her boss. He parted his few long strands of black hair just above his left ear and combed them across the top of his head in an attempt to hide the baldness. Travis had nicknamed him Barcode.

9

"If he made you happily—I mean happy, Travis would accept him. I know he would."

"The way you've accepted Nate?"

Matt said nothing.

"Baxter used to make me laugh. But now he's got long-term plans, follows me around like a lovesick teenager. I don't know what I ever—"

"Travis and I, we've always been straight with each other." He pleaded for her to understand. He awkwardly pulled on his underwear, losing his balance each time he tried to stand on one leg. Finally, he sat on the edge of the sofa.

She jerked a cigarette from the drawer in the coffee table. "You don't get it, do you? Travis won't blame you. I'm the one he'll be angry with. Ever since he got involved with Jennifer and her crazy religion, he's been a different kid. The Church of the Narrow Way. What the hell kind of a name is that?"

"He's a teenager," Matt said, trying hard to make his mouth form the words. "He...I mean, he probably just goes there to spend more time with Jennifer."

Crystal shook her head. "We had a big fight about it last night. Travis said if I forced him to choose between me and that church, he'd choose them." She shook her head. "I'm surprised Jennifer's parents even let her go to Marana's spring dance. I wish they'd put her in a Christian school where Travis would never have met her." She paused, started again. "He blames my lack of faith for everything—even the fact my two sisters won't speak to me and that his father died. Like if I'd only gone to that church, the whole damn Vietnam War would never have happened. Believe me, Travis will hate me forever if you tell him."

Matt wanted to reassure her Travis could never hate her, but he didn't have the clarity of thought. After a sharp pain that made the contents of his stomach rise, he rushed into the bathroom and vomited, then rinsed out his mouth, washed his hands and returned to the living room.

"You'll feel better now," she said, then took a long draw on her cigarette. She looked away from him when she exhaled. "I've got a lot of problems these days. Decisions to make. Things you and Travis don't know about." She grabbed his forearm. "Promise you won't add this to them."

Matt lowered his head. He felt so sick he wasn't sure how much longer he could sit up. "I can't," he mumbled. "I mean...I've never lied to him."

Crystal's eyes flashed. "This is my life. Understand me? This is none of Travis's business."

Travis would be horrified by what they'd done. He'd feel betrayed by both of them. Matt thought about his own mother and knew exactly how he'd feel if Travis had sex with her. Disgusted.

"I have to go now. My dad...my dad will be worried."

"I can't let you do that." She snuffed her cigarette out in the ashtray. "Your dad wouldn't want me to."

"Why the hell not?"

"Think about it. You're eighteen, not even old enough to drink, let alone drive drunk. What kind of mother do you think I am?" She put her hand to her mouth for an instant, then let it drop by her side. "Besides, if the police stop you, I could get in trouble for providing the beer." She glanced away.

When she looked at him again, her eyes were filled with tears. "Sleep it off in my bed. Travis won't even know you were here. I'll wake you in a couple hours. Then you can go home and pretend like you dreamed the whole damn thing. Pretend it never really happened. But please, I'm begging you. Don't get all righteous and tell Travis."

She picked up his tuxedo pants, the shirt he'd draped over the recliner, then shoved him toward her bedroom and pushed him onto her bed. After placing his clothing on the chair beside her window, she took off his shoes and socks, tucked them beneath the chair. When she left the room, she pulled the door partially closed behind her.

A moment later, he heard the refrigerator open, the sound of a cap popping off a bottle. Another chorus of the Arizona fight song.

For the next hour and a half, he drifted in and out of sleep.

Cradled by the night sounds of the desert outside the open window, each time a memory emerged, his thoughts thickened and folded back into sleep. At one point, he heard water running for a bath. A little later, he heard a car outside. *Oh God, please don't let it be Travis.* He stumbled to the window and opened the curtains. In the street, two long rectangular taillights moved away, turning south onto Oracle Road.

Matt leaned against the wall, staring at the sunflower sheets on Crystal's bed. The same bed he and Travis had jumped up and down on when they were eight. The digital clock read 10:38pm. His head throbbed. He needed to close his eyes. Crystal would wake him in time to leave before Travis got home. He fell back onto the bed.

When he woke up again, the room was very dark. He wore only his boxers and a white T-shirt his mother had insisted upon—claiming his usual dark one would show through his tuxedo shirt. As if the color of his T-shirt could ruin her perfect wedding. But he'd been ingenious and found another way to ruin things for his mother. He turned toward the empty space beside him. It took a few moments for him to realize where he was. He closed his eyes, shook his aching head to clear it. Crystal was his best friend's mother. What the hell was he doing in her bed?

He thought he heard the sound of the front door open, then close again. *Oh God, please don't let it be Travis.* His eyes adjusted to the darkness. One event at a time, he remembered everything.

Fully awake now, he shot from the bed, rocking for a few seconds before he achieved balance, then hurried to the window. The moon hung over the mountaintop, its light silver and unforgiving. Crystal's driveway was empty. Whoever he'd heard, it wasn't Travis. On the other side of the street, an engine started. This time the taillights were round. Definitely not Crystal's Escort. The car turned north on Oracle Road.

Matt let out the breath he'd been holding and glanced at the digital clock—its red letters told him it was 11:20pm. He needed to get dressed and leave. The dance ended in forty minutes and Travis would head home. He grabbed his tuxedo pants and shirt from the chair. His hands shook so hard he could barely work the fly and the button on his trousers. He slipped into his shirt, then sat on the edge of the bed. As if he had the flu, his head throbbed and his stomach felt queasy.

He rushed down the hallway toward the bathroom. And when he did, he saw the puddle of blood on the floor beside the bathtub. He hurried across the room, jerked open the pale green shower curtain.

Crystal lay naked in a bathtub filled with blood-colored water. Her hair, her beautiful blonde curls, had been chopped off, shorter in some places than others, as if a small child had done it. Some of the curls were floating on top of the water.

For a strange moment, everything remained calm and slow.

Her head was propped against one of those blow-up pillows attached to the back of the tub with suction cups. The tint of her skin was pale and slightly blue. Crystal's eyes were open and staring straight ahead—looking at something he couldn't see. Blood splattered the white tiles that surrounded the tub. It dripped down them like wet paint. One of her hands flopped over the side of the tub. A single thick drop fell from her index finger into the crimson pond congealing on the linoleum floor. It covered her neck and shoulders. Tiny bubbles of frothy blood still oozed from the gash in her neck.

An empty Smirnoff bottle sat in a puddle of blood on the tub's rim, beside a straight-edged razor blade.

The bathroom was so quiet. Nothing but the sound of his own breathing. He clenched and unclenched his hands. His body grew numb. "Oh no. Oh God, no," he said, the words thickening in the air in front of him. His head filled with strange sounds—the drone of insects humming, violinists tuning their strings. "What have I done?"

The contents of his stomach rose. He crouched in front of the toilet and heaved until nothing more came up. Then he started to rock, back and forth, muttering what he already knew was a useless prayer. *Please, just let her be okay.* He said it over and over like an unstoppable mantra. If only he could keep saying the words, maybe he could reverse this unthinkable thing.

Maybe she was still alive. He straightened up and stepped over to the bathtub to check Crystal's neck for a pulse. As he bent closer, he smelled the metallic scent of her blood as it mixed with her perfume and the stale, metabolized smell of alcohol seeping through her skin. He placed two fingers on her neck, searching for her carotid and pressed. His fingers slipped into the gaping hole. It felt wet and warm. He screamed and jerked them out. They were covered in blood.

He swiped his hand on the front of his shirt, then checked the other side of her neck for a pulse. *Please, just let her be okay.* Nothing. He shook her by the shoulders, then tried again. Still no pulse. At that moment, he stopped his mantra.

Though he knew she was dead, he held her hand—soft and still warm. It belonged to Crystal, who'd taught him to line dance, who liked hot buttered popcorn with cheddar cheese grated on top. Crystal, who was sometimes irresponsible and drank way too much. Crystal, who'd cheered for him at bat in Little League, cheered just as loud as she had for her own son. Crystal, who'd always be sitting in a bathtub of blood. "I'm sorry." He squeezed her hand, then let go. "And I swear to you, Travis will never know what happened between us."

Struggling to his feet, he headed for the kitchen phone to call 911. Halfway to the bathroom door, he stopped. Blood smeared the front of his white shirt. And there was still blood on both his hands, drying beneath his fingernails. His body was slick with fear. He smelled it, tasted it, and felt it coming out of his pores like sweat. His mind told him to call the police, to tell the truth. His heart told him to keep his promise to Crystal. It was the last thing she'd ever ask of him.

He dropped his chin and stared at his shirt. Holy shit. If anyone saw him like this, they'd think he'd killed Crystal. The thought stopped him. Had he? Was he capable of doing something so heinous?

The bubble of panic in his throat got bigger. He hurried across the bathroom to wash his hands. There were more clumps of hair in the sink and a hardened blue streak of toothpaste. He used toilet paper to pick up the hair clumps and dropped them into the trashcan. Looking at the uncapped tube beside Crystal's toothbrush, he felt as if something had been cut out of his chest. He grabbed the sides of the sink, stared at himself in the mirror. The face staring back resembled no one he'd ever seen before. Was it the face of a murderer? Had he just pushed someone else to her death? He shook his head—breathing in short gasps, like a swimmer gearing up for a plunge. His lungs burned as if he were being swept away by a strong current.

When the memory of his cousin's death surfaced, as it often did, Matt used his fists to hammer the stranger's face he saw reflected in the medicine cabinet. The mirror fractured, sending out long cracks in every direction. The face split into interlocking parts like an abstract puzzle. One jagged sliver fell into the sink, breaking in half. It left a black and empty space in what had once been the mirror.

He held onto the sides of the sink again and rocked slowly in front of it, still staring at the blood on his hands and under his fingernails. "You're all right," he said, but could barely hear the words, the sounds inside his head were so loud.

In his mind, he saw himself letting go of the sink and getting as far away from this nightmare as possible. But it would destroy Travis to come home and find his mother like this. Matt had to intercept him.

He washed his hands, then rinsed the blood from the sides and bowl of the sink, recapped the toothpaste and tucked it into the medicine cabinet. He wrapped the shards of mirror in toilet tissue, careful to avoid getting his fingerprints on the glass, and placed them in the trashcan, jagged sides down. There were no towels in the bathroom, so he wiped his wet hands on his pant legs. Panic rolled in, sucked him under.

What should he do? Call the police? His father? 911? If he did, there'd be a recording of his voice and he'd have a lot of explaining to do. The police often suspected 911 callers. They might take his DNA. What if they found semen inside of Crystal? What if they matched it to Matt's DNA? If that happened, they'd know. It would be in the newspapers. It would hurt Travis. He couldn't let that happen.

He hurried back into Crystal's bedroom. Hands shaking, he sat on the edge of her bed and put on his socks and shoes. Then, as if he were someone else, running through an obstacle course, he went into the kitchen and gathered the empty beer bottles. He took them out into the garage and carefully placed them in their cardboard carriers. Next, he wiped the kitchen table, closed the open drawers, loaded the dishwasher, emptied the ashtrays, then made Crystal's bed with fresh sheets. He tossed the sunflower sheets into the washing machine and started the cycle, careful to wipe his prints from the lid and dial. With the same cloth, he wiped down the edge of the plastic shower curtain, then pulled it closed—the way he'd found it. For the most part, his fingerprints were easily explained. He'd spent almost as much time in Travis's house as his own.

Matt stood in front of the coffee table. He heard the candles guttering, smelled the wax melting. He blew them out, then picked up the clothes Crystal had discarded in the hallway beside the bathroom door. Folding them neatly, he then placed them on the chair beside her window. He grabbed her red cowboy boots from the living room and set them beneath the chair. It was the least he could do for Travis.

The clock on the stove read 11:45 p.m. The Narrow Way didn't allow opposite sex teenagers to spend unsupervised time together. Jennifer's parents would pick her up from the dance. That meant Travis would be leaving for home soon.

If Matt hurried, he could intercept him, convince him to spend the night with Matt and his dad. He raced into Travis's bedroom, jerked open the drawer where he kept his T-shirts. Surely he had a plain black or a dark blue one somewhere. Matt lifted the stacks of folded shirts until he found one, then ripped off the tuxedo and stained T-shirt, slipped Travis's shirt over his head, then grabbed his jacket from the kitchen chair and hurried outside.

On the back deck, insects clustered around the light fixture, high-pitched, insistent and frantic. The sound reminded him of Crystal's voice when she'd pleaded with him not to tell Travis. Why hadn't he agreed?

In the carport, Matt unlocked the trunk of his Mustang, a restored nineteen sixty-seven Grande that had been his mom's first car, and dropped both the jacket and the bloodstained shirt inside. Silence ballooned into the night air around him, a strange silence with a ticking heartbeat. Then he remembered the cufflinks. Crystal had tucked them into his shirt pocket. He checked. They weren't there. He plunged his hands into his pants pockets and then the tuxedo jacket. No cufflinks. He didn't have time to go back inside. He had to stop Travis from coming home.

When he climbed into the front seat, he looked out through the windshield, but the dome light inside the car and the darkness outside had changed the glass into a mirror. He turned away. His face was the last thing he wanted to see.

CHAPTER THREE

Detective Winston Radhauser played the song, *For The Good Times*, over and over on his wife's old upright piano, the way he'd done every night for a solid year. He played until everything inside him collapsed—played until his shoulders slumped and his arms rested on the keyboard. He dropped his throbbing head onto his forearms and closed his eyes. Tonight, he was remembering their first date and the way it felt to hold her in his arms on the wooden dance floor. One dance, one song, and it was as if they'd been dancing together their entire lives.

The telephone rang. His eyes shot open.

The Pima County Sheriff's Department dispatcher reported paramedics, responding to a 911 report of an injury, had found a dead woman in a bathtub out in Catalina. No sign of forced entry or struggle. Most likely a suicide, but the two deputies at the scene had requested investigative backup.

"Can you go out there?" Lottie asked.

He looked at the photo of Laura and Lucas he'd unpacked an hour ago and set on the piano top between two lit candles. It had been taken under their blue spruce tree, the Christmas before the accident. Laura had been thirty-two years old and Lucas thirteen. "This isn't a good night for me, Lottie."

"I know," she said quietly. "I haven't forgotten what today is, but none of the other investigators are answering their phones. I'm sure they'll blame it on the power outage. It's hit half of the county, but right now you're the only one I can reach. I'm really, really sorry, Wind."

He sighed, knowing it was the job that had kept him as sane

as he was—which wasn't saying much. "All right, give me the address." He jotted down the location.

"Should I try to contact Crenshaw?" Lottie asked.

He thought of the Pima County Medical Examiner with his round body and slightly yellowish skin. They called him Melon behind his back. Radhauser was glad he'd earned *his* nickname because he ran faster than any other runner on the high school track team. He got teased about it occasionally, a little bathroom humor, but at least it wasn't because he looked like a cantaloupe.

"Wind? Are you still there?"

"Unfortunately," he said.

"What about Crenshaw?"

"Melon is a pain in the ass and thinks every dead body is his own personal property. I'll phone him after I check things out."

"You know the policy," Lottie said. "And you know how he gets."

"He'll be pissed. So what's new? I'd rather have Officer O'Donnell out there first, if you can get a hold of him."

Radhauser had worked a murder case with Tim O'Donnell over a year ago, and found him to be a damn good investigator.

"I'll do what I can," Lottie said. "And, Wind, I wish I could say something that would—"

"Yeah, I know. Thanks, Lottie."

He glanced at the photo again, blew out the candles and hung up the telephone. He slipped on his favorite bolo. It had a large turquoise slide attached to a black leather band, with tooled silver tips on both ends. He grabbed his western-cut jacket. Though he'd never told anyone, he dressed in western garb for his son, for the boy who'd wanted to be a rodeo cowboy. He touched the silver belt buckle that had been Lucas's most prized possession. Just weeks before he died, Lucas took first place in the junior calf-roping event at the annual youth rodeo in Florence.

He grabbed the steel gray Stetson Laura had given him that Christmas, four months before the car accident. He measured everything that way now. One week after the accident he'd packed away their photographs because he couldn't do anything but look at them. Five months after the accident he'd sold their house and moved into an apartment. Seven months from the day of their funeral, Lucas would have turned fourteen. Radhauser supposed he was destined to measure time that way; first the days, then the weeks and the months. And finally, one year after another.

He sighed, picked up the camera bag where he kept his 35mm Canon, slung the strap over his shoulder, locked his studio apartment and headed for the parking lot. The late night air was cool, the sky dotted with stars and a moon hanging white and full.

Once he'd passed Oro Valley and the new El Conquistador Resort, Radhauser drove fast on the empty two-lane road. To be safe, he flipped on the switch that turned his headlights into strobes. Ten minutes later, he arrived at the scene. The house sat on a dirt cul-de-sac, with a scattering of others, a few miles north of Catalina State Park. It was lit up like one of those porcelain shops in the Christmas village Laura had set up each year—every window glowing with yellow light. No power outage here.

An ambulance from Catalina Search and Rescue blocked the driveway, its dome light swirling, casting red and blue shadows on the white landscaping stones on either side of the walkway. Inside the ambulance cab, a paramedic he didn't recognize talked into a radio.

Radhauser parked his Ford Bronco on the street behind the patrol car, grabbed his camera and headed toward the house, just as two deputies stepped into the yard. They wore the Sheriff Department's brown pants and brown short-sleeved shirt with its gold and blue deputy patch. Hastings and Mudrow introduced themselves.

Hastings updated Radhauser on what they'd found upon arrival, stated they'd determined the victim was deceased, done a security sweep, and secured the scene by taping off the bathroom entrance. "We saw nothing to indicate anyone had broken into the house. No sign of any struggle. Nothing much out of place. But there's a straight-edged razorblade beside the body. I've never seen anyone use one on their neck before, but I guess it's possible," Mudrow said.

"Who called 911?"

"A woman. But she didn't leave her name. The front door was unlocked. No one around when we got here. So, we called for backup."

Radhauser nodded his approval. He preferred a uniform make his mistakes on the side of being too cautious, even if it did mean a middle of the night trip to Catalina. "I'll take it from here." He made a mental note to have the phone call traced.

Radhauser snapped a few photos of the outside of the house in relationship to its neighbors, overviews for the big picture, then headed inside. His process was to inch through the house, open drawers and closets, learn what he could and get a feel for the victim's life, before focusing on the actual scene of death. It looked like a rental house; white walls, dark but neutral carpet, and those cheap plastic window blinds they sell at K-mart. It had only one bathroom that opened into the hallway between its two bedrooms.

"She's in the bathroom. Down the hall, second door on the right," a clean-shaven paramedic said. "I left the shower curtain open. Better prepare yourself. It's not pretty."

"Was it closed when you got here?"

The paramedic nodded.

Radhauser put on a pair of latex gloves and shoe covers, then walked down the hallway, paying attention to the walls and carpet. He took a quick look in the bathroom without disturbing the yellow crime scene tape. He'd investigated some gruesome scenes, but this one hit him hard. The bathroom smelled like excrement and lavender bubble bath. The victim was small with blonde curly hair that looked as if it had been hacked off with hedge clippers.

When he stepped back into the living room, the paramedic was stuffing a stethoscope and blood pressure cuff into the bag that held his gear. He closed the zipper. "We just got another call down in Oro Valley. Sounds like gallstones."

Radhauser told him to go ahead, O'Donnell was on his way and when they were finished, they'd call the Medical Examiner to transport the body. "You figure she lives alone?"

"She's got a kid," the paramedic said, his voice tight. "From the looks of the other bedroom, a high school boy who's smart and good at sports." He wheeled around and headed out the front door.

* * *

Matt parked his Mustang in the Marana High School lot, then paced up and down the rows of cars, searching for Crystal's 1981 Escort. When he found it, he perched on the hood. There were big pockets of unspilled tears behind his eyes. His throat ached. And he was about to see Travis, still innocent of any knowledge of his mother's death.

Innocent. How long had it been since Matt felt innocent? He longed to go back to that summer before his cousin, Justin, died. When the three of them had made themselves blood brothers, then spent hours developing a secret handshake—linked fingers, knuckles tapped three times against the forehead, a left elbow grip followed by two handclasps and a high five—a routine so complicated no one would ever be able to copy it. With stars trembling in the black sky above them, Matt had believed their magic worked and they would be joined, like three brothers, forever.

But he'd destroyed that dream.

Until tonight, losing Travis's friendship had been Matt's greatest fear. Now there were much bigger things to worry about. He couldn't imagine what would happen to Travis without his mother. His father was dead. Travis was only seventeen. The state might put him in a foster home.

Matt tried to focus only on Travis, but other fears kept rising. The police might suspect Matt had been there. They might even discover he'd had sex with Crystal. How could he face Travis? He shook his head, trying to clear his mind. He wondered for one second if it could be a suicide, then dismissed the thought. No way Crystal would take her own life. Someone murdered her, but he couldn't imagine who or why.

A horn beeped. He opened his eyes and braced himself against the windshield of the Escort, holding himself tight. Travis would be coming out soon. Stay calm. Matt wanted things to appear normal for as long as possible, wanted to keep the remaining threads of brotherhood from unraveling. A short string of vehicles lined up around the circular entrance to the school. Strict parents, like Jennifer's, picking up their kids. He spotted Travis bouncing along as if he had springs instead of joints in his knees. He wore a white dinner jacket with a wilted blue carnation in the lapel. His blond hair was long and curled up over his collar.

Matt slipped off the hood and jogged toward him. They leaped into the air, thrust their lanky bodies forward and slapped their right hands together, then launched into their secret handshake. It was their signature move, perfectly choreographed. But it was unbearable to Matt. Every second worse than the one that had preceded it.

"What's up, man?" Travis slapped Matt on the back, then glanced at the tuxedo pants, not so different from the ones he wore, and the black T-shirt Matt hoped Travis wouldn't recognize. "You look like shit, dude. Did Nate give you hell for redesigning your tuxedo?"

The ball in the base of Matt's throat hardened. He cleared it, tried to keep his voice from cracking. His legs trembled. He reseated himself on the Escort's hood. "Yeah," he said. "I went a little mental at the wedding, but it's not like I took a piss in the punch bowl or anything."

Travis threw his head back and laughed.

Matt wanted to hold onto the sound for as long as he could. He wanted to keep Travis safe and happy. Once he knew the truth, would Travis ever laugh again?

"What happened to your shirt, dude?" Travis's gaze lingered on the T-shirt.

Please. Please. Don't let him recognize it. "I spilled something on that lame-ass tuxedo shirt at the wedding. How was the dance?"

"Kick ass." Travis waltzed around the car as if still holding Jennifer in his arms. "I know you'll be shocked 'cause I'm usually such a cool dude, but I think she's the one." Travis's blond curls flopped over his forehead and he shook them away, a gesture Matt had seen a thousand times.

He raised his eyebrows. "Let me get this straight. Are you talkin' about love?"

Travis nodded, his curls bobbing up and down.

Matt watched him for a moment, not wanting to take one second of this hopeful time away from Travis. He wanted to make him laugh—for them to joke around and punch each other in the shoulder like they always did. He wanted to keep postponing Travis's horror at learning his mother was dead. Again, Matt felt his fingers slip into the wound on Crystal's neck. He shoved his hands into his pockets.

Travis took a deep breath and launched into one of the slapstick routines he and Matt performed whenever the opportunity presented itself. "*Love*," Travis said, drawing out the word. "Let's talk about *love*." He paused for effect and smiled, his eyes twinkling with practiced sincerity.

It was a routine Matt had borrowed from a television evangelist's sermon in the movie, *Oh God*. Their performance had dissolved the audience into peals of laughter and won them second place in the Senior Class Follies. His thoughts shifted to Crystal, the way she'd slapped them both on the back after the performance, told them she planned to call Johnny Carson.

Now, Travis was on a roll. "You can love your brother or your sister. You can love your husband or your wife. You can love your new britches. Mah new car. You can even walk by the pet shop and just *love* that little doggy in the windah." He paused and flashed another wide grin—Matt's prompt to take over.

Despite the blood pounding in Matt's head, despite the flashing mind photos of Crystal lying on the sofa in only her underwear, the routine was so familiar and automatic he didn't miss a beat. "Now some folks say *love* is what they done seen in a porn-o-graphic movie." He spread out his arms, palms raised, beseeching the skies, then shook his head, jiggled the flesh on his jowls like Richard Nixon. "But that is *lust*, my friend." Matt waited a second, opened his eyes, wide and astonished, then whispered, "Not love." He took a breath. "Is that what you want? Is that what you're talking about?" He shook his fist at the sky in a parody of rage, gave a long, drawn out sigh, then slumped his shoulders. Another photo flashed. Crystal in a bathtub of blood.

"No, my friend," Travis said. "The kind of love worth talking about is the kind that calls for a *sacrifice.*" He bellowed out the last word, then carried on in earnest. "Are you willing to make the sacrifice?"

Travis held his stomach in an attempt to stop laughing, then flashed his most ingratiating grin and held it for a good thirty seconds. "You can start, Matthew Garrison, by digging *deep* into your pockets."

Matt slid off the hood of the Escort. He planted his feet wide apart on the asphalt, jerked out the linings of his pants pockets and said, "Nothin' there but lint." He gave Travis a punch on the shoulder. "So, what is it you really feel for Jennifer, my man? Is it love or lust?"

A voice in Matt's head mocked him. *And what were you feeling when you had sex with Crystal?*

Travis's face grew serious. "You okay, man?"

Matt swallowed, said nothing.

Travis shrugged. "No room for lust in Narrow Way. I guess that means I'm sacrificing my boner."

This was Travis at his best. Matt laughed in spite of himself. "What do you say we chill at my house? We can grab some of my dad's beer, hang out in my room or by the pool. We can philosophize about lust and love. It'll be like old times."

"Smells like you started without me."

"Please, Travis. You can talk to me about Jennifer. And I'll freak out about shouting 'bullshit' at my mom's wedding."

"No way, dude," Travis said. "You didn't."

"I know. How lame can I get?"

"I have Miss Crystal's car, and I need to pick her up at work."

Matt looked at Travis's shoes for a moment, then back up at his face. "She'll understand. I'm sure Barcode will give her a ride."

"I'm sorry, man, I really am. But Crystal doesn't want to encourage the Barcode." He looked at his watch. "I said I'd pick her up. You know how she is. She'll want to hear what Jennifer wore, if the flowers matched. And after the fight we had last night—" he stopped, started again, "well, I figure I owe her that much."

Travis's hope he could make it right again with his mother was something Matt could feel, something he could almost touch. He couldn't let Travis face that bathtub alone. "You could call The Spur, leave a message I'm all messed up and need your help."

Travis laughed and soft punched Matt on the shoulder. "You're just bent out of shape because of the wedding, but your mom and Nate will get over it."

"Please," Matt said. "I'd do it for you."

Travis stared at him for a moment, then shook his head.

Matt's stomach growled as if it had just digested gravel. If only he could back up time, he would be happy for his mom and Nate, offer a toast at the reception. He'd dance with his mom and his sister and stay until the party was over. Couldn't he have one more chance?

"Look," Travis said. "I'm sorry. But I have to keep my promise to Crystal."

Every excuse Matt came up with sounded limp and contrived. He crossed his arms in front of his chest, held his shoulders and said nothing. He wanted to cry, but the tears remained clenched behind his eyes like fists.

Travis gave him a questioning look. "Dude, you really are bent."

Matt swallowed. "I've had cooler days," he said, his voice almost gone.

Something softened in Travis's face. "Why don't you come home with me? We'll pick up Crystal and then camp out on the living room floor like old times."

Matt's thoughts were coming too fast. The blood spattered on the bathroom tiles. The shattered mirror. The oozing wound in Crystal's neck. His hands started to shake. "You should go. Crystal is probably waiting for you."

Matt knew his behavior would give him away if he had to see

Crystal in that bloody bathtub again. He couldn't let that happen. He had to keep his promise to her.

Travis touched Matt's arm. "I'll call you tomorrow," he said, then opened the car door, got in and backed out of his parking place. He'd turned on the radio and the Indigo Girls were singing *Love's Recovery*. Through the windshield, Matt saw him smile as he cranked up the volume.

Matt headed for his Mustang, ashamed of his lack of courage. He caught up with Travis at the stop sign just beyond the school parking lot. He rolled down his window.

Travis did the same. He turned down the Indigo Girls.

"How about I follow you to The Spur," Matt said. "You can leave the Escort in the parking lot for Crystal."

Travis grinned. "Excellent."

CHAPTER FOUR

The parking lot at The Silver Spur Steak House held only three other cars. Matt rolled down the window and called out to Travis. "Leave the keys in the ignition. No way she can miss the car." If Travis found out Crystal hadn't showed up for work, he'd rush home to make sure she was okay.

Travis jogged over to the Mustang. "No can do, man. I dissed her last night and I need to apologize. I'll be back in two." Travis headed for the backdoor, throwing his keys into the air and catching them, a happy spring still in his step as he walked.

Matt flipped on the radio. A news broadcaster droned on about Chinese students protesting for democracy in Tiananmen Square. He changed the station. Madonna sang her hit, *Like a Virgin*. He turned it off.

In the silence, with no way to force the memory back this time, Matt heard the fear in Justin's voice so vividly that he had to brace himself to keep from turning around to look for his cousin. An instant later, Matt was back in Lake Powell, twelve years old and kicking his legs to stay afloat.

* * *

All around him rusted mountains rose—carved by nature and mirrored on the water's surface. The lake was cool with only the slightest ripple. To his left, a tuft of white cloud peeked over the ridge of Gregory's Butte. Everything was quiet except for the slapping sound of waves caressing the shoreline in Mountain Goat Cove. On a rock ledge about twenty-five feet above Matt, Justin's hair gleamed like polished mahogany in the angled sunlight. The sky behind his cousin was so bright it hurt to look up and Matt had been momentarily

28

blinded before the sun dropped behind a cloud and turned the lake to sapphire.

Matt heard the soft slapping sound of Justin's wet feet on the rocks.

"Don't be a chicken," Matt had yelled up from the water. "Get a running start like I did."

"I can't," Justin shouted. "I'm scared."

The rock canyon amplified and echoed sound as if it had a voice of its own. Scared...Scared...Scared.

"Yes you can. Be brave. It's so easy." Easy...Easy...Easy.

Justin stood as still as a statue.

Then Matt said the worst thing he could think of. "You're acting like a little girl. A sissy crybaby."

Justin still didn't move.

Matt swam towards the shore, got out of the water and climbed up the cliff until he stood directly behind Justin. "You jumped off the high dive at the YMCA pool. You can do it," he said. "I know you can."

Justin's arms went out to his sides like a tightrope walker as he inched to the edge. He stood for a moment looking down at the water, his legs visibly trembling. "I can't. I'm too scared."

"Yes you can." Matt gave him a small nudge.

Justin stumbled forward and dropped off the ledge. His legs scissored back and forth for an instant, then dangled loose as if they'd become disjointed from his body. When the wind caught his bright red bathing trunks, they billowed out like a balloon. His chin dropped to his chest and he seemed to hang in the air for a moment.

Justin looked so amazing as he fell that Matt applauded. Justin would love the thrill of the fall, the way his heart beat faster and his body felt free and light as a hawk. Justin would get over his fear and next time they'd jump together and land side by side.

And then everything slowed down. Another cloud passed over the sun, leaving a golden ribbon across the lake. It was into this ribbon, near the rocky edge, that Justin entered the water. Concentric circles grew bigger and bigger, then disappeared.

Matt got a running start and jumped from the ledge. Once he entered the water, he opened his eyes and looked for his cousin. Bubbles rising from his nose, he sunk deeper into the lake. He saw nothing and decided Justin had already risen to the top.

When Matt's head popped out of the water, he skimmed the lake's surface, searched the cove, but saw no sign of his cousin. "Come on, Justin. You're scaring me."

As Matt waited for him to surface, for the shining wet head to bob up, the cliffs reflected by the water moved with the lake's ripples like spirits dancing.

He waited and waited, but Justin didn't resurface.

Matt dove so deep, his fingers and toes tingled, then went numb. A dull roaring sound filled his ears as he dove again and again. Dove until his stomach hurt and his eyes and lungs burned as if the lake were on fire.

His arms aching, his breath coming in short gasps, he fought his way back to the yellow dinghy he and Justin had pulled ashore. Matt had to get help. Alone, he paddled faster than he'd ever paddled before. When Aunt Kelsey, Mom's twin sister, spotted the dinghy with only him inside, her dark eyes widened and her face went white as she looked from him to her sister and back again.

A hollowness filled his chest, as sharp and brittle as a skeleton. "Justin and me," he said, choking out the words. "We jumped into the lake. He didn't come back up."

For a moment, everything was still. And then orders were shouted. "Radio the marina to call search and rescue. Get the speedboat."

A motor started, strong arms pulled him out of the dinghy and into the already moving boat. Uncle Bryce grabbed his shoulders and shook him hard. "Show me the exact spot where he went in."

Dad and his uncle dove again and again. The terror-filled minutes elongated into a lifetime, then collapsed like a stack of dominoes. Uncle Bryce had found Justin, his right foot wedged between two boulders jutting out from the canyon's rock wall.

For six years, Matt had believed that afternoon at Lake Powell would always be the worst time of his life, but he'd been wrong. He closed his eyes and tried to focus on Travis. Matt had never seen Travis cry, not even at Justin's funeral. Travis could have a breakdown like Aunt Kelsey did after Justin died.

Light from the restaurant windows seemed to scatter into

meaningless splotches. Matt leaned his head back against the seat. There was a horrible nakedness in the silence. It was hard to breathe. He opened the driver's side window and sucked in some air. It smelled like the hamburgers his dad used to grill on their backyard Weber.

On the other side of the lot, the backdoor of a gray Toyota Camry opened. The dome light came on. Under its glow, a man and a woman tried to arrange their bodies into one small backseat. *Oh shit.* He tried to remember if Crystal had closed the blinds before they'd started to dance. If the candles had given off enough light for them to be seen through the window. Dancing? What was he thinking? They'd had sex without a condom. The police would find his semen inside her. Travis could disappear from Matt's life the way Justin had.

On television, they never let the victim bathe until after the rape test was done. Crystal had sat in a bathtub of water for a couple hours after they'd had sex. That might change the results. He unclamped his hands from the steering wheel and wiped them on his thighs.

Travis returned, stood by the driver-side window. "She never showed up for work. Gracie said as soon as I drove off, Crystal got in some fancy car. Figures. No wonder I hate her."

Matt swallowed. "Don't say that. Don't ever say that."

Travis's eyes widened. "I just wish she'd stop screwing everything up for me."

Matt stared at the steering wheel. Travis was about to get his wish. Crystal would never screw anything up again. She'd never laugh at their antics or teach them another dance step. Never see them graduate from high school. Never watch a NCAA game where Travis played for the Arizona Wildcats and slammed the baseball out of Kindall field.

"She's going through a bad time," Matt said.

Travis cocked his head, gave Matt a suspicious look. "How do you know?"

Above them, the moon slipped behind a cloud, rearranging the shadows on Travis's face.

There was an awkward silence.

"I don't know for sure," Matt said. "And maybe you don't know what she's going through right now either. But your mom is the best person I know."

"She's been drinking too much, man." Travis slapped the Mustang's door. "Go on home. She's probably waiting for me. I'll make sure she's okay and then be right over."

"If she got a ride, what's to worry about? You can call her in the morning."

"I'll change and be at your house in a half hour," Travis said. "What's the big deal?"

"Do you want me to go with you?"

"If she's drunk and passed out, she'll be freaked you saw her that way."

"I can help you get her into bed."

Travis shook his head sadly, then lumbered away, his shoulders slumped, his head down.

A better friend would have gone home with Travis, no matter the cost. Matt thought about the blood, the wound in Crystal's neck. A wound that would soon belong to Travis. And no amount of stitching could ever close it.

CHAPTER FIVE

Radhauser stood at the living room window for a moment, thinking about the victim's son. Had his own son lived, he would be entering high school this fall.

As the paramedic backed the ambulance out of the driveway, a white Ford Escort screeched to a halt on the road in front of the house. The driver's door opened and a tall, lanky boy wearing a white dinner jacket dodged the ambulance and raced across the landscaping stones to the front walk. His hard-soled shoes clicked against the paved walkway like manic drumsticks.

The front door was flung open. The boy ran into the room. He had blond curly hair and pale skin with a scattering of blemishes spread across his forehead like freckles. "What's going on?" There was more than a trace of fear in his voice. "Has something happened to my mother?"

Radhauser's blood turned to ice water in his veins. *How does a kid recover from something like this?* He removed a leather case from the inside pocket of his jacket, flipped it open and flashed his badge. "I'm Detective Winston Radhauser from the Pima County Sheriff's Department." He slipped the case back into his pocket and took out a small black notebook with a ballpoint pen clipped to the cover. "What's your name, son?"

"Travis Reynolds. I live here with my mother. Was she in that ambulance?"

"No," Radhauser said, jotting down the boy's name and the time he'd arrived on the scene, realizing he'd probably given the poor kid a seed of hope his mother wasn't hurt badly enough for an ambulance.

33

"I need you to wait outside until my partner arrives and we finish up in here."

"Finish up what?" Travis ran into the kitchen, as if looking for his mother, then returned a second later and tried to push past Radhauser and into the hallway.

Radhauser grabbed Travis from behind and pinned his arms to his sides. "You need to stay out of there." Radhauser knew the house had been compromised by the paramedics, but intended to treat the bathroom like a crime scene until he'd had time to investigate. He led Travis back into the kitchen.

"How bad is it?" Travis asked.

"I'm sorry, son. But it's about as bad as it gets." Radhauser saw something pass over Travis's face that told him he knew the truth, but wasn't ready to face it yet. He'd give the boy some time—let him ask questions for which he already knew the answers.

"Why did the ambulance leave? If she's hurt so bad, why aren't you taking her to the hospital?" Travis's pulse thumped in and out of his neck like a frog's throat. The ceiling light threw a dark shadow across his face. "Where is she? Where's my mom?"

Radhauser gently pushed Travis into a chair at the kitchen table.

For a moment Travis sat, unmoving, his mouth open like a fighter who'd just taken a wicked blow to his head. And then he asked the question his blue eyes had been holding. "Is my mother dead?" His gaze lingered on Radhauser. Travis's eyes were bloodshot and full of pain, but Radhauser could see them reaching for a negative answer.

"No," Travis said. "She can't be dead."

Dead. The word echoed back at Radhauser, separate and hard as a stone. *Dead.* He shook his head to clear the old memory of the emergency room the night his family had died, and tried to focus on Travis. "I'm so sorry, son."

With no warning, Travis leaped from his chair and grabbed Radhauser by the shoulders. "What happened to her?"

"We don't know yet," Radhauser said, though he was about ninety-five percent sure she'd been murdered. "The first officers on the scene thought it presented like a suicide."

The boy's eyes grew wide and uncomprehending. "She wouldn't do that. Please," he said, his hands tightening on Radhauser's shoulders. "Can't you just tell me where she is?"

"Come outside with me."

Travis didn't budge. "Why can't I see my mom?"

Radhauser understood the need.

He'd been out on a domestic violence call and had gotten to the hospital too late. In the basement morgue, he'd sat with his wife and son for hours, trying to understand how they could be present in the world one minute and gone the next.

"I know I can't say anything to dissuade you," he said. "But until we're certain a crime didn't happen here, we have to protect the scene."

"I'm not going to do anything to your scene. I just want to see my mom."

The kid's eyes held so much pain Radhauser had to look away. Knowing he'd behave the same way in Travis's position, Radhauser kept his voice calm. "It's procedure. You understand that, don't you, Travis?"

Travis reseated himself at the kitchen table. "Yes, sir," he said, and dropped both arms onto the tabletop, rested his head on his folded hands and closed his eyes.

Radhauser watched him from the doorway for a moment, then walked into the living room to look out the window for O'Donnell.

When he heard the sound of a chair falling over in the kitchen, Radhauser turned back, just as Travis raced down the hallway. *Shit.* He should have seen that coming.

Before he could stop him, Travis burst through the crime scene tape. One long yellow ribbon dangled against the doorframe when Radhauser caught up.

Travis stepped into the bathroom and froze.

Radhauser grabbed him by the shoulders and turned him around. Travis had a wide panicked look in his eyes. His skin, even more pale than before, mottled with color as bright as welts. A tear dropped from the corner of his right eye and ran the length of his cheek, dropping straight and fast, like sweat on a summer glass. *Jesus Christ.* Maybe he should have kept those two deputies on the scene. What the hell was taking O'Donnell so long?

He pulled Travis into the hallway and wrapped his arms around him. As he held tight to the sobbing boy, Radhauser stroked his back, real gentle, the way he'd want his own son treated.

A siren pealed in the distance. *Thank God.*

Travis pulled away and reeled down the hallway toward the kitchen.

Radhauser replaced the tape over the bathroom entrance.

The siren grew closer. A loud thumping sound came from the kitchen. Radhauser hurried toward it.

Travis stood in front of the refrigerator, leaning into it with both hands as if he were holding it up. Between his two palms, an indented spot marred the smooth, avocado-green surface where he'd smashed it with his head so hard the force of it rattled the stack of trays and cookie sheets stored on top. When he turned to face Radhauser, Travis's forehead dripped blood.

For one long moment, Radhauser stared at the boy, understanding exactly why he'd done it. Anger came first. Then grief rolled in and settled over you like a thick and unrelenting fog. He pulled Travis away from the refrigerator, shoved him into a chair, then grabbed a dishtowel from the drawer, wet it under the faucet and pressed it against the boy's head. The cut was in the hairline.

"Her hair," Travis said. "Why would someone cut off her hair like that?"

Radhauser cleaned the wound, applied pressure and kept checking the bleeding. "She may have cut it herself." As head wounds often do, it bled for what seemed like a long time. When it finally stopped, he wrapped ice cubes in another towel and handed it to Travis.

"She wouldn't do that. She cared about how she looked."

After a few moments, Radhauser checked the cut. It was a one-inch gash, didn't appear to be deep, but he'd better watch for signs of concussion.

"At the dance, I was talking to Jennifer about Mom," Travis said, his voice soft and choked with sobs. "About how excited she was and how she'd probably ask me a zillion questions about the dance and..."

The more Travis talked, the more sympathy Radhauser had for him. Radhauser was a grown man and still had nightmares about the mangled Ford station wagon. He still wished he'd taken the night off, as Laura had begged him to do, and been behind the wheel. Maybe he could have prevented the accident, driven fast enough to be long past the ramp where the Dodge pickup driver, drunk and confused, had headed south into the northbound lanes.

Unlike this poor kid, Radhauser had coped with grief for a year—long enough to know the memory of his wife and son was a weight he'd always carry. He scratched his cheek, felt the beginning of his nightly stubble. "Do you have a first aid kit?"

"Mom keeps it in the top drawer of her dresser."

"Are you okay to go get it?"

Travis nodded.

"Then I want you to sit and hold the ice on your head for a few more minutes."

Travis headed down the hallway toward his mother's bedroom. When he returned with the first-aid kit, Radhauser put some Neosporin on the wound, used the butterfly strips to close it, and then sat quietly with Travis in the kitchen for a few minutes, hoping the boy would calm down enough to answer a few questions. Radhauser tried to assess what he saw and heard with the unbiased eyes and ears of a cop, but it wasn't easy to do when the grief in the room was so thick it made it hard to breathe.

With the screech of a patrol car coming to a halt outside, the siren ceased. After what he'd seen, there was no way Travis would return to that bathroom. No longer worried about protecting the boy, Radhauser met O'Donnell at the front door. "It's about time you got here."

Tim O'Donnell was a short, solid, and shaved-bald man in his forties. He wore the navy blue uniform of the Tucson Police Department—his badge pinned above his breast pocket. Each time he saw Tim, Radhauser imagined a dark chocolate-colored fire hydrant. Tim had a sprinkling of even darker freckles across his nose and cheeks. He carried a long-handled police-issue Maglite that looked big enough to light up a movie screen.

He looked over Radhauser's attire, pausing for a moment at the hand-tooled boots, custom-made in Nogales. "What's with the cowboy suit? You used to dress like a professional. Did you get called while two-stepping at the Get Up and Dance Saloon?"

"Save your wardrobe critique for another time," he said, then brought O'Donnell up to date on the scene and the teenage boy in the kitchen who'd tried to bash his head in with a refrigerator.

O'Donnell raised his eyebrows. "Guilt?"

"More like grief," Radhauser said.

Tim held up his flashlight. "I'll start outside."

"If your siren got any neighbors out of the sack, go talk to them. See if they saw or heard anything. The 911 call was made by a female. See if one of the neighbor women will admit to calling."

Radhauser asked Travis to join him in the living room. When the boy was settled on the sofa, Radhauser asked generic questions at first to put him at ease. He got Travis's age, information on where he went to school, and what he'd been doing that night. He asked for Jennifer's last name, address and phone number. Travis's mother's full name and where she worked. He wrote everything down in his notebook. "How old was your mother?"

"Thirty-four," he said. "She had me when she was seventeen."

"What's your father's name?"

"Mitchell Travis Reynolds."

"Is he in the picture?"

Travis stared at the floor for a moment, then looked back up at Radhauser. "He was a helicopter pilot shot down in Vietnam a month before I was born," he said so wistfully Radhauser could almost see the wish he'd known his father fall out of the boy's mouth. Poor kid. He was pretty young to be an orphan.

A moment later, as if someone had just lit a match under him, Travis shot up from the sofa. "Something is wrong here. My mother." He stopped. Started again. "I know this sounds weird, man, but my mom doesn't do a lot of cleaning. She doesn't even make her bed. I mean like never. She's hardcore about it. I'm the one who empties the ashtrays. I take out the trash and beer bottles. Everything is way too clean tonight."

A single drop of blood oozed from the cut and dripped down his forehead and onto his nose. Travis didn't seem to notice. "You need to listen to me. Somebody cleaned up around here. And it wasn't me."

"I am listening. And believe me, I'll check out every lead." Radhauser examined the cut again. "It looks pretty superficial, but you might stop by the emergency room and see if you need a stitch or two."

"It's no big deal. I'm not dying." With the word *dying*, another spasm of grief passed over Travis's face.

Radhauser's pity was almost palpable. He'd only realized after the death of his family how shameful it feels to be pitied. He hammered a box of unopened cigarettes against his wrist and then removed the wrapping. He'd stopped smoking six months ago, but still carried a pack in his pocket, still felt the occasional need to stick one in his mouth.

"You can smoke," Travis said. "My mom does." He dropped his gaze to the empty ashtray. "I mean, she did."

Radhauser took out a cigarette. "I know this is hard, and there's no good time to do it, but I have a few more questions. Are you up to it?"

"I guess."

With the unlit cigarette dangling from his lips, Radhauser looked at Travis for a moment. He sat on the edge of the coffee table, close enough to Travis that their knees were nearly touching. "Does your mother make a habit of leaving the doors unlocked?"

"Only when she's home. We've lived here almost my whole life. No one ever bothered anything."

"When did you last see her?"

"I dropped her off at The Silver Spur Steak House at five forty-five pm. She had a six to two am. shift, but Gracie planned to cover her last hour. The bar closes at one, then the waitresses clean up and reset the tables."

"Do you have any idea how your mother got home?"

He told Radhauser about his plans to go home with Matt, and what Gracie had said about Crystal getting into a car right after he'd dropped her off. "Knowing Crystal, she might have thumbed it."

Radhauser made a note in his book to interview Gracie and the other waitresses at The Silver Spur.

"Why do you call your mother by her first name?"

"She was a kid when she had me. It was just the two of us and we were best friends." He lowered his head.

Radhauser gave him a moment. "Does she have a history of taking rides from strangers or other dangerous behavior?" The unlit cigarette moved with his lips when he talked.

"Are you going to smoke that thing?"

"I'm trying to quit," Radhauser said. He repeated his last question.

"Not when she's sober," Travis said.

"Do you have any idea who may have phoned 911?"

Travis looked dazed. "Someone called 911?"

"That's how the paramedics knew to come out here. Is your mother close to any of the neighbors? Do any of them drop by?"

"She pretty much keeps to herself."

"The caller was a female. Does she have a friend who might have been with her?"

"She's pretty tight with Gracie, but she was at work."

"I'm sorry to put you through this, son," Radhauser said. "Do you want to call a relative? An aunt or uncle, your grandparents?"

"Call?" Travis repeated the detective's word as if it were a foreign language. "It was mostly just Mom and me. I have a couple aunts in Mesa. But I haven't seen them for years. I'm closer to my friend Matt and his parents."

Radhauser took the unlit cigarette from his mouth and replaced it in the pack. "I'll leave the calling up to you, son. Has your mother ever intentionally hurt herself?"

Travis hesitated. "I already told you she drinks too much.

40

Sometimes she passes out. But something about this house isn't right. Somebody cleaned it. My mom wouldn't do that. She just wouldn't. And who broke the bathroom mirror?"

"People can be unpredictable, especially in a crisis," Radhauser said. "Sometimes they drink too much. Or dress up or down. Sometimes they're angry enough at themselves to cut off their hair or strike out at their reflection." He paused and stared at the coffee table. "Sometimes they light candles and clean house."

"What if she took a ride with some sleazebag? What if he followed her into the house? What if he—" Travis winced, and something bitter and hopeless washed over his face.

Though Radhauser knew the sample would most likely be compromised, he made a note to request a rape kit.

When Radhauser glanced up from his notebook, Travis had gone pale and was breathing way too fast. The kid was having a panic attack. "Put your hands on your thighs. And take long, slow breaths."

Travis did as he was told.

Radhauser placed a hand on the boy's shoulder. "I hate to keep you any longer. But I need forensics to fingerprint you. It's routine. We want to eliminate the prints that belong to people who spend a lot of time in the house."

"You should fingerprint my friend, Matt Garrison, then. He's here almost as much as I am."

"Anybody else, son? Think hard. It's important."

"Gracie. And Baxter. Maybe Millie, she's another waitress, but I don't think she and my mom hung out much."

Radhauser jotted the names in his notebook. In order to preserve the already compromised scene, he walked Travis outside to the Bronco. "You can wait here where it's warm," he said. "Is there someone you'd like me to call to be with you now?" He opened the back door for Travis.

"Matt," Travis said as he slipped into the backseat.

"Give me his number. My mobile phone doesn't work out here. But I'll radio dispatch to call him. While Matt is here, we'll have forensics fingerprint you both."

Travis gave him the number.

Radhauser was glad to know Travis had a friend. He wished he'd had someone, anyone, with him the night he got the news about his family.

He stood by the open car door for a moment, feeling bad about leaving Travis alone. He poked his head back inside. "I don't give up easy, son. If someone killed your mother, I'll figure it out and I won't stop looking until I find him." Radhauser closed the door and returned to the living room.

Tim O'Donnell rounded the corner of the house, shaking his head. "I think it's a suicide."

"How many suicides have you investigated where the victim used a razor blade on anything but their wrists?"

"None," he said. "But that doesn't make it impossible."

"Tape off the entire area. I still need to photograph the bathroom and take one more look around. Make a list for forensics."

"The forensic boys can handle the photographs."

"You know I prefer to take my own," Radhauser said.

A muscle along the side of O'Donnell's jaw throbbed like a heartbeat. "You're the boss." He didn't sound happy about it.

Radhauser didn't have time to worry about anyone's mood. This was his case, and he wouldn't label it a suicide until he was absolutely sure.

CHAPTER SIX

While Tim O' Donnell walked the outside perimeter and flagged it with yellow CRIME SCENE tape, Radhauser slipped on a pair of latex gloves and a pair of disposable shoe covers. He started in the kitchen. There were no dishes in the sink. He opened the dishwasher. It held a couple glasses, two plates and a cereal bowl. Though it always pissed them off, Radhauser started a list of things to be bagged for the forensic guys. Glasses. Plates. A cereal bowl. He rummaged through the cupboards, but found only the usual things; flour, sugar, cake mixes, boxes of cereal, peanut butter, and a loaf of wholewheat bread.

He checked under the sink, found cleaning supplies and dishwasher soap. He emptied the garbage can, which was lined with a white plastic bag, onto the counter.

On the evening his wife and son died, Radhauser had forgotten to empty the kitchen trashcan. When he returned home from the morgue where he'd said goodbye to Laura and Lucas, their German Shepherd, Witka, had pulled every paper towel, egg shell, potato peel and apple core out of the can and scattered them over the floor. The crusts of bread from the wholewheat toast Laura still trimmed off for Lucas had lain, hardened and still, against the doorframe. It had seemed odd to Radhauser then, and again now, that Witka hadn't eaten the bread. Maybe she'd known.

Now, he set Crystal's empty garbage can back on the floor. Aside from some paper towels, a few wadded-up tissues, an empty pack of cigarettes, about a half-dozen Pabst Blue Ribbon bottle caps and another six Corona, the garbage held nothing unusual. He added tissues, a cigarette pack and bottle caps to his list. He photographed her bulletin board, removed the pushpins from her calendar, took a photo of each month, then pinned it back onto the cork.

Next, he tackled the victim's bedroom. The bed was neatly made and still held the smell of detergent. He turned it down and examined the sheets and pillowcases. He found a dark pubic hair, added it and a long straight hair on the pillow to his list. Trace evidence that could easily be overlooked. He bagged both hairs for forensics.

The bedroom trashcan yielded nothing of significance. The victim's red leather purse sat on the dresser. He picked it up and emptied its contents. The usual. He opened the wallet. There was a picture of her son behind the little plastic window where most people kept their drivers' licenses. Travis stood in a batter's box wearing a yellow and green baseball uniform.

Radhauser stared at the photo for a moment, wondering if Lucas would have played high school baseball. After the funerals, Radhauser had packed away his photographs of Lucas and Laura, even their wedding album and Luke's baby book. He'd believed he had to hide those images in order to keep on living. Now he wondered. Was it possible to find a place for grief that didn't erase the faces of the wife and son he'd loved?

He examined the rest of the wallet, where he found three dollars and forty-two cents. A checkbook with a balance of forty-six dollars and seventeen cents. A tube of hot pink lipstick. A pack of cigarettes. A teal blue Bic lighter. A book of matches from The Silver Spur Steak House.

After he finished, he headed down the hall toward the bathroom with his camera. As always, he tried to clear his mind. He needed to observe the scene and the victim with absolute clarity. He moved slowly, taking in the doorway, the linoleum floor, and the missing piece of the broken mirror over the sink. The toilet with its lid lifted as if a male had been the last one to use it. Could someone have used the bathroom? Not likely, he thought. Not with the victim in the tub and Radhauser standing guard. The paramedics would know better. There was something reddish brown splattered on the underside of the toilet seat that looked like vomit.

He glanced at the empty liquor bottle. Maybe the victim had been so drunk she'd lifted the toilet seat and vomited before getting into the tub.

As he looked around, Radhauser searched for anything out of the ordinary. There were two chrome towel bars on the bathroom wall, but no towels hanging on them. He looked around the bathroom for a linen closet, but found none.

He made a note to ask Travis if there were towels on the racks when he'd left for his dance. Radhauser purposely avoided looking at the bathtub until he'd had time to take in the rest of the room.

He noted the mirror shards wrapped in toilet tissue in the trashcan and added them to his list for forensics, along with a blue smear of what looked like toothpaste he'd found hardened on the sink.

At the bathroom window, O'Donnell's flashlight bobbed along the east wall. If any evidence lurked around the perimeter of the house, Tim would find it.

Radhauser set up remote flashes on mounts that lit up the bathroom as if it were still daylight. He photographed the scene and the victim from every angle, then placed plastic numbered tents near the body, the sink, the toilet, and the puddle of blood on the floor, the blood splatters on the tile and tub, the single-edged razor blade, and the vodka bottle.

Paramedics told him the shower curtain had been closed when they arrived, but the blood spatter didn't support it being closed when the victim bled out. It was too clean. If she'd killed herself with the shower curtain closed, the inside of it would be bloodied. Someone closed the curtain after the victim was killed. Who? A frightened 911 caller who'd wanted to protect Crystal or couldn't bear to see her that way might have closed it. Or a remorseful murderer. A fly buzzed angrily against the bathroom window.

Radhauser closed off his thoughts to speculation and made sure every possible angle and object was preserved on film. He tried not to think about what he shot or to whom the body belonged, that she was a parent, a woman who worked hard for a living. A person who mattered—at least to that boy waiting in the back seat of Radhauser's Bronco.

Lastly, he focused on the body. The victim wore only a pair of gold cross earrings, no rings or other jewelry. Her hands were small and neatly manicured, her nails polished red. No visible trace evidence under her nails. But he added them to his forensic list. Though her hair had been cut off in clumps, there were no scissors in sight. Maybe she'd used the razor blade. Or maybe she'd dropped the scissors into the bath water. Or maybe some angry murderer had cut her hair.

Though he was no splatter specialist, the blood on the back wall seemed consistent with a severed carotid. A plume hit the wall and made a big spot, splattered pretty evenly and dripped back down the tiles and into the tub. One thing was for certain, if someone severed it for her, they'd have her blood on their body and clothing. And that could explain the missing towels. Could one of the pieces of glass in the trashcan have been a murder weapon? He gathered up his evidence tents. The forensic guys would bring their own props. Radhauser headed back to the living room.

Tim poked his head around the front doorframe. "I found nothing." He grinned, shot Radhauser a raised eyebrow look. "By the way. You look like a fag in that necklace."

"It's a bolo, but thanks," Radhauser said, and blew him a kiss.

Tim laughed.

"I want to know what you think went down here, but before you tell me, talk to the boy in the back seat of my car. He seems like a good kid. But I want you to assume he's hiding something."

O'Donnell stood in the doorway for another moment, staring at Radhauser.

"What?" Radhauser said.

"I hope I grow up to be just like you."

"Oh yeah," Radhauser said, slightly amused. "And what would that be?"

"A cowboy pitbull on steroids."

Radhauser laughed and grabbed Tim's flashlight, then picked

up his camera and went out the front door to Tim's patrol car. He didn't want to disturb any prints the 911 caller may have left on the house phone. And he didn't want Travis to hear what he had to say. He radioed Lottie. "Time to call Crenshaw," he said.

"You think it's a homicide?" she asked.

"I'm sure leaning that way."

"What should I tell him?"

"Tell him we've got a woman with her throat slashed in a bathtub of blood. Tell him her hair has been chopped off and clumps of it are on the floor and in the bathroom trashcan. And some of it is floating in the tub. Tell him I made a list for the forensic guys. And I bagged a couple of hairs."

"He'll love that."

Radhauser gave Lottie Matt Garrison's phone number, signed off, then retraced O'Donnell's steps around the perimeter of the house. Radhauser moved slowly, shooting the flashlight about. He photographed some smooth-soled footprints in the pollen on the back patio. They were probably useless, but you never knew. He'd wait for forensics to dust for fingerprints. If his instincts were correct, Crystal Reynolds didn't take her own life. And there was bound to be something, somewhere in this scene, that pointed directly to the person who did.

CHAPTER SEVEN

Loren Garrison, professor of Philosophy at the University of Arizona, sat at the oak game table in front of the fireplace, waiting for his son to return. He glanced at the clock. 12:30am. Matt always phoned when he intended to be late. When Nate Sherman dropped Sedona off to spend the week with Loren and Matt, he mentioned Karina wanted to see Matt before they left on their honeymoon and asked him to have Matt call her at Hacienda del Sol.

Loren stood, opened the door into the west wing of his house, and paced the hallway that led to the children's bedrooms. Sedona's door was closed, but the light still burned. He considered talking to her about Matt, but as he stepped closer to her room, Loren changed his mind. His daughter hadn't spoken an unnecessary word to him since she and her mother moved out.

He opened the door to Matt's bedroom and flipped on the light. The walls were crammed full of masks, some of them so grotesque they frightened Loren.

After Karina and Sedona moved out, he came home one night to discover Matt had painted all the walls of his bedroom black. He'd sold his baseball cards, including some classics from Loren's own childhood collection, like Babe Ruth and Willie Stargell. Matt took his sports posters down and hung masks from Nigeria and Ghana, faces of animals like the Great Monkey Spirit and King Gorilla, later adding Balinese Theatrical, Buddha and Brazilian carnival masks.

Loren stared at the latest addition, a yin yang mask Sedona had brought back from the Oregon Shakespeare Festival. One

48

she believed her brother would like because of the way the faces entwined like the living and the dead. He grimaced. A mask like that was the last thing Matt needed.

Less than a month ago, Matt's English teacher assigned a paper on the place each student most wanted to visit. Matt wrote about a quaint mountainside village in the German Alps where the dead gathered, awaiting the people they loved to join them. He'd written it well, filled his village with specific sensory details, employed active verbs and used both poignant and appropriate metaphors. He'd received an A for his efforts. But in the wake of the Cleveland School Massacre, the principal couldn't be too careful and called Loren in for a consult—wanting to be certain Matt wasn't assembling bombs or keeping loaded guns in his closet.

The grandfather clock in the entryway chimed 12:45am.

The first time he'd held Matt, his whole newborn head had fit into the palm of Loren's hand, and he vowed he'd never disappoint this boy—nothing bad would ever happen to his son. But Loren had failed miserably. He was a philosopher, the author of textbooks on ethics and morality who possessed neither virtue.

When he'd finally told Matt at least part of the truth—it was the affair Loren had that ruined his marriage, Matt had acted like it was no big deal. But he'd always been obedient and polite, had always strived to please his father. His teachers commented on his good manners, even after Justin's accident, after Matt had given up baseball and birthday parties—had lost twenty pounds and bitten his fingernails into bloody half moons. Even after the circles under his eyes had grown as dark as bruises, Matt had completed all his assignments and brought home stellar report cards.

* * *

It was nearly 1am. when Matt tiptoed into the house, hoping to avoid his father, but Loren Garrison, already dressed for bed, sat reading in the family room. His long, pajama-clad legs crossed at the knees and a short burgundy robe tied around his waist.

Under the reading light, his hair looked whiter than the steel gray Matt had always associated with his father. Matt swallowed back a little lump of sadness at this reminder his father was getting old.

His dad set his journal on the mahogany lamp stand beside his chair. "Are you all right, son? You look terrible."

Everything seemed to collapse a little; the room, the air, and Matt's insides. His throat tightened and he turned away so his dad couldn't see his face. "Tired," Matt said, feeling the slow coiling pressure of panic building inside him. He knew it wouldn't be long until he got the dreaded call from Travis. On the ride home from Catalina, Matt had tried to convince himself Crystal committed suicide, but it wasn't happening. Sure, she was upset and worried Travis would find out what had happened with Matt, but Travis Reynolds was destined to be a star. Crystal wasn't the kind of mother who'd miss something like that.

He gave voice to his thoughts. "Dad? Do you think Crystal Reynolds is the type who'd hurt herself on purpose?"

His father's steel gray eyes were the kind people told the truth to. At the same time, they looked both concerned and skeptical. "No, I don't," he said. "But where did that come from?"

Matt sucked in a breath. Shit. Now he'd blown it for sure. "I might write a paper on suicide. And I was wondering what kind of people…you know, actually do it."

His father's brow furrowed. "You're not having those dark thoughts again, are you, son?"

Matt shook his head. "No. Nothing like that."

"Dr. Thompson said we could call him anytime."

"I'm okay, Dad. I don't need a shrink anymore."

His father stared at him for a moment, as if trying to make his own assessment of Matt's mental state.

"It was the worst night of my life," Matt said, his gaze on the floor. He dried his palms on his wrinkled trousers and hoped his dad wouldn't say anything more about the wedding.

His dad stood, dropped a hand on Matt's shoulder. His eyes appeared darker behind his reading glasses. "Watching your mother marrying someone else must have been difficult."

Yeah, difficult, Matt thought.

With his hand firmly planted on Matt's shoulder, his father babbled on. "But what molds us is often what wounds us as well. It seems like a high price to pay, I agree, but what we learn from disappointment and pain can be priceless."

Matt cringed a little, fought the urge to jerk away or tell him to save his philosophical platitudes for his students.

"Nate said you left the wedding early. Where have you been?"

Matt's head throbbed and his stomach still felt queasy. "I drove around, parked and thought for a while, then met Travis after his dance. He's coming over to spend the night," Matt said, trying to sound cheerful, to sound like there was a chance it could be true.

His father glanced at the mantel clock. "Aren't you working at UMC tomorrow?"

For the past two years, Matt had volunteered at University Medical Center on Saturday and Sunday mornings, transporting oncology kids—something his dad claimed would look good on college applications. And Matt had been surprised to discover he liked working with the kids and sometimes entertained them by wearing a clown nose and acting goofy.

After an awkward moment, his dad removed his hand from Matt's shoulder and said, "I'm glad you're home, son. I think I'll hit the sack." He took off his glasses and rubbed the space between his eyes. "It's not been my best day either."

For the first time all evening, Matt understood this hadn't been easy for his dad. He'd screwed up, had an affair with someone he worked with, but he'd never stopped loving Karina. Matt had slept with Crystal, something that could devastate his best friend. If he hadn't been so upset, he would have told his dad he understood how a man could betray someone he loved—something he hadn't known before tonight. Sometimes the pieces of who you thought you were don't add up to who you really are.

When he heard the click of his father's door closing, Matt hurried into the hallway.

His sister waited outside her bedroom. She wore a long, pink robe, her feet sticking out beneath the hem, toenails painted bright blue. Her hair, sprayed into perfection for the wedding, was matted and flattened on one side. Mascara was smudged beneath her eyes. She looked like a little kid who'd been experimenting with her mother's makeup. "You look wasted," she said. "And you smell like you've been swimming in a keg."

"Thanks. But what do you know about kegs?"

She raised her eyebrows. "Probably more than my studious brother. You do realize, mister most-likely-to-succeed, you blew your cover and behaved like a clueless dweeb at the wedding."

"Why are you acting like this?" he said.

"Like what?"

"Look, I know I screwed up. Really bad. And I don't need my little sister to tell me."

She took a step back, her eyes widened, and for a moment she looked almost frightened. "I'm sorry," she said, looking at the floor. "I…I just wanted everything to be perfect for Mom."

"Grow up. Nothing is ever perfect." Unable to face her tears, Matt hurried into his bedroom and slammed the door, hating how obscene and messed up his world and everything he touched had become. He shouldn't have been such a coward. He should have called 911 and waited for the paramedics to arrive. He could have told them he stopped by to see Travis and found Crystal dead. A better friend would have been there when Travis got home.

He looked at the black walls with their rows of masks—all screaming the word "asshole" at the same time. Head spinning, he closed his eyes. The anger all around him wrenched his chest, wrung it hard. Crystal was dead. A deep longing for revenge was brewing inside him. He could hear the awful noises it made as he fought to find a breath. He opened the closet door, pulled aside his jeans and shirts, then punched the back wall so hard his fist broke through the drywall and into the linen closet. The pain brought tears to his eyes.

Seconds later, when he heard Sedona's footsteps in the hallway, he flipped the lock on his door. He leaned against the frame and slid to the floor. Why was he treating his little sister like this? He was the one who needed to grow up. He was five years older and should be setting an example for her—making her understand his mother deserved to be happy again. But Sedona was the one who'd accepted their new stepfather. Nate had taught her to horseback ride in the desert wash behind their mother's new house. Matt loved horses and longed to ride, too. Why did he think it was a betrayal of their father if he joined them? Nate was a good man and wanted nothing more than a little respect. Matt's dad was the one who'd ruined everything. Why did his happiness mean so much?

Sedona tapped her fingernails across the wood in the secret code he'd taught her years ago. A knock like the introduction to a Sousa march rolled on snare drums. When he didn't respond, she tried the knob. "You dick." She kicked the door, then slipped an envelope under it. "Mom asked me to give you this. Personally, I can't imagine why she tries so hard to make you love her."

When he heard his sister walk away, he picked up the envelope. His hand throbbed and his knuckles were scraped and red.

Outside his window, in the fenced yard where he'd once spent hours playing with his little sister, a miniature wind chime rattled; a whimsical, irregular sound, like children laughing.

The phone rang twice, then stopped.

Travis. It had to be Travis. Matt braced himself, hoping Sedona had answered it and not his father.

She knocked on his door. "It's some police lady."

He groped the bookcase that topped his waterbed for the phone and yanked the receiver to his ear. "Hello."

"Is this Matthew Garrison?"

"Yes," he said, scared to the center of his bones. He'd expected a call from Travis, but not from the police.

"My name is Lottie and I'm a dispatcher with the Pima County Sheriff's Office. I'm calling on behalf of Travis Reynolds. There's been an accident. He wants you to come to his house in Catalina. Are you able to do that?"

"Is he…I mean, is Travis okay?"

"Yes," she said. "He's unhurt."

"Tell him I'm on my way."

He hurried into the hall.

Sedona stood in her bedroom doorway.

He told her what the policewoman had said. "His mother..." He stopped, realizing his mistake. "The woman said there'd been an accident. Travis needs my help."

"I'm coming with you," Sedona said.

"No way."

"I care about Travis, too, dickhead."

"I know you do, but I think something terrible has happened."

"Is he hurt?"

"You're just a kid, Sedona. Mom wouldn't want you there."

"I'm thirteen, but I might as well be five." She stepped back into her bedroom and closed the door.

He drove sixty miles an hour and got to Catalina in fifteen minutes. A black Bronco and a police car were parked in front of Travis's house, blue and red dome lights swirling. Backed up to the front walkway, a long, black van waited—the words *Pima Country Medical Examiner* painted on the side panel.

Travis sat on the front steps with his head in his hands. When he spotted Matt, he looked up, tears clinging to his eyelashes. "My mother's dead."

CHAPTER EIGHT

Wanting nothing more than to get the questioning over with and go home, Matt stood with Travis on the front yard as two men from the Medical Examiner's office maneuvered the gurney with Crystal's body. Her right arm slipped from under the black plastic sheet, and through the clear bags that covered her hands, Matt saw the bright red polish on her fingernails. He remembered the warm weight of her hand on his neck as they'd danced. The way her nipples had hardened at his touch. He stopped. He couldn't let himself remember.

One of the men tucked her arm back under the sheet and turned to Travis. "Let us know when you've made arrangements and we'll call the mortuary. They'll handle her transport."

Travis didn't respond—his gaze was glued on the van waiting for Crystal. Someone had flung its back doors open. The men slid the gurney inside.

After the Medical Examiner's van drove away, Detective Radhauser stepped outside. The detective's skin was tanned and weathered—like Matt imagined a real cowboy who herded cattle in the desert sun would look. Not at all like the rumpled, rain-coated men in mystery novels who always came to mind when Matt pictured a detective. Radhauser shook Matt's hand.

He swallowed a grimace at the pain in his knuckles and tried to look straight into the detective's dark blue eyes, but he stood at least four inches taller than Matt's five-feet ten. *Welcome to Tucson,* Matt thought, *where even the police dress like cowboys.*

"I'd like to ask you a few questions," Radhauser said. "And then maybe we can call your parents to come get you both."

Matt thumbed Travis's T-shirt into his tuxedo pants. "I have my car. I can drive us."

Ignoring Matt, Radhauser asked Travis to wait outside. "If you're cold, you can go back to my car."

Matt followed Radhauser into the kitchen. It smelled like fresh-brewed coffee.

The detective offered Matt a cup.

He drank the scalding liquid, burning his mouth as he swallowed—a red knot of pain in his throat and chest. He absorbed it, knowing no matter how bad it felt it would never be punishment enough.

Radhauser pulled out the chair across the table from Matt. "What happened to your hand?"

After setting the cup on the table, Matt studied his knuckles. "I punched a hole in my closet wall."

"Any particular reason?"

He told him he was pissed off at himself and took it out on his wall.

"What were you so angry about?"

He shrugged. "My mom got remarried tonight. I went a little mental at the ceremony. What do you think happened here?"

"We don't know yet." Radhauser stared at him for a moment and then asked him for his full name, age, where he went to school, the nature of his relationship with Travis, and what he was doing that night.

"Crystal wouldn't kill herself." Matt told Radhauser about Travis's scholarship—how proud she was of him and how she'd never missed a single game. "Does the evidence really point to suicide?"

Radhauser raised his eyebrow. "What evidence?"

"I don't know," Matt said. "You're the detective. I figured you'd be looking for evidence. Like did she leave a note? Don't people usually leave a note?"

"Some do. We'll know more after the medical examiner gives his report."

Matt looked at his shoes, but felt the heat of Radhauser's gaze on the crown of his head. The walls seemed to be closing in, and the weight of air was heavy against the skin on Matt's arms.

Radhauser made notes. He asked for Matt's mother and stepfather's names, the time and location of the wedding. The detective sniffed the air, then cocked his head. "Have you been drinking?"

"I know it's against the law, but I had a beer," Matt said, cupping his hands on the tops of his knees.

Radhauser lifted one thick black eyebrow. "Where'd you get it?"

Matt had to think fast. "At the wedding reception," he lied. "I nabbed one when no one was looking."

"Tell me if I got this right. You were at your mother's wedding at Hacienda del Sol. Travis was twenty miles away at the Marana spring dance."

"I left the wedding early. I was upset because I wanted my parents to get back together. After that I drove around for a while." As soon as the words were out of his mouth, he realized saying them was a mistake, given he'd just admitted to the beer. "Then I went out to Marana to meet Travis. I needed to talk to someone."

"Kind of late for a social visit, wasn't it?"

"Not for Travis and me. We're nocturnal."

Radhauser smiled. "Teenagers," he said, and then the smile disappeared and his handsome face seemed to tighten into something brittle and easily broken. "And then what happened?"

He told Radhauser the truth—he'd followed Travis to The Spur to leave the Escort for Crystal but she wasn't there. Travis had told Matt to go ahead, he'd drive home and check on his mother then come over to Matt's house. "A little while later, I got the call from the policewoman."

"Do you have any idea who may have phoned 911?" Detective Radhauser's gaze bored straight into Matt's eyes. He could almost see the knotted thoughts in Radhauser's mind, as if he suspected Matt knew more than he told. "I don't have a clue. I mean… maybe one of the neighbors or whoever drove her home from work." He looked at his hands resting in his lap and wondered if the detective could see what was going on inside him, like some internal lie detector.

"The caller was a female. Do you know if she has a friend who may have been with her?"

Matt's breath caught in his throat. He inched back against the chair. It was just a look, he thought. It didn't mean anything. "I don't know any of her friends."

"Travis seems to think someone cleaned up the house. He said his mother didn't do a lot of cleaning. Would you agree with that?"

"I don't know," Matt said, trying to keep his voice steady. "Travis is a neat freak, but I guess I don't notice stuff like that."

Radhauser studied him for another moment, then stood. "Will it be okay with your parents if Travis stays with you for a few days?"

Matt nodded.

"Call them," he said, ripping a paper towel from the roll on the counter. "Use this to hold the receiver. Forensics tried to lift fingerprints. That carbon is hard to get off your hands."

Matt looked down at his fingertips. He wondered if he'd completely removed his fingerprints from the shower curtain. They could have already found his cufflinks in Crystal's bedroom. Could already know he was here earlier and lying about it.

"I can drive Travis to my house," Matt said. "It's not far and you won't have to wake up my dad or interrupt my mom on her wedding night." He was talking too much. It made him look like he was nervous. He was nervous. The detective's big hands and the way he wrote things down made Matt nervous.

"Travis is a minor and I prefer to release him into the custody of one of your parents."

The last person Matt wanted anywhere near this house tonight was his mother, who'd always been able to tell when he'd done something wrong. But he looked up the number for the Hacienda del Sol where she and Nate were spending their wedding night and called her anyway. Unlike Matt, Travis hadn't blamed Karina for the divorce. She was closer to Travis than Matt's dad. She'd know what to do, how to comfort him.

"I'll need you both to stay clear of this house for the next few days," Radhauser said. "I'll let Travis know when it's okay to come back."

Matt couldn't stop thinking about his cufflinks. He had to find them before Detective Radhauser did. "Could I get a box of tissues for Travis out of the back bedroom?" he asked, hoping for an opportunity to search.

"No," Radhauser said. "This is a potential crime scene." The detective's stare was level. He took a neatly folded white handkerchief from his pocket and handed it to Matt. "I don't need it back."

* * *

Radhauser stepped into Matt's path. The kid had a flashlight and was obviously searching the ground between the back deck and the carport. "Lose something?"

Matt flipped off the flashlight. "No. I was just…just looking for anything suspicious."

Just what Radhauser needed—a kid who wanted to be a detective. "That's my job. You wait in the car with Travis."

When he heard the car door open and close, Radhauser checked in with Tim O'Donnell. His shaved head was shiny with sweat. "I'm thinking suicide with an outside chance of homicide."

Whenever they investigated a late night case, most officers hoped for an accident or suicide. It meant they'd turn it over to the Medical Examiner and be finished except for the paperwork that could wait until morning. But this case didn't feel right to Radhauser. Women usually opted for pills or carbon monoxide. They rarely did something as violent as slicing their own carotid. "That means you're not sure."

"Isn't suicide on your mind, too?"

Radhauser nodded. "Always."

Tim's eyes shone with sympathy. He quickly looked away as if he knew how Radhauser still felt about losing his family. "Her kid said she'd been drinking and missing work. That they didn't have enough money to pay the rent last month. Sounds like depression to me."

"Yeah. But somebody drove her home. And it was a female who made that 911 call at 11:44."

"Maybe the victim placed her own 911 call. The place is pretty neat. No sign of a struggle. Wouldn't she kick and fight like hell if someone tried to slit her throat? Wouldn't there be water splashed all over that bathroom? A trail of blood?"

"Maybe," Radhauser said. "But what if she was so drunk she passed out in the tub? An unconscious woman wouldn't put up much of a fight. And what if the murderer, frustrated by what he'd done, broke the mirror?"

"Maybe she didn't like the way she looked and broke it herself."

"Would she have carefully wrapped the shards and put them in the trashcan?"

"If she didn't want her kid to get cut, she might have," Tim said. "It's the only bathroom in the house. Obviously a perp couldn't shower before he left the scene. Forensics will do their thing, but her fingernails looked clean to me—no trace evidence I could see. And Luminal showed no bloodstains on the carpet in the hallway or the living room either. Not even the front door knob."

This was one of the things Radhauser liked about working with O'Donnell. He questioned everything. Looked at all the angles. "And what if the killer used the bathroom towels to clean up most of the blood on his body and clothing?" Radhauser said. "What if he took off his shoes and wrapped them in the towels, washed his hands at the bathroom sink—used one of the washcloths to open the door and then took everything with blood on it with him?"

"And what if the victim washed a load of towels and forgot to hang new ones? What if you're looking for something that doesn't exist?"

"Travis said there were four towels on the bars when he left for the dance. He said his mom had bought them to match the new paint in the bathroom. Routinely, he used the two dark green ones. His mother used the light green ones. And each of them had a matching washcloth."

"She still could have washed them," Tim said. "And a woman about to kill herself wouldn't be worried about having a towel to dry herself off."

60

"That's probably true, but I checked the washing machine and the dryer. The washer had a set of sheets and a dishtowel. They were still wet. I checked the hallway linen closet, too. As far as I can tell, those towels disappeared."

"Maybe she dropped them off at the Laundromat. Or maybe they did have blood on them and the Good Samaritan who called 911 took them home to wash."

"Maybe," Radhauser said. "But the broken mirror, the unknown person who drove her home, the absent caller, the clean shower curtain, and the missing towels are enough to investigate it like a homicide, at least until we talk to the 911 caller or Melon says otherwise."

CHAPTER NINE

As the headlights from Nate's pickup truck swept over the yard, Matt read the words *crime scene* on the yellow tape stretched across the driveway and the borders of the property. His chest tightened. Even the dazzling night sky seemed panicked. He wanted to see his mother, wanted to get Travis away from here. Matt leaped out of Detective Radhauser's Bronco and opened the passenger door before Nate could turn off the ignition.

His mother slipped out of the truck and tried, unsuccessfully, to smile. She wore a pair of white slacks, a navy and pink striped shirt, and pink running shoes. Over her right shoulder, she carried a multicolored striped purse, big enough to hide Portugal—obviously an outfit she'd purchased for the honeymoon.

"Thanks for coming, Mom." There was no other living adult who loved Travis as much as she did. Matt led her away from the truck. "I'm really sorry about the wedding."

She looked terrible, exhausted, and as if she'd been crying for hours. "It doesn't matter now."

"The police won't let you inside. Detective Radhauser is helping Travis pack a few things and then they have to secure the—"

Her gaze landed on the yellow tape. "Crime scene? Do the police think Crystal was murdered?"

He looked away. His Mom had eyes so dark the iris made one color with the pupil, giving them an intensity that could make Matt uncomfortable, especially if he tried to hide something. "I don't know. Maybe."

"Are you cold, honey?" she asked. "You keep rubbing your hands."

Matt dropped his hands to his sides.

Under the glow of the porch light, their eyes met and she held his gaze for a moment—so many unsaid things between them. She stared at the T-shirt he was wearing. "What happened to your tuxedo shirt?"

He told her he'd spilled something on it and put it in the trunk of his car, along with the tuxedo jacket.

"Don't look so worried," she said. "I'll wash it out."

"I can handle it. And I can take it back on Monday, along with Nate's if you want."

"Some stains can be tricky to get out," she said. "Especially after they dry."

"I've become quite the laundry expert since you—"

A pained look spread over her face. "I'm happy to reapply for the job. Anytime you're ready."

He heard the eagerness in her voice and had a hard time meeting her gaze. He waited for her searching to settle, waited for her to see whatever answers she looked for on his face.

Her gaze dropped to his hands—his fingertips stained black. "They fingerprinted us," he said. "The ink is hard to get off."

"I don't understand. Are you and Travis suspects?"

He told her what Detective Radhauser said about eliminating prints of the people who spent a lot of time at the house.

Her face relaxed. She touched his shoulder. "I'm glad you're here. Travis is lucky to have such a good friend."

The word pounded away inside Matt's head like machine-gun fire. *Friend. Friend. Friend.*

Travis and Detective Radhauser stepped through the front door. Radhauser carried a suitcase, Travis's backpack of books, and the dirty baseball uniform he hadn't gotten around to washing after his last game.

His mom gathered Travis into a hug. "I'm so sorry, honey." She held him until his shoulders stopped shaking. "You'll stay with Nate and me," she said, still patting his back. "You can have the room we fixed for Matt. For as long as you want it." There were tears rolling down her cheeks.

Travis wrenched away. "What about the honeymoon? You guys are leaving tomorrow."

"No, we're not. And don't give me any fuss about it either. How could I go to Aruba knowing one of my boys needed me?" She hugged him again.

Though he wanted to, Matt was too scared to cry. He turned away, afraid Travis might read something in his face, then Nate's arms folded around him. For one moment Matt forgot Nate had ever been the enemy, the man he'd hated for taking away any possibility Matt's family would be reunited. His stepfather had understood any words, even kind ones, would have filled the space where Matt's sorrow needed to be. Sometimes the world cracked open and revealed its goodness in a single instant.

After a few words with Detective Radhauser, Mom and Nate took charge of Travis.

While Nate carried Travis's things to the truck, Matt stood outside Crystal's bedroom window with his hand on Travis's shoulder. The moon sat full and impossibly bright in the early morning sky. Travis cupped his hands over his eyebrows and stared into the window, as if trying to memorize this place filled with Crystal's clothes, magazines and jewelry—a bed he'd probably shared as a small boy after a nightmare. *A bed she'd shared with his best friend*, Matt thought.

Travis sighed and walked away.

Matt followed him, grabbed his arm and tried to pull Travis into a guy hug. Though he knew he couldn't say the words, he wanted Travis to know Matt was sorry, a prick, a real fucking jerk.

Travis pushed him away and kept walking. "Don't go all homo on me."

"I don't know what you want," Matt said, running to catch up. "I don't know how to help you."

Travis stopped and turned, a runaway train of sadness barreling straight toward Matt. "I want her back."

Radhauser asked for an address and telephone number where he could get in touch with both Matt and Travis. He jotted Karina and Nate's names and number in his notebook, along with Matt's father's phone number.

When Radhauser gave her a questioning look she added, "Matt lives with his father."

As soon as she said it, Matt realized he couldn't go back to his father's house. There was no way he could leave Travis now. Matt tried to imagine what this loss must feel like to Travis. Before he'd left for the dance, his mother was alive. And after he returned, she was dead. Those two parts, the before and the after, how could Travis ever put them back together?

Matt hung his head.

* * *

It was nearly 3am when Matt stepped outside and sat on the porch steps in front of his mother's swimming pool. He'd showered and changed out of the tuxedo pants and into a pair of Nate's pajamas and a pair of Reeboks a half size too big. The pajamas smelled like the detergent his mom always used and a hint of Nate's Stetson cologne. The bottoms were too long and Matt had rolled them up to his ankles.

He needed to process everything that had happened with Crystal and his role in it. Right now, he wasn't a suspect. But if the police proved he was there and had sex with Crystal, he'd have to tell the truth. He worried about the cufflinks. He'd searched the area between the house and the carport. There were only two other places they could be—her living room or, God forbid, her bedroom.

Despite the drinking, Matt had been cognizant enough to hear the sound of water running. A car on the road at 10:38. He was pretty sure he'd heard the front door open and close around 11:20. Saw another vehicle turn right on Oracle Road. If he'd heard all of that, he couldn't have slept through a murder, could he?

He thought about that for a moment. He didn't know what was worse—if she'd died on purpose because of what they'd done, or if someone else had entered the house while he'd been in a drunken stupor and murdered her. Either way, Matt was not blameless. He knew he should make a plan, decide what to do next, but he couldn't focus.

When he'd awakened, Crystal's bedroom door was open. He remembered her pulling it closed when she'd left him. But maybe she came back for something before her bath. If someone else had entered the house and murdered Crystal, that person would have seen Matt's car and maybe him asleep in her bed. Why hadn't he been killed, too?

He had to go back to Catalina and find the cufflinks before it was too late.

As kids, he and Travis had played robbers, practicing their cat burglar moves so many times they'd kept a narrow putty knife over the back frame around the sliding glass door. All Matt needed to do was slide the knife into the gap between the door and its frame and lift up on the latch.

Through the kitchen window, he saw Nate and Travis at the table. The house had been recently purchased and this was the first time Matt had been inside since his mother, sister, and Nate had settled in.

Behind Travis, on the long family room wall, Matt's mother had arranged a series of framed photographs of her children. Half the space designated for Sedona, the other half recorded events of Matt's childhood. A dark, curly-haired toddler clad in a sagging diaper, forever standing at the edge of the ocean, the surf slapping, like foamy wings, against his plump brown feet. A dorky snapshot in his band uniform, his saxophone thrust out in front of him. An eight-by-ten enlargement of Matt and Justin—cousins born three days apart. Cousins who looked like brothers, their arms flung around each other's bare shoulders, that summer they'd learned to water ski on Lake Powell. Matt quickly looked away.

His mom called out to him. "You need to eat something." She'd made grilled cheese sandwiches and tomato soup. The meal she'd always fixed for him when he stayed home sick from school. Matt didn't feel hungry, but he stepped back inside and washed his hands at the kitchen sink. Three rinsed-clean rocks were lined up in the windowsill. Matt stared at them for a moment, remembering the way his mother carried one home from every new place she discovered and loved. The way she'd carefully mark the rock's underside with the location she'd found it. She believed you could feel the spirit of a place, just by warming its rock in the palms of your hands.

Over the years, she and Matt had gathered them along Oak Creek in Sedona—his mother's favorite place and the source of his sister's name. They'd filled their pockets along the Delaware and Colorado Rivers, on a hike at the edge of the Grand Canyon, and then carefully sorted them later, choosing the perfect one to represent each new place.

Now, he stared at the three rocks in the window—thought about his mom's new life with Nate. Heat built behind his eyes—a pathetic, self-indulgent loser, about to cry over some stupid rocks when his best friend's mother was dead. He looked out the window and tried to make himself think of something else.

"There's plenty of soup left," Nate said.

The kitchen smelled like buttery grilled bread, basil, and grief. "I'm not hungry. I think I'll head home and pick up a few things. I'll be back in an hour," Matt said, hoping it would give him time to drive out to Catalina and retrieve his cufflinks.

Travis took a bite of his sandwich and left the rest on his plate. His soup remained in the bowl, untouched. He wrapped his arms around his shoulders and rubbed them vigorously—looking so shaken Matt changed his mind. He couldn't leave Travis now. There had to be another way.

CHAPTER TEN

Matt checked the time on the clock radio on the nightstand between their twin beds. It was 5am. Travis snored softly. The Valium Matt's mom gave Travis had worked. This was Matt's chance to go back to Catalina and search for his cufflinks.

He slipped out of bed, grabbed Nate's shoes, pulled the door closed behind him and tiptoed barefoot down the hallway, through the kitchen and out the back door.

He sat on the porch steps and put on the shoes. He closed the redwood gate as quietly as he could, released the parking brake, shifted into neutral and drifted down the driveway. Close to the end, he started the ignition and headed toward Catalina.

As he neared Travis's street, he pulled the car over and parked. The early morning air smelled like sage and Palo Verde blossoms. Matt opened his trunk to get out his flashlight.

The tuxedo jacket and shirt were gone. His white T-shirt, too.

He turned on the flashlight and checked the corners of the trunk.

Shit. Radhauser must have taken them when Matt wasn't looking. No, his Mustang didn't have an automatic trunk release inside. And the keys had never left Matt's pocket.

Then it dawned on him—his mother had asked about the shirt and jacket. She already had his shoes and tuxedo pants. With her key to his Mustang, she'd probably taken them out of the trunk while he sat on the porch steps. Now she'd see the blood. And he'd have a shitload of questions to answer.

Matt shuddered, then pushed that worry aside. Right now, he had to make certain his cufflinks weren't in Crystal's bedroom. Or

68

in the living room where she'd taken them off.

He flipped off the flashlight. The last thing he needed was to draw attention to a lone, pajama-clad walker at 5:30am in a neighborhood as spooked as this one must be. After closing the trunk as quietly as he could, he started to walk, praying the police car and Radhauser's Bronco would be gone.

Five minutes later, he circled around the empty house and stood on Crystal's back deck. He reached above the door and found the putty knife. Thirty seconds later, he lifted the latch, replaced the knife, and stepped inside the kitchen. A gnat flew around his ear and he swatted at it. Predawn light fell in through the sliding glass door and pooled on the floor. He turned on the flashlight.

He stood very still, waiting for his eyes to adjust, then crept down the hallway, pointing the flashlight at the floor. As he passed the bathroom, still cordoned off with yellow tape, he paused and flashed the light inside. The bathtub was still filled with bloody water, though the level had dropped much lower now that Crystal's body had been removed. Blood still spattered the tile walls surrounding the tub. The puddle on the floor had congealed into something thick and dark, like motor oil.

Before tonight, he'd seen only one dead person. He hadn't known the patterns blood could leave on white tiles. Or how the skin turned a grayish color when most of the blood had been drained from the body.

By the time he'd seen Justin, someone had closed his eyes. Until tonight, Matt hadn't understood how the absence of life left a person's eyes as dull as stone.

He turned and hurried down the hallway and into the living room. The blinds were closed, but he couldn't remember if Crystal had closed them or Radhauser. He glanced at the leather recliner where he'd dropped his shirt, but saw nothing. He shined the flashlight along the woodwork and under the tables. He stared at the candles, remembering the way Crystal's skin had glowed in their light. He quickly moved the flashlight over the surface of the sofa, then reached behind the cushions—found some loose change and a couple of popcorn kernels, but no cufflinks.

He checked the leather recliner again, pushing his hands deep into the space between the back and seat cushions. When he found nothing, he slipped down the hallway and into Crystal's bedroom, careful to keep the flashlight beamed at the floor. On his hands and knees, he searched under the bed and the chair. He ran his fingers along the baseboard and the edges of her dresser, reached behind it as far as he could on both sides. He found nothing except dust and some spider webs with dead insects caught inside them. He sat on the floor for another moment. If he'd left his cufflinks inside Crystal's house, Radhauser had already found them.

Matt headed back down the hallway.

The kitchen light came on.

He flipped off the flashlight, ducked into Travis's bedroom and flattened himself against the wall behind the partially open door. His heartbeat pounded in his ears.

Footsteps shuffled on the linoleum, and then were muffled by the carpet in the hallway.

He held his breath. Fear pricked his skin. A thousand tiny hairs stood upright on his arms, offering their useless protection. Dammit. How stupid of him to leave the sliding glass door unlocked.

"Is anyone here?" It was a man's voice, but not Radhauser. Matt smelled sweat and cigar smoke. Through the crack between the door hinges, he saw the man was older, wearing house slippers and a raincoat over his pajamas. He carried a tire iron in his right hand. He must be one of Crystal's neighbors. Matt shifted away from the crack, hoping the man couldn't see him.

Ten seconds felt like an hour.

The swishing sound of slippers on the carpet passed by Travis's door and stopped in front of the bathroom. The man flipped on the light. "Holy shit. Holy mother of Jesus." The man began to breathe in short gasps.

For a moment, Matt worried the old man would have a heart attack.

The man turned and hurried back down the hallway. Again, Matt held his breath, listening to the slap of slippers against the kitchen floor. The lights went off and the sliding door slammed shut. Matt exhaled a long stream of air, leaned his back against the wall and considered his options. The man might go home and call the police. If Radhauser had returned to the Catalina Sheriff's Station, he could be back here in ten minutes.

Matt wanted to run, but couldn't risk being seen or a tire iron bludgeoning his skull as he stepped onto the deck. Five minutes. He'd wait five minutes, then carefully slip out the back door and head for the desert wash where he and Travis used to build their fires. He could follow it to the road where he'd parked his Mustang.

The curtains in Travis's room were thin, and the rising sun cast a golden light over everything inside. As Matt's eyes adjusted, he saw the framed posters of Nolan Ryan and Mike Schmidt, Travis's heroes, and the watercolor print of a little boy walking along the railroad tracks tossing a baseball into the air. A bulletin board with pictures and articles Travis had cut from the paper—most of them about Ryan and Schmidt. A neatly-made bed stood beside a bookshelf that held trophies, framed honor society certificates and his collection of paperback books. For as long as Matt could remember, Travis had made his bed without being told. Something Matt could barely imagine.

In the corner, beside the closet, the Nolan Ryan autographed, JSA certified, Rawlings Big Stick was propped against the wall. Matt looked away, determined not to remember the autumn day six years ago when he'd given it to Travis. But there it was, a home movie, unwinding behind his eyes.

It had been three months since Justin's death. The monsoons had come and gone, leaving the cactus pears plump, the branches of the ocotillo still leafy and green.

Travis and Matt wore their swim trunks and sat outside at the picnic table beside the pool. They ate potato chips and the peanut butter and jelly sandwiches Matt's mother made for them and stared at the empty space where Justin should be seated. The roses were in their second blooming, perfuming the air around them like the funeral parlor where they'd stood awkwardly, side-by-side, in front of Justin's open casket. Travis had leaned forward and placed his Nolan Ryan autographed baseball into the coffin.

Matt pushed the bag of potato chips aside. "I'll be right back." He hurried into his bedroom, picked up the bat his uncle had given him, and walked back outside. In the bright sunlight, little flecks of salt from the chips glistened on Travis's chest.

Matt held up the bat. "Justin would want you to have this."

Travis took it, ran his hands along the smooth wooden surface, admired Ryan's signature for a moment before handing it back.

"Nolan Ryan was his hero, too," Matt insisted. "And besides, baseball isn't my sport. Not anymore." After what he'd done to Justin, it didn't seem right for Matt to play a sport his cousin had loved so much.

Travis stood, brushed the salt from his bare chest, picked up the bat and assumed his stance, taking a few hard and level swings. "But he was your cousin. It should stay with you."

Matt thought about all the stuff that had stayed with him the last three months, all the words not said after Justin died because it hurt too much to say them. He couldn't remember a good moment in his life that hadn't included Justin. And suddenly the mere mention of his name seemed to cast a dark spell on everything. "I don't want it," he said, then burst into tears.

Travis carefully placed the bat on the picnic table and sat beside Matt on the bench, draping his arm across Matt's shoulders. They stayed like that for what seemed like a long time.

"The whole jumping from the cliff thing was my idea," Matt finally said, his voice breaking. "Justin said he was scared and didn't want to do it. I shoved him."

Travis moved a little closer and tightened his grip on Matt's shoulder.

It was the first time Matt had said those words out loud to anyone. And the relief had been as big as the Grand Canyon.

Matt shook his head to clear the memory and looked around. Nothing in Travis's bedroom had changed since they were boys. And it felt wrong. Matt wanted to cry, but he couldn't. The room should be different now.

It should be a man's room.

CHAPTER ELEVEN

In his bare feet, Loren Garrison paced the length of his family room, again and again. He wanted Matt to come home, wanted to know his son was all right. Ever since his ex-wife's call, he hadn't been able to stop the hammer blows of guilt and remorse. Crystal was dead. In his mind, he saw her sitting in the bleachers with Karina, head thrown back, the sound of her laughter ringing through the dusty air—back when Matt, Justin, and Travis had played baseball together.

Loren thought of Crystal now, her empty body probably inside a drawer in the morgue. She'd been so young, a little more than half Loren's age. He shuddered, felt colder than he had in years.

He turned up the thermostat, made a pot of coffee, and reviewed the facts as he knew them. Travis must have come home from his dance, found his mother dead and called Matt.

Loren understood Matt's need to be there for Travis. But that didn't stop his anxiety about his son. He was still a boy, not equipped to cope with another death. It had taken two years of counseling before Matt could even whisper Justin's name. And clearly, he still wasn't over it.

Loren tried to convince himself both Matt and Travis would be all right. But his worry remained beside him waiting as the coffee slowly dripped into the glass pot—a sound as loud as a drum in the dark and quiet house. Before he knew it, he was crying for Crystal and for Travis. There was no one home to see him so he just let the tears fall. Eventually, he blew his nose, wiped his face with a napkin, then poured himself a cup of coffee. He sat in the rocker and lit his pipe.

He never cried, not even when his parents had died. He'd choked up when Bryce pulled Justin from the lake, but no tears had actually fallen. Maybe this was another sign of his aging.

It was 6:30am. He'd been awake since the phone call, thinking about Crystal and obsessing over his life, over the many mistakes he'd made.

Loren shook his aching head. He'd really messed things up this time.

When he heard the sound of tires on gravel, he picked up a philosophy journal and pretended to read. He waited while Matt took off his shoes and tiptoed in his bare feet through the brick archway into the family room. He wore only a T-shirt and a pair of flannel pajama bottoms, rolled up at the ankles.

Loren set the journal on the mahogany lamp stand beside his chair. Matt's face was drawn, his eyes red-rimmed.

"Your mother called. She told me what happened. I've been so worried about you."

Matt wiped his hands on the pajama bottoms. His gaze skimmed Loren's face, then flicked away. "The police wanted to talk to us. They asked a lot of questions and—"

Loren's pulse quickened. "What kind of questions?"

"The usual, I guess. But I'm not okay." Matt's voice was curt and flat. "How could I be okay?"

Loren stood and took a step towards him, lifted his arms, then let them fall back at his sides. "Dumb question, huh?" He wanted to feel connected to his son again, to do what he could to help. "I need to ask you something."

Matt planted his gaze on the fireplace. "I'm pretty tired of questions."

Something wasn't right. There was a terrible squeezing under Loren's breastbone. "Did you know Crystal was dead when you asked me if I thought she was the type of person who'd commit suicide?"

Matt looked at him and shook his head. "No way."

But Loren saw it—the flash of a lie, that brief sidestep of eye contact.

"How could I?" Matt continued. "Travis called me after he got home from his dance. After you went to bed."

"Where is Travis now?"

"When I left, he was asleep at Mom and Nate's house. I guess you know they cancelled the honeymoon."

"They didn't have to do that. Travis is always welcome here."

"I think he needs to be with Mom."

Loren swallowed. His throat was tight, and once again his eyes filled with sudden tears. He hooked an arm around his son's neck, wedging Matt's head against his shoulder. God, how he loved this kid. "You know you can tell me anything, right?"

Matt drew away. "I need to pack some things. I'll be staying with Travis for a while."

Despite the obvious truth of what Matt had said, Loren wasn't ready to let him go. "Do the police have any idea what made her do it? Did she leave a note or anything?"

"They're investigating it like a homicide. Until they're sure."

"A homicide? Why would they think that?" Loren careened toward the fireplace, thrust out his right hand to support himself. The bricks were rough against his palm.

Matt closed his eyes. "I don't know. For Christ sakes, I wasn't there." He shook his head, again and again.

There was something final and forbidding in the gesture, as if he'd seen things he never wanted to see or talk about again, and Loren had the sudden urge to shield his son. He wanted to give him something to look forward to after this nightmare ended. Something that might get the currents of conversation and connection moving between them again.

"I thought it might be good for us to get away before you head off to college. After your finals. How about a trip to Europe? We could see some theater in London." As soon as the words were out of his mouth, he realized how insensitive they might sound.

An odd look crossed Matt's face—one Loren couldn't identify—then it was gone.

Matt took a step back. "Travis's mother is dead. They found her with her hair all whacked off in a bathtub of blood, and you...you want to go to the theater?"

Loren missed a beat. "I'm sorry, son. I merely wanted—"

"The police want us to stay in town," Matt said. "All this shit coming down. It's too much." He turned and walked away.

CHAPTER TWELVE

Matt intended to pack his textbooks, a couple of poetry books, his journal, his Walkman, a few CDs and some clothes, but instead he flopped down on his bed, buried his head in his pillow and finally slept.

Later Sunday morning, as the arrows of sunlight pierced through his bedroom windows, Matt rolled onto his stomach, crimped the pillow tight around his throbbing head. Behind his closed eyes, Crystal's face emerged in candlelight and the soft skin of her breasts pressed against him.

He threw the pillow onto the floor and bolted upright in bed. Perspiration beaded his forehead. He wiped his wet face with his T-shirt. Grief, as much as guilt, wracked his brain and haunted his sleep. The skin on his chest, belly and butt still felt hot, as if it had been branded with her fingertips everywhere she'd touched him. Picturing Crystal dead was like trying to visualize the ocean dried up, or the Catalina Mountains flattened. He couldn't imagine Travis's life without his mother anymore than he could imagine a night sky without the moon and stars.

Finally, unable to take it any longer, he checked the clock. It was 9:30 a.m. The unopened letter from his mom lay on the bed beside him. Hoping it would distract him from his thoughts of Crystal, Matt tore off the top of the envelope and read.

Dear Matt,

I'm sorry I've disappointed you. I had no right to expect you to be happy about something that changed your life so drastically. I never wanted to do anything that would cause you pain. I love Nate, but that doesn't take anything away from my love for you or from the feelings I once had for your father. All I can do now is hope the love we share will win and eventually heal us all. Mom

His hand trembled. He stared at the way she'd underlined the word *Mom*, as if trying to reclaim her role. It seemed to Matt this note had been written in a time of innocence, when he'd still been a stupid boy angry with her for moving out and falling in love with someone else.

He picked up the phone and dialed his mother. "Did I wake you?"

"No, honey. Nate took Kelsey and Bryce to brunch, then to the airport. Where are you? I didn't hear you leave."

He told her he couldn't sleep, decided to pick up some of his things and had fallen asleep on his bed.

"Travis is out cold," she said. "I don't expect to see him before noon."

Good. Travis would never know he'd left before dawn. "I'll be there later. And Mom?"

"Yeah?"

"Thanks."

"For what?"

"For…I don't know. I guess for just being there."

He tucked the letter into his bookcase headboard, padded across to the window and opened the shutters. A thick spring morning pressed against the glass as he stared into the fenced play yard with its tree house and rusted swing set. Scenes from endless childhood hours, picnics in the tree house with Sedona, fighting over matchbox cars and Lincoln logs. The time they'd discovered a Gila monster, a large and venomous lizard, and thought it was a dinosaur flashed before his eyes. He'd been a dick to her last night. He needed to apologize.

Sedona's door was closed. Matt softly tapped out their Sousa march.

"It's unlocked," she said.

He opened the door. She sat on her canopy bed, reading the song lyrics to Dépêche Mode's *Personal Jesus*. She wore a yellow, sleeveless nightgown with rubber ducks floating along the hem.

One of her bare feet rested on top of the other.

"Nice outfit," he said.

"Yeah. When I was ten. I really need to bring some decent clothes over here."

"Why don't you do that?"

She lowered her gaze, but not before he saw the sadness in her eyes. "Because I don't want to."

Matt knew it was because she didn't want to admit this was still her bedroom, still the house she'd grown up in, still the place where they'd once been a family. "Don't you ever sleep?" he asked.

"Not in this house. Not anymore."

"Why do you hate it here so much?"

"It's the way Dad protects his image, the perfect husband and father. That's why he makes me sick. He's such a fake. Such a—" She lifted her hair and flipped it to one side. Little flecks of glitter from the eye shadow she'd worn to the wedding glistened on the white skin of her neck. "Such a dweeb."

He was too tired and sad to defend their father. "Look, I'm sorry about last night. I was mad at myself. But I shouldn't have taken it out on you."

"You've been mad at yourself for six years." She moved over on the bed, patted the space beside her. "I miss Justin, too."

It was a blow he hadn't expected.

His body felt liquid and loose. He sat on her bed and leaned back against the pillow for a moment, waiting for the dizziness to pass so he could tell her Crystal was dead.

She reached into her bedside table and pulled out a cigarette.

"What are you doing?"

She lit it and inhaled deeply. "I'm smoking. What's it look like I'm doing?"

"You're thirteen. Nicotine is a drug. You promised you'd never do drugs." He'd smoked a few cigarettes himself, even tried marijuana a couple times, but this was different. This was his little sister.

She held the smoke for a moment, then exhaled, a white cloud curling above her head. "Oh yeah," she said, between coughs.

"That promise. Well, I broke it. Breaking them runs in our family. A gene we inherited from our Garrison side." She made a throwaway gesture with her right hand. "I found a half pack on the school playground. Are you gonna have me arrested?"

If anyone deserved to be arrested, it was Matt. The smell of the cigarette smoke brought back images of Crystal at her kitchen table. He pushed them away and thought about the past two years, wished he'd spent more time with his sister—another childish attempt to punish her and their mother for leaving.

Sedona replaced the Dépêche Mode lyrics in her cassette case and snapped it shut. "Sometimes I get so sick of being your sibling. It makes me gag when I watch the teachers' faces. *Oh, you're Matt Garrison's little sister.* They think I'll be brilliant and well behaved. Dorky, but perfect."

"I'm about as far from perfect as a person can get."

"Yeah, right. Whatever you are, I'm not like you. I'm like me. And I just want that to be good enough."

He opened his mouth to tell her about Crystal, then something burst inside him and his shoulders began to heave. He leaned into his hands, and though he felt as if he sobbed, no tears fell.

"If you're gonna go ballistic on me, I'll stop. I'm not addicted or anything." Sedona crushed the cigarette out on a saucer that still held the crust of a peanut butter sandwich. "Besides, it's not like I'm free-basing cocaine or dancing with Mr. Brownstone."

"About last night," Matt said.

"Oh my God, that's right. Is Travis okay?"

Matt shook his head. "His mother is dead."

"Holy shit," Sedona said, tears already welling in her eyes. "What happened?"

He told her she'd been found dead in their house, leaving out the bathtub, the blood, the whacked off hair and the razor blade, though he was sure she'd learn about it from someone else.

"Did she kill herself?"

"She would never do that to Travis," he said. "I think the cops are treating it like a homicide."

"Where's Travis?"

He told her Travis was with Mom and Nate. How they'd canceled their honeymoon.

She leapt to her feet. "Drive me home. Please."

"You are home."

"This will never be home to me again. Please. Travis is my friend, too."

"Fine. I'm going over in a little while. But you have to try harder with Dad. Stop acting like Nate took his place."

Sedona snapped to attention, cupped her right hand over her eyebrow and saluted. "Only problem is, I really like Nate. And you would, too, if you gave him a chance." She studied him for a moment. "But you can't let yourself like anyone Mom loves."

He thought about the way Nate had comforted him in Catalina. "I like you. Most of the time." He glanced at the clock on her dresser. It was 9:50am. He stood, but before he left her room, he turned to her again. "I need you to understand something," he said, waiting for her to look at him. "No way I'm a saint. Not even close." He looked away, the remainder of his words directed at her pink gingham bedspread. "I'm not what everyone thinks. You want to know the truth?"

"Sure. Tell me Ted Bundy was just falsely executed for your crimes. Or you rob 7-Elevens and beat up old ladies on street corners."

He held up a hand to stop her. "I don't do any of those things, but I'm a lousy person who goes around pretending he's somebody special, somebody who does the right thing."

Sedona laughed.

* * *

Matt poured himself a bowl of Fruit Loops and sat at the kitchen breakfast bar, postponing seeing his mother and Travis. Outside in the pool, he heard the steady slapping of the water as his dad swam his hundred laps, a weekend ritual. Matt checked the kitchen clock. 10am. His father was as reliable as an alarm clock.

The doorbell rang.

Sedona rushed to answer.

Within seconds, Matt heard the garage door open.

"Who was that?"

"I took care of it," she said. "Some dude from Anderson's Garage Doors—We Do It Up and Down." She paused and smiled. "No kidding, that's what was painted on the side of the truck."

"You should be more careful about letting in strangers."

"Because of what happened to Crystal?" She pinched his cheek. "Don't go all paranoid on me."

"I'm not paranoid. I just want you to be safe."

Sedona sighed. "When can you take me home?"

"Later."

"What's wrong with now?" She picked up the telephone and dialed their mother, asked if Nate could pick her up. She listened for a moment. "Oh. Okay. Well, as soon as he gets home."

"What's the matter? Your personal taxi driver quit?"

She told him what he already knew. Nate had taken their aunt and uncle to the airport. After Justin died, Aunt Kelsey and Uncle Bryce had buried him in the family plot in Delaware, then sold their house in Tucson and moved back. "Mom doesn't want Travis to wake up and find nobody home. It wouldn't kill you to drive me over there."

"I'm not ready yet." Matt returned to his cereal.

Sedona stomped into her bedroom and slammed the door.

The cereal had turned the milk in his bowl pink, like the Strawberry Quick powder Crystal used to put in their milk. She'd claimed it was fruit and surely better for them than chocolate. He picked up the bowl and dumped the cereal into the garbage disposal.

He needed some time away from Travis to figure out what really happened last night. Matt shuddered. Someone could have planted a razor blade to make it look like suicide.

Once again, he forced himself to remember everything he could—drinking beer and dancing with Crystal, their lovemaking, the argument about telling Travis, her anger, and then her insistence he sleep before driving home. He had a vague memory of water running and assumed it was Crystal running her bath. He'd been confused, but was certain he'd heard the sound of two cars. One at 10:38 and the other at 11:20. The second time he'd heard the front door open and close and a car door slamming across the street, which he'd confirmed by looking out the window. The sound of a motor turning over. He'd watched both cars drive away, only the glow of their tail lights recognizable. One of those cars must have held Crystal's murderer.

Crystal's neighbors were mostly old people. And Mrs. Lawrence, the woman in the house across the street, went to bed early. She had for years. It didn't make sense she'd have visitors leaving so late.

His sister would be pissed when she learned he'd left without her, but he wanted her to spend some time with their father.

And Matt needed to ask Mrs. Lawrence a few questions.

CHAPTER THIRTEEN

It was nearly 11am on Sunday when Radhauser stopped by the Safeway and picked up a bouquet of yellow roses, Laura's favorite. His wife and son had been dead for three hundred and sixty-five days. He should head out to The Silver Spur to interview Baxter and the two waitresses Travis had mentioned, but Radhauser had something important to do first.

With the scent of roses filling the car, he drove through the arched gates into Hope Lawn Cemetery. He took the winding asphalt drive to the left and parked his Bronco in front of the row of graves where Laura and Luke were buried.

He opened the tailgate and lifted the weighted lariat with the rawhide Hondo Lucas had spotted at the Grange Co-op a few weeks before the accident. The boy had looked up at him and grinned, the braces on his teeth glinting under the fluorescent lights. *Please, Dad. I'll wash your car for the rest of my life.*

Radhauser shook his head, as if that gesture might clear the memory. The new lariat would be stolen before the day ended, but it didn't matter.

The air smelled of mowed grass, which had been cropped as close as a golf course. Like green confetti, small, damp blades stuck to his boots as he walked. The sky was bright blue and the wind played in the Desert Willows, sunlight bouncing off their leaves.

He'd chosen burial over cremation because he knew there would be days like this one when he needed a grave to visit, someplace where his family felt tangible—within arm's reach, just six feet beneath his hands.

During the past year, the ragged edges of sod had knitted

together in a green carpet as thick as velvet. The headstone, large enough to cover three graves, had the name Radhauser carved in block letters across it.

Though he'd come bearing gifts, he didn't intend to get sentimental. He wasn't the kind of man who'd convinced himself his life with Laura had been perfect. She could be a pain in the ass, especially about the overtime hours he spent on the job. But they'd had moments of real happiness he hadn't questioned while living them.

He looked away. *Moments*. Maybe they were the secret of love.

A family of three quail strutted single file along the paved walkway.

His car radio bleeped.

He ignored it, placed the lariat on top of Lucas' grave and struggled to remember his son's face. But each time he tried, it was Travis Reynold's face Radhauser envisioned.

His hand trembled as he arranged the roses in the copper vase in front of the gravestone, using the hose at the end of the row to fill the vase with water. When he finished, he sat on the grass and stared at his wife's name. *Laura Jane Radhauser*. "It was a good idea to start that college fund for Luke," he told her. "You'd be surprised by how much it's grown."

The radio squawked again. It seemed louder this time. He heard Lottie's voice. "Where the hell are you, Wind?"

Radhauser scrambled to his feet. "Shut up, dammit! Can't I have ten fucking minutes with my family?" Then he felt bad. He was glad Lottie couldn't hear him. It wasn't her fault. She was just doing her job.

He patted the headstone above his son's name. "I miss you, cowboy," he said, then headed back to his car to take Lottie's call.

Ordinarily, he'd stop by another grave. Tyler Meza, a six-year-old who'd been abducted from the Dennis Weaver Little League Park in 1980. Tyler was Wind's first kidnapping case and it had come down all wrong. After the funeral, Wind had Tyler's name tattooed on his wrist beneath the face of his watch. A hidden reminder to never forget the mistakes he'd made.

But he didn't have time to visit that grave today. There was another boy, a seventeen-year-old living boy, depending on him to find the person responsible for his mother's death.

* * *

Matt parked in Mrs. Lawrence's driveway. To his relief, Radhauser's Bronco was nowhere to be seen.

He rang the bell.

No one answered.

He rang again.

Finally, the old woman made her way to the door. She looked through the peephole. "I'm not dressed for company."

"I want to talk to you for a few minutes, Mrs. Lawrence. It's Matt Garrison. I'm Travis's friend. We used to pick up groceries for you, remember?"

She opened the door. Mrs. Lawrence wore a blue cotton robe snapped down the front. Yellow buttercups dotted the hem. The old woman looked as if she'd shrunk a few inches since the last time Matt had seen her. She invited him inside.

Her blue slippers made a shuffling sound as they crossed the hardwood floor, her movements slow and labored, but her face was perfectly made up, her hair permed into little white ringlets that bounced when she talked. She sat on the sofa. Matt took the rocking chair across from her.

"You're the boy who drives the Mustang." She batted long, dark eyelashes that were obviously false, as if she wanted to make sure Matt noticed them. "I get the groceries delivered from the Casas Adobes Market now."

"I'm not looking for a job," Matt said. "I wanted to ask a couple questions about last night."

She nodded, her curls bobbing. "A terrible thing. Poor Travis. And he's such a nice young man. Imagine him getting that scholarship. Henry, he lives next door to Crystal, went over to check on things. The back door was unlocked so he went on in. Let me tell you, he was white as a ghost this morning when he told me about it. It must have been awful for that boy."

"You're right. Travis didn't deserve any of this," Matt said, his words tripping over each other like someone running away from a crime scene.

She fiddled with the hem of her robe, swishing the buttercups. "Where is Travis? He's not staying in that house, is he? I bet it will never sell. Something like that happening taints a place, you know?"

He told her Travis was staying with his mother and stepfather. "Did you have visitors last night? Someone who left about 10:38pm, then someone else who left about an hour later?"

"Heavens, no. I go to bed at 8pm. And you will, too, when you're my age. Mark my words."

"Did you hear anything? A car starting or a door slamming around that time?"

"I take my hearing aids out at night. But I did hear Crystal having a terrible fight in the driveway with some man. I looked out the front window. He was good-looking. Dressed real nice, like a lawyer or something. When he left, she chased him down the road and threw a rock at his car."

"What time was that?"

"Aren't you a little young to be working for the police? Besides, I already told that nice detective in the cowboy hat all about this."

"Do you remember anything about the car? How about the shape of the taillights?"

"Son," she said, batting her eyelashes again, "I don't even remember my own birthday anymore."

Matt asked her again about the time.

"It was definitely after my supper. I eat around 6:30. So maybe it was around 7:00 or so."

He thanked her and headed to The Silver Spur Steak House to talk to Crystal's co-workers, see if one of them knew who drove her home last night.

* * *

Matt crossed the creaky wooden plank floor and stood for a moment to let his eyes adjust to the dim light. The inside walls were covered in old barn wood and decorated with lassos and bridles, horseshoes, and fringe-trimmed suede chaps spread out into the shape of bowed legs. Patterns from dozens of branding irons had been scorched onto the wood. He'd been here with Travis enough times to know the waitresses.

He headed toward an oak podium where Gracie stood, wearing the same outfit Crystal had worn last night. Grief crept up his throat, tightened it. He looked away, swallowed back the memory.

"Matt," she said, looking toward the front door. "Is Travis with you? I can't wait to hear about his dance."

"No. But something terrible has happened. And I really need to talk to you."

She led him to a small table near the front of the restaurant. "Is Travis okay?"

He told her Crystal was found dead in her home last night, leaving out all the details.

Gracie's face scrunched up like a child's. A moment later, she started to cry. "I can't believe it. She was so happy when I saw her yesterday. Where's Travis?"

He told her Travis was staying with his family, and assured Gracie his mom would take good care of him.

"That poor kid. He doesn't have anyone now."

Matt looked away. "He has me. And my family. Do you have any idea what Crystal was so happy about?"

"I never pegged Crystal as the type to have enemies that would..." She trailed off.

"Why was she so happy?"

"I don't exactly know. But she said she'd gotten some good news and needed to share it with her boyfriend." There went Matt's theory she'd gotten bad news at her doctor's appointment on Friday afternoon. If she was happy on Saturday when Gracie saw her, then something changed between the time Crystal left work at 6:00 and the time Matt saw her around 7:45pm. Maybe the so-called boyfriend didn't think her news was good.

"Wasn't she supposed to work last night?"

"She asked me to cover for her."

"Do you know this boyfriend's name?"

"She was so proud of Travis getting that baseball scholarship.

She planned to go to every single game."

"I know," Matt said. "But do you know the boyfriend's name? Maybe he could help us understand."

"Crystal was pretty private about him. She wouldn't want me talking behind her back."

"Look. I'm just trying to help Travis figure out what happened to his mom. She was your friend and that makes it your business. Didn't you ever get a look at his face or hear his name?"

Matt sensed the presence before he saw Radhauser standing beside the table, listening and obviously furious. "You need to leave." He shot Matt a look that could have melted stone.

"I'm not finished talking to Gracie."

"I'm equipped to handle it," Radhauser said. "Get out of here. Now."

"You talked to Mrs. Lawrence. You know Crystal had a fight with some man earlier last night."

Radhauser glared at him. If someone lit a match, the space between them would blow up. "You have no business questioning my witnesses."

"I'm just trying to help Travis. He had a fight with his mom. And he never got to say he was sorry."

"It's my job to find out what happened," Radhauser said. "Now get the hell out of here before I arrest you for interfering in a police investigation."

Matt didn't respond. He felt a thousand miles of desperation inside, stretching out like a long, dusty road with no gas stations in sight. But he'd keep walking if it meant he might find the truth. What choice did he have?

* * *

After Matt drove away, Radhauser opened his Levi jacket, took his badge out of the inside pocket and introduced himself. Gracie was in her early twenties, he guessed, and wore a short denim skirt, a low-cut sleeveless white blouse, with a red bandanna around her neck and scuffed red cowboy boots that rose almost to her knees. Just like the clothing he'd found neatly folded on the chair in Crystal Reynolds' bedroom. He thought about what Travis had told him. If Crystal didn't make the bed or empty the ashtrays, would she have been so careful with her clothes, placed her boots so precisely under the chair?

"I can't believe she's dead," Gracie said. "I have to tell Millie and Baxter."

"I'd appreciate your waiting until after I've talked with them." With homicides, some witnesses were eager to talk, while others clammed up. "Is there a place where we can talk in private?"

"I'm on duty," she said.

The Silver Spur smelled like beer, peanuts, and beef grilling over open flames, and something sweet, brown sugar melted in butter. It smelled damn good. Much better than the fast food places Radhauser usually frequented for lunch. "Ask someone to fill in for you while we talk."

"It's Sunday morning," she said. "And only Millie and I are working. I'm already behind because of Matt."

"This won't take long." He nodded toward Millie. "Ask her to help you out."

Gracie led him around a horseshoe-shaped bar with about thirty chrome-based swivel stools, their seats covered in red vinyl. The bar, along with a dance floor, occupied the entire center of the restaurant, with seating areas for dining on either side. It was just about noon and already half the stools were filled with jeans-clad men watching a baseball game and drinking beer from frosty mugs, their elbows planted on the bar.

"Millie," Gracie said to the older woman who tended bar. "I need you to watch my tables for a few minutes."

Millie shot her a look that could have wilted cabbage. She was dressed just like Gracie, except her red cowboy boots looked brand new. "What am I, college girl, the babysitter?" she asked, her face half hidden behind her teased blonde hair. Though she appeared to be in her fifties, she had one of those irritating, high-pitched little girl voices and a slight southern accent. She poured Jim Beam into an oversized shot glass.

Radhauser took out his badge. "I'll need to speak with you, too. When I finish with Gracie."

Millie stopped pouring, raised her left hand to her mouth for an instant, then returned her attention to the bar.

At one end of the counter, a knot of sports enthusiasts stood arguing over an umpire's call. The floor by the bar was littered with peanut shells. When one of the men, wearing a white baseball cap, took a step forward to pick up his beer mug, the shells crackled like insects under his boots. None of the bar's patrons glanced up at Radhauser as he maneuvered past their stools. The murmur of their conversations continued uninterrupted.

Gracie stopped in front of a small booth in the far corner, away from the customers.

Radhauser slid across the bench. The window overlooked the parking lot.

Gracie took the seat across from him and put her hands on the table. Her nails were manicured, polished bright red to match her bandanna, and she wore a class ring on her right ring finger.

The table was covered with red and white checked oilcloth, already set with a red napkin wrapped around silverware and a wooden lazy susan that housed condiments. An old-time jukebox hung on the wall, just below the window frame.

"So, you're a college student?" Radhauser asked in an attempt to break the ice.

"Millie likes to make fun of me, but I take classes at Pima College," she said, looking up at him through a dark fringe of bangs. "I'm studying to be a nurse."

"Good for you. I hear there's a shortage."

She nodded, but said nothing more.

"When was the last time you saw Crystal Reynolds?"

"I see her often," Gracie said. "She is, I mean she was, my friend and she worked here." Her dark eyes pooled with tears. It was pretty obvious she cared about Crystal.

"Did you see her last night?"

Gracie clamped her eyes shut as if she didn't want to see herself talking to a detective about her friend. "In the parking lot. A little before six. Travis dropped her off, before his dance. It was a big night. Even that guy she used to—" She stopped abruptly and brought her hand to her mouth. Color rose on her cheeks.

Radhauser leaned forward in the booth. "That guy? Crystal was with a guy in the parking lot last night?"

"Please, I didn't mean to say that."

"But you did say it."

"It was just an old friend of Crystal's. Someone she lived with when Travis was a baby."

"Does this old friend have a name?"

"She didn't say."

"Lying to the police is perjury and it could put you in jail."

"Crystal swore me to secrecy."

"I won't tell her," Radhauser said.

"And you won't tell Millie or Baxter?"

Radhauser shook his head. "So, this old friend of Crystal's was in the parking lot on Saturday night?"

She nodded. "He came by Friday and he wanted to see Travis, but Crystal was adamant. She threatened to get a restraining order. But he kept begging, and finally she agreed he could see Travis when he dropped her off yesterday, but she made the guy swear not to say anything to him."

"Did she tell you his name?"

"No."

"Did the person who'd wanted to see Travis wait?"

"He sat in the cab of his truck. An old Ford, black with one red fender."

"What happened after Travis drove away?"

Across the room, a customer clicked his spoon against his coffee cup and glared toward Radhauser and Gracie. "I'm not paying for cold steak fries," he said.

Gracie stood.

"We're not finished," Radhauser said.

Millie shot Gracie another of her cabbage-wilting looks, then took a plate from beneath the warming lights and delivered it to the disgruntled customer's table.

"I need to get back to work," Gracie said. "This job pays my tuition."

"The quicker you answer my questions, the sooner you'll do that. Now, what happened when Travis drove away?"

She slid back into the booth. "Crystal was dressed for work, but she didn't come inside and start setting up her tables like usual. She just stood there—leaning against the building so Baxter, he's our boss, wouldn't see her. When she spotted me crossing the parking lot, she put her finger to her lips and beckoned me over. She looked happier than I'd seen her in months. That's what makes this so…"

"What was she happy about?"

Gracie wrung her hands and stared at the tabletop. "She didn't tell me. But I could tell by the way she behaved."

Radhauser got the distinct feeling she was lying. "Are you sure she didn't tell you?"

"Listen, Crystal and I were friends. We shared some of the same dreams. And we told each other things in confidence."

"She's dead, Gracie. And if she was murdered, you'd want justice for her, wouldn't you?"

Gracie's eyes widened, then filled with tears.

Radhauser gave her a moment to compose herself.

She wiped her cheeks and then blew her nose on a napkin. "Crystal didn't have time to say very much. Someone came to pick her up. She asked me if I'd cover her shift, waved and was on her way."

"Did you recognize the driver?"

"No. But it was a very nice car. Big. And expensive-looking."

"Are you sure you didn't recognize the driver of the car?"

"No. He had on a cap, like a chauffeur wears. But I've seen the car before."

"Where?"

"Here, in the parking lot."

"Describe it for me."

She talked with her head in her hands, the way someone might cradle an aching jaw, as she described what had to be a white Lincoln Continental, one of the Marks, with the tire well on the back and a blue Landau roof. Radhauser knew the car. His father, a World War II vet, had considered it his dream car.

"It had a little oval window on the side."

He nodded, realized he was closer to answering the question of how Crystal had gotten home last night. "Did her friend in the truck leave then, too?"

"He followed them out of the lot."

"Which way did they turn?"

"Both of them turned south, towards Tucson."

"You've been very helpful, Gracie. Would you ask Millie to join me now?"

Gracie slid out of the booth and stood. She brushed her bangs away, her brown eyes wide beneath them. As she walked away, someone put quarters in the jukebox and the Mamas and the Papas sang California Dreaming.

Millie slid into the booth. "What's this all about, sugar?"

"Crystal Reynolds," he said, showing her his badge.

Millie leaned across the table, exposing her ample cleavage. "Has something bad happened to her?"

Radhauser hadn't anticipated that question. "Why would you think that?"

"I don't know. It just popped into my head. But Crystal had a way of pissin' people off."

"When was the last time you saw her?"

"Is she missing?"

"I'm asking the questions," Radhauser said.

"My policy is to always cooperate fully with law enforcement, especially when he has blue eyes as dark and pretty as yours are."

Radhauser had no trouble imagining Millie chatting up law enforcement. "When did you last see Crystal?"

"I see her all the time. She works here. Well she's supposed to, anyway."

Radhauser waited.

"All right. I saw her Friday night. We both had the 6pm to 2am shift all weekend. Not that she hung around for hers last night. You can tell me, sugar, is she in some kind of trouble?"

"Did Crystal seem upset to you? Angry or depressed in any way?"

"No, she was happier than she'd been in a long time."

"Do you know why?"

"I suspect it had something to do with getting back together with her hot-shot boyfriend."

"Did you ever meet this boyfriend? Hear his name?"

"No, but she claimed he had a lot of money and would take care of her, send her to college so she could make something out of herself."

"Claimed? You didn't believe her?"

Millie smiled. "You never knew with Crystal. She used to watch reruns of Perry Mason when she was a kid. I reckon that was where she got her big dream of being a lawyer." Millie rolled her dark eyes. "Fat chance. She never even graduated high school. Not that she isn't smart as a whip, especially with men."

A group of about eight people entered. One of them rang the bell at the hostess podium.

"I have to seat those folks," Millie said, sliding to the edge of the booth.

"Gracie can seat them."

When Millie saw Gracie heading toward the podium, she settled back into the booth.

"How did Ms. Reynolds get along with your boss?"

"If you ask me, she should have stuck with Bax. He was plum crazy about her. And he would have helped her go to college, too." She waved her right arm, encompassing the restaurant and bar. "He owns this joint."

"So, Ms. Reynolds and Mr. Baxter were lovers?"

"I doubt she loved him, but they did the nasty, if that's what you mean." She grinned and looked up at him as if waiting for a comment on her cleverness.

"Does Mr. Baxter have a first name?"

"Yeah. It's Thomas. But we all call him Bax."

"Did he work last night?"

"Yeah, he was here."

"What time did he leave?"

"A little before 10pm. It was supposed to be his night off, but when Crystal didn't show, he worked a few hours until the rush was over."

"Was he angry she didn't show up for work?"

"Bax was used to being disappointed by Crystal. She broke his heart about fifteen different times. But he had perspective. Bax had real tragedy. His little girl, Becka."

"What happened to her?"

She held a pencil in her hand and twirled it in her fingers like a miniature baton. "I don't much like talking about the dead. My momma used to say it was bad luck."

Radhauser was glad he hadn't told her about Crystal. "How did Becka die?"

"Oh, all right. Bax didn't see her in the rearview mirror. Can you imagine? And then his wife just up and left him. For a while afterwards, we all thought his cheese had slipped plum off the cracker." Millie shook her head. "That poor man won't even park at the K-mart unless he can drive straight out of the spot. It's like one of them fetishes or something."

Jesus, Radhauser thought, realizing he could at least blame the drunk driver for the loss of his family. He wondered how a man could live, knowing he was the one responsible. But people were resilient. He'd had a breakdown after botching the Tyler Mesa case, spent a couple weeks in Palo Verde Psychiatric Hospital, but somehow he'd gone on. He still thought about it a lot—a little boy dead because of him. He couldn't imagine how much worse it would be if it had been his own kid. He sometimes thought God had paid him back by taking Laura and Lucas.

"Earth to Detective Radhauser," Millie said. "Where'd ya go, sugar?"

"Sorry," Radhauser said. "Do you know where Baxter went after he left?"

"He claimed he was going right to bed, but I heard his television blasting when I emptied the trash around 11pm. So, if Bax needs one of those alibi thingies, I can give him one. He has a motion light over his garage. It shines right on the cash register for at least five minutes. Bax don't go nowhere at night without me and

95

Gracie knowing about it."

Radhauser slid out of the booth. "Why would he need an alibi?"

She gave him a big smile. "In case Crystal pulled a heist at the 7-11 with some ex-boxer dude sporting a comb-over."

He laughed. "Where is Thomas Baxter now?"

She looked around the restaurant. "He was horsing around with the guys at the bar, but he left. He lives in that brown house right next to The Spur. Ain't that convenient?"

CHAPTER FOURTEEN

Radhauser rang the bell.

Thomas Baxter answered the door, wearing a tank top and a pair of navy blue sweat pants. He was about fifty, olive-skinned with a barrel chest, a hard belly, and arms that bulged as if they were stuffed with small cantaloupes. His feet were large and bare, and his toes had little tufts of black hair growing out of them. He looked like the kind of man who swaggered when he walked.

Radhauser silently cautioned himself not to judge too harshly. He and this man were in the same fraternity. *I survived a dead kid.*

"I'm not buying anything," Baxter said. "I don't care if you're selling Girl Scout Cookies in drag."

Radhauser showed him his badge. "I'm here about Crystal Reynolds."

"Maybe you should offer that worthless bitch a job in the Sheriff's office doing the donut run, because if she doesn't show up again today, I plan to fire her ass."

Radhauser studied Baxter's face. Either he was a very good actor who'd practiced his script or he had no idea Crystal was dead.

"When did you last see Ms. Reynolds?"

"Is the bitch missing?"

"Answer the question, Mr. Baxter."

"Go home, Detective Radhauser."

"You can either answer my questions here or you can answer them at the Sheriff's Department."

Baxter stepped aside.

Radhauser entered. It was one of those modular homes, delivered to a site in two pieces—sparsely furnished, but neat and orderly. On the long bar between the living room and the kitchen, a nearly finished dollhouse occupied most of the available space. It looked like a replica of a southern plantation, with white wooden siding, six white pillars in front, an upstairs balcony, and black shutters at all the windows.

On an orange towel spread out beside the house, tools lined up as neat as surgical instruments. He'd used different wallpapers for each room and covered the floor with carpet. A miniature staircase, complete with a polished mahogany banister, led to the top floor.

"That's a real work of art," Radhauser said. "Is it for sale?"

Baxter shook his head. "It's for my daughter." He smiled then, as if the mere thought of his daughter made him happy. It was a warm and likeable smile.

Radhauser searched the room for evidence of another child. All the available wall space held enlarged and framed photographs of a smiling toddler with curly, raven-colored hair. In one of them, she rode a pink pony on wheels. In another, she sat, belted into a yellow plastic swing, Baxter behind her, his big hands grasping the chains on either side.

Radhauser looked away. Maybe Millie was right. Maybe Baxter had his own mental breakdown after his kid died. Pretty damn hard not to. Maybe it eased some of the grief to pretend she still lived. Radhauser shook his head. Hadn't he used a similar coping mechanism this morning when he'd left the lariat on Lucas' grave? If he told anyone, they'd think he was headed back to Palo Verde.

Baxter stood in front of the television. Phillies swamping the Dodgers. Mike Schmidt at bat.

As he picked up the remote and muted the sound, Radhauser thought about the posters on Travis's bedroom walls.

"Why don't you sit down, Mr. Baxter? This won't take long."

The springs creaked as Baxter dropped into his recliner.

Outside the sliding glass door, Radhauser spotted a patch of newly mown and edged grass—rare for Tucson. "Nice yard," he said, trying to put Baxter at ease. "Do you have a sprinkler system?"

"Yeah, I do, and a gardener. You may think it's faggy, but I like plants, especially flowering ones. Are you with the water police?"

"Just noticing, that's all."

"Well, I'm noticing you're taking up my time on my day off. What do you want?"

"When was the last time you saw Crystal Reynolds?"

"Friday," he said, without hesitation. "I shoulda seen her on Saturday, too, cause she was scheduled to work the late shift all weekend, but she didn't show. After all I—" He stopped, started again. "Well, suffice it to say, I was pissed."

"Does she miss work often?"

"Yeah," he said. "Too often lately."

Radhauser leaned forward, his elbows on his knees, and focused his attention on Baxter's eyes to see his reaction to the news. "I'm afraid she no longer needs your employment. Crystal Reynolds was found dead in her home last night."

Baxter sat up straight and grimaced as if the news had physically hurt him. "Oh shit. I…I don't know what to say. You must think I'm some kind of emotionless prick."

Yeah, Radhauser thought, *I do*. But he gave Baxter a moment, watching him carefully for any sign Crystal's death wasn't news to him.

Baxter slapped his forehead. "You stupid fuck. She was dead. Now I know why she didn't come to work. Oh God. How's her kid doing? How's Travis?"

"As good as anyone could be," Radhauser said. "Given what he came home to last night."

"How did she die?"

"A severed carotid artery."

"Jesus Christ," he said, real shock on his face. "You mean Travis was the one who found her?" Baxter hung his head for a moment, and when he lifted it again his eyes filled with tears.

Radhauser gave him a moment before he asked, "Do you know if she had a boyfriend? Or dated anyone?"

Baxter hesitated and fiddled with the controls on the side of his chair, raised the footrest, then lowered it again. He lifted his hands, palms up, empty, as if holding no answers. "Women," he said. "You know how it goes. I might as well tell you. Me and Crystal had an off-and-on thing. I was never all that serious about her. Good thing, I guess. For the last couple months, it's been mostly off. That is unless she was lonely, horny or drunk. Or if she needed to borrow money. She'd get all lovey-dovey, promise me anything, and I looked real good to her then."

"This is a routine question," Radhauser said. "I'm asking everyone who knew Crystal. Where—"

"I was right here," Baxter said. "I worked tables until about 10pm, then crashed in front of the tube. Never left the premises."

"Can anyone confirm that?"

"Ask that nosey Millie. She watches my place like a hawk. I keep meaning to get rid of that motion light over my garage."

"Have you ever seen Crystal with another man?"

Baxter laughed. "A guy waited for her in the Spur parking lot a few times. Fancy dresser. I suspected…but Crystal, she always denied anything romantic."

"Do you know his name?"

Baxter shook his head. "Crystal may have introduced him once, but I'm not good with names."

"Do you know what kind of car he drove?"

"Yeah. A gas-guzzler. Lincoln Mark V. Four years old but looked brand new. Pretty thing. White with a baby blue top."

Radhauser's gaze returned to the dollhouse. There was something about it that wouldn't let him go. He nodded toward the wall of photographs. "That's one beautiful little girl. She yours?"

"She was," Baxter said, his face stripped of color. He stood, crossed the room, straightened one of the frames, took a step back to examine it, then straightened it again.

For a moment Radhauser felt as if this man had turned inside out in front of him, as if Radhauser were witness to something between a father and his child as intimate as a bedtime story.

"Do you believe in reincarnation?" Baxter asked.

"I don't know much about it."

Baxter's dark eyes sparkled. "Sometimes, when a person dies young, they come back real quick because they didn't get the things done they were supposed to. I just hope I recognize my Becka when she does."

Radhauser nodded, thanked Baxter and left.

From the phone booth outside The Silver Spur, Radhauser called O'Donnell and asked him to do a check with the motor vehicle department and see if they could get a list of 1985 Lincoln Mark V owners. There probably wouldn't be more than a few hundred in the metropolitan Tucson area. O'Donnell bitched about it, called it a needle in a haystack. But, what the hell, they had to start somewhere.

CHAPTER FIFTEEN

With all four windows rolled down, Matt drove the short distance to his mother's house, hoping he could help Travis with Crystal's memorial. The spring desert smelled like dust and creosote. As he turned onto her dirt road and drove straight toward the northern face of the Catalina Mountains, the wind tossed his hair across his face, scratching his eyes.

The suburbs of Tucson hadn't spread this far north yet and the Sonoran Desert was still pristine. Prickly pears sported bright yellow wax-like flowers. Ocotillos flew red blossoms from the tips of their branches like flags. There were barrel cacti crowned with rings of orange flowers, and both teddy bear and longhorn cholla. Giant Saguaros rose in clusters around him, their thick green arms pointed toward the blue and cloudless sky.

When he pulled into the gravel driveway, Phaedrus, Nate's German Shepherd, ran alongside the car, a yellow Frisbee dangling from his mouth. Matt parked the car, opened the door and stepped out. Phaedrus dropped the Frisbee at Matt's feet, licked his hand and turned in circles around him. He smelled of damp fur.

Matt knelt in the gravel, patted the dog for a moment, scratching his ears and rubbing his muzzle. He picked up the Frisbee and tossed it down the driveway. Phaedrus raced after it.

The hacienda-style ranch house had thick adobe walls, arched windows, and a mission tile roof that blended with the colors of the desert. A Mexican-tiled courtyard opened off the front room. The backyard pool was enclosed within another half-moon shaped adobe wall. Behind it, the rugged northern face of the Catalina Mountains rose, a backdrop as striking as a postcard. He hurried around back and entered through the kitchen door.

His mother stood in her bare feet at the laundry room sink, staring at the brown stains smeared down the front of his tuxedo shirt. She plugged the sink, started the cold water and then sprayed stain remover on the shirt. She let it sit for a moment, then thrust the shirt into the water and swished it around a few times, but the stain remained.

Matt stepped up behind her. He stared into the sink, as tiny red swirls that were unmistakably blood undulated in the water like smoke curling from a chimney. "I told you I'd take care of that stain."

She flipped around to face him, stared at him for a long time. "You know you can talk to me about anything, right?"

Right, Matt thought. He could tell her how he'd had sex with Crystal. How he'd drunk himself stupid. He said nothing.

"That stain on your shirt is blood, isn't it?"

Matt turned away.

She grabbed his arm. "Is it Crystal's blood?"

"You think I killed Crystal? You think I'm capable of killing someone I loved?"

"No, honey. Of course not. I know you were upset at the wedding and I thought you may have gone to Catalina looking for Travis. Thought maybe you'd found Crystal and tried to help. If that's what happened, you need to tell Detective Radhauser."

"I was crying," he said. "After your wedding. And then I had a nosebleed. Are you happy now?"

She stared at him for a moment, then hurried into the kitchen, grabbed a bowl, held it under the ice dispenser until it filled with cubes, then dumped them all into the laundry room sink.

"Let me do it," Matt said. He rubbed the stained spots with an ice cube until his hands were so cold he could barely feel them. When the blood began to lighten, he left the shirt to soak. A few minutes later, the ice had done its job, broken down the hemoglobin and most of the stains were out.

"Put a cup of bleach in the machine," his mother said. "It will take out any residue."

Matt did as he was told, set the dial for a small load and when the washtub began to agitate, he dropped in the shirt, hoping that would be the end of it.

He sat at the counter in the kitchen. The silence in the house seemed to vibrate and hum. Sunday's newspaper lay folded on the blue tile countertop, but he didn't open it. "How come you and Crystal stopped being friends?"

Karina glanced at the clock that was part of the front panel of the stove. It made a constant grinding noise, which Matt thought of as the sound of time passing.

"I should be working on the Eagle Dancer," she said. It was the Hopi Kachina stained-glass window she'd been commissioned to make for the new bank on Oracle Road.

"Did you have a fight or something?"

"No. It was nothing like that. You stopped playing baseball, my business took off, then your father and I—"

Travis stumbled into the kitchen. It was one in the afternoon. He looked exhausted, his blue eyes bloodshot, his hair wild and sticking out on both sides as if he'd spent most of the night tossing. A sleep crease stained the right side of his face red.

He stared at them brokenly. "It was only a bad dream, right?" His face and eyes puffy with sleep, he sounded like a much younger child.

Karina set down her coffee mug, swiveled the stool around and opened her arms.

Travis stepped into them.

"No, honey. I'm so sorry. But it wasn't."

He dropped his head onto her shoulder for a moment. "It was always Crystal and me," he said. "Now I…"

Karina stroked the back of his head and neck.

He rocked in her arms, his hands up between them, clenched into fists on his chest. He let her hold him, but only for a moment. "What am I gonna do now?"

"Your mother would want you to go to college and play baseball—just like you planned."

"I used to think college was important…"

The phone rang.

Karina answered, listened for a moment, then put her hand over the receiver and turned to Travis. "It's Reverend Williamson from Narrow Way Church. He wants to talk to you." She handed him the phone, then beckoned to Matt and they left the kitchen to give him some privacy.

When they heard him hang up, they returned.

"I'm supposed to meet him at 2:30," Travis said. "He's gonna help me plan a memorial service for my mom."

"That's wonderful," Karina said. "Do you want Matt or me to drive you over or go with you?"

He shook his head. "Jennifer and her parents will meet me at the church. I can take Mom's Escort."

Matt knew there was no earthly help for this kind of pain. Maybe a church was what Travis needed now. God looking on with His eye on the sparrow.

"How about some breakfast before you go?" Karina asked.

"I'm not hungry."

"You have to eat. You'll get sick if you don't. And that won't help anyone."

"So why did you and my mom stop hanging out? Did you have a big fight or something?"

She bent to pull a frying pan from beneath the stove. "Why would you think that?"

"You used to do stuff together. Make banners for our teams and cupcakes for class parties."

"You and Matt outgrew team mothers, cupcakes, and banners. And after the divorce…well…I guess I needed to lick my wounds." She told him the same thing she'd told Matt; her glass business had taken off and she didn't have time for friends.

She set the pan on the stove and put her hand on Travis's shoulder for a moment. "The important thing for you to remember is she loved you more than anything and was very proud of you," she said, then headed to the refrigerator.

She fried up a pound of bacon, scrambled six eggs, toasted four pieces of wholewheat bread, and set two plates in front of them.

"It's a feast," Travis said, and to Matt's relief he began to eat and was still eating when the front doorbell rang.

Matt hurried into the entryway and opened the door.

Phaedrus sat on his haunches, his snout pointed up at Detective Radhauser who crouched down, rubbing the dog's ears.

Matt sucked in a breath. *Please, don't let him be here for the tuxedo shirt.* "I hope he didn't jump on you," he said, his heart thumping. "Phaedrus can be quite the lover."

Radhauser tipped his Stetson and smiled. "I like dogs, especially Shepherds," he said, his right hand still resting on Phaedrus' head. "I gave one to my son for his sixth birthday."

"How old is your son now?" Matt asked.

Radhauser cleared his throat and when he spoke, his voice was steady and strong, but his pauses were off, as if he'd started on the wrong breath. "My son died when he was thirteen." He looked over the acres of undeveloped desert. "It's great you live in a place where your dog can run free."

"Actually, it's Nate's dog."

Matt's mother joined him in the entry. "The land was one of the reasons Nate and I bought the house," she said. "But it's Sunday. Don't you ever get a day off?"

He stared at her silently for a moment. "Not when I'm working a case. I hoped you could help me with something. It will only take a minute or two."

"Are you any closer to discovering how and why she died?"

"We'll know more after the autopsy."

Matt held his breath. If Radhauser asked for the shirt, he'd have to tell him it was in the washing machine. If he got anywhere near it, he'd smell the bleach in the water. He held that piece of information like a hot stone in his chest.

"It's nothing to worry about," Radhauser said. "I'm establishing a timeline for everyone involved and need to verify where Matt was last night."

Karina stuffed her hands into the pockets of her sweat pants. Her fingers twitched inside them.

"Matt's not involved. He's a good boy, an honor student. He's never been in any kind of trouble," Karina said, as if Matt weren't in the room. "Besides, he was at my wedding last night."

The detective's expression softened. "It's part of a routine investigation."

Matt breathed. Radhauser hadn't come for the shirt.

"What time did he leave?"

"I'm not sure," she said. "It ended early. Travis was at his dance. Knowing my son, he was probably hanging out at the mall with Danni and her friends." She stepped aside so Radhauser could enter.

He took off his Stetson, fiddled with it for a moment, creasing and denting the crown. "I'll need addresses for Matt's friends."

"My address book is in the kitchen," she said.

Both Radhauser and Matt followed. "Don't bother, Mom. When I left the wedding, I was upset and I drove around for awhile. Later, I headed out to Marana to see Travis after the dance."

Travis stopped eating, pushed back his barstool and swiveled around to face the detective. "Have you found out who killed my mother?" There was an accusation in his voice, a hint of anger in his eyes.

Radhauser retracted a step and shook his head, a careful and almost sad gesture. "We haven't completely ruled out a suicide."

"There is no way my mother would do that." Travis blinked and tilted his head back, like Matt had seen men do when they tried to keep tears from spilling, but Travis's tears fell anyway. He wiped them with the back of his hand.

"I'm working hard on the case, son." He described the car Millie had seen Crystal get into last night. "Do you know anyone who drives a vehicle like that?"

Travis looked frozen—his eyes wide and unblinking, his fork full of scrambled eggs poised an inch from his mouth.

Matt locked gazes with him for an instant and then opened his mouth to speak, but nothing came out. A grenade thrown into the room could not have shocked him any more.

Radhauser's description of the car repeated itself like white noise inside his head with the volume turned up.

"Matt's father drives a car like that," Travis finally said.

CHAPTER SIXTEEN

At his interview with Matt's girlfriend, Danielle Warren, Radhauser learned Matt had left her house around 7:30pm—angry enough to rip a necklace from her throat.

Travis Reynolds' dance ended at midnight. That was a lot of time unaccounted for. And the kid seemed squirrelly—more nervous than he should be. Radhauser needed to talk to Matt again without his mother or Travis present. But not as much as he needed to talk to Loren Garrison.

It was a little after 2pm on Sunday when Radhauser pulled up in front of the sprawling stucco and adobe ranch house. He drove around the center island, expertly landscaped with boulders and giant multi-limbed Saguaros, and parked in the circular driveway. He walked through the arched façade and onto a Mexican-tiled porch with pots of hanging petunias someone had recently deadheaded—probably a gardener.

He rang the bell.

Matt opened the door.

The kid hadn't wasted any time getting back here. Radhauser hoped he'd listened to him and not warned his father about the car.

Matt took a step back, a look of fear spreading over his face. "Detective Radhauser. Is something wrong?"

A walnut-haired girl, dressed in black denim jeans and a bright red T-shirt with a sequined peace sign on the front, stood behind him.

Matt moved aside.

Radhauser stepped into the entry, one of those fancy Italiantiled rooms with a huge cherry-wood grandfather clock set against the wall. The brass pendulum made a faint ticking sound as it swung. He took off his Stetson and held it in his left hand.

Matt introduced his sister, Sedona.

"When I was little, I read all the Nancy Drew mysteries. I wanted to be a detective." She paused and smiled. "Of course, I was ten. Now I'm aspiring to be a movie star." She did a couple of tap dance steps, then bowed from the waist.

Matt soft punched her shoulder. "Her thirteenth birthday was Thursday. This time last week, she was mere child of twelve."

Radhauser smiled and offered his hand.

She took it.

Her hand was small and impossibly soft. "Winston Radhauser," he said. "But you can call me Wind." He encouraged the familiarity with kids, believing it disarmed and sometimes led to revelations that might not ordinarily be made.

Sedona raised her eyebrows and gave him a dazzling white smile.

This kid would break some hearts. And she took good care of her teeth, too.

"As in breaking wind," she said, deadpan.

Radhauser laughed. So much for familiarity. He'd heard that one before, but never from a thirteen-year-old girl. "Exactly. You can imagine the caliber of jokes I endured in high school. That one doesn't even make the top ten."

Matt shook his head. "She's like that with everyone. Totally obnoxious."

A door opened on the other side of the living room and a silver-haired man stepped out and hurried toward the entryway. Radhauser guessed him to be about six-foot-two—his body slender and hard muscled. He wore a pair of navy blue trousers and a crisp white shirt, professionally laundered and left open at the neck. The initials LPG were embroidered in pale blue on the cuffs. His cordovan loafers were polished to a soft luster, and they sunk deep into the white carpet as he crossed the room.

As the man moved closer, Radhauser recognized Loren

Garrison from a photo he'd seen in the *Arizona Daily Star*. The professor had a career in philosophy stretching back three decades. Radhauser did the math. Though Garrison looked younger, he'd have to be in his late fifties or early sixties. The article Radhauser read was about a textbook Garrison published. Both Harvard and Yale had committed to using it as their introductory text. No wonder he could afford Italian tile and a gardener.

"I'm Doctor Garrison. May I help you with something?" The man had an air of superiority—a man used to commanding respect—but there was a cord of tension in his neck that told him Doctor Garrison was nervous.

Radhauser introduced himself. "I'm here about Crystal Reynolds."

The smile froze on Garrison's lips. "I'm aware she passed away last night. It's a real tragedy. Especially for Travis. What can I do to be of help?" He led them through the entry, under a used brick archway, and into a family room with a matching fireplace surrounded by cherry cabinets and bookshelves crammed with leather-bound books.

Sedona and Matt followed. As Sedona passed by the fireplace, she kicked a bulging pink duffel bag closer to the hearth.

Radhauser stopped and picked up a new textbook from the table in front of the fireplace. He studied the front cover. *Debating the Issues of Modern Morality through Intellect, Reasoning and Ethics.* "That's a mouthful. Congratulations. Quite an impressive article in the *Daily Star*."

"The title is too long," Garrison said. "Not my first choice." He indicated a leather sofa and loveseat. They were positioned into an L, giving occupants the choice between a view of the fireplace and the wall of windows.

The kids hung back for a moment before Matt took a seat at a game table with a chess set that looked as if it had a match in progress. *Nice life*, Radhauser thought.

The aspiring actress stood off by herself, watching her father, her back against the windows.

Radhauser took a seat on the sofa. The windows overlooked

the northern side of the Catalina Mountains and a landscaped yard with a swimming pool and waterfall. Most of the landscaping was desert but on either side of the waterfall, multicolored rose bushes bloomed. "You have a beautiful place here." He set his hat, crown down, on the coffee table.

"May I get you something to drink?" Garrison asked. "A cup of coffee. Or a glass of ice water or lemonade?"

Radhauser declined.

Garrison sat on the loveseat facing the fireplace.

"Do you want to go someplace more private to talk?" Radhauser asked.

"I have nothing to hide from my children."

"I don't know how well you knew Ms. Reynolds," Radhauser said. "But it seems you were one of the last people to see her alive."

"No. That can't be true." His tone was soft, almost mournful. He closed his eyes for a moment as if he didn't want anyone to see how he reacted. But he continued to shake his head, eyes closed.

Radhauser gave him a minute. This guy had some strong feelings going on behind his closed eyes. "What was your relationship with Ms. Reynolds?"

Garrison's eyes shot open. "She is, I mean she was, the mother of my son's best friend."

Sedona moved closer and stood silently a few feet away, observing her father with no less intensity than Radhauser.

"What kind of car do you drive, Mr. Garrison?"

"It's Doctor Garrison. And I'm not trying to be evasive. I really want to know why you're interested in my car."

Radhauser was used to being a voyeur looking into the cracks and crevices of other people's lives. And nothing surprised him much. "Because it's my job to ask questions."

Despite everything he'd seen over the years, Radhauser liked to keep his perspective, liked to think his role was to assist people to be forthcoming, rather than punish them for being reticent and suspicious. He waited a few seconds, then asked the question again.

"I drive a 1985 Lincoln Mark V," Garrison said. "What

difference does it make?"

"Could it be white, by any chance? Blue Landau top?"

"Yes. Exactly. What is this all about?"

"Seems a car fitting that description was seen picking Ms. Reynolds up in the parking lot of The Silver Spur yesterday around 6pm."

Garrison's gaze shifted off Radhauser and landed on the floor.

"Was she upset?" Matt asked. "Did you do something to make her sad?"

"I'm conducting this interview, Matt," Radhauser said, then turned his attention back to Garrison. "These are routine questions, Doctor Garrison. I'm establishing a timeline for the victim. Travis dropped her off at The Spur a little before 6. One of the questions that came up during my investigation was how she'd gotten home."

Garrison looked up at his daughter. "Would you and your brother excuse us for a few moments? I'd like to speak privately with Detective Radhauser."

Matt took one more shot. "Gracie said she was really happy before you picked her up. What did you do to her?"

Sedona stepped closer, cocked her head and looked directly at her father, eyes wide and innocent. "You got something to hide, Mr. Morality and Ethics?" she asked, as if going for her Oscar.

Matt stood up fast and took her arm, nearly pulling her out of the room. He opened a door at the back of the family room that obviously led to a wing of bedrooms. A moment later, Matt and Sedona disappeared, closing the door behind them.

So much for the nice life. It sure looked like Sedona had issues with her distinguished father.

The doorbell rang.

Sedona burst back in and raced through the family room, grabbing the duffel bag on her way into the entry.

From where Radhauser sat, he could see her open the front door. "Hey, Nate," she said, handing him her bag. "Goodbye, Wind," she yelled, then closed the door and left without a word to her father.

There was an awkward silence.

"My daughter blames me for the divorce."

Radhauser said nothing. He gave Garrison a moment to collect himself. "What was the nature of your relationship with Crystal Reynolds?"

Garrison's expression grew thoughtful as if he were remembering a particular moment—something he'd refused to face earlier. His hair was so neat it looked like fine strands of pewter. This was a man who cared about appearances.

"Crystal has been a family friend for years," Garrison said. "She called me yesterday afternoon. Said she was in trouble and needed to talk. When she asked me if I'd pick her up at The Silver Spur around 6, she sounded upset. So, what could I do?" He shrugged. "I drove her home. We had a beer together." He paused. "We talked for about an hour. When I left, around 7pm, I assure you she was very much alive."

"Can you account for your whereabouts after you left Ms. Reynolds' house?"

"Do I need to?"

"You might," Radhauser said.

"I came directly home and was here all evening. Sedona was to stay with Matt and me while my ex and her new husband honeymooned. I didn't know what time they'd drop her off or if they'd call me to pick her up at the reception."

"And what time did they phone?"

"They didn't. Nate dropped her off around 9:30."

"What did Ms. Reynolds want to talk about?"

"Do I need a lawyer?"

"You're certainly entitled to one. We can meet at the police station and finish this conversation there."

"Crystal had something private she wanted to confide."

"This could be a murder investigation, Doctor Garrison," Radhauser said. "Nothing will be kept private."

Garrison's normally calm face dropped its mask for a moment, in which Radhauser saw a flash of something that looked like fear. "Murder? Who would want to hurt Crystal?"

"That's what I'm trying to find out." Radhauser repeated his question.

"She wanted to borrow money. I wrote her a check."

"Why would she come to you for money?"

Garrison's brow furrowed. "We've bailed her out before. Back when Karina and I were still married. And Crystal always paid us back."

"Did she tell you why she needed it?"

"I assumed rent or groceries."

"Is that what she told you?"

"No, it's what I assumed."

"How much?"

"A thousand dollars."

"That's a hell of a lot of groceries." Radhauser had gone through her purse and wallet and found no check. Travis had the car. The banks would have been closed, even if Crystal had a way to get to one. "Did you happen to see where she put it?"

Garrison checked his watch. "No. But check behind that baseball picture of Travis she keeps in her wallet."

He sounded like a man who'd seen Crystal's wallet before. Travis had mentioned his mother drank too much and had fallen behind in the rent. Radhauser hadn't removed the photograph when he'd searched her wallet. Garrison's check could very well be there. He made a note to follow up.

"Are we through here?" Garrison asked. "I've got a radio interview in less than an hour."

"Thank you for your time, Doctor Garrison. Would you mind getting Matt for me?"

"What's my son got to do with this? He was at his mother's wedding until late. Crystal was already dead by the time Matt got to Catalina."

Radhauser wasn't surprised Matt hadn't told his father he'd left the wedding early. Most teenaged boys never told their parents anything, unless backed into a corner and the information bulldozed out of them. "I need to talk to your son, sir."

Garrison left the room and returned a moment later, Matt

trailing behind him.

The boy looked stunned, his face red, as if he'd been caught doing something he shouldn't have.

"Could you stop by the sheriff's office today?" Radhauser asked. "I'll be there until 7pm or so. It's nothing to be alarmed about. I'll be asking you the same questions I asked last night, but departmental policy dictates I tape the interview." This wasn't true, but Radhauser didn't want to raise the boy's anxiety level. "Just routine," he assured him. "I'll be calling Travis in, too."

Matt seemed to relax a little. "No problem."

"I'm coming with him," Garrison said. "And I'm bringing my lawyer."

"It's okay, Dad. I'd rather you didn't. I'm eighteen and I don't need a parent or a lawyer present. Besides, I'd like to speak privately with Detective Radhauser."

If Doctor Loren Garrison noticed the echo, the mocking tone in his son's voice, he made no comment.

CHAPTER SEVENTEEN

After his father's Lincoln cleared their driveway, headed for University Boulevard and the KUAZ Radio station, Matt raced through the living room to his dad's bedroom and its attached study.

Detective Radhauser said his dad was seen picking Crystal up at The Silver Spur yesterday—he was one of the last people to see her alive. He could be the boyfriend Gracie talked about. The man Mrs. Lawrence saw Crystal fighting with in the driveway. His dad could be the reason Crystal had been crying. His dad was a jerk, an asshole for wrecking their family, but he had better sense than to get involved with Travis's mother. At least, Matt hoped he did.

Matt rummaged through his father's roll-top desk, looking for anything that might connect his dad to Crystal. He found nothing. *Good*, he thought. It was all his imagination. Maybe Crystal needed a ride home. Maybe she tried other people and they weren't available. Maybe she'd gotten sick. She was a family friend, after all.

Or maybe she realized it wasn't the best night for Loren Garrison, with his wife remarrying. Maybe she wanted to give him something to do. To make him feel useful. Crystal was a kind and loving person. Maybe she intended to cheer his father up.

He checked the dresser drawers, lifted the neat stacks of boxers and undershirts, but found nothing. He examined the carved wooden box where his dad kept his watches and class rings. Matt discovered a silver ID bracelet with thick links of chain he'd never seen his father wear. He picked it up. It was shiny and new-looking, engraved with the name *Lore* in a fancy script—a nickname he'd never heard his mom call his father. He turned it over and found an inscription. *All my love forever, C.*

As if it were scalding hot, Matt let go of the bracelet. It fell to the floor. It was hard for him to say what he felt. A horror about the events of last night, but beneath it a jittery fear neither he nor his father was the person Matt had once believed them to be.

Don't jump to conclusions, he warned himself. It could be a bracelet his dad had kept from college, or from a high school girlfriend in a time before he knew Karina. He thought about all the names that began with the letter C. Connie. Coleen. Catherine. Cecelia. Christine. Carole. Dozens.

When his dad had finally confessed to his affair, the real reason for the divorce, Matt asked him about the other woman. His father claimed it was someone he worked with—someone Matt had never met. No matter how hard he tried to get his mind around the idea, he couldn't believe his father would have an affair with Crystal.

Matt dropped to his knees, searched the thick white carpet, found the bracelet and studied it again. Even if it were old, it would still look new if his father had never worn it. Matt stood, and dropped the bracelet back into the box. He shouldn't be spying on his father like this. He would be livid if his dad rummaged through his things.

Despite his efforts, Matt couldn't stop himself. He needed to find something else—something more definitive. His father was a fanatic about record-keeping. Matt rummaged through the file cabinets, found the folder for his MasterCard bills and pulled out the last three months. He ran his finger down the list of charges. Roses ordered three weeks ago from Desert Florist. There was a delivery charge, but no record of where they'd been delivered.

Matt pulled out the telephone book, looked up the number and dialed. "This is Loren Garrison. I ordered flowers a few weeks ago, and I've been out of town and just discovered they were never received. Could you verify the delivery address for me?"

The woman on the other end of the line looked through her records. "Where did you intend for them to be delivered, Doctor Garrison?"

Matt took a chance and gave them Travis's address in Catalina. He braced himself.

"I'm sorry, sir, but our records indicate they were delivered to an address on Edison on April 1st and signed for by a Wilma Southwick."

Matt breathed. It was his father's long-time secretary. He'd wanted to send Wilma flowers to celebrate the publication of his textbook—for all the extra work she'd done for him.

"My mistake," he said. "Sorry to trouble you." He didn't know what the hell was wrong with him. Sure, his dad lied to him about the affair, but most parents would lie to protect their kid. Matt had lied to Travis for the same reason. It was as if Matt were two people. The Matt who kept hoping Crystal's death had been a nightmare—that none of it had ever happened. And then there was the sex-craved, wannabe poet Matt, who'd had sex with his best friend's mom just hours before her death and wanted someone else to blame.

* * *

With the squeak of the redwood gate's hinges, his mother glanced up at him and smiled, her dark eyes lit from the inside. She was kneeling in front of the rose bed, plucking weeds. She wore a pair of jean shorts, a blue sleeveless T-shirt, an old set of his soccer kneepads, and a floppy denim hat with a dorky silk sunflower glued to its upturned brim. "No one home but me," she said, then told him Travis hadn't returned from his meeting with Bryan Williamson. "Nate took Sedona to the movies."

Matt kicked some dirt back into the rose bed. The scent of the blooms reminded him of real love—of the roses he'd sent to Danni last Valentine's Day. "I should be the one helping Travis with the memorial. At least I knew Crystal."

His mother gave him a closed-mouth smile. She picked up a pile of discarded leaves, deformed and yellowed with dark spots that looked like blackheads, dropped them into her bucket of weeds and stood. "I couldn't focus on the stained-glass window, so I decided to take care of the roses." She took off her garden gloves and touched his shoulder. "I've got mac and cheese in the oven.

Lots of black pepper and sharp cheddar, the way you like it."

"I'm not very hungry."

Her gaze wandered to his chinos, the open-collar button-down shirt, and the slightly too big navy blazer his dad had insisted Matt wear. "You look nice. Do you have a date with Danni?"

He swallowed, looked away for a moment, then told her about his meeting with Detective Radhauser.

Her face paled. "Why?"

"Some routine questions about last night. No big deal."

She cocked her head and studied him for a moment. "Is there something you want to talk about?"

A slow panic built inside him. He forced his back straight, squared his shoulders and returned her gaze. "Like what? Why do you keep asking me that?"

"Why won't you talk to me?" His mother's voice sounded fragile. She dropped a hand on his shoulder. "Danielle called. She's worried about you."

There was a dull roaring sound in his ears. Danni had reached out to him. "Did she ask to talk to me?"

His mother paused, seemed to measure her words. "She wanted to talk to me."

"Did she want me to call her back?"

"Did you have some kind of misunderstanding?"

Matt cringed, fought the urge to tell her there was no misunderstanding what the linebacker from Tucson High School meant, but he remained silent.

"You can tell me anything," she said. "You know that, don't you?"

He couldn't tell her he'd had sex with Crystal two hours before she died. That Crystal's death made him remember everything about Lake Powell and how it was his fault Justin was dead. Like she'd even believe him if he did. He couldn't tell her any of it. They were his burdens, not his mother's. He deserved them and so much more.

She tightened her grip on his shoulder. "Are you sure you're all right? The hospital called. They said you didn't show up this morning."

He twisted away.

"Don't worry," she said. "I told them what happened. Of course, they understood. They just wanted to make sure you were all right."

"How can I be all right? How can anything be all right again?"

"Listen to me. What happened to Crystal is terrible. But it wasn't your fault. People die. All we can do now is help Travis as much as we can."

Matt stared at his shoes, the cordovan loafers his dad had polished. The air held the faint smell of rain and he could almost feel the dry desert floor reaching up to meet the sky.

She glanced at her watch. "It looks like Travis is going to be late. The mac and cheese is done. Please. Have some dinner with me before you talk to Detective Radhauser."

When he nodded, she headed through the side door into the garage, her gait slightly askew from the kneepads slipping down her legs and settling around her ankles. She took them off and tossed them, along with her gloves, into a deep wicker basket beside the kitchen door.

With the scent of melting cheese and toasted breadcrumbs drifting into his nostrils, he followed.

At the table set for three, she asked if he was nervous about talking to Detective Radhauser.

He shrugged.

She waited a moment as if giving him time to formulate a better response. When he said nothing, she made a suggestion he write Danni a note—tell her how much he wanted to work out their misunderstanding.

Matt kept his head down to avoid having to look into her dark eyes. But it didn't matter. He still felt their heat—those eyes that could peel him away in layers. He ate his salad and macaroni in silence.

"Danielle called because she was worried about you. Maybe you need to take a step in her direction now."

Matt thought about the poem he'd written for Danni about their bodies being like wings, flying in and out of each other. The poem her mother had found. His ears and neck grew warm. "She didn't ask to talk to me, Mom. What am I supposed to do? Beg?"

"I'm not suggesting you beg, only that you meet her halfway."

"Does she know about Crystal?"

"I'm sure she would have mentioned it if she did. As far as I know, it hasn't made the news yet. Detective Radhauser may have a reason to keep it quiet for now."

She pushed the salad around on her plate.

The clock on the stove ticked loudly, like someone had turned up the volume, the way clocks sounded at midnight when no one else was awake.

"So," she finally said, a hint of defeat in her voice. "Have you made your decision about colleges yet?"

"I'm leaning towards Iowa," he said, relieved for a subject that didn't make his skin crawl. "I need to accept and get the deposit in by May first."

She lifted her eyebrows and nodded, a slight smile on her face.

"It has this really cool program where they design a freshman curriculum and a reading list based on my questions. I already have three good ones. 'Can a person do something horrible and still find redemption?'"

Her smile disappeared. She unraveled a thread at the armhole of her shirt, glanced at the photo of Matt and Justin at Lake Powell.

Matt had an unmanageable lump in his throat. He drank some water. "Do you want to hear my other two?"

She nodded.

"'What does it mean to be human?' And 'do we have an immortal soul?'"

Her face brightened again. "That school sounds perfect for you. Send off your acceptance letter."

"Dad wants me to go to Penn, like he did."

"It's your decision, not your father's."

"I'm also thinking about the University of Arizona."

"I know it doesn't seem like it now, but Travis will be okay," she said. "He'll hit homeruns for the U of A. He'll be a superstar. We'll be around to cheer him on. And if Travis needs anything, Nate is very good with young people."

Matt's new stepfather was the guidance counselor at Marana High School. According to Travis's girlfriend—a student there—the kids rushed to him with problems they couldn't tell their parents. And Mr. Nathan Sherman kept their confidences as if he were a priest. Matt imagined Travis hanging out with Nate—the two of them buddies, going to games or a movie together while Matt was in Iowa. A surge of jealousy spread through him. He checked his watch, stood. "I have to go. I don't want to keep Detective Radhauser waiting."

* * *

When the doorbell rang, Loren hurried into the entryway, flipped on the porch light and opened the door. Karina stood under the yellow glow. She wore a pair of denim cutoffs, a teal blue T-shirt with a pink flamingo on the front, and pink running shoes—looking as if she'd just come in from a game of badminton behind her college dorm.

He had no right to it but jealousy stabbed him hard. "Karina. Is Matt okay?" He stepped aside so she could enter.

Loren had always been able to gauge her moods from a distance of fifty feet. She was scared, a little nervous, and definitely on a mission.

"I'm sorry to barge in on you like this, but I'm worried." She told him what he already knew, Matt was in Catalina being re-interviewed by Detective Radhauser.

"It's routine. Nothing to worry about," Loren said. "He'll be bringing Travis in for additional questioning, too."

She looked everywhere except into his eyes. "It's more than that." She told him about the blood on Matt's tuxedo shirt.

Loren tried to remain calm. "Did you ask him about it?"

She tossed him a sideways look. "Nosebleed."

"Is there some reason you don't believe him?"

She followed him into the family room. "Yes. He's lying. And if Radhauser discovers it, Matt will be implicated in Crystal's death."

Loren knew better than anyone his ex-wife could spot a lie from half a mile away.

"At first, he said he'd spilled something on the shirt. Later, when I confronted him with the blood, he invented the nosebleed." She talked fast and Loren heard a tremble in her voice. "There was a lot of blood—smeared all over the front, like he'd used his shirt to clean his hands." She set her purse on the table and either ignored or didn't see the copy of his new textbook.

"The wedding wasn't easy for Matt."

Karina sighed, took a seat on the burgundy leather sofa, crossed and then uncrossed her legs. She wore the perfume she'd always worn, Oscar de la Renta, and the powdery scent unnerved him.

"Aren't you even a little bit concerned Matt may be implicated in a murder case?"

"She committed suicide."

"I don't know how you can be so sure when the police aren't," she said.

Loren sat on the platform rocker, leaned back and lit his pipe, giving himself a chance to regroup. The cherry-scented smoke wafted into the air. "No," he finally said. "I'm not worried. I know my son. I trust Matt. But you know as well as I do he's been different, darker and less talkative, since…"

Karina grimaced. "It's been almost six years. Why do you still think everything Matt does is connected to Justin's death? What about the divorce? Haven't you read studies about depression and anger in teenagers with divorced parents?"

The stone smoothness of her words chilled him. He stood, paced around the family room for a minute, puffing on his pipe and trying to find an appropriate response. The grandfather clock in the entryway chimed 7:30.

He forced his back straight, his shoulders square—the ramrod posture of self-confidence once enforced by his military father. "I didn't mean to hurt you or break up our family," he said for the hundredth time. "Surely you know that."

She steepled her fingers. "What I know is you're so concerned about your image you can't see our son could be in trouble."

"That's not fair. You know how much I love Matt."

"Then talk to him. Make him understand that lying to the

police will make him look guilty."

"Guilty of what?" He glanced at her hands—at the diamond solitaire and matching wedding band from Nate. Loren wondered what she'd done with the marquis-shaped diamond ring he'd given her. "Matt had nothing to do with Crystal's death."

Through the big wall of windows, the sun was setting, dropping its pink blanket of light over the mountains.

"Truth has a way of coming out," she said. "I still believe Matt needs to hear it from you."

"I know I haven't been a perfect father, but I'm better at it now that Matt's growing up. I'm not a liar, by nature. I couldn't stand the idea of Matt not trusting me."

He'd seen what even justified suspicion had done to Karina. It was like acid, everything it contacted corroded. It ate through shiny surfaces, sometimes even its own container, and left permanent scars in its wake—scars he'd hoped his son would never have to bear.

She looked at him with her dark eyes, both brave and a little apprehensive. "I'm scared, Loren."

He stood. With every ounce of his being, he wanted to go to her, to wrap his arms around her, to make her feel safe again. Instead, he took a step back, lost his balance and fell into the rocking chair. He smiled. "As you can see, I'm the picture of grace and composure."

She laughed.

"It's going to be okay." He wished he were half as sure as he sounded.

Karina, whom he knew would never shy away from self-examination, looked off into space for a moment, her brow furrowing. "It's human nature. We all like to hide the selves that aren't moral, ethical or smiling," she said, with sadness, not judgment, in her voice. "But no matter how deep a hole we dig, they get hungry, like bears just out of hibernation."

"Matt's not like me," he said.

"Matt adores you. He's emulated you since he was a toddler."

"I talked to the volunteer supervisor at UMC. The oncology

staff and the lab all love him. Not to mention the kids." He kept his voice soft and modulated. "He doesn't have any indicators for violence." Loren thought about the phone call he'd gotten from the high school principal, the essay Matt had written about the place where the dead congregated. They were passive gestures. And then Loren remembered the fist-sized hole he'd found punched into Matt's closet wall.

"For God's sake, Loren. I'm not suggesting he killed her. Only that he was there. Maybe he was looking for Travis, stumbled on her body and tried to help her. You know how fond he was of Crystal." Abruptly, she stood.

"Do you want me to talk with him about the blood?"

"No. I've probably made too much out of it already." As she passed through the family room, she stopped and lifted his textbook from the table. She turned the book over and examined the author photo for a moment, before returning the book to the table. "Congratulations. You look proud. Loren Garrison, the expert on morality and ethics." She gave him a closed-mouth smile.

There was a moment of silence. Words dangled on Loren's tongue. He wanted to say something to make the awkwardness between them go away. He wanted to tell her, despite his wandering, he'd loved her more than anyone.

"Look," she said, as if still able to read his thoughts. "I didn't mean for things to get antagonistic. I just wanted to give you a heads-up about the blood." She told him how they'd washed and bleached the shirt. "I plan to return it to the rental shop in the morning."

"So Radhauser didn't ask for it?"

"No. And after the bleach, I doubt there is anything left to identify. But you need to pay attention, Loren."

His nerves crawled like worms beneath his skin. "Maybe you need to believe what he tells you."

Two circles turned red on her cheeks. She closed her eyes for a moment as if there were no other gesture that could convey her exasperation. "Where does the truth fit into your life, or is

125

that something you don't worry about anymore?" She pushed her hands into the back pockets of her shorts—a familiar gesture.

A fist of remorse unfurled in Loren's gut as he watched her turn away and walk through the front door. When the crunching of the driveway gravel stopped, indicating she'd driven onto the paved street, Loren hurried into Matt's bedroom. He flipped through a stack of papers on his son's desk, stopping at a partially finished poem Matt had titled *The Real Room*. Loren read the first stanza.

Inside the real room there are mirrors—
Stained, scratched, shattered.
I am everywhere. And the worlds I've destroyed
Lie in pieces all around me.
In their deaths, the mourning begins.

Inside the real room there are masks,
And I have worn them all.

His son had attempted another half dozen or more lines, but had smudged many of them out.

He struggled to read the last legible stanza, his hands shaking.
The real room is a battlefield filled with corpses.
In their blue hands they hold pieces of my shame.
When I pry them out, my blood, impossibly red,
Flows onto their gray and lifeless skin.

He returned the pages, careful to place them exactly how he'd found them, then opened the bookcase headboard on Matt's bed.

A recent issue of *Playboy* magazine sat on top of a line of books, most of them classics. He smiled. Boys will be boys, even studious and well-mannered ones. He pulled out *Tom Sawyer*, wanting to re-read the inscription Karina had written. It was then he noticed a black leather journal Matt had hidden behind the other books.

Loren picked it up, stared at the cover. He'd never snooped in his son's room before. In truth, he didn't believe it was right. A journal was a private thing. But he was a parent, worried about his son. Afraid he may have done something—Loren stopped. He wouldn't allow himself the thought.

The journal held only one entry, dated September 8, 1983— less than two months after Justin drowned. Loren read the words Matt had printed.

Justin Speaks From His Grave

Before I plunged into the water, I took a deep breath. My heart pounded and I felt both brave and excited, like the time we went on Space Mountain at Disneyland. You were right, Matt, I could do it.

I sank and sank. Went down deeper than I'd ever been before. My right foot grazed the rocks, then wedged between two boulders.

At first I thought it was no big deal, but when I couldn't get my foot loose, I panicked and tried with all my strength to pull my foot out. It started to bleed. I needed to breathe. My body accumulated carbon dioxide and that made me want to breathe even more. I tried not to. I knew I shouldn't, but I couldn't help it. I sucked in a breath, but it wasn't air, it was lake water.

When water reached my upper airway, I coughed and then I swallowed more lake water, coughed again and swallowed even more.

I was more scared than I've ever been in my life—even the time we rode the roller coaster at Hershey Park. Like the baby you said I was, I cried for my mom.

My throat began to spasm when water reached my lower airway. It was my body trying to seal off the path to my lungs. With nowhere else to go, the water went into my stomach. It felt like I'd eaten three Earthquakes at Baskin Robbins. I wanted to barf. And then I stopped fighting and lost consciousness. I didn't feel this, but my throat relaxed and water went into my lungs. No one could have saved me. I was dead in two minutes.

At the bottom of the entry, Matt had entered one more line.

I miss you Justin and I'm sorry. It's all my fault.

Loren dropped the journal onto Matt's bed. His twelve-year-old son had obviously researched drowning. He'd wanted to understand and feel everything Justin had felt. Loren knew Matt blamed himself, but had no idea the depth of that little boy's guilt. No wonder he'd shut down.

What had carrying that kind of weight for six years done to him?

The sun hid behind the mountains and the light in the room seemed to thicken and gather around him like smoke. He replaced Matt's journal behind his row of books, then hurried into the family room where he sat in the dark, worried sick about his son.

CHAPTER EIGHTEEN

In the Catalina Sheriff's Department interrogation room, while Detective Radhauser peeled off his Levi's jacket and adjusted the thermostat, Matt stood in front of a rectangular green-legged table and tried to stop his knees from shaking. He was determined to stay calm, to answer questions as if he were completely innocent and wanted only to help—as if he knew nothing about the events leading up to Crystal's death.

The room smelled like burnt coffee, banana peels and cigarettes, with a trace of pine deodorizer. Two metal chairs with worn tweed seat cushions were placed across from each other. A single box of tissues sat on the tabletop.

Just like on television, one of the walls looked like a mirror. Matt moved closer. A reflection stared back, his own features so foreign he reached out and touched the glass to make sure it was real.

"There won't be anyone watching us," Radhauser said.

Under the fluorescent glare, a green plastic trashcan—the type used in kitchens—overflowed with empty soda cans, old newspapers and the tattered remains of food wrappers, tissues, and coffee cups. As he took a seat at the table, Matt wondered how long it had been since anyone emptied it. He wanted to take it out into the hallway so he wouldn't have to smell the rotting banana peels. He wanted to wipe the top of the table with a sponge. Then he thought about the mistake he'd made in cleaning Crystal's house. The crucial mistake that had raised both Radhauser's and Travis's suspicions.

Anxiety built inside Matt—his lies stacking up like a toddler's tower of blocks. He sat on his hands for a moment to see if he could stop them from shaking.

When Radhauser offered a Coke and a bag of potato chips, Matt welcomed the salt and the stomach-settling soda.

Radhauser dug in his pocket for change and stepped into the hallway. The change clinked as it dropped. "Piece of crap machine." He kicked it hard. The can fell out with a thud. Radhauser stepped back into the room and set the chips and Coke in front of Matt.

Radhauser set up a tape recorder, just like the ones physicians at UMC used to dictate patient notes. It was small enough to fit inside a shirt pocket.

Matt ate a couple of chips and drank from the Coke can. When his hands started to shake, he sat on them again.

Without any warning, the memory of Crystal on the sofa came back to him. The way she'd unbuttoned his shirt and ran her fingers down his chest and into the waistband of his tuxedo pants. The smell of her wildflower perfume and the warm softness of her hands, the taut skin stretching across her shoulder blades. Her smooth, slightly rounded belly. The weight of her breasts in his hands. A ripple of desire passed through him.

He wanted to slap himself. Would there be a day when he could say, "the night Crystal died" without an explosion of guilt consuming him?

Finally, the detective set down his clipboard with its attached yellow-lined tablet and pulled out the other chair. He took his black notebook from his pocket, then draped his jacket over the chair back and sat directly across the table from Matt. Radhauser paged through the notebook for a moment, then flipped on the tape recorder.

He dictated the time and date and the fact he interviewed Matt Garrison, the first layperson after the victim's son to arrive at the scene of Crystal Reynolds' death. When Radhauser finished, he set the recorder on the table between them and asked Matt to state his name, address, and age for the record.

Matt did.

Radhauser looked Matt directly in the eyes. "I want you to be straight with me. I realize you were probably in shock last night, but some things you said didn't check out."

Matt's head buzzed and his vision blurred around the edges, like smoke. "What things?"

"This is the way it works. I ask the questions." Radhauser watched him intently. "You answer with the truth."

"Am I in trouble?" Matt could barely hear his own voice over the pounding in his head and ears.

"Should you be?"

"I don't know." Matt looked at the tabletop. "It's confusing." He shook his head and a strand of hair slid over his forehead. He brushed it away.

"It feels intimidating. These rooms are designed that way. But you've got nothing to worry about. Just tell the truth. And let me sort things out."

There was something in Radhauser's voice that made Matt look up. The detective's eyes were blue. Not the usual blue color— deeper, like the startling sapphire of a lake he'd visited with his parents in Oregon. Crater Lake. "So, you acted like a jerk at your mother's wedding and left right after the ceremony."

"I don't deny that."

"Where did you go?"

"I wanted to see my best friend."

Radhauser stared evenly at Matt. "Didn't you know your best friend was at the Marana spring dance?"

Matt told him the truth—he had known, but been so upset he'd forgotten.

"I've had about enough of your lying bullshit."

"I'm telling the truth."

"You wouldn't know the truth if it kicked you in the ass."

"You have to believe me."

"I don't have to believe anything."

"I do know the truth," Matt said. "I do."

"Then tell it."

"It's not that simple."

"Bullshit," Radhauser said. "The truth is always simple. What time did you leave your mother's wedding?"

"I don't know the exact time, but right after the ceremony, so it was probably around 7:30." He told Radhauser what had happened at the wedding and how he'd sat in the Hacienda del Sol's parking lot for a few minutes, trying to compose himself. He then drove to Danni's house and was there for a while before he headed over to see Travis.

"What happened when you got there?"

"Halfway to his house, I remembered about the dance."

Radhauser made notes again. Notes Matt knew he'd review later, reconstructing Matt's version of the night piece by piece, like a house of cards.

"What time did you leave Ms. Warren's?"

Matt stiffened. "Was Danni's mother there when you talked with her?"

"I'm asking the questions, remember?"

Matt told him about finding Danni with another guy, how they'd argued for a minute or two, and how he'd ripped the heart pendant from her neck.

"Good," Radhauser said, as if Matt had just confirmed something the detective already knew. "So, you were angry when you left Ms. Warren's house. What time was that?"

Matt thought about Danni, the way her eyes had darkened before she closed the door. "I was hurt. I thought she loved... It was maybe around 8pm."

Radhauser paged back in his notebook as if to see if the time matched what Danni had told him. "Did you tell me you'd changed into the black T-shirt before going to Ms. Warren's house so you wouldn't look like a dork?"

Matt took another drink of Coke, slumped down a little in the chair. Radhauser had talked to Danni. He already knew the truth. "I had a nosebleed," Matt said, deciding to stick with the same story he'd told his mom. "After I left Danni's house. It happens sometimes when I'm upset. It dripped onto the shirt and that's the reason I changed it."

"What did you do with the shirt?"

"I left it in my car. And then my mom asked me to give it to her. So she could take it back to that rental place in the mall."

Radhauser cocked his head. His index finger absently tapped his cheekbone. "I don't get it. That's a perfectly legitimate reason for changing your shirt. Why perjure yourself by telling me you spilled something on it?"

Matt set the Coke can down, rapping it too hard against the tabletop. The sound echoed in the small room. People went to jail for perjury. "I was scared. I thought if I told you there was blood on my shirt you'd think I had something to do with Crystal's death."

"Did you?"

Matt's face burned. The pockets behind his eyes burned, too. He couldn't cry. Not now. He straightened his back. "I swear to you. I would never hurt Crystal." He thought about the way Crystal's eyes sparkled with tears when she'd heard about Travis's baseball scholarship. Matt swallowed several times, but couldn't get any moisture into his mouth. He felt claustrophobic in the tiny, windowless room.

"Did you drive directly from Ms. Warren's house to Catalina?"

"I already told you I remembered the dance. So, I turned off on Golder Ranch Road. I drove out that way for a while and parked so I could think."

"Where exactly did you park?"

Matt settled his gaze on Radhauser for a moment, then drew it away. "It's a dirt road. But somewhere near Casa Tucson—that drug and alcohol treatment center. I saw their lights. My mom made stained-glass windows for their chapel a couple years ago. I helped her deliver them. It's really beautiful out there. And quiet. A good place to think."

"Did anyone see you?"

"I doubt it."

"I know it was dark, but did any cars pass you on the road? Any walkers?"

"Not that I remember."

"How long were you there?"

"Until about 11:00 or 11:30, then I headed out to Marana to wait for Travis."

The detective leaned back. "You parked on a dirt road and thought for three hours?"

"Yes, sir, I'm a poet and that's what I do sometimes." The sweat dripped into Matt's eyes. He blinked it away, wiped his forehead with his arm.

"What were you thinking about?"

"My life. Mostly what a jerk I'd been at the wedding." He closed his eyes briefly, still trying to fathom everything that had happened.

Radhauser handed him a tissue. "It's warm in here. Why don't you take off your blazer?"

Matt wiped his face, then stood and struggled out of his father's jacket and draped it over the back of his chair. He smelled his own sweat. Under his arms, the oxford shirt was stained and wet.

Radhauser pulled a pack of cigarettes from his shirt pocket, put one in his mouth, but didn't light it. "Tell me how you felt about Crystal Reynolds." The cigarette flapped up and down when he talked, like a finger waving.

"She was my best friend's mother. I've known her since I was six." He told Radhauser about the way Crystal had taught them to dance in sixth grade. "And I loved her. Not in any weird way. More like the way you love your own mom." His voice broke when he realized that wasn't true anymore. Last Friday night, he hadn't loved Crystal like a mom. He'd loved her sexually—the way a man loves a woman.

"I take it you were pretty upset about your parents' divorce."

"Yeah. But that was two years ago."

"Ms. Warren said you were furious with your father last week. After you learned the real reason for the breakup."

"She shouldn't have told you that."

"Do you ever take your anger out on other people?"

"No," Matt said, thinking about the way he'd treated his sister last night. "What are you getting at?"

Radhauser raised his eyebrows.

"My father lied to me for two years," Matt said. "Of course I was angry."

"Parents have private lives, too. Things they don't discuss with their kids."

"I'm not a kid anymore."

For a long moment, Radhauser said nothing. "Your father is kind of a big shot, isn't he?" he finally asked.

"I guess."

"I read that article in the paper. I'll bet he'd do almost anything to keep an affair quiet."

"Why are you asking me about my father?"

"Everyone is a suspect until we piece it all together and figure out what really happened." He studied Matt's face.

Matt shriveled inside.

"What was your father's relationship with Ms. Reynolds?"

Matt shook his head, hard. "I didn't know he had one." What did the detective want from him? He'd been as surprised as anyone to learn his dad had driven Crystal home. But it didn't mean anything. One time his dad had driven Crystal and Travis to and from an all-star baseball game in Casa Grande when her car was in the shop.

"Why would he give her a thousand dollars?"

He could see the map in Radhauser's head, and felt himself being dragged along one of the back roads to the place where it all ended with Matt's father. "Because she needed help."

There was a faint smile on Radhauser's face. "I think that's enough for today, Matt. I want to thank you for your cooperation and your candid answers."

Matt stood, grabbed the blazer and reached into the pocket for his keys.

"Stick close to home and school for the next week. After we've canvassed the neighborhood and the autopsy findings come in, I may need to ask you a few more questions."

"It's finals week. Seniors have a pretty light schedule. If I'm not at school, I'll either be at home, my mom's house or with Travis," he said, then stood and left the room. He felt pretty good—felt as if Radhauser had believed what he'd said.

A few steps down the hallway, Matt remembered something, turned around and went back. He wanted to ask the detective when Travis could pick up the rest of his things. He wanted to make sure he was with Travis when he went back inside that house. "Detective Radhauser," he said, "I wonder—" Matt stopped, unable to finish his sentence.

Radhauser had a rubber glove on his right hand as he tucked Matt's Coke can into an evidence bag.

Matt forgot his question. He'd read a newspaper article about the first man convicted of a rape in Virginia based on DNA evidence. He pivoted, hurried from the room and down the hallway. His palms slapped against the heavy wooden door to the men's room and pushed it open. He lunged toward the stall, stumbled inside, then closed and latched the metal door behind him. He leaned back against it and shut his eyes, wanting nothing more than to hide from himself. Ten minutes ago, he'd felt confident he'd slide through this interview, answer the questions in the same way he'd done last night. But something changed.

It was clear Detective Radhauser didn't believe Crystal committed suicide. Radhauser had collected Matt's DNA. He was in big trouble—a suspect in her murder. What if the police discovered he and Crystal had sex just hours before she died? Matt hung his head. Even if he didn't kill her, he deserved punishment. He was Judas. He'd betrayed his best friend, and when Travis found out, nothing would ever be the same again.

CHAPTER NINETEEN

On Monday morning, Matt woke up with his neck and forehead covered in sweat. He'd been dreaming about sex with Crystal. After they'd finished, she pulled a pistol from under the pillow and held it to his head. It turned into a snake that slithered across the bed, up the wall, and out through the open window.

It was only a dream, he told himself. But it didn't stop the pounding in his chest. He wiped his face on the bottom of his T-shirt and listened for a sound that would tell him Travis was awake, but heard nothing.

On the end table, between the two twin beds, the red numbers on the alarm clock read 4:30am. The bedroom smelled like new paint and sweaty gym socks.

As Matt's eyes adjusted to the darkness, he saw Travis lying on his back on top of the comforter, hands behind his head, eyes open.

"You okay?" Matt whispered.

"Yeah. Fine," Travis whispered back. "And I'm going to school today, man. If I miss practice, I can't play in Friday's game. Baseball is the only thing—"

"Coach would make an exception. Mom can call and explain. We could stay in bed all day or play video games. Nab some of Nate's beer and hang out by the pool."

"I need to play baseball," Travis said.

"Maybe you could just show up for practice."

"If I want to ace the English lit final, I gotta hear Singleton's review."

"We can call the office, ask someone to tape it."

"Are you listening, dude? I'm going to school."

Matt pulled the comforter up to his neck, the washed cotton soft against his skin. It smelled like laundry soap and the pool towels his mother used to dry in the sunshine. "We should try to sleep."

"My brain doesn't have an off switch anymore. And you've been pretty noisy. Tossing around and yelling out."

For a moment, Matt couldn't say anything—his throat scratchy and hot. He threw the comforter off again. "I had a nightmare."

"You called out my mom's name. And then you said, 'please' like you wanted something." Travis sat up and swung his legs over the edge of the bed. He flipped on the table lamp and stared at Matt.

Matt froze. "I can't remember. Probably a Twinkie. You know how dreams are." He rubbed his eyes and yawned, giving himself a few extra seconds to think before he sat up and propped his back against the headboard. "It was confusing."

Travis tapped his bare foot against the floor.

A giant wave of guilt hit Matt hard. "If you want to go to school, we need to get some sleep." He reached over and turned off the light.

"I keep expecting to dream about her," Travis said. "I really want to."

Matt's hands curled into fists. "Don't be so sure. In my dream, she had a gun."

Travis was quiet for a moment before he whispered, "My mother wouldn't kill herself."

"Dreams are fucked up," Matt said.

For a moment, Travis said nothing. "I know, but at least you got to see her again."

Matt was glad it was dark in the room. "I did want something from her," he whispered. "I wanted her to live."

After a quiet minute or so, Travis got back into bed and pulled the comforter over him. "Before she started drinking so much, I thought I had the best and coolest mom in the world."

"Back then," Matt said. "I used to…"

"You used to what?"

Matt swallowed and forced himself to finish the sentence. "I used to wish she was my mom, too."

* * *

Matt sat on a kitchen barstool and watched his mother pack lunches. She wore a short yellow robe over her nightgown and a pair of ridiculous duck slippers Sedona had given her. Karina stopped spreading honey mustard on rye bread and turned to Travis. "I wish you'd reconsider and stay home for a couple days, honey."

Travis sat on the other stool, his hands cupped around a mug of coffee.

Karina busied herself picking out apples from the fruit bowl on the counter.

Travis shuffled his uneaten scrambled eggs around on his plate. "I know you want to help. But I…" He hung his head.

The silence in the room was a ticking clock.

Karina cut the ham sandwiches in half and dropped them into Ziploc bags. "You want life to feel normal again." She shot Matt a raised-eyebrow look that said *watch out for him.*

Matt gave his mom a quick nod. "I'll drive."

Travis slipped off the bar stool, picked up one of the lunch bags, and headed toward the back door. "No thanks. I want to drive the Escort."

"I'll ride with you."

"Dammit," Travis said. "Stop stalking me. I still have a life."

Karina touched Matt's shoulder. "Give him a moment," she whispered.

Halfway to the door, Travis stopped and turned toward Matt. "I have baseball practice after school. I know you've got exams to study for. You don't need to wait around for me."

"I like to watch you practice," Matt said. "And that way I'll be around if you need…"

Travis stared out the back door into the desert. Once again, the clock on the stove ticked into the silence. "Just leave me alone," he finally said, keeping his eyes on Matt a beat too long.

Matt walked a few steps toward Travis. Words dangled on his tongue. He wanted to say something that would make the distance between them disappear. No matter what, he and Travis had always found a way to talk to each other.

"I'm not some pathetic orphan," Travis said, carefully examining Matt's face. "Don't you get it? Every time you look at me like that, Crystal dies again." Travis raced through the back door, across the porch and down the steps. The redwood gate slammed.

Karina handed Matt his lunch, then draped her arm around his shoulder and gave it a hard squeeze. "Give him some space," she said. "But not too much."

* * *

Matt pulled his Mustang into the Canyon del Oro student parking lot next to Crystal's Escort, and turned off the ignition.

When Travis didn't get out of the car, Matt hooked his backpack over his shoulder, picked up his lunch, and hurried over to the driver's side window.

Travis sat, stone-faced and unmoving.

Matt tapped on the glass.

Travis lowered the window.

"I can drive you back home," Matt said.

Travis repeated the word *home*, then shook his head.

Matt bit the inside of his cheek. They walked across the parking lot in silence.

Inside, the pale yellow hallways smelled like apples rotting in old lunch bags, and hair gel. They were walking toward their bank of lockers when Chad Rawlings marched right up to Travis and stopped just inches from his face. He wore a CDO jacket that announced he'd lettered in football. The all-star quarterback. King of the senior class. "I heard about your mom," he said. "Gruesome."

Travis shrugged and looked at his shoes.

Matt grabbed Chad's arm and pulled him aside, trying to get him away from Travis. "What did you hear?"

"Have you been out of the country, Garrison? It's all over the morning news. Some old guy who said he'd seen the bathroom." Chad clenched his fist and lifted it high into the air, making a stabbing motion. "Norman Bates does Tucson."

Travis ran down the hallway toward his locker, a sea of students parting to let him pass.

Matt reeled back and punched Chad hard in the face. "Shut your fat-assed mouth." The words were little more than croaks, but Matt forced them out.

Chad put his hand to his nose, then stared at his bloody fingers. "You're a fucking psycho, Garrison." He wiped the blood from his hands and face. "What's wrong with you?"

"Me?" Matt said. His already injured hand—the one he'd punched through the drywall in his closet—throbbed. "His mother just died, asshole."

Chad gave Matt a disgusted look and then allowed a girl to take his arm and walk him toward the nurse's office. He left a trail of blood on the floor behind him.

Matt stared at the drops for a moment, then quickly turned away. Chad weighed a good twenty pounds more. Matt was lucky Chad hadn't beat the shit out of him. Until this morning, Matt thought he hated fighting. But it felt damn good to slug that asshole. He stood in the hallway for a moment, breathing hard while the other students lost interest and headed toward their lockers.

Mr. Baker, the vice principal, rounded the corner and headed directly toward Matt. "Everything okay here, Mr. Garrison?"

"Just fine, sir," Matt said, and headed toward his locker.

The lockers at CDO were half-sized, painted bright yellow and green, the school colors. They stacked one on top of the other in neat rows along the first floor corridor. Matt's was on the upper tier, directly across the hall from the one Travis occupied. Matt twisted the dial. The lock didn't open. His fingers felt too thick. He tried again, hand shaking. Failed. With the third try, it popped open.

On the inside of the steel door, Matt had taped a photograph of Danni sitting on the hood of his Mustang. He stared at it for a moment, wanting to go back to that day, to press his forehead against hers. He wanted to smell her hair.

He looked away, grabbed his English lit book, put his lunch bag on the top shelf, and then closed the door. The warning bell rang and he hurried to catch up with Travis. They had first period AP English together. Danni was also in their class.

"I hear you decked Chad," Travis said.

"He's an imbecile." Matt tried to open his fist. It wasn't happening.

Travis stepped into the classroom, Matt at his heels. Everyone froze, like when the music stopped in that stupid kid game they once played at birthday parties. Travis straightened his shoulders.

Danni was the first to move. She walked over to Travis, looked him in the eyes for a long moment, then hugged him hard. She wore a pair of blue jeans with sequin flowers on the back pockets and a pale yellow T-shirt tucked in at the waist. When she released Travis, she kissed him on the cheek and returned to her seat.

Like magic, the room started to buzz with conversation again.

Almost everything Danni did got to Matt. If they walked across the schoolyard and she fitted her hand into the back pocket of his jeans, he felt the caress of her fingers all the way down to his toes. When she tossed a glance at him as they passed in the hallway between classes, they'd lock eyes in a way that excluded everyone else. Danni had been the first and only girl he'd ever made love to. The only one before Crystal.

He hung his head for a moment, unable to breathe or move.

Travis sat two rows in front of Danni.

Matt took his usual seat next to her, then leaned into the aisle. "Can I talk to you at lunch?"

She leaned away. "It's not about my mother," she said. "It just isn't a good idea."

"Please," he whispered. "I need to talk to you." Danni and Travis were the only people he'd told the entire truth about what happened to Justin. And she'd made him feel better, made him consider his motivation for the push, made him believe it could have been an accident. It probably wasn't a smart thing to do, but he thought his head would explode if he didn't tell Danni about finding Crystal.

Before she could respond, the bell rang.

Mr. Singleton, a short and stocky man with gray springy hair and round wire glasses, clapped his hands—his usual call to action—and class began. He gave them a warm-up exercise—"pretend you are Raymond Carver, and write the first three paragraphs of a short story using his blue-collar characters and minimalist style."

Matt, typically one of the first to begin, wrote nothing.

Mr. Singleton walked around the room, his rubber-soled shoes making farting sounds against the linoleum.

The girl behind Matt giggled.

Singleton checked journals to see homework assignments had been completed, making little red pencil marks in his grade book. He smelled like garlic and Irish Spring soap. "I'm giving you some slack, Garrison." His gaze found Travis. "But I expect you to complete that Carver assignment by tomorrow."

After Mr. Singleton reviewed the material for the final exam, he dismissed the class with an assignment to rewrite their Raymond Carver paragraphs into their journals.

Matt stood outside the doorway for a moment, watching Travis head to their second period, history, then turned in the opposite direction, following Danni to her French class.

She was about ten feet in front of him with her best friend, Lindsay. The sight of Danni's hair, the golden brown flag that waved across her back, released something inside him and his muscles loosened. He'd be okay if he could tell her what happened. He'd leave out the sex with Crystal, but he'd tell her everything else.

As if Lindsay had sensed his presence, she turned and glared at him, then stuck her arm out in front of Danni. "It was her cousin, asshole."

Matt opened his mouth and then closed it. That football player from Tucson High was her cousin? He thought about that for minute. Danni had mentioned something about her mother's brother moving to Tucson last summer. But she'd said they weren't close. Matt saw himself ripping the necklace from her throat. Lindsay was right. He'd behaved like an asshole.

Melanie Abrams and her posse of cheerleaders stopped to watch—their heads swiveling from him to Danni and back again. Most everyone in the senior class knew them. Matthew Garrison and Danielle Warren had been voted the senior couple most likely to marry.

Danni's whole body tensed. She reached out with both arms, fingers up, as if to stop him from coming closer.

He tried to take her hands.

She pulled away. "I don't know you anymore. You scare me."

He saw the red mark on her neck where the chain had scraped her skin as he'd ripped it off. He wanted to reach out. He wanted to kiss her throat.

Lindsay tried to take Danni's arm and lead her down the hallway. "She doesn't want to talk to you."

Danni jerked away, grabbed Matt by the elbow and pulled him into an empty classroom. "I think you're an asshole. You humiliated me in front of my cousin. And didn't give me a chance to explain." Her face and ears were red. She touched the scraped band on her neck. "I loved that heart pendant and everything it stood for. I wanted to keep it forever." Danni started to cry. She covered her face with her hands.

"I'm sorry," Matt said. "I think I'm an asshole, too."

Danni's face softened—a hint of a smile in the slight deepening of the dimple on the left side of her mouth.

The late bell rang. Neither of them moved.

He stepped toward her and placed his hands on her shoulders. "I need to talk to someone. You're my person, Danni," he said, pulling her head against his chest. Her breathing grew slower.

"If I'm your person, why didn't you give me time to explain on Saturday? And why didn't you tell me about Travis's mother? I had to hear it on the news this morning."

"I didn't call you, because I thought you never wanted to see or talk to me again."

She shook her head sadly. "Then you don't know me very well."

She slipped out of his arms and left the classroom, closing the door softly behind her.

Matt headed toward his history class, then changed his mind and started out in the opposite direction. He hated being late. Hated the way it felt to have a classroom of eyes looking into him, watching his every move. Someone, no doubt that busybody new nurse, had probably reported him to the principal by now for decking Chad.

With all the blood rushing into his head, Matt took off, running down the hallway and out the closest set of doors. He didn't stop until he stood beside his Mustang. His hand hurt. The knuckles were already red and swollen. He unlocked the car and sat for a few moments, flexing his hand on the steering wheel, then started the car.

Hitting the speed bumps going at least forty miles an hour, he ignored the crossing guard at the front gate who tried to wave him down. He drove without thought of where he headed and then turned into Danni's neighborhood as if the car had a plan of its own.

He thought about the necklace, his tenth grade Valentine's Day present to her, and how the tiny gold heart had balanced in the shallow cave between her collarbones for more than two years. He liked the idea of Danni wearing that symbolic heart, carrying a vital piece of him with her always. He had to find it.

When he believed he'd traveled about the same distance from her house as he had on Saturday night, Matt parked his Mustang. He searched the desert for more than an hour and had nearly given up when he spotted the necklace with its broken clasp, dangling from a prickly pear cactus and sparkling in the morning sun. For a moment, he believed in God's existence—believed this was a sign Danni would forgive him and they'd be together again. He picked up the necklace, clutched it in his left hand, then tucked it carefully into the empty pocket over his chest.

CHAPTER TWENTY

Radhauser stopped at the Tucson mall and picked up the tuxedo Matt Garrison had rented. To his relief, the garments hadn't been cleaned. Though wrinkled and obviously worn, there were no visible stains on the black trousers or jacket. When he pulled out the shirt, it was spotlessly clean and smelled like it had been recently bleached. Someone had washed it.

Though he was pretty certain they'd find nothing of value, he dropped the tuxedo and shirt at the forensic lab and headed to Catalina for another look at Crystal's house.

The blinds were closed. He flipped on the lights and looked around the living room. Everything appeared to be just the way he'd left it. He hurried into the kitchen to check the sliding glass door. It was unlocked. That would explain how the neighbor he'd seen on the news had gotten inside. Radhauser had talked to the old man. He thought he'd seen a moving light that might be a prowler inside the house.

Killers sometimes returned to the scene of their crime. Whatever had happened that night, Radhauser remained positive he'd left the sliding door locked. There wasn't anything he could do about it now.

He didn't know what he specifically looked for; anything he might have missed the night Crystal was found. He studied the candles on the coffee table, wondered why she'd burned them the night she died. He took the CD out of her player—love songs from the sixties. Maybe she'd been entertaining a man—or just nostalgic, half drunk, and looking back on happier times. Radhauser could certainly identify with that behavior.

Looking through a dead person's home and possessions always made him feel a little guilty, like a peeping tom, and so he tried to make up for his invasion by being respectful and diligent in leaving things the way he'd found them.

From a bookshelf in the living room, he picked up a pair of bronzed baby shoes that must have belonged to Travis. For an instant, Radhauser was back in the hospital with Laura, the night Lucas was born. The nurse, a big woman in surgical scrubs, had a voice like warm, thick molasses. He remembered the delivery room, Laura bearing down for one last push, and the way Lucas's head had appeared, his fine hair matted with blood and milk-colored mucus. Radhauser could recall every detail, the purple umbilical cord he'd cut, the first high-pitched angry wail—the way Lucas had stared, open-eyed and unblinking, into his father's face. The moment his entire world changed and he metamorphosed into a father.

Radhauser swallowed, set the shoes back on the shelf. He had to stop letting everything remind him of his family. He had to focus on the job. The captain wouldn't keep him around if he failed again.

He slowly examined every room, pulled out each drawer in the living room and kitchen. Re-checked the pantry shelves and the cabinets, then moved on to Travis's bedroom, where he searched his closet, bookcase and dresser drawers.

He stood in the bathroom doorway for a few minutes, glanced at the bloody water and the spatters on the tile surrounding the tub, then stepped carefully inside and opened the small medicine cabinet slowly, hoping what was left of the mirror would remain intact. He searched for the scissors Crystal had used to cut her hair. The cabinet held the usual cough medicines, Vicks VapoRub, aspirin, Excedrin, a prescription for an antibiotic Crystal must have been taking for an infection. A tube of toothpaste, bottle of mouthwash—nothing to indicate Crystal had any serious medical problems that may have led her to take her own life. And no scissors.

She'd cut some of her hair while in the tub, but there were no scissors in the water either. It seemed unlikely she could do that much damage to her hair with a razor blade. Radhauser closed the door and continued down the hallway to Crystal's bedroom.

He flipped on the light and went through the same procedure, checking each dresser and nightstand drawer. He found a gold cross pendant that matched the earrings Crystal wore. He picked it up, stared at it for a moment, wondering why she'd put it in the drawer instead of her jewelry box on her dresser. He looked under the bed and was about to leave when he changed his mind. He pulled the chair beneath the window into her closet and parted her skirts and dresses. Her clothing released a smell that reminded Radhauser of the wildflowers he'd picked for Laura on their mountain top honeymoon in Whistler.

Everyone told him the first year was the hardest, that it got easier after all the anniversaries had passed, but so far, two days into his second year without his family, he saw no traces of the grief easing up.

He stood on the chair and ran his hand along the top shelf of Crystal's closet. Tucked into the far back corner, he felt a small rectangular box and pulled it out. The shoebox held two stacks of unopened letters, each secured with a wide blue rubber band. They were addressed to Travis Reynolds and postmarked from the Arizona State Prison in Florence—from an inmate named Mitchell T. Reynolds. Either this was Travis's grandfather or Crystal had lied to her son and his father was still alive.

Radhauser took the box into the kitchen, sat at the table and leafed through the letters, checking the postmarks. The first one was sent in August of 1974. Travis would have just turned three years old. The last one sent in February of this year. Radhauser lifted out both stacks. On the bottom of the shoebox, he discovered a folded piece of paper with Travis's name neatly printed on top. Radhauser opened it.

Dear Travis,

I know how kids like to snoop, so don't think I'm mad at you for finding these letters. But if you're reading this note, it means you know I lied to you about your father. I was seventeen and Mitch was only a year older—much too young to be married with a baby. There never seemed to be enough money, and after you were born he started running with a bad group of boys. He got into drugs and alcohol. Mitch was a mean drunk and I was often afraid for you and me. To tell you the truth, I was relieved when the cops arrested him. I figured you'd have enough to cope with having me for a mother.

School kids can be cruel and I wanted to spare you the shame of having a father in prison. So I moved us away from Phoenix and down here to Tucson. You're a smart boy, Travis. I wanted you to feel good about yourself and where you came from, so I made up the story about your father being shot down in Vietnam. I could have thrown his letters away—but I saved them, planning to give them to you on your eighteenth birthday. I thought about opening them, but they were addressed to you, so I didn't. Sometimes men turn themselves around in jail, get their GEDs and even take college classes. I hope with all my heart Mitch is one of them. He's paying for what he did and, who knows, maybe someday he can be a real father to you. Believe it or not, I hope so. It's hard being a single mom. I didn't always do it right. But I always wanted to.

Love, Crystal

There was something vulnerable and deeply honest about her letter. Crystal would remain alive to her son as long as he learned new things about her and what she'd wanted for him. He read it again. Crystal had done what she'd believed was the right thing for Travis.

Radhauser carefully refolded the page and returned it to the bottom of the shoebox. He placed the two stacks on top, then tucked the box under his arm, turned off the lights, locked up the house and got back into his Bronco. It went against police procedures to take the letters, but he needed to do it. They weren't evidence related to the case. And even if they were, he needed to honor Crystal's wish that Travis receive them on his eighteenth birthday. And he needed to track down Mitch Reynolds.

CHAPTER TWENTY-ONE

After his calculus final on Tuesday morning, Matt drove to the Mountain View Clinic in Catalina. He'd seen the appointment with Dr. Cunningham on Crystal's calendar. Maybe the doctor had given her a reason to be depressed that had nothing to do with Matt or his father. Maybe she had cancer or something.

Once inside, he found the bank of elevators, checked the list of physicians on the plaque between the doors. Cunningham was an obstetrician and gynecologist. Not a doctor Travis was likely to visit. Restless energy burned through Matt. He pushed the button for the third floor, then changed his mind and ran up the three flights of stairs.

He took a moment to catch his breath, then stepped up to the receptionist window, praying Travis had never come here with Crystal. Matt's hands curled into fists at his sides. The room smelled like new carpet.

"May I help you?" The receptionist's blonde hair sparkled under the fluorescent light. She was in her early twenties. Over her chinos she wore a bright red smock printed with teddy bears.

Matt stared at it for a moment, wondering if he would ever be able to look at the color red again without seeing that bathtub of blood. For a moment, he couldn't breathe.

"Did you want to make an appointment for someone?"

Matt avoided making eye contact. "I'm Travis Reynolds. My mother, Crystal, was a patient of Dr. Cunningham. He saw her last Friday."

She nodded.

"I know this is an unusual request," Matt said, a slight tremble in his voice. "But my mother died Saturday night and I'd really like to talk to her doctor."

"I know about her death," she said. "A police detective was already here."

Holy shit. Radhauser didn't waste any time. Matt tightened his elbows against his sides to keep himself upright. He told her about coming home from the dance and finding his mother.

Her green eyes widened. "You poor boy," she said, just as Matt had hoped. "Could you show me some identification?"

Oh crap. He hadn't anticipated this. "You mean to prove I'm really Travis? What do you need?"

"A driver's license or insurance card would do."

He slapped the back pocket of jeans. "I'm such an imbecile. I left without my wallet," he said. "I've been so messed up since it happened. My backpack is in the car. I probably have a textbook with my name inside. Or a blue book essay I wrote for English. Would that do?" He paused, looked her straight in the eyes and shrugged. "I mean, really, who else would I be?"

"Let me see if Dr. Cunningham is available." She directed him to wait in the lobby.

Matt took a seat and watched her walk away. Her hair danced across her back in a golden sheet when she moved. She twisted it in one hand and pulled it forward into a glossy rope over her shoulder.

A few moments later, she called out Travis's name. "Dr. Cunningham will see you now."

Matt looked around, half expecting Travis to be standing in the doorway.

She ushered him through a door, down a hallway with examining rooms on both sides, and into an office with an oak desk, corner windows, and pictures of a family on the credenza. "Have a seat," she said, gesturing to a chair facing the desk. "He'll be with you in a few moments."

Matt sat and looked around the office. Dr. Garrett Cunningham was a graduate of the University of Arizona's Medical School. He'd done a residency in OB/GYN at UC San Francisco. He was a father to three boys and one girl. The room smelled like pipe tobacco, something more orange than the one his dad smoked.

The door opened and Dr. Cunningham entered. He was short, round-faced, and slightly overweight. He wore his white lab coat unbuttoned, his belly hanging a couple inches over the belt of his dark pants.

Matt stood.

"Your mother talked about you a lot, Travis," he said, giving Matt a firm handshake. "She was very proud of you." His horn-rimmed glasses were thick and made his golden brown eyes look huge. He was sandy–haired, and had a dark mole on his cheek where women sometimes drew one. "I'm truly sorry for your loss." His voice was deep and his hands as big as catchers' mitts.

Matt smelled their clean, soap and water scent.

Cunningham pulled out his chair and sat behind his desk. "Now, how can I help you?"

Matt's voice came out in a long, strangled rush. "I had a fight with my mother right before she died. When I came home, she—" He stopped and gazed out the window into the desert where two ocotillos were still in full bloom, a flag of red flowers waving from the tip of every leafed-out branch.

"What do you want from me, son?" Cunningham's voice was gentle, as if he talked to a child.

Matt tried to crawl inside Travis's skin, tried to think and talk the way he would. "What did you say to her on Friday, man? Was there some test result that made her feel hopeless? Like did she have cancer or something?" Matt couldn't believe he wasn't crying. But ever since Crystal died, the tears seemed to have dried up and disappeared. "I want to know it wasn't my fault."

Cunningham shook his head sadly, but didn't look at Matt. "Patient confidentiality prevents me from discussing this with you or anyone else. I told the police detective he'd have to get a warrant."

"I'm not a detective. I'm her son. And what difference does confidentiality make now? My mom's dead. They're doing an autopsy," Matt said. "So eventually I'll find out. Please, you have to help me. I won a full baseball scholarship to Arizona, but how can I go, thinking I caused her to—" He stopped, swallowed, decided he didn't need to say more.

There was a knock at the door. The receptionist opened it and stuck her head inside. "It's Dr. Richardson about Mrs. Parker's biopsy."

Dr. Cunningham's brow furrowed. He picked up the phone, made some notes on a pad beside the phone. "No, that's okay. I'll call her." When he hung up, he steepled his fingers on the desk and looked over them at Matt. "The autopsy report will reveal anything I may have told her."

"Yeah," Matt said. "Like they'll give me a copy of that."

"It's public record," Dr. Cunningham said. "All you need do is request a copy. They'll mail it to you or you can stop by the Medical Examiner's office and pick it up. You may have to pay a fee."

"Don't you think I've paid enough? I'm so upset I can't think straight. It's finals week. If I don't take them, man, I might even lose my scholarship." Matt tried to mimic Travis's speech pattern.

Dr. Cunningham looked down, as if gathering words, preparing himself to say something he really didn't want to say. "Your mother came in because she'd missed three menstrual cycles. She suspected early menopause. She had some other vague complaints that led me to do an internal examination."

"And?" Matt didn't know much about menopause, but could understand why it might make Crystal feel as if her life were slipping by. "Was it?"

Another knock on the door. "It's your wife. Line two."

"Tell her I'll call her back," he said, a hint of impatience in his voice. He turned to Matt. "I need to cut this short. I've got patients to see. Your mother was about three and a half months pregnant."

Matt leaned over and gripped his knees with his hands—a dark ball of dread in his stomach. "Pregnant? My mother?" Stupidly, he wondered for one terrible instant if he could have impregnated Crystal with their unprotected sex. And then he realized it was impossible. But he was vaguely repulsed by the idea he'd had sex with a pregnant woman. "Was Mom upset when you told her?"

The doctor stood. "It was hard to say. She was shocked, of course. We did a sonogram to confirm."

"Was she depressed?"

"Not really," he said, taking a step toward the door. "As I mentioned, she was shocked, but after a few minutes she seemed almost excited about it."

"Did my mother tell you who fathered the baby?"

"I wouldn't disclose that information if she had." He opened his office door.

Matt hastily thanked Dr. Cunningham for his time, tried to smile at the receptionist, then stumbled out into the hallway.

In the windowless stairwell, the overhead light bulb fizzled, then flickered out. With the darkness, Matt was consumed by exhaustion. His arms and hands, even his legs, seemed to thicken, and when he started down the stairs, his body moved heavily as if he'd just taken on a burden.

Outside, drawn by the sound of water, Matt headed toward the front of the building where a man-made waterfall cascaded over rocks. It flowed into a pond filled with orange, yellow and white Koi swimming in circles. It smelled like fish food and garden soil after rain had fallen.

Matt stood in front of it, staring into the dark pond, its rock sides too high for the fish to ever escape. The harm he'd done to Crystal and to Travis seemed bottomless. The sound of water striking the pond's surface got louder—white noise cranked up. It was as if his brain could no longer filter out what didn't matter. Everything mattered.

* * *

On Tuesday afternoon, Radhauser tapped on Crenshaw's office door. The Medical Examiner sat at his desk, still wearing his lab coat. He stood and motioned Radhauser inside. "I'm glad you're here," Melon said. "I completed the autopsy on your waitress and found something interesting." Crenshaw paused and grinned. "Sometimes I just love this job." He was so excited his yellow-tinted skin flushed—ripe as a peach.

Out of respect for the dead, Radhauser removed his Stetson.

Melon liked to show off in front of the detectives, and often took them into the autopsy room. "Follow me."

Radhauser would stroke Melon's ego if it meant getting the autopsy results more quickly than waiting for his written report.

Crystal Reynolds' body was laid out on a stainless steel table with a drain at one end and a lip around all four edges. On a steel cart beside the table, Crenshaw's gleaming instruments lined up as neatly as a surgeon's. As usual, when he listened to Melon pontificate in his autopsy suite, Radhauser wished he had sunglasses. The room smelled of disinfectant, formaldehyde, and some other, darker odors Radhauser never tried to identify.

Melon slipped his hands into a pair of latex gloves and pulled back the sheet.

Again, Radhauser was struck by her small body—her resemblance to Laura.

"I haven't dictated the report yet. But I knew you'd want to see this right away."

Crenshaw tossed a pair of gloves to Radhauser, then grabbed a small, stainless steel measuring device—a narrow ruler about six inches long. He slid it into the wound on Crystal's neck. His excitement was palpable.

Radhauser pulled on the gloves.

"Read that," Crenshaw said.

Radhauser bent over the body. "Three and a quarter inches."

"Good," Crenshaw said. "You can read. Now what else do you notice?" He did a little dance around the table.

"Now that it's cleaned up, I can see that the cut is smooth, but looks a little like a z."

"That's right. There's still hope for you, Radhauser." Crenshaw smiled his gap-toothed grin. "And here's another thing. When cutting is associated with suicide, there are almost always hesitation wounds—less severe cuts caused by attempts to build up resolve to inflict the fatal cut. As you can see, our victim has none."

Crenshaw walked over to his supply cabinet and came back

with a single-edged razor blade. He set it on the table and placed the ruler beside it. "Well?" Melon wore his excitement like donut glaze, shiny on the surface of his skin.

Radhauser checked the measurement. "Looks like a half inch," he said, knowing exactly what it meant. There was no way Crystal Reynolds slashed her own carotid with a razor blade. The cut was far too deep and wide. But Melon loved to make his pronouncements, so Radhauser played dumb.

"The official cause of death was exsanguination," Crenshaw said. "But this was overkill. This little lady's neck was cut deep enough to scrape bone. Scissors leave a wound that is broader than a typical knife because the scissor blades are much thicker. That z you noticed reflects the one scissor blade over top of the other." Melon flashed Radhauser a big smile. "Look for a pair of scissors with about four to five inch blades. And a murderer who was really pissed off."

"Could the victim have cut her hair with the same scissors?"

"Almost certainly," Melon said.

"What about the razor blade?"

"No traces of hair on the blade, just some sage green paint. I suspect she used it for cleaning the tile. It looked to me like the bathroom had been recently painted. Looks like you've got yourself a double homicide."

Radhauser shot him a questioning look.

Melon grinned again. "Pregnant."

Radhauser understood what Dr. Cunningham was so reluctant to tell him—no warrant needed now. "Can you pinpoint the time of death?"

"No rigor mortis. A small amount of post-mortem lividity and the body temp was 95.2. But, of course, we have the temperature of the water in the tub to take into account. I withdrew fluid from her eyeball to determine the level of potassium. It rises after death at a predictable rate. All things considered I'd say she died between 10:30 and 11:30pm."

"Did you do the rape kit?"

Crenshaw rolled his eyes. "You're not dealing with an amateur here, Radhauser. There were no vaginal tears or visible signs of bruising. She had some semen in the vaginal cavity. Very possibly compromised because of the long bath, but I sent it off. The water in the tub may have affected body temp. Time of death might have been as early as 9:00 or as late as midnight."

"The 911 call came in at 11:44, so we know she was dead before then."

Radhauser's thoughts shifted to Loren Garrison—his suspicion Crystal had been more than a family friend. He wondered if Mister Morality and Ethics would kill his pregnant girlfriend in order to avoid a scandal.

CHAPTER TWENTY-TWO

Matt was cramming for Thursday morning's Advanced Placement chemistry final when Travis stepped into the bedroom they'd been sharing. He'd gotten his hair cut short, and dressed differently. All he needed was a necktie and he'd look like one of those Mormon boys proselytizing door-to-door. Tempted to tease him about his church-approved outfit, Matt held up the study guide instead. "You want to quiz each other on all those laws of gas we memorized?" He made a farting sound and waited for Travis to pick up on the joke.

Travis's shoulders slumped. There was a raw-looking outbreak of acne on his cheeks. "I've got stuff going on. You'll ace the exam, you always do."

Matt remained silent.

Travis fiddled with a stack of papers on his bed and avoided Matt's gaze. "Some friends are coming here tonight to do a sin study with me. You cool with that?"

"You mean like here in our bedroom?"

Travis nodded.

"If you're sure that's what you want, I can hang out in the kitchen unless you need me for moral support. Or to supply the sins." Matt grinned, still trying to cross the distance between them. If only Travis would take one step in Matt's direction.

"I'm thinking about becoming a real member of Narrow Way."

"Why not wait, check it out and make sure it's everything you think it is?"

Travis gave him a questioning look. "What's your real problem?"

"There was a documentary on *60 Minutes*—" Matt hesitated.

158

He wanted to tell Travis everything, but he was afraid that if he did, the gap between them would grow even wider.

Travis stared at him for a moment in which Matt became aware the two of them drifted toward something dangerous. "I have to give up some things," Travis said.

Pushing his chair away from the desk, Matt stood, then slammed his chemistry book shut. "Like me. Is that what you're trying so hard to say?"

"I'm not saying anything like that. It's just I need a quiet and private place."

"Are you suggesting I move out of here?"

"I wish I had another option, but I don't. We'll see each other all the time at school. You're still planning to help me clean out the house tomorrow, right? And you'll come to the memorial." There was a soft edge of emotion in Travis's voice.

Matt stood, looped his thumbs in the waistband of his jeans, but said nothing.

"You sleep better in your waterbed anyway. Please, Matt. I told Karina we'd study harder for our finals if we're separated." Travis paused and smiled. "She was all over it."

"I'll do whatever you want," Matt said. "But Mom taped that *60 Minutes* segment. I just wish you'd—"

Travis slid his hands into the pockets of his Dockers. "You could at least see for yourself before you judge."

They eyed each other across the room.

"You know I'd do just about anything for you," Matt said softly. "But not that."

Again, Travis studied him. "Are you so sure you've done nothing that needs to be forgiven?" His look was withering.

It was a look Matt deserved. He'd give anything to go back and undo the mistakes he'd made last Saturday. His mom's happiness with Nate had become clear to him during the few days he'd lived in their house. She sang when she cooked and there was a bounce in her step that had disappeared for a while after she and his father split. At night, he heard Nate and his mother laughing in their bedroom.

His dad was a jerk. He didn't deserve the loyalty Matt had shown him. A loyalty that ruined his mother's wedding and, in the aftermath, took his best friend's mother. He wanted to drag a razor blade over his skin so he could feel something other than shame, but he didn't have the courage to do that either.

Matt's mind scrambled for the right combination of things to say. And when no words came, he turned his face away and crammed books into his backpack.

* * *

Matt stumbled from his bed and looked out the window. It was nearly dawn and the moon still hung in the sky like a ghost of itself. He watched it for a moment, then sat at his desk, pulled out a yellow tablet, and wrote a poem. It had happened to him before, this awakening with a fully-written poem inside his head, but the experience still surprised him. He read it twice, made a few changes, then returned to bed.

Hours later, his face buried in his pillow, Matt stuck his hand out to punch the knob on his trilling alarm clock. School let out early in Tucson, the entire high school finished by the second week of May. But this was seniors' week, and they were expected to show up only for their final exams. Matt was free today.

If things had gone according to plan, Travis's two aunts would have rented a U-Haul truck and carted off whatever items they could use to their house in Mesa. Given how estranged they'd been from Crystal, Matt couldn't believe Travis had called them and made the offer.

Matt climbed out of bed, got showered and dressed. He was tying his shoes when his father knocked on the bedroom door. "I need to talk to you. Is it okay if I come in?"

Matt opened his door.

Loren, carrying an oversized glass ashtray and his pipe, looked tired and older than Matt had ever seen him look. Normally he'd have left for work by now, but he was still dressed in his pajamas and short, burgundy robe. There was a strain to his breathing. For a moment, Matt felt sorry for him—for the way their once solid relationship had changed over the past few days.

"I'm glad to have you back in your own room," his father said. "I missed you."

"I was only gone for three nights."

"It seemed much longer. By the way, your mom called about the missing cufflinks from your tuxedo rental. The store inquired about them."

Again, he saw Crystal undo them and drop them into his shirt pocket before she'd rolled up his sleeves. *Oh my God.* What if her fingerprints were on them? The police had surely found them by now. Why hadn't Radhauser questioned him about them?

"I guess I must have lost them."

His father nodded, didn't appear to think missing cufflinks was a big deal. "Could we sit down for a minute?"

Matt slumped into his desk chair, his hands falling limp at his sides.

His father set his ashtray on Matt's bookcase. He didn't seem to know what to do with his hands. He put them in his robe pockets, then pulled them out and wiped them on his pajama bottoms. Finally, he sat in the small leather chair beside the bookcase. It creaked a little with his weight.

"Travis expects me. I've got to get going."

"It's sure to come out now. And as difficult as it is, I think it's better if you hear it from me."

Matt sat up straight. "I'm listening."

His father cleared his throat, looked at the floor. "I'm not going to lead up to this or try to justify it in any way, I'm just going to say it." He talked quickly, like someone determined to get it over with. "Crystal Reynolds was the other woman in my life."

Their eyes met. "No," Matt said. An image rose of Crystal lying on the sofa in only her red bikini panties and lacy bra. He tried to push it away. Then he saw his mother's pale face, the tears when he'd stood, statue-like in the driveway, refusing to move into a condo with her and Sedona. The trip he and his father had made to the ER after Sedona called them and said his mom wouldn't wake up. It all jumbled together with the basketball net his mom and Nate had hung on the garage of their new house. The bedroom she'd kept for him. Mom and Crystal laughing in the stands at a little league game, back before Justin died when Matt played third base. The images came so fast he could barely recover from one before another arrived. "No," he said again. "You were only trying to help her."

His father's face froze for just a moment and the strain in his breathing returned. He coughed, cleared his throat again. "I've been involved in a sexual relationship with Crystal Reynolds for three years. I tried on several different occasions to break it off, but the break never lasted more than a couple months. And that's the reason your mother left." Something in his dad seemed to collapse.

For a moment, Matt just stared, open-mouthed. "Why tell me this now?"

"Because it's the truth. And Detective Radhauser will eventually discover and disclose it. I never planned to keep it from you indefinitely. But the longer I didn't tell you, the more difficult it got to bring it up."

Matt shut his eyes, tried to relax, but felt only the steady tightening of a coil inside his chest. He thought about Mom and how angry he'd been at her for leaving. "She was Mom's friend. My best friend's mother." Matt was being a hypocrite, but he couldn't hide the judgment in his voice.

His father looked away, slipped his pipe from his jacket pocket, and drilled out the bowl. He tapped it methodically against the side of the ashtray, emptied the bowl and then repacked it. "Yes. I'm not proud of it. When your mother told me she was leaving, I promised I'd break it off for good, but it didn't matter. Karina was finished with me and filed for divorce."

The coil inside Matt snapped. He crossed the room in three strides and knocked the pipe out of his father's hand, spilling tobacco onto the carpet. "Stop hiding behind your pipe."

His father leaned forward and picked up the pipe and set it in the ashtray.

Matt took two steps backwards. "Can you blame her?" he shouted. "Can you honestly blame her?"

"No," his dad said softly. "I can't."

It all seemed so sick. Both he and his dad had slept with the same woman.

A part of him wanted to lash out even more, wanted to whip his dad with the details of how Crystal had looked in that bathtub of blood with her hair all chopped off. He wanted to tell his father how she'd needed comfort, how her eyes had filled with tears when she'd talked about how hard it was to lose someone you love. She'd been talking about his dad. He thought about what Travis had said about Crystal's hotshot boyfriend. "Does Travis know?"

"Your mother, Crystal, and I agreed not to tell you or Travis."

"How do you think he'll feel when he finds out?"

"I can only guess. I've already disappointed too many people I care about."

Matt stared at him in disbelief. *Disappointed?* What a weak word. It sounded like he'd missed a school play or a band concert. His father didn't have a clue. "Yeah, you care so much about disappointing Travis you aren't even going to show up at his mother's memorial service." Matt spoke between nearly clenched teeth, his voice so low he barely recognized it as his own.

His father jerked back as if he'd been slapped. "Your mother said she'd wait and let me tell you myself."

Matt's eardrums thundered. He didn't want to get his mother in trouble. When he realized he was holding his breath, he exhaled quietly. "Travis hung out here all the time. You taught him to swim in our pool. Mom used to make his Halloween costumes and take him trick-or-treating with Sedona and me. No meeting is more important than Crystal's funeral. A woman you loved— or did you? Maybe you just used her for sex and threw her out afterwards."

"I think you know the real reason I won't be there. I don't want to put Karina through that."

"Did you know Crystal was pregnant?"

"Yes," his father said. "And I'm wondering how you knew."

"Maybe she told me. In case you didn't know it, I loved Crystal, too."

His father stared at him, but said nothing.

Matt dropped his gaze to the floor. "Did you break up with her on the night she died? Is that why she was so sad?"

His dad cocked his head and gave Matt a puzzled look. "Did you go there?" He stopped himself as if he didn't really want to know the answer.

Matt saw what the last few days had done to his father, the toll they'd taken. His eyes were red and swollen from lack of sleep and large brown crescents hung beneath them, but Matt couldn't stop. He paced five steps across his room and then five steps back to his desk. Despite his suspicions, Matt was leveled by his father's confession. "Mom was the one most hurt by what you and Crystal did." Again, Matt flashed on that night in the emergency room. "And I can guarantee you she'll be there for Travis."

His dad hung his head for a moment, then looked at Matt. "Your mother is a far better person than I am. And I thought it would be easier on her if I didn't attend."

"That's bullshit. It's not like you and Mom haven't been together lots of times since the divorce. She and Nate even invite you over for dinner with no reason. And in case you can't see for yourself, she's happy with him, happier than she ever was with you."

The arrow hit its mark. His father's eyes filled with tears. "I don't want your mother to watch me mourn the woman she blamed for the breakup of our family."

Shame as well as understanding washed over Matt. He had no right to accuse his dad. At least Matt knew his father's big secret now. Would anyone ever know Matt's? He covered his face with his hands. They smelled like sweat and anger.

"Does Sedona know about Crystal? Is that why she hates you so much?"

He winced. "Neither your mother nor I told her. But I suspect she knows."

"You'll have to excuse me if I don't hang around to hear any more confessions. I need to help Travis clean out the only home he's ever known, Dad." He drew out the word dad, made it sound long and disgusting, then grabbed the poem he'd written that morning, pivoted, and walked to the bedroom door.

"No one is perfect, son," his dad whispered, more to himself than to Matt. "We all have secrets."

Matt stopped for a moment. His father was right. At only eighteen, Matt had made some colossal mistakes, done at least two terrible things. He hurried down the hallway and across the family room, as if he could walk fast enough to leave his guilt behind him. But it tracked him as he walked, an ugly dark shadow on the carpet.

CHAPTER TWENTY-THREE

When Matt, still shaking with anger toward his father, turned onto the dirt road leading to Travis's house, the Mustang skidded. He tightened his grip on the steering wheel and pumped the brakes. Just as he got the car under control, he spotted Detective Radhauser's Bronco parked in front of the house across the street. The texture of the air changed and Matt's chest tightened with the effort to breathe. Radhauser was questioning Mrs. Lawrence. He would figure out it was Matt's dad who'd been fighting with Crystal.

Other neighbors had likely seen his father's car in her driveway. If he'd been having an affair with Crystal for three years, surely his Lincoln had been parked there often. It wasn't a car people missed.

But neither was Matt's Mustang. The carport was on the backside of the house. One of the neighbors could have been walking in the desert and seen it in the carport last Saturday night.

It was then Matt thought about Crystal's pregnancy. His father had just admitted to an affair with Crystal. Of course—his dad had to be the baby's father.

He parked in front of Travis's house, took a stack of boxes and a roll of packing tape from his trunk, and hurried around back. As he turned toward the deck, two doves darted out from beneath it. The air filled with the beating of wings.

Travis sat on the edge of the deck facing the back desert.

Matt apologized for being late, said his father wanted to talk. He wished he could tell Travis the truth, but knew it would only hurt and confuse him more. "He keeps going over the same old shit. He fucked up and the rest of us had to pay."

Travis shot him a look. "Your father had an affair. He made a mistake. Maybe you just learned about it, but it's history, man. And he's the one who ended up alone."

He stood and opened the sliding glass door into the kitchen. "I know you'll think I'm a real wuss, but I couldn't go inside by myself."

Matt gave Travis a soft punch to the shoulder. "I'm glad you asked me to help." Matt walked through the door first, dumped the boxes on the kitchen counter, then followed Travis around the house while he checked out every room. After Radhauser released the house as a crime scene, the owner had hired professionals to clean the bathroom. It smelled like the sheets Matt's mother used to hang out on the clothes tree to dry.

When Travis stepped into Crystal's bedroom, Matt followed.

The room felt like it belonged in a haunted house. Matt wanted to run from it as fast as he could, but he stood behind Travis as he stared at the items his mother had arranged on her dresser—a metal tree that held her earrings, a clay ashtray Travis had sculpted for Mother's Day in second grade, a framed poem Matt had helped him write for Crystal's birthday. *I learned change from the ocean tides, but Mother, I learned love as a boy by your side.*

It was Crystal's life the way she'd assembled it, and Travis seemed to have a need to pick up each object, run his hand across the surface or hold it against his chest. And every time he did, a new sliver of guilt pierced Matt's skin. The air in the room thickened with memories and things that could never be said. Travis picked up an old framed photograph of the three of them— Justin wedged between Matt and Travis. They wore bright orange soccer uniforms smudged with dirt—the winter they'd won the state championship in the eight-year-old division.

Three boys grinning from ear-to-ear, their newly-acquired adult teeth too large for their mouths. A time of unbridled happiness for Matt. At that moment, he had loved his life so much it hurt. He loved his beautiful young mother, his distinguished father, his funny little sister, Justin, and Travis, with a kind of fierceness he'd felt in every muscle of his body. And even the memory of it now had the power to call him back to another time, another possibility. That was the amazing thing about photographs. They proved life could be perfect, even if it was only for the split second the camera's shutter flicked open and closed.

Travis set the photo back on the dresser. "Remember when you wrote that paper about wanting to visit the place where the dead go?"

Matt nodded.

"I totally get it now, man."

Matt had no response. No way out of the hopelessness.

"I'll grab the rest of the boxes and the packing paper." Matt hurried outside to his car. Radhauser was still parked across the street.

When Matt returned, Travis sat on the floor in his mother's bedroom, taping boxes together. He stared up at Matt in silence, studying him intently as if trying to see into his brain. "You're hiding something."

For a moment, Matt wondered if the secrets sitting in the pit of his stomach had a smell, if Travis could detect them each time Matt entered the room. He glanced at Crystal's bed and imagined her and his dad nestled together, naked and spent. He shook his head fast and hard.

"Is there something you want to tell me?" Travis asked.

Matt braced himself. "Like what?"

"Like why you have trouble looking me in the face."

"It's the church. You spend way more time there than you do with me."

"I've been spending time with Jennifer for months."

Matt swallowed.

Travis's gaze darted over Matt's face, then quickly flicked away. "Haven't you ever had the urge to start over? Be a better person?"

His questions seemed to swim in front of Matt's eyes. There'd been so many times he'd wished he could start over, erase the past and be the person he'd planned to be. He hadn't intended to have sex with Crystal and he hadn't intended to push his cousin to his death. Maybe we make mistakes that eventually define us. Maybe we don't get to choose the people we ultimately become. "You've always been a good person," Matt said.

Travis looked at the floor. "I hurt Crystal. I said something awful, and I don't even know if it was true, man. I told her I'd choose the church over her. She was my mother and..."

Matt thought about his father—all the mixed-up emotions. He wondered how he'd feel if he came home and found his father dead. He wanted to listen to Travis now, wanted to track what he said, but the words had too many meanings and traveled in too many directions. He turned his head toward the bedroom window where an image of Crystal's face appeared for an instant, then disappeared like haze on a bathroom mirror, first the edges, then all of her.

There was a long, empty moment before Travis spoke again. "Jen says I should have tried harder to get Crystal saved."

Matt tried to imagine Crystal in the strict confines of Narrow Way. "She wouldn't have fit in. And she would have hated all the rules."

Travis locked gazes with Matt. "You don't know that. Being part of something important—something bigger than we are—it sets you free, man." He smiled, and for a moment he looked like the old Travis.

Matt thought about all the sleepovers he'd had at Travis's house when they were younger. The way Crystal had ordered pizza and ate it with them inside the tent they'd pitched in the backyard. He tucked the poem deeper into his shirt pocket. It no longer felt like something he could share.

Travis reached over and pulled it out. "So, that's what you've been hiding. You wrote another one." He unfolded the paper and read out loud.

The Circus Tent
Leaning on a vast shadow, it crouches,
Yellow and white and I enter its cathedral, born anew.
While in another world, my body tosses and perspires.
With gathered peals, laughter turns back on the mouths

*That made it and I scream: "Step into the light and
Mourn the mirror's mock of your painted life."*

When Travis paused, Matt reached out and grabbed the poem. It had been a mistake to bring it.

"Since when do you have secrets from me?"

Matt tried to hold Travis's gaze, but looking straight into his eyes was a weight Matt could only carry for a few seconds. He looked away.

"It's good, man. One of your best. I want to read the rest of it." Travis jerked the poem from Matt's hand. The top corner tore. Travis apologized, then read on.

*A windowpane clings to the face of stolen moonlight
And it soothes me with its purifying brightness.
While in its glass, I am captured, grotesque and ashamed.
I stare at myself, pressing my red rubber nose to the pane.
As I struggle to pry the smile from my painted lips
I weep out loud for the man I no longer am.*

Travis scanned the poem again, then handed it back. "I read something about poems being like dreams. They're filled with stuff we don't realize we know. Seems you're ragging on yourself not to pass judgment on the clown before you've worn the rubber nose. Maybe something else about masks and wearing them to hide." Travis stared at Matt for a long moment. "You got more masks on your walls than anyone I've ever known. You were just a kid, goofing around on that cliff the way kids do. It wasn't your fault, man."

Matt refolded the poem and tucked it back into his pocket.

Travis looked around the room, his gaze landing on a photo of himself with Crystal. "What's really got me freaked is the more I lose her, the more she still has me."

CHAPTER TWENTY-FOUR

Matt watched Travis remove a stack of nightgowns from a shelf in Crystal's closet, his hands thick and heavy against the flimsy fabrics.

When he piled them on the bed, Matt recognized a pale blue gown with a lace-covered top identical to one his dad had given his mom. *That asshole bought one for Crystal, too.*

Travis abruptly turned to Matt. "I can't do this, man. I'm sorry. But I can't. I'll go pack my room." He hurried out of Crystal's bedroom.

Matt jerked a large box from the floor, unfolded it, taped the bottom and set it on the bed. He picked up the blue nightgown, studied the label for a moment in which he saw his mother untie the big red bow and open the gift. She'd smiled at his father and held the nightgown against her body—the last Christmas his family had spent together.

Matt ripped Crystal's nightgown down the center—the sound was like an adhesive bandage being torn away from skin. He stuffed the nightgown into the bottom of the box, crammed the other gowns on top, closed the lid and sealed it with tape.

When he looked up, Detective Radhauser stood in the doorway, holding his Stetson on his index finger. For a moment, he didn't say anything, just stood watching. "I heard a ripping sound," he said, stepping into the room. "Was there something about that particular nightgown pissed you off?"

Should he protect his father and hide the truth from Radhauser? His father said Radhauser would find out. Matt had already lied about too many things. "I'm pretty sure my dad bought it for

171

Crystal. But please…please don't tell Travis."

Radhauser looked skeptical, but said nothing.

"It's the Lord and Taylor label," Matt said. "We don't have that store in Tucson."

"Are you saying your father and Ms. Reynolds were more than friends?"

"My father said you'd find out and he wanted me to hear it from him first." Matt could taste his own bitterness.

Radhauser's dark blue eyes bored into Matt with a level of invasion he'd never experienced from anyone besides his mother.

Matt looked away. After what had happened with Justin, Matt knew better than anyone you could do a horrible thing, lie about it, then spend years trying to atone for it.

"I'm here to speak with Travis," Radhauser said.

"He's packing up his bedroom. You aren't going to tell him about my father, are you?"

"No," Radhauser said. "But eventually these things have a way of coming out." He left without saying another word, had probably stopped outside Travis's door to make notes in that damn book of his. Matt had made another mistake. He should have been more protective of his dad.

Matt stuffed the remainder of Crystal's clothes into cardboard boxes. As he piled them into the corner, he heard the reckless sound of her laughter, exactly like when they'd danced. As if laughter were a set of arms she allowed herself to fall into. But he'd been the one to fall. He wondered if his father might be right. If everyone on Earth walked around with at least one unbearable secret. Maybe it was part of growing up. Maybe if he went to his mom and confessed everything she'd say, *"Don't be silly, Matt. Everyone has hurt someone else. Each of us has pushed a button that could drive someone they love over the edge."*

The front door opened, then closed again. Noises that brought back the memory of the sounds he'd heard the night Crystal died. Matt stood at the window for a moment and watched Detective Radhauser put on his Stetson, then head down the street toward the house next door.

Matt found Travis sitting on his bedroom floor in front of his bookcase, surrounded by books, honor society plaques, and sports trophies. He'd stopped packing, and studied a five-by-seven piece of yellow construction paper. He handed it to Matt. "Remember this?"

Matt settled on the floor beside him and stared at the drawing of a baseball player swinging a bat, obviously made by a child. He read the words he'd printed beneath it. *My wish is for Travis Reynolds to be a famous baseball player who beats Hank Aaron's homerun record.*

In third grade, Mrs. Zeeb had asked the class to make a wish and illustrate it. Matt did the math. "You saved this for nine years?"

Travis kept his head down, the roots of his hair soaked with sweat. "I wished for a Big Wheel. Half the other kids did, too. Or a house with a swimming pool."

Matt handed the drawing back to him. "I was such a dork. I should have wished for a million dollars." He punched Travis lightly on the shoulder. "Instead of bet on a sure thing."

Travis tucked the drawing into the front of a book, then carefully placed it in the box. "Mrs. Zeeb tacked the wishes on her bulletin board. I slipped this one off when no one was looking. I don't know why. Or at least, I didn't back then."

"And now you do?"

Travis shrugged. "I was a little jealous. You had the Big Wheel and the swimming pool. But you also had real parents, grownups, and you never had to worry about the rent or getting evicted." Travis paused for a moment and stared into space. "I don't know, man. Your making a wish for me...it made me feel, well...like I mattered."

Words tumbled around inside Matt's head, but nothing felt right. Everything that had gone before, what now felt like the best times in their life together, seemed precariously balanced. Happiness was a kind of arrogance, a gift he'd taken for granted.

Travis taped the box closed. "Radhauser wanted to know if I'd come across the missing bathroom towels."

"Did you?"

He shook his head. "I found the two other washcloths that matched, but no towels." He nodded toward the dark and light green washcloths folded neatly on his bed. "Oh yeah, and he wanted to know if you ever drank beer with Crystal."

Matt's toes curled in his shoes. "Why would he ask that?"

A silence fell between them.

"I suspect he found your fingerprints on some of the bottles he took from the garage." Travis's tone was neutral, but his eyes held a question.

A little chill went through Matt and he felt himself flush. "What did you tell him?"

"That we both did. Every chance we got. Did you want me to lie for you?" He held Matt with his gaze.

"Of course not." Matt looked away. "I think I'll grab a soda. You want one?"

Travis shook his head.

Matt stood and headed for the kitchen. Crystal's calendar still hung on the bulletin board above the telephone—a record of the last few months of her life. Matt stared at it for a moment, then removed the pushpin and took it down. The square of cork where the calendar had hung was a lighter brown than the rest of the bulletin board—a visible sign of something missing.

He sat at her kitchen table and wondered if she'd recorded the days she'd seen his father, marked them with a star or a heart.

Radhauser opened the sliding glass door and stepped into the kitchen.

Matt started. He stood so quickly his chair wobbled on its back legs for a moment. He tried to replace the calendar on the corkboard, but his hands shook too hard to hold the pushpin in place.

"Find anything interesting?"

"No," Matt said. "I was just—"

"Looking for evidence of your father's affair with Crystal."

* * *

After they'd loaded everything left in the house into the Goodwill truck, Matt stood in the driveway, in the perfect stillness that fell when the truck disappeared around the corner. It was as if everything happy and bright about the childhood days he'd spent here with Travis disappeared, too.

Matt waited beside his Mustang as Travis pulled Crystal's loaded Escort out of the carport for the last time.

Travis rolled down the passenger window. He looked different—more lines and shadows on his face, as if the events of the past week had aged him. He gave a quick wave as he pulled out of the driveway.

Heat rose behind Matt's eyes. After the Escort turned onto Oracle Road and disappeared, he walked out into the desert behind the house, to the wash where they'd built their boyhood campfires. Matt studied the circle of rocks, picked them up, one by one. It was difficult to choose. After five minutes, he finally decided on a flat, round, bluish-gray stone with veins of turquoise and coral. Closing his eyes, he held it in his palm for a moment to feel the heat, to make sure it was the one to hold his memories, then he slipped it into his pocket.

He stood in front of the empty house for another moment, listened to the harsh *char, char* sounds of cactus wrens calling from the mesquite trees.

An era had just ended.

CHAPTER TWENTY-FIVE

At the sound of the back door opening, Matt's mother glanced up from her chopping board. "So, how'd it go?" She met his eyes briefly, then brought her attention back to the mound of sliced carrots she'd chopped. She scraped them into the round, wooden salad bowl. She wore a pair of white slacks and a black T-shirt with a red dragonfly on the front.

"It was hard for Travis to pack her clothes and stuff."

She looked up at him again and smiled. "So, like a good friend, you did it for him."

"Love is action. Never just words."

She laughed, then faked a look of total shock, throwing her hands into the air, her mouth forming an O. "I don't believe it. You actually listened to me." She glanced toward the back door as if waiting for Travis to appear.

Matt told her about Travis's plans to spend the evening with Jennifer at a church potluck.

She shook her head, looked worried. "After the boys from the church left last night, Travis cried for two hours. I heard him through the door, but he didn't want comfort. When he finally came out, I asked him if he was okay and he said it felt as if an abscess had been drained from his body."

Matt remembered what Travis had told him about starting over and being a better person. "Maybe they were good tears." He stopped and gave his mother a wicked grin, moved his eyebrows up and down like Groucho Marx and pretended to hold a cigar. "Maybe this whole church thing is a way of getting closer to Jennifer. If you know what I mean."

176

She laughed and slapped at his arm. "Did you happen to find the cufflinks?"

"No," he said, unable to meet her gaze.

"Don't worry about it. I'll pay for them. They were hardly fourteen carat."

He shook his head. "Cheap silver. Can I ask you something hard, Mom?"

Outside the kitchen window, the porch wind chimes rang.

"Don't look so worried," she said. "I'm sure people lose them all the time."

"It's not about the cufflinks."

"What then?"

"Why didn't you tell me Dad had an affair with Crystal?"

An uncomfortable silence hung in the kitchen for a minute, as if every molecule of air had been broken.

"You shouldn't pay attention to gossip." She kept her gaze on the cutting board where she'd set out a cucumber, some scallions, and four radishes. "It's evil."

"I heard it from a reliable source."

She bit her lip and looked away. "Sedona has read so many mystery books she thinks she's a detective."

"I didn't hear it from Sedona."

Karina's hands gripped the sides of the salad bowl. Her voice was tight and cautious as she asked, "Who then?"

"Dad told me."

Her eyes softened. She lifted her hands slowly, then dropped them to her sides as if the strings had been snapped. "Neither your father nor I wanted you or Travis to have to choose between a parent and your friendship. It wasn't fair."

"Travis doesn't know, but even if he finds out, we'll be okay. What wasn't fair is I made a choice without all the facts," Matt said. "I chose to live with my father and I regret it."

"Your father messed up. And it hurt me deeply. But it doesn't have anything to do with his love for you and Sedona."

Matt decided not to tell her about Crystal's pregnancy. Maybe she'd never have to find out. His own hypocrisy didn't escape him as he wrapped his arms around her, the first hug he'd initiated in more than two years. Matt knew she would say or do anything to help him, and he treasured the safety of that, like a child falling asleep in the back seat of a car, believing his parents would remain awake, keeping watch through the dark.

He heard the sound of her swallowing, drew away from her then and looked directly into her eyes. "I understand why you didn't tell me."

She touched his cheek with the back of her fingertips— something she'd done for as long as he could remember. "I love you, Matt. You're my son. Nothing can ever change that."

"I don't deserve it. I behaved like a complete spoiled brat at your wedding, and I'm sorry. I really am. I can see you and Nate are happy together."

"I won't argue with your self-analysis. But what I said still goes."

"What's for dinner?"

"Pork roast and red potatoes. That mushroom wine sauce you used to like and a salad."

"Do you have enough for me?"

"Are you kidding? I could feed the entire senior class."

He asked about his sister.

"She's in her room, throwing her math book against the wall."

Matt headed down the hallway towards his sister's room. He drummed his fingers in the Sousa tap on her door.

"It's open," she said. "Unless it's the dweeb who screwed up Mom's wedding." There was a smile in her voice.

"The dweeb has repented and been granted a pardon." He opened the door a few inches. "If you ask me, math sucks. Who needs it?" He used the high-pitched whiney voice they'd invented as children for their stuffed animals.

Sedona sat at her desk, bent over her math homework. She wore a pair of black sweatpants and a vintage T-shirt with the Rolling Stones on the front. Her hair was loose and falling into her face. Through the Walkman speaker he'd bought her for her birthday, Richard Marx sang *Hold On To The Nights*.

She looked up at him and grinned. "What's happening, dude?"

Matt stepped inside and turned down the volume. "I have a question."

"I'll confess to anything, even let you turn down my tunes, if it means you'll lend me your math brain."

"It's about Dad."

"Let me guess. He finally told you about his love life."

When he nodded, her eyes widened. Something crossed over her face that told him she knew. "It was Crystal, wasn't it?"

Again, he nodded.

"Holy crap. I knew it. You get why I'm so pissed at Dad now?"

"Totally. But how did you know?"

She grinned. "Women's intuition."

"Yeah, right."

"Oh my God," she said. "I just thought of something." Sedona's eyes grew even wider as she stared at him. "If the police find out about Dad's affair with Crystal, they might blame him for her death."

The palms of Matt's hands were dry and icy cold. "The police already know about the affair," he said, thinking about the fight in the driveway, the thousand dollars their dad gave Crystal—most likely for an abortion—and the terrible sadness in her eyes when Matt had arrived that night. "I've done a little investigating on my own," he continued, wishing what he was about to say was true. "It's possible Crystal did kill herself."

"How would you know?" Sedona asked. "You weren't there. She didn't leave a note."

Matt took a deep breath. "Not everyone leaves a note."

He told his sister about their father's loan of a thousand dollars, but decided not to tell her about Crystal's pregnancy—the child that might have been their half brother or sister. Sedona already hated their father enough. A thought entered his mind that he'd just lied, tried to protect his mother and sister in the same way his dad had tried to protect him from the affair.

Matt had tried to protect Travis by hiding all evidence of what he and Crystal had done. He couldn't imagine how hard it was to be a parent. The lengths they'd go to save their kids from pain.

"Holy shit," Sedona said. "A thousand dollars. Do you think they already suspect him?"

Matt sat on her daybed. "I think you watch too much *Matlock*."

"In books, lots of characters try to make a murder look like suicide. It's practically a cliché."

He stared at the floor, felt his sister's dark gaze brush across his face. "I really want to know why you were so certain Dad had an affair with Crystal."

"My astute powers of deduction. Mom and Crystal stopped hanging out. And Dad looked guilty every time her name was mentioned." She paused and grinned. "Besides, Arielle's parents saw Dad with her. I tried to tell you, dorko. But you wouldn't believe me."

Sedona was right, she had tried to tell him, but he was too hardheaded to listen. Worst of all, he'd lost two years with his mom and little sister. What an idiot he'd been.

He punched his fist into Sedona's pillow, then picked it up and hit her over the head with it.

Sedona grinned, grabbed another pillow and charged toward him. "The repentant dweeb is in big trouble now."

CHAPTER TWENTY-SIX

The memorial service took place on Thursday evening in the Chapel of the Narrow Way, a building that seemed too small to hold Travis's grief. Crystal's coffin rested on an oak podium, no more than five feet away. It was only a prop—she'd been cremated. But each time Matt glanced at the coffin, a chill dashed up his spine and he had to look away.

A crude wooden cross hung on the wall behind the pulpit— powerful in its simplicity. The casket a blue so dazzling it looked as if someone had chipped it from the Tucson sky. Matt's eyes were drawn back to it again and again. The closed top held a spray of tiny pink rosebuds. A ribbon with the word *Mother* in gold letters draped over the casket's side.

Matt thought about all the roles Crystal had played in his life, how years from now his wife or girlfriend might ask about prior women he'd made love with. Before he could stop himself, he imagined a ribbon with the words, *Dance Coach, Team Mother, Friend, and Lover* in a silver script.

"I wish my dad had lived long enough for me to have a memory of him," Travis said. "Like maybe when he tossed a ball with me in the yard."

Karina patted his leg.

"Maybe he wasn't even a good guy," Travis said. "Maybe he would have come home from Vietnam all screwed up and evil." When he leaned forward, Karina rubbed his back.

Above their heads, in the high cedar ceiling, fans stirred the air and the delicate scents of roses, chrysanthemums and giant peonies mingled. Mourners filed down the aisle and Travis pointed out Barcode and some of the other waitresses from The Silver Spur. Millie and Gracie wore their short denim skirts, red cowboy boots, and the low-cut blouses, as if in tribute to Crystal.

Jennifer's parents kept their heads down.

Matt stole a look at Danni.

She smiled at him.

The muscles in his body seemed to loosen up.

A parade of young and old people stepped over to Travis and clutched his hand, whispering condolences before taking their seats in available pews. "Brothers and sisters from the church," Travis whispered.

And though Matt was happy Travis had other people who cared about him, he had the usual pang of jealousy at Travis referring to someone else as his brother.

Players from their school soccer and baseball teams wore their uniforms and carried banners Crystal and Karina had made.

The chapel filled to capacity. Despite the obituary in last night's paper, Travis had worried no one would come. The piece had included a photo of Crystal in a white blouse with a round collar, smiling like a member of the church choir. Matt was surprised by the way there was no mention of a police investigation, suicide or murder. The obit did a strange dance around the facts: the woman had died suddenly at her Catalina home. He closed his eyes and another version printed itself. *Crystal Reynolds may have killed herself because of the guilt she felt for having sex with her son's best friend.*

When the organ music dwindled away and everyone was seated, Matt scanned the chapel, hoping his father had changed his mind.

Loren Garrison wasn't there.

But Detective Radhauser, wearing a navy blue suit that looked as if it had just been picked up at the drycleaners, leaned against the back wall, holding his gray Stetson in his hands. When he spotted Matt, Radhauser gave a quick nod.

Matt took a sharp breath that felt as if something had wedged between his ribs.

Bryan Williamson, wearing a white clerical robe, slipped through the side door and approached the pulpit, confidence in his attitude and his walk. He looked comfortable in his own skin—blameless and pure.

"Love never fails." With the commanding sound of those three words, Williamson lifted his robed arms like the snowy wings of some glorious bird, reborn into this man of God. There was something so charismatic and hypnotizing about his presence, Matt could understand why Travis was impressed with him.

"Have you ever stopped to think about the enormity of God's love for you? A love so great He sent His only son to die on the cross for your sins." He paused and turned his head toward the cross on the wall. "I want you to close your eyes and think about that for just a moment. Those of you with children, ask yourself is that a sacrifice you could make?" Williamson slowly shook his head. "I know I couldn't."

He waited a moment, then began again. "In this world, nothing lasts forever. Our loved ones leave us, they die. More and more families dissolve every day. It's a world filled with sin and confusion, and only God can clear the way for salvation. Only God's love is everlasting. In His family, there is no divorce, no separation, and no death."

Williamson paused and looked toward the casket. "Crystal Reynolds has come before the Lord for His judgment. None of us can presume to know what was in her heart. But God does."

And I do, Matt thought. She was thinking about her son and how to protect him from what she and Matt had done.

Williamson paused again and his gaze traveled over the first row of mourners until it lighted on Travis. "We ask you to comfort her son and all the ones who loved her. Ease their pain, Lord, and let your solace and mercy spread like a healing ointment on their sad and weary hearts."

From deep in the congregation, church members whispered "Amen" in unison. Barcode cried loudly into a white handkerchief, then blew his nose.

"Grief is a powerful force that can transform sinners."

Williamson paused and smiled. "When the heart is hurting, it often cracks open and lets God enter." He let that sink in for a moment, then invited the sinners in the congregation to step forward and be saved.

Williamson's hypnotic voice rose into the high ceiling of the chapel. "If there is anyone who hurts, who has sinned and regretted it, or who is disillusioned with earthly families and wants to become a member of God's family, I invite him or her to come forward and begin the journey back to forgiveness and everlasting life."

Usually indifferent to prayers, Matt perched on the edge of the pew, listened so intently he almost believed he could grab hold of the preacher's words and float with them straight to the place where he could undo the wrongs he'd done to Crystal and Justin, and find forgiveness. Matt started to rise. His mother cupped her hand over his knee and pressed down, as if she knew his thoughts. A tremendous pressure seemed to release and dissipate. His shoulders relaxed.

Travis cried.

Matt's mother lifted her other hand from Travis's knee, riffled through her purse to find a Kleenex.

Travis stood. It was as if an invisible hand guided him up the aisle and to the altar, where he knelt at Bryan Williamson's feet.

Matt wanted to grab Travis and pull him back into the pew, but it was too late. Matt lowered his head. This would change everything between them.

Williamson took Travis's hands. "Welcome, son. We've been expecting you. Welcome home."

After the ceremony, Matt cornered Baxter. His eyes and nose were red from crying and he clutched his handkerchief in his right hand. "Okay if we talk for a minute?"

"Sure," Baxter said. "Any friend of Travis is a friend of mine."

Matt cleared his throat. "I was wondering if you could tell me anything about the night Crystal died."

"Nothing for me to tell, kid. She didn't show up for work. End of story."

"But Travis dropped her off in the parking lot."

"I think you already know someone picked her up," Baxter said.

"I know you used to date Crystal."

"Off and on for a few years now, kid. But Crystal always had her sights set higher."

"Were you in love with her, Mr. Baxter?" Matt asked, thinking about his father.

Baxter stared at Matt for a moment. His dark eyes went soft. "Don't worry. It's not so weird for a boy your age to have a crush on an older woman."

* * *

Matt slipped off his shoes and was halfway across the entryway when his dad flipped on a dim lamp in the living room where he'd been sitting in the dark, his pipe still smoking in the ashtray. He held an empty bottle of Johnny Walker Black in his hand, ripping a path through the label with his thumbnail. He wore a worn denim shirt, a pair of paint-splattered khakis, and sported a two-day beard. Even his hair, usually parted so carefully, was tousled on top. "Are you sick?" Matt whispered.

"I guess that depends on whom you ask." His father stood, walked a little unsteadily toward Matt, draped his arm around Matt's shoulder and squeezed. "Did you get that acceptance letter off to Penn yet?"

Matt pulled away. "I'm not going to Penn."

His father jerked back. "What do you mean? I thought it was already decided."

"If I go anywhere, it'll be Iowa." The statement surprised Matt even as it tumbled out of his mouth. There was no if. College had always been a given for him and his sister—the next step after high school. And there was nothing Matt wanted more now than to get the hell away from Tucson and the ghosts that haunted him here.

His dad moved closer. "Is this another way to show your anger at me?"

Matt said nothing.

"This behavior isn't like you, son. It doesn't matter where you go. But you're too smart not to go to college. Without it, you won't have much of a future." His voice sounded uneven.

"I once wanted to go to Penn," Matt said. "Once, I actually wanted to be you." It stabbed him to realize a relationship that had once seemed unbreakable could slip apart so easily. "Now, I don't even know who you are or how you could hurt Mom the way you did."

"The people we love are rarely worth it," his father said. "And maybe none of us deserve the burden of that love either." His breath smelled like scotch. "I'm sorry I lied, son. But I haven't lied to you about anything else. I'm ashamed of what Crystal and I did. Maybe someday you'll..."

Matt was silent for a moment, realizing this was his opportunity to talk, and trying to gauge what would happen if he actually told his dad the truth. "Believe me, I understand shame."

His father's gaze stayed fastened on Matt. "Then you understand how difficult it was for me to talk about her—especially with you."

Matt shifted from one foot to the other. He couldn't hold his father's gaze. There'd never been a time when he'd felt such strong and conflicted emotions. He loved his father and he hated him. He trusted him and he didn't.

"What do you want to know?" his dad asked. "Come on. Ask your question."

Matt turned his back to his father and closed his eyes. Another burst of shame at the meanness of his own deceit rose. For a moment, he could neither move nor answer.

"Come on, Matt, step into the ring. Don't lose your nerve now." He put his hand on Matt's shoulder and jerked him around so they were face-to-face, moving him into position like a boxer. "Come on, spit it out, Mister Too-Smart-for-College."

There were patches of sweat under his dad's arms, and clusters of pine needles on his shirtsleeves.

Matt felt a moment of guilt for not helping him remove the overgrown Aleppo Pine from the back yard. "Was Crystal pregnant by you?" Matt twisted one of the buttons on the front of his shirt so hard it snapped off and flew across the room.

His dad smiled bitterly. "I'm not sure I like the direction this conversation is taking." The light in his steel gray eyes flashed. He stared straight back into Matt's eyes and held them, and Matt, motionless.

Finally, Matt looked away. "It's true, isn't it?"

"Truth rarely exists as an absolute. This is not true. In fact, I had a vasectomy. But if you need someone to blame for Crystal's death…" He stopped, shook his head. "You better get some sleep, you have a final exam tomorrow."

Without another word, his dad turned away, strode into his bedroom and closed the door.

Matt hurried down the hallway and into his own room. His closet door was open. The gaping hole he'd punched into the wall stared back at him, jagged and angry. He wanted to punch out another one. His father had set this whole tragedy in motion. If he hadn't become involved with Crystal, Matt's parents would still be together. There would have been no wedding to Nate Sherman. Matt would never have done something else that shamed him, something that could hurt Travis so much. And Crystal might still be alive.

Once again, the black walls of his bedroom seemed to close in on him, the rows of masks he'd so carefully arranged looked grotesque—all of them empty-eyed. This time they screamed the word *liar* in unison.

But it wasn't the lies that haunted him now. It was the secrets. No one had asked him if he'd had sex with Crystal. No one had asked if he'd pushed Justin off that ledge. Secrets were far worse than lies. And the secrets that shamed Matt, the ones he couldn't seem to set straight, were his own, not his father's.

CHAPTER TWENTY-SEVEN

Unable to sleep, Loren paced the length of the master bedroom again and again. Outside the sliding glass door that led to the pool, insects flew in frantic circles around the porch light. He turned it off. He could still feel the heat of his son's eyes on him as he'd left the living room.

He could never explain his relationship with Crystal to Matt. The boy he used to lift into the air and spin in a dizzying whirl. The son he'd taught to swim, throw a curveball, and ride a two-wheel bike. All the hours that had elongated into their lifetime together had collapsed like a row of dominoes.

Oh, come on, he told himself. *Don't get melodramatic*. Matt was an adolescent. Boys were competitive at that age and wanted to take on their fathers, wanted to figure out who they were without their dads. Loren was guilty of bad judgment, but that didn't make him evil. Only people with a conscience anguished over what others thought of them.

As soon as Karina had discovered his affair with Crystal, Loren tried to break it off. But, even during the weeks he'd stopped seeing Crystal, she was there, sitting at the dinner table between them. She hovered over his pillow whenever he tried to make love with his wife—her presence so real he couldn't look Karina in the eyes without seeing Crystal.

If only he hadn't been home feeling an undeserved sadness about Karina's wedding when Crystal called on Saturday. If only he'd said no, this tragedy might have been avoided or at least unfolded in a different way. His car wouldn't have been seen picking up Crystal at The Spur, and it was unlikely the police would have learned his name. But, like always, he'd been lured by her voice, by her professed need of him.

"Loren, baby," Crystal had said in that throaty whisper that raised the hairs on his neck and sent shivers down his arms. "I need to see you. I have such good news. The Spur parking lot. 6pm. Please."

Though he could never explain it to anyone, his hunger for her was like a pulsing ache that crept into every cell of his body. For him, her beauty didn't come so much from her physical appearance. It came from the way she let go of herself and melded into him. When they were together, her body was the liquid air he breathed. She made him laugh harder than he'd ever laughed before. He was more real and alive in her presence. For the hours he held her in his arms, he was unaware of getting older and closer to death.

At exactly six, he'd slipped on his chauffeur's cap, a standing joke between them, and pulled into the gravel lot at The Silver Spur. When she slid into the front seat and turned toward him, her short skirt rose, exposing the black lace of her slip. He smelled her wildflower perfume as she leaned across the console to kiss him.

His gaze moved past the blouse that revealed her silken breasts and stopped at the white flash of her smile—the place he wanted to linger for a moment.

"Come on, let's get out of here," she said. "Before Baxter handcuffs me to the bar."

Loren drove with his left hand on the wheel, the other one holding Crystal's hand on top of the console.

She wouldn't tell him anything until they sat at her kitchen table with a glass of ice-cold beer.

"I know you love me," she finally said. "And I realize you think we can't be together because of our boys. But I'm pregnant, Lore."

She paused for a moment, as if waiting for him to speak. When he didn't, she continued. "At first, I didn't know how to feel about it, but then on the drive home from the doctor yesterday, the road looked all glittery, like New Year's Eve. And the sky was so blue and wide there was room for everything. And I realized this baby will be related to you, me, Travis, Matt and Sedona. No one can resist a baby. Matt and Travis are already closer than most brothers. Don't you see? This new little person will make us into a real family."

Loren couldn't have been more shocked if she'd kicked him in the chest with the pointed toe of her cowboy boot. The ceiling fan he'd installed above her kitchen table whirled like an angry bird, bringing with it the smell of bacon, a hint of cigarette smoke that mingled with Crystal's perfume.

When she laughed, he heard hope in the tingling sound and for a moment he wished he could be a different man, one who'd welcome a chance to parent any child.

"You should see the look on your face," Crystal said.

"I already have two children, and that's more than enough for me."

She lowered her gaze and was still for a moment, her hands caressing the sides of her glass. "I know it's sudden," she said, without looking at him. "Believe me, I was shocked, too. But I don't think either of us has much choice now."

Silence splintered the air between them, as sharp as glass. "I've got plenty of choices and being a surrogate father to your child is not one I intend to make." He was both surprised and relieved he'd said it, but also a little ashamed of himself for not being more tactful.

Crystal opened her mouth, a slight tremor in her chin and bottom lip. "Why are you being like this?"

He swallowed hard and looked around the kitchen where they'd spent so many stolen hours—drinking coffee, laughing, eating gourmet foods he'd brought from the deli, and talking about anything and everything.

Outside the window, the desert sky had darkened a little, but remained molten at the edges of the Rincon Mountains behind which the sun had just begun its slow descent. "How far along are you?"

She paused, seemed to be doing some math in her head. "It

must have happened when we were in Bisbee. About six weeks ago."

"You're lying. I told you from the beginning I was sterile. There is no way I fathered your child. And that can only mean one thing." The level of betrayal he felt amazed him. He'd broken off the relationship so many times—only to return a few weeks or months later. He could hardly blame her for a fling with someone else.

She rolled her eyes. "Maybe you were wrong. You fathered Matt and Sedona, didn't you?"

"I had a vasectomy after Sedona was born."

Her eyes widened. "Karina never mentioned anything about that." She took a sip of her beer and slowly set the glass back on the table. "Everybody knows those vasectomies aren't foolproof."

His anger built to a point where he had to look away from her. "Listen to me. Vasectomies fail at a rate of about one in every forty-five hundred performed—and those failures usually occur in the first few months after surgery. Face it. I'm not the father of this child. And you're not equipped to take care of a baby, especially one that may be born with—"

"Born with what?"

He stood to leave, holding onto the back of the chair for a moment to steady his legs. Despite the warmth in the kitchen, even his face felt cold. "You're drinking too much, Crystal."

Her eyes flared. "I'll quit then." She pushed the beer away from her. "Besides, I drank when I was pregnant with Travis. I even smoked a little pot. And he's every bit as smart as Matt."

She was right. Travis was an exceptionally bright boy. "You were lucky," he said, as he lumbered out the sliding door and onto the back deck, his legs heavy and thick as tree trunks.

She rose to her feet so quickly her chair tumbled over. Not bothering to pick it up, she followed him out into the driveway. "What do you expect me to do?"

"I'd consider an abortion."

"But what about our being a family? You have that big house. We could turn the guest bedroom into a nursery. I saw this adorable—"

"I'm sorry, Crystal. But that's not going to happen." He reached for the car door handle.

She grabbed his arm.

When he turned toward her again, tears rolled down her cheeks. "I can barely pay the rent this month, Lore."

For a moment, he felt sorry for her. He slipped his checkbook from his inside pocket, used the front fender of the Lincoln for a desk, wrote a check, and handed it to her. "Please, don't call me again. It's over. And this time I'm sure of it." He climbed into his car, closed the door and started the engine.

Crystal pounded both fists on the hood and screamed. "You're an arrogant bastard, Loren Garrison. I'm good enough for you to fuck for three years, but not good enough to marry and raise our child."

As he drove away, he saw Crystal in the rearview mirror, red-faced and still screaming at him from the driveway. "I'll get a paternity test. I don't care what you say, I'll prove the baby is yours." She picked up a rock and heaved it toward the car.

He'd driven as far as Catalina State Park when he pulled the Lincoln into the lot and parked beneath a cluster of Palo Verde trees. He shivered, turned on the heater, and rested his head on the steering wheel. After a moment, he'd driven home.

Now, Loren stopped pacing his bedroom. Crystal had been right. He was an arrogant bastard who could have handled it differently. A better man would have supported Crystal, taken her to the doctor and held her hand through the procedure, no matter who'd provided the sperm. Maybe if he'd agreed only to do that, Crystal would still be alive.

Outside, in the distance, a car turned onto his street—its headlight beams plunged through the bedroom windows, swelling the shadows of the furniture for a moment before it turned into another driveway and the light disappeared.

The things for which he'd fervently prepared as an older father to Matt and Sedona—death, a debilitating disease, or unemployment—didn't turn out to be what was needed to protect his family. Their undoing had come waltzing in through a separate door. One Loren had opened of his own volition.

Perhaps when enough time had passed, he and Matt would be able to move forward. But even as he hoped for that day, he understood relationships, like mended teacups, were always weak at their fracture lines.

CHAPTER TWENTY-EIGHT

In the high school courtyard, Matt sat alone on a small bench under the shade of an olive tree, trying to act normal. It was lunch hour, and all around him students gathered in small clumps, signing yearbooks and comparing the answers they'd given on their final exams. He heard the traffic sounds on Oracle Road, the high-pitched and rhythmic chants of the cheerleading posse as they practiced on the football field for the upcoming state competition.

Danni sat down beside him. "What's up?"

Matt felt a rush of joy so alive and energizing it was all he could do to remain seated. "Just hanging out," he said, trying to sound casual. "Watching people scribble trivia beside their mug shots. What about you?"

She smiled, a bright burst of happiness on her face. "I just got accepted to the nursing school at U of A."

"That's way cool. Congratulations."

They'd just agreed to meet at Coco's at 3pm, when he spotted the two police officers walking across the courtyard, directly toward him. One was about six feet tall, with a long and determined stride. The other was short, his blue-shirted belly hanging over his belt buckle. He struggled to keep up with the tall one.

They paused to question Tom Riley.

Tom pointed toward Matt.

The policemen continued across the grassy courtyard, stopped in front of the bench, and introduced themselves as Officers Dunn and Rodriguez. "Are you Matthew Garrison?" Dunn asked.

"I am," Matt said.

All around the courtyard, students stopped what they were doing and watched.

"We need you to come with us," Rodriquez, the tall one, said.

Matt stood. His chest felt as if it were collapsing, as if it had suddenly realized its own pathetic hollowness. "What's this about?" he asked, even though he had a damn good idea.

Danni's face was so red, you'd think she was the one they were taking away. "You can't just drag him off like some kidnapper. He's a United States citizen. He has rights."

Dunn cleared his throat and looked at Matt. "You're wanted for questioning in the Crystal Reynolds case. You can come voluntarily or we can arrest you. Your choice."

"I'll come," Matt said.

Danni stared at Matt in silence, her face pale and slick with perspiration. She studied Matt as if trying to see inside his head, trying to determine exactly what Matthew Garrison was capable of doing. But this time she said nothing.

Clumps of shocked students gathered and watched as the officers led Matt to the patrol car—their honor student, the one they'd elected most likely to succeed. Matt tried to keep his head still, to look straight ahead. But he felt their eyes on his back—unasked questions following after him like a kite's tail.

* * *

Radhauser stood in front of the one-way mirror into the interrogation room, watching. He hoped having Matt picked up at school and brought in for questioning would finally scare the truth out of him. Radhauser had worked with lots of boys over the years in Eagle Scouts and Outward Bound programs, and studied Kinesics. He could read things in gestures and body language. The lab had found no blood on Matt's tuxedo and the shirt had been too compromised to show anything.

In spite of the lack of evidence, he'd bet money on Matt being the one who'd found Crystal. But he couldn't figure out why the kid wasn't talking about it. Given the closeness of his friendship with Travis, it made sense he'd leave and try to intercept his friend. Matt was smart. Way too smart to make a 911 call if he didn't want anyone to know he'd been there. But who made that call? Radhauser had listened to the tape several times. The caller's voice was muffled, but definitely a woman.

Matt's fingerprints were on several of the beer bottles in the garage, but that didn't mean much. Radhauser remembered drinking beer with his friends in high school.

He didn't really think the kid had anything to do with her murder. But there was another, more likely, possibility. Matt could be protecting his father. Maybe Matt arrived at the house in Catalina to find his father's Lincoln parked in the driveway. Maybe the kid witnessed something that incriminated Loren Garrison.

Radhauser stepped into the interrogation room, pulled out the chair across from Matt and sat. "Here's the problem. I talked to Security at Casa Tucson. They encourage their patients to walk after dinner. But drug addicts and alcoholics are inventive. They've been known to get a buddy or naïve family member to meet them on the road with drugs or booze. Security patrols Golder Ranch Road from dark until dawn—at least once every half hour. I also talked to three neighbors who claimed they'd walked their dogs between eight and ten. No one saw you."

Matt sat at the table, back erect, his hands folded neatly in front of him. He bit down on his bottom lip and looked directly at Radhauser. "I didn't hurt Crystal."

Radhauser drew his notebook from his jacket pocket. "I need to know where you really were between 7:30 or so p.m. when you left Ms. Warren's house, and midnight when you met Travis at the dance."

"I got to the parking lot before midnight. I sat on the hood of Crystal's Escort for a long time. I'm sure some parent picking up their kid saw me."

Radhauser stood, walked to the corner of the room and leaned into it, watching Matt intently, trying to get a sense of what went on in the kid's brain, noting the unmistakable fear that seemed to surround him like cheap cologne. "Were you sitting on the hood for an hour?"

"Not that long."

Radhauser returned to his seat, asked the question slowly, trying to keep his voice steady and not lose patience. "Then where were you between 7:30 and 11:30?"

"I already told you I drove around for a while. Maybe I was wrong about the name of the street."

Radhauser leafed through his notebook until he found the right page, skimmed his notes. "You were pretty specific. Even mentioned seeing the lights from Casa Tucson. You'd been there before, helped your mother install windows. Am I wrong?"

"No," Matt said. "You're right."

"I won't waste any more time going over things we've already talked about. I think you crossed over some line, Matt. I don't know what, but I can read it in your eyes and your body language. You've done something that's forcing you to wonder about yourself."

The kid's hands were shaking as if he were about to sing the National Anthem into a microphone. "I…I didn't hurt Crystal. I mean…at least not in the way you might be thinking."

"Look," Radhauser said, seeing the kid's nervousness. "I'm not saying I suspect you killed Crystal. At this point, I don't. But I do think you know more than you're telling."

"Have you ruled out suicide? I've learned some stuff that makes me believe it's possible."

'I told you to leave the investigating to me."

"Just stuff Travis and my dad told me."

"I know you talked to Mrs. Lawrence."

"Oh yeah, I forgot about her."

"So where were you Saturday night? Just tell the truth, I'll do the unraveling."

"I don't know how to begin."

Radhauser sighed. "Maybe this will help you. A rancher said one of his llamas got loose Saturday night and he had to chase it down Golder Ranch by flashlight. Three of his kids and some neighbors helped out. No one saw your Mustang, Matt, because it wasn't there."

"All right," Matt said. "All right. I was at Danni's house."

Radhauser groaned. "We've already been through this, Matt. She said you left around 7:30 or so."

"I did, but I came back."

"Why?"

Matt shifted in his seat. His shoulders slumped as he dropped his chin and studied the chips in the Formica tabletop. The kid looked weighted down by something too heavy to carry. "I just wanted to watch her house, see if she left with that football player. I didn't know until Monday it was her cousin."

Jesus, Radhauser thought. Matt's teachers claimed the kid was smart. The volunteer coordinator at UMC described him as a quiet, but good kid—kind, intelligent, and likely to go places. The kind of kid Radhauser had dreamed Lucas would become. But they must have Matt confused with someone else. This was one stupid, mixed-up boy. "Why the fuck didn't you say so?"

When the kid finally looked up at Radhauser, there were tears in his eyes. "I didn't want Danni to find out. To know how desperate and screwed up I am."

Radhauser shook his head. Now that excuse sounded ludicrous enough to be true. "You'd rather be accused of a crime than of being a screwed-up teenager in love?"

Matt hung his head.

Radhauser felt a moment of pity for the kid. That first breakup could be rough.

Before the accident, Lucas had just started to get interested in girls. On the spring morning he'd planned to invite Alyssa Jordan to the sixth grade dance, Laura had caught Lucas sneaking into the back yard to pick a bouquet of zinnias from her flower garden. Wind wanted to tease him about it, but Laura had insisted he remain silent.

He got Matt a glass of water, offered a friendly smile, and gave him a moment to calm himself. "I have one more question. Why did you wash the tuxedo shirt before returning it?"

The kid looked relieved, as if he'd finally been asked a question with a simple answer. "I didn't. My mom did. I told you I had a nosebleed after my fight with Danni. Mom's good at getting stains out."

"Okay," Radhauser said. "Thanks for your cooperation."

Matt looked at his watch. "Are you saying I can leave now?"

When Radhauser nodded, the light in Matt's eyes returned. "I'm supposed to meet Danni at 3 o'clock, but my car is parked in the school lot."

Radhauser suppressed a smile. Maybe things were looking up for this kid. "Good luck. Officer Dunn will drive you back."

* * *

Matt slipped into the booth at Coco's across from Danni, determined to talk to her about the night Crystal died. The restaurant served breakfast all day long and the freshly-baked smell of apple pies and blueberry muffins mingled with the sizzle of bacon, sausage, and hamburgers on the nearby grill. "Have you been waiting long?"

"No," she said. "Are you all right? What did the police want?"

"It's a long story. But after we order, I'll tell you if you're willing to listen."

She leaned forward, her voice soft. "I'm sorry about the other night. I should have invited you inside and told you right away Larry is my cousin. But I didn't want my mom to find out you were there. I never meant for it to hurt you."

They ordered slices of apple pie with vanilla ice cream and coffee, made small talk about Danni's acceptance to nursing school until the waitress delivered their order. When she stepped away from their booth, Matt started to talk. "Did you mean it when you said you wanted to keep the heart necklace forever?"

"No, I just said that to make you feel bad." She gave him a closed-mouth smile to make sure he knew she was being sarcastic.

"I found it. It's at the jeweler to have the clasp repaired."

She smiled with her whole face this time. "Now that makes me very happy."

Tenderness for her brushed over Matt. He remembered how safe she'd once made him feel, the way he'd turned to her with his guilt over Justin, and again when things at home got crazy and out of control, just before Mom moved out. He wanted to touch her, but held back.

The wadded-up thing in the pit of his stomach started to unfold. He told her what had happened at the wedding. "My mom has every right to hate me."

"She could never hate you," Danni said. "She loves you too much. Did you know she called my house Saturday night looking for you? She said she couldn't go to Aruba without making sure you were all right."

Matt didn't know what to say. He didn't deserve that kind of understanding from his mother or anyone else. He told Danni about the way he'd felt when he saw her with someone else. How he'd driven out to Catalina to talk with Travis and found him gone. How Crystal had invited him inside and they'd drunk way too many beers. The way she wouldn't let him drive home without sleeping it off, and how he'd awakened to find her dead in the bathtub. Everything except the dancing and the fact he'd had sex with Crystal.

He waited for Danni to say something, but she remained silent, her eyes focused inward, unreadable. A moment later, she reached across the table and took his hand, then looked straight into his eyes. She had a light dusting of freckles across her nose, the same golden brown color as her hair. "Are you asking me for advice?"

Matt didn't know what to say. He'd needed to tell at least part of the truth to someone safe, to say the words out loud. "Advice? Yes, I guess that is what I'm asking for."

"I think you should go back to Detective Radhauser and tell him exactly what you just told me. Everything you did was understandable. You were trying to protect Travis. He's your best friend. No one can fault you for that."

Matt swallowed. "But what if they blame me for her death? What if they think I killed her?"

"I thought it was a suicide."

"Radhauser believes she was murdered."

With her free hand, Danni lifted the blanket of hair from her back and twisted it into a knot at the nape of her neck. "Who'd want to murder Crystal?"

He told her about Crystal's affair with his father, the way she'd called him on Saturday to pick her up at The Spur, and the fight they'd had in Crystal's driveway, overheard by Mrs. Lawrence. That Crystal was pregnant, and his dad had given her a check for a thousand dollars.

"Oh my God," she said. "Do you think your dad is the baby's father?"

Matt shrugged, told her about the vasectomy.

"Do the police suspect him?"

"How could they not?" Matt said.

She squeezed his hand. "But you were there. You know your father wasn't. You have to tell them before it's too late."

CHAPTER TWENTY-NINE

Just before 7am on Saturday, one week after Crystal's death, Radhauser parked his car in the circular driveway behind the Mustang. He'd called the Arizona State Prison and learned Mitch Reynolds had been released on parole nearly three weeks ago. Could he have been the "old friend" waiting in the parking lot to get a look at Travis?

The prison authorities told Radhauser that Mitch lived in a halfway house in Florence and went to work at 10am. If Radhauser wanted to get there in time to see Crystal's ex-husband, he'd have to be on the road by 8:15.

It was at least an hour drive and could take him another half hour to find the house. But he also wanted to catch Loren Garrison, detain him if necessary, so his Lincoln would be available when the other officers arrived with the search warrant.

Radhauser strolled around the Mustang once, admiring the sleek, but squared-off lines, the deep turquoise paint job, the white racing stripes on the back fenders and doors. He cupped his hand over his eyebrows to block out the sun's glare and peered through the driver-side window. The blue and white upholstery was new—but original-looking—as was the carpet. Someone had spent big bucks on restoration.

When he rang the bell, Matt answered, his hair neatly combed but still wet from his shower. He wore his usual black jeans and a black button-down collar shirt with the sleeves rolled up. He held his car keys in his hand. "Thank God you're here. I came by the Sheriff's office to see you last night, but you weren't there."

Radhauser tipped his head toward the Mustang. "Nice ride.

You sure keep it clean. Those spoke wheel covers are a bitch to wash."

The kid smiled. "I try. Did you get my message? Is that why you're here?"

"No. I came to talk to your father. I'm in a bit of a hurry."

"Why do you want to see my dad again?"

"Some questions I need to ask. Is he around?"

"His bedroom door was closed when I got up. I can check and see if his car is still in the garage."

While he waited, Radhauser twirled his Stetson and studied the Mustang—the distinctive fender emblem—a wild horse racing across red, white and blue stripes. Pieces of his old life coalesced around him.

In 1967, the year he'd graduated from Camelback High School in Phoenix, Radhauser had driven a beat-up Ford pickup with rusted fenders, and upholstery that always reeked of cow manure. It had belonged to his uncle, a cattle rancher Radhauser had been sent to live with after his mother's breakdown. He'd lusted for a Mustang, listed it in the yearbook as the set of wheels he'd most wanted to own.

He thought about Lucas then, wondered what kind of car his boy would have dreamed of owning. Maybe they'd have bought a Mustang and refurbished it together in the driveway, with Laura watching them through the kitchen window as she loaded the dishwasher. Instinctively, Radhauser fingered the silver belt buckle.

Matt returned. "He'll be right with you."

"You headed somewhere?" Radhauser asked.

"The grocery store. We're out of everything, even Fruit Loops." He shrugged and jingled his car keys in his left hand, as if to validate what he'd said. "I can wait if you have time. But I need to talk to you in private. Without my dad."

The judge had granted Radhauser a warrant to search the Lincoln, and he hoped Matt wouldn't be home when the officers arrived. "We can talk this afternoon," Radhauser said. "After I return from Florence."

"I'm helping Travis spread Crystal's ashes after work."

"I'll be in the office until late," Radhauser said, then stood on the porch for a few moments, watching the kid drive off and thinking about the way Laura had kept their pantry stocked with Lucas's favorite cereals and snacks. The way she'd joked about the huge quantities of food their pencil-thin son could pack away.

A rust-colored dog raced out of the neighbor's driveway, yelped, and chased alongside the Mustang. Matt's brake lights came on. He rolled down the window. "Go home, Meyer." He pointed toward a neighbor's driveway. The dog obeyed, and when it was halfway down its own driveway, Matt's brake lights went out and he continued down the road.

A gate squeaked. Footsteps crunched in the gravel. Loren Garrison stepped around the corner of the house, through a redwood arbor covered in bright pink bougainvillea blossoms and into the driveway. He was unshaven, dressed in work clothes, and had a pair of pruning shears in his gloved hand. Sweat wet his brow and a streak of dirt spread across his right cheek. He could have easily been mistaken for a gardener working for minimum wage. "Sorry for the wait," Garrison said.

Maybe Radhauser had pegged him wrong—maybe Garrison, despite his notoriety and subtle arrogance, deadheaded his own petunias.

Garrison wiped his shoes on the mat, opened the front door and ushered Radhauser inside.

In the entry, Garrison set the shears on a small Mexican-tile topped table, took off his gloves, wiped his right hand on his pant leg and held it out. There were circles of perspiration beneath his arms and he had the distinct musky smell of male sweat and last night's alcohol. "What brings you here so early?"

Radhauser shook Garrison's hand. "I have a few more questions about you and Ms. Reynolds. I'm sorry to bother you on a Saturday morning, but it won't take long."

Garrison led him into the family room.

The plantation shutters covering the wall of windows into the backyard were closed, and it took Radhauser's eyes a moment to adjust to the dim light.

Garrison opened them and the sliding glass door to the back yard. The air held the faint smells of chlorine, pine, and wet soil as they seated themselves across from each other at the table.

"Crystal's neighbor, the woman across the street, claimed a white Lincoln with a blue top was parked in Crystal's driveway last Saturday until around 7pm."

Garrison waved his hand casually, as if batting away a fly. "I already told you I left Crystal's house about that time."

"The neighbor claimed you and Crystal were involved in a pretty heated discussion. Would you mind telling me what you argued about?"

Garrison looked away. "I haven't been entirely forthcoming with you about my relationship with Ms. Reynolds." He told Radhauser about their affair, the many times he'd tried to break it off and couldn't, Crystal's pregnancy, her assertion he'd fathered the child, and the vasectomy he'd had years ago.

"I know about the affair," Radhauser said. "I subpoenaed your office and home phone records for the past three years."

"And you found phone calls to Crystal's house and her place of employment—not unusual when you're in a relationship with someone."

His new attitude of cooperation surprised Radhauser. "Then you won't mind me swabbing your cheek for a paternity test." He didn't really expect his captain to spring for DNA testing, but Radhauser could learn a lot from the suspect's attitude about providing a sample.

"Be my guest."

Garrison opened his mouth and Radhauser swiped the swab against the inside of his cheek, replaced the cap, then sealed it in the evidence bag.

"The way I see it, you'd have a lot to lose if Crystal blabbed about you being the father of her child."

"I'm not the father."

"By the time you proved that, a lot of damage could be done to your reputation, to Harvard's endorsement, and the sales of that new textbook of yours."

"What are you trying to say?"

Radhauser cocked his head, gave him a sympathetic but inquisitive look. "That you had motive."

"Motive for what? Didn't Crystal commit suicide?"

Radhauser was quiet for a moment, trying to decide how to play out his next move. A double murder in a town as small as Catalina was a big deal. The story could be a headliner in tonight's paper, tomorrow's at the latest. If Garrison read it first, he'd have time to recover, to plan his next move. Radhauser would miss his initial reaction.

"No, she didn't." Radhauser's gaze never moved from Garrison's face. "The razor blade threw us off. Either someone tried to make it look like suicide, or the blade was superfluous—there because Ms. Reynolds used it to clean the tiles or to shave her legs. The ME established the wound was too deep to be self-inflicted with a razor blade. He's calling it a double homicide."

Garrison went pale. He pressed his fingers into his temples. "Please, don't do this. I had an affair with her while I was married. That was wrong. But you can't think I'd kill Crystal."

"I'm not paid to think," Radhauser said. "I'm paid to gather evidence and follow its trail until I get at the truth. And that trail leads me straight to you. Her neighbor said Crystal ran after your car, crying and screaming she'd prove you were the father. Sounds to me like a world of hurt."

Garrison studied him for a moment, as if he were a specimen in a glass case. "You're a bit of a pitbull, aren't you, Radhauser?"

Radhauser laughed. "It's the job. I've been called that and worse."

Garrison's complexion had gone from pale to ruddy. "Like anyone would be, I was hurt by her obvious betrayal and the way she tried to blame the pregnancy on me. But I didn't kill her. For Christ's sake, I couldn't even break up with her to save my marriage. She had that strong a hold on me. I'm not a perfect man, but I could never murder anyone. You already told me this nosy neighbor confirmed I drove away around 7pm, just like I told you?"

"Yes," Radhauser said. "She did. And the ME put the time of death between 10:30 and 11:30—with the possibility of it being as early as 9-9:30, depending upon the temperature of the bath water." He waited a moment to see if Garrison responded. He didn't.

"Did you return to her house, hoping to make things right?"

"Absolutely not."

"There aren't any streetlights out in Catalina," Radhauser said. "The houses are set on two-acre lots. As you probably know, most of the folks are older, stick to themselves, and go to bed early."

Garrison looked down. Radhauser had no way of knowing how what he'd said had affected him.

"But I didn't return. I remained here. Nate dropped Sedona off at 9:30. I answered the door fully dressed—my hair wasn't wet from a shower. I was calm and relaxed, working on a lecture. And I most certainly wasn't covered in blood. If you don't believe me, ask Nate."

"I intend to," Radhauser said. "Did you give Crystal the thousand dollars to keep her quiet about your affair?"

"No," he said, meeting Radhauser's gaze. "Absolutely not." He told Radhauser about his concern the child would be born with fetal alcohol syndrome, and how he'd suggested Crystal consider an abortion. "She claimed she had no money. You may find this hard to believe, Detective Radhauser, but I tried to help her."

"After you broke up your family for her, I'll bet you were pretty pissed off she'd been making it with someone else."

"I didn't leave my wife. Karina left me."

"The end result was the same. I asked if you were angry."

Garrison shook his head. "The truth is, I was relieved. The hold Crystal had on me for years disappeared." He looked at the detective, as if checking for a reaction, but Radhauser said nothing.

Maybe he was wrong about this guy. Maybe he'd better start thinking about Matt, Mitch Reynolds, and other potential suspects. There was something about the waitress, Millie, and her concern over the way Crystal treated Thomas Baxter that seemed slightly suspicious. And Baxter must have been pretty pissed off, too.

At the sound of a car coming down the driveway, both Radhauser and Garrison looked toward the entryway. Matt stepped inside, carrying two bags of groceries. "I can't believe it. I must have run over a nail. I could barely get down the driveway."

Damn, Radhauser thought. He'd hoped the kid wouldn't be home when the officers arrived with the warrant.

"I guess it's time you learned how to change a tire," Garrison said. "I'll help you when I get back. Call UMC and tell them you might be a little late this morning. Detective Radhauser and I are going out to CoCo's for a cup of coffee."

Matt gave his father a long look as if trying to read his thoughts, then set the bags on the kitchen counter and began unpacking and putting them away, leaving out the box of Fruit Loops. He opened the refrigerator and removed a carton of milk.

Radhauser checked his watch. "I'll drive. I've got thirty minutes."

CHAPTER THIRTY

Matt sat on a barstool at the kitchen counter, eating cereal and wondering what his dad and Radhauser were talking about. He thought about what Danni had said about telling the truth. He should have insisted Radhauser take the time to listen.

For a moment, Matt felt sorry for his dad, understanding how the events of your life could become a tsunami. He made himself some toast, but couldn't decide what to put on it, so he ate it dry.

Without a clean shave and three-piece suit, his father had looked more vulnerable than Matt had ever seen him before—the way he'd pressed his fingers to the side of his head as if it could help him think more clearly, as if thinking was one more gift of youth that didn't come so easily to him anymore.

The telephone rang.

Matt leaped up to answer.

Travis called to remind Matt they'd meet at UMC around one o'clock to take Crystal's ashes to Gates Pass. They were about to hang up when Travis said, "I feel bad about something, man."

"Let me guess. Your conscience is bothering you for kicking me out of my own mother's house."

"It's not that," Travis said, no trace of amusement in his voice. "I've kept something important from you. And it doesn't feel right."

"Then spill it."

"My mother was murdered."

Matt dropped his gaze to the floor.

"It's not just what I think," Travis said. "The Medical Examiner confirmed it. I told you, man. Crystal would never kill herself."

He explained what the pathologist had discovered about the depth and width of Crystal's wound, and the impossibility of it being made with a razor blade. The high probability it had been made by a pair of scissors, possibly the ones used to cut her hair.

Matt stared at his right hand, felt his fingers sink again into the gaping hole in Crystal's neck. Felt the warmth and stickiness of her blood. "Are you okay?" Matt's voice sounded hollow.

"I'm not okay," Travis said. "But at least I don't have to blame myself anymore. Radhauser said he believed me from the beginning. He had a hunch. And something didn't feel right."

"Can you think of anyone who'd want to hurt her?"

"Radhauser has a suspect. He's getting a search warrant. That's why he didn't want me to say anything. Keep it between us, okay? Don't even tell your parents."

* * *

Matt emptied the remainder of his cereal into the garbage disposal and loaded the bowl into the dishwasher. The word *murdered* remained inside his mouth, and each time he tried to force it down, it rose again. Someone saw his dad pick Crystal up at the Spur. Radhauser had told Travis they planned to get a search warrant. Of course, they'd want to search the Lincoln. Maybe his dad really did have something to hide.

Matt hurried into the garage. He knew something awful was about to happen. He felt it in the air around him, as if time itself had somehow become electrified, each individual second standing straight up on its end.

The entire garage seemed to be holding its breath. He kept telling himself it couldn't be true. They couldn't believe his father killed Crystal. His dad wasn't a violent man. Even when he'd been livid with Sedona for shoplifting a tube of lipstick, he hadn't laid a hand on her.

Matt maneuvered his way through the garage, opened the driver's side door and popped the hatch for the trunk. It was spotless. The four-year-old carpet looked new.

He opened the passenger side door, checked under the seat and in the glove compartment. He flipped the visor down and looked into the small, lighted mirror at a face he barely recognized. He was not himself anymore. He was a different person altogether.

After hurrying around to the driver's side, he opened the door, ran his hand under the seat, and that's when he felt it—something nubby like an old beach towel. Maybe his dad left a towel under the seat from when he'd last washed the car. Matt pulled it out. It was a pale green washcloth wrapped around something solid and hard.

He carefully unwrapped the washcloth and found a pair of scissors with orange handles like the ones he and Travis used to wrap Christmas presents every year. The blades were stained with something that looked a lot like dried blood.

His hands shook so hard he could barely hold the scissors. How did Crystal's scissors get into his father's car? Holy shit. Could he have been wrong about his dad? Matt had been wrong about the affair and even more stunned to learn it was with Crystal. Loren Garrison, the renowned expert on ethics, had lied to him for three years. Maybe he was capable of murder.

No. It had to be a mistake. His father couldn't kill anyone. He rarely raised his voice and had never so much as spanked Matt or Sedona.

Matt went back and forth. He didn't know what to think, but he couldn't let Radhauser find the scissors. He had to get rid of them before his dad and the detective returned. It wasn't smart to hide them on their property, but he didn't have another choice. He couldn't drive the Mustang with a flat tire. And at least getting them out of the Lincoln would buy him some time. He could retrieve the scissors later and dispose of them where no one would ever find them.

He hurried into the back yard, out the redwood gate and into the desert behind their house. It was way too quiet. The air broke around him like twigs.

Along the edge of the sandy wash, he walked faster and faster, dodging cholla cactus and boulders. He feared turning around to see someone behind him. He didn't have much time.

He spotted the five-armed Saguaro with a woodpecker hole

the size of an orange in its trunk. Matt knew from summer camp at the Desert Museum the Gilded Flicker nested higher up in the more mature Saguaros, but left a much larger hole than the Gila Woodpecker.

The Saguaro would have bled its resinous sap into the cavity between its spines to heal the wound. The resin hardened into callus tissue and formed a Saguaro boot inside. Woodpeckers nested in them—a safe place hard for a predator to find. He stood on his toes. But the hole was too high for Matt to reach.

Out in the cul-de-sac, he heard the sound of a car idling. He hoped it wasn't Detective Radhauser and his father. The sound lingered in the still air for an instant, before it accelerated, then slowly disappeared.

Matt left the washcloth-covered scissors on the ground and raced back to the garage for his dad's tallest stepladder. Blood buzzed in his head as he climbed up to the third from the top rung. His legs were shaking so hard the ladder shook with them.

Sweat dripped into his eyes as he pushed both the washcloth and the scissors through the hole and into the boot. It landed with a dry rustling sound like paper being crushed.

* * *

Matt had just rehung the ladder in the garage and poured himself a glass of water when the doorbell rang.

Two uniformed police officers stood behind the screen, their patrol car parked in the driveway behind his Mustang.

"Good morning," the taller one said, his voice deep and resonant.

The shorter one took off his hat, his dark hair styled in a fifties-type flat top. He had a small scar in the shape of a fishhook on the left side of his mouth. "We're here to see Loren Garrison."

"I'm his son. Is there something I can help you with?"

"No," the flat top said. "We need to see Mr. Garrison."

"He and Detective Radhauser are at CoCo's."

"May we come in?"

"I'd rather you wait until my father is home."

"We have a search warrant for a 1985 Lincoln Continental

Mark V," the tall one said. "Is it here?"

"It's in the garage."

"The law doesn't require your father, or anyone else, be home."

Matt's hands trembled as he fumbled with the handle on the screen door for an instant before he managed to open it.

The officers wiped their feet on the welcome mat, then stepped inside. Their rubber-soled shoes made squeaking sounds against the entryway tile as they followed Matt into the family room.

Within seconds, Matt heard the sound of a car door closing. "That must be my dad. He's home now. I'll get him."

He rushed through the front door and onto the porch, his legs shaking.

His father stepped out of Radhauser's Bronco.

"It's the police, Dad. They have a search warrant for the Lincoln."

Loren studied Matt quickly, then looked at Radhauser. "Thanks for the heads-up. But they won't find anything in my car."

As his dad turned toward the house, Matt hurried over to the Bronco. "You're right. I've been hiding something. And I need to talk to you. Now."

Radhauser glanced at his watch. "I'm sorry, Matt. But I have a suspect to interview in Florence. I'll miss him if I don't leave now. Stop by my office when you finish up with the ashes. I'll be there until 8 o'clock tonight." He drove away.

Matt watched him for a second, then hurried inside.

His father stood in the family room, one hand braced on the game table. "What exactly do you think you'll find?" Loren asked the officers. "A stash of drugs hidden in a shoe box?"

"We have our orders," the tall one said, then told Matt's dad to stay out of the way.

Matt wanted to follow them into the garage, but knew he'd be sent back inside. His father had always been so above reproach. It was hard to see him humiliated. Yet at the same time, Matt thought about the rage he'd seen in his father's eyes last night when they'd argued about colleges.

If his father had driven back to Crystal's house on Saturday night, if he'd seen his son asleep in her bed, he might have been enraged enough to murder. *Oh my God*, Matt thought. He shouldn't have hidden the scissors. What was wrong with him? He'd made one bad decision after another in an attempt to protect Crystal, Travis, and now his father. Matt cradled his head in his hands, tried to think. But he could no longer choose between right and wrong. Maybe his dad had killed Crystal. Maybe Matt had made a huge mistake. But it was too late to go back and undo what he'd already done.

He was still standing in the family room when his dad and the two police officers returned.

The flat top wore a pair of latex gloves.

Matt gave his father a questioning look.

"They found absolutely nothing," he said.

The officer wearing the gloves shrugged.

Matt's father shook his head, as if he couldn't believe this had happened to him.

"Stay close to home, Mr. Garrison. A tow truck is on its way. We're impounding your car." He nodded toward his partner. "This is Officer Harrington. He'll wait in the garage until the truck has left with the Lincoln."

"When will I get it back? I need it for work on Monday. This isn't right. I'm calling an attorney." But instead of moving toward the telephone, his father stood very still, his eyes cast down at the floor, his hands clenched together.

The flat top shrugged, then walked through the family room, into the entry and out the front door without another word.

Matt stood behind the screen door and watched as the police car backed up, circled the center island, and drove out of the driveway and onto the street, moving slowly, as if it were in a parade. Through the small gap in the driver side window, the radio crackled with snippets of conversation—other police personnel talking in coded sentences.

A vein throbbed in Matt's neck. He didn't know what to do. If he told his dad about the scissors, he'd probably insist Matt remove them from the Saguaro and take them to Detective Radhauser.

214

And then both Matt and his dad would be in deeper trouble. He took a breath, tried to keep the heat from rushing to his cheeks, and let the air out slowly. Matt doubted anyone, except maybe a Gilded Flicker woodpecker, would ever find those scissors.

The police car rounded the corner and the radio sounds disappeared.

When Matt spotted the tow truck headed up their cul-de-sac, he turned to his father.

He was observing Matt—such a simple, fatherly, thing to do. "It's all a misunderstanding. Let's change that tire before you're late for work. Don't look so worried, son. Aside from the affair, I didn't do anything wrong. Everything will be all right."

And Matt watched him, too, searching for one misplaced movement—something that would give his father away.

CHAPTER THIRTY-ONE

Loren Garrison sat in his study, reviewing lecture notes. Something registered in his peripheral vision. His gaze followed two heads moving along behind his five-foot high patio wall. As he focused, he realized they were police officers. What the hell did they want now?

He stood and hurried to the front door, opened it and stepped outside onto his porch. A white van was parked in the cul-de-sac with the words *Pima County Sheriff's Canine Unit* painted in black on the side.

Loren rushed into the desert behind his house. Two huge and straining dogs pulled at their leashes. "What are you doing? This is private property."

A barrel-chested uniformed cop gave the dogs a signal with his right hand. They immediately calmed and sat back on their haunches.

"And who are you?" one of the officers asked.

"My name is Loren Garrison. I own this land."

"I'm Officer Walters. And we have a warrant to search these grounds, Mr. Garrison."

"It's Doctor Garrison, and I was already humiliated with one of your warrants earlier today. One that yielded absolutely nothing, I might add."

Walters nodded to the dogs. "Columbo and Friday," he said, as if he expected Loren to kneel down and shake their paws.

The other officer, younger and much taller than Walters, held a white cloth that looked like a handkerchief soaked in blood.

"Ready."

Walters nodded.

The tall officer held the handkerchief under the noses of the bloodhounds until they picked up the scent and Walters released them.

Loren watched the dogs for a moment as they raced around the desert, stopping to sniff rocks and barrel cactus, the remains of lizards and other small animals. Then he shook his head and returned to his work.

Five minutes later, Walters walked back to the van and returned with a ladder. Loren nearly laughed as he opened his sliding glass door and walked behind the pool for a better view. The dogs stood at the base of a huge Saguaro cactus, looking as if they were starved and the Saguaro dangled a steak from each of its five arms.

Walters, wearing a pair of latex gloves, climbed the ladder. A few minutes later, he descended, holding something that appeared to be wrapped in a light green washcloth.

Garrison stepped closer. "What have you got there, the beginnings of a woodpecker's nest?"

"Possible evidence in a murder case."

"Whatever it is," Loren said. "It's not mine. And I sure as hell didn't put it there."

Walters shrugged. "I'm just doing my job, sir." He handed the washcloth to the tall officer while he picked a few cactus thorns from his wrist.

"Come on," Loren said. "A washcloth."

"They're used to clean off dirt," Walters said. "You got any dirt you need cleaned, Dr. Garrison?"

"What's it wrapped around?" Loren demanded.

Neither officer answered.

"The Fourth Amendment gives me some rights. You are required by law to leave an inventory of what you take from a private residence."

"We didn't take it from your residence."

"Well, from my property then."

The taller officer ripped a form from his clipboard and wrote. "Here you go," he said. "One blood-covered pair of scissors and one green washcloth."

"What the hell are you talking about?" Loren asked. "Let me see them."

"Detective Radhauser wants them untouched."

"I understand the chain of forensic evidence. I won't touch anything."

Walters carefully opened the washcloth.

It took a moment for Loren to believe what he saw. His knees felt wobbly and he braced himself against the patio wall. He had a horrible vision, a fear for which he had no real evidence, and yet he couldn't get it out of his mind. One by one the suspicions registered and added up to something Loren couldn't face.

The blood on the front of Matt's tuxedo shirt.

Karina's certainty Matt had lied to her about it.

His anger and disillusionment with his father.

The fist-sized hole in his closet wall.

The disturbing poem he'd found on Matt's desk.

All of it tied to Loren's foolish affair with Crystal. Had he turned his own son into a murderer?

Walters carefully rewrapped the washcloth around the scissors. "Stay close to home, Doctor Garrison. I suspect Detective Radhauser will want to talk to you after we have this analyzed and blood-typed."

* * *

Radhauser believed it no coincidence Mitch Reynolds had been released from the state pen just weeks before Crystal died. He wouldn't be the first ex-con to murder the wife who didn't stand by him while he served his time. As he neared Florence, Radhauser checked the clock on his dashboard. 9:15am. He had 45 minutes before Reynolds left for work.

Driving down Florence's Main Street was a trip back in time. In the mid-eighteen hundreds, it had been a prosperous mining town. If he closed his eyes, he could almost hear the clippity-clop of horse-drawn wagons and piano music coming from the open windows of its many brothels and saloons.

Lucas had loved Florence because of the Junior Parada—the

oldest youth rodeo in the world. From the time their son was two, they'd brought him here in late November for the parade down Main Street and the rodeo. He competed in western pleasure events at five years old. Until Lucas died, they'd never missed the Parada.

The silence in the car rang in Radhauser's ears. Haunted by flashbacks of his wife and son, he lowered all the windows. The fresh air rolled through the car and puffed up the damp hair on the back of his neck. He smelled the musty brine of the Gila River as he drove on.

The halfway house, a small adobe bungalow out on Diversion Dam Road, was probably built after the war. It nestled in the Sonoran Desert at the end of a long dirt drive in a compound of about a dozen similar dwellings—the gray-blue Mineral Mountains looming in the distance. Radhauser parked, waited in his car for the dust to settle, then got out, walked up onto the porch, and rapped on the door.

It opened. A lean, tall man stood in the doorway, absently picking his teeth with a wooden matchstick. He wore a worn flannel shirt with the sleeves rolled up to reveal a couple of dragon tattoos, rumpled gray Dockers, and a pair of black shoes that hadn't been near polish in years. His reddish-brown hair swept back into a ponytail and he had a thin red moustache. "What ya sellin', cowboy?"

"I'm looking for Mitch Reynolds."

His brow furrowed. "He a friend of yours?"

Radhauser pulled out his badge.

"Jesus." The man's lips fluttered around the matchstick. "Mitch is one of my good ones. Why do you want to talk to him?"

"Part of a routine homicide investigation." Radhauser tucked his badge back into his inside coat pocket and pulled out his notebook. "Is he here?"

"Homicide? Are you shittin' me?"

"Is he here?"

"I heard his wife died last week, but Mitch said she was high strung and maybe it was suicide."

"Mitch was wrong. What's your name?"

"Simon Pierce. I'm the house manager." He puffed up a little at the word 'manager'.

Radhauser jotted the name in his notebook.

"I don't want no trouble," Pierce said.

Radhauser pocketed his notebook and stepped inside. "I'm not here to make trouble. Just to ask some questions."

"He's been here about three weeks now," Pierce said. "Far as I know, he's mindin' his own business. He shows up for meals and does his share of the chores. Got a job right away, makin' deliveries for the *East Valley Tribune*, six days a week."

Radhauser decided to take a chance, to assume it was Travis's father who'd waited in The Spur parking lot to see his son. "Witnesses spotted Mitch Reynolds in Tucson last Friday. And again on Saturday—the night his ex-wife was murdered."

"I know all about his bein' there," Pierce said. "He got a weekend pass from his parole officer. Mitch's boy lives there and he wanted to see him—to make things right. Makin' amends is a big part of the program here."

"Do you know what time he got back?"

Pierce shook his head. "I didn't hear him come in. But that don't mean nothin'. I'm a heavy sleeper. I can check the sign-in sheet, if you want."

Pierce stepped over to a small desk beside the door and leafed through a notebook.

Radhauser looked around the room. It was clean and well-organized, with the standard fare for halfway houses—a sagging brown sofa, two side chairs, end tables, and a coffee table in front of the sofa. A card table with four folding chairs set up in the corner—a deck of cards and a stack of jigsaw puzzles on top. The floor, white linoleum with blue speckles, was partially covered by a braided hooked rug, the kind seen in country farmhouses. A dining area with a round maple table and eight chairs was set off from the living area with an arched plaster wall painted army green.

"Says here he got home at 6:30 Sunday mornin'. We use the

honor system. And far as I know, Mitch ain't had no infringements."

Plenty of time to kill Crystal, get cleaned up and drive back here, Radhauser thought. Casa Grande had a truck stop off Interstate 10 with showers for rent. He could have packed a change of clothes, worn a raincoat, and dumped his bloody clothes there. "Is he here now?"

Pierce nodded, confirmed what Radhauser already knew. "He don't go to work until 10. Second door on your right. I can get him for you, if you want."

"Is there a place I can talk to him in private?"

"Sure. There's a conference room down the hall on your right, just past the indoor swimming pool."

Just what Radhauser needed, a wise ass.

Pierce grinned. "I'm just shittin' ya. The bedroom's set up for four, but the other residents do construction. Out of here by dawn six days a week. I run a tight ship."

Radhauser tapped on the bedroom door. An instant later, it opened.

He didn't know what he'd expected, but it wasn't what greeted him. Mitch Reynolds was a handsome man, with sand-colored hair, strong features, and white teeth that would have been perfect if they hadn't overlapped slightly in the front. His eyes had an unmistakable sincerity to them and were the same laughing blue color as his son's. With his clean shave and boyish grin, he looked more like a country western singer than an ex-con, right down to the cleft in his chin and the absence of any visible prison tattoos. He wore a blue plaid western shirt tucked into a pair of Levi's that looked as if the creases had been steam pressed—his cowboy boots polished like new.

Radhauser introduced himself.

Without changing his expression, Mitch stuck out his hand. "Pleased to meet you."

Radhauser shook it.

The small room was crowded with two sets of bunk beds, neatly made with brown corduroy spreads tucked into the mattresses with military corners. A shared desk wedged into the space between them held a big ashtray that had been recently emptied, but not washed.

"You want to sit?"

Radhauser pulled out the desk chair, took off his hat and placed it on the desktop, then turned the chair around so it faced into the room.

Mitch sprawled out on what Radhauser assumed was his bunk. "My guess is you're here about Crystal." He shook his head. "Damn shame. I wish I'd known she was in such a bad way when I seen her. Looked to me like she was on top of the world, had a date with some older guy driving a fancy Lincoln."

Radhauser moved his chair a little closer. The legs made a scraping sound on the linoleum. "What else can you tell me about your visit with Crystal?"

Mitch told Radhauser he'd stopped by The Silver Spur on Friday. He'd wanted to see Travis, but Crystal was adamant and threatened to get a restraining order if he tried. He said she'd finally agreed he could wait in the parking lot and catch a glimpse of his son when he dropped her off between 5:30 and 6 on Saturday.

"I was so excited I got there an hour early," he said. "At first, I was pretty pissed off about her telling Travis I died in Vietnam. But it's not like I ever paid her a dime of child support. When she told me why she'd done it, I understood. It worked, too. That boy is something else. Crystal planned to tell him about me when he turned eighteen."

He paused and grinned. "July fourth. I used to call him my little firecracker. I got a lot of making up to do with that boy." He gave Radhauser a quick nod. "I plan to do it, too."

Mitch sounded sincere, and Radhauser admired the way he validated Crystal's position and didn't try to make himself the injured party. This man had a steely capacity to endure what life offered without the usual ex-con bitterness. Radhauser saw it in his eyes, the depth of the injuries he'd inflicted on his son and his willingness to heal them.

"Did you follow Crystal home when you left The Silver Spur on Saturday?"

He swung around and sat on the edge of the bed. His eyes narrowed, like someone farsighted trying to read the small print. "I told you she had a date. My sister lives on Campbell Avenue, near the medical center. I drove to her house, had dinner around seven o'clock with her and her husband and two of their neighbors. We watched a baseball game on her television. They had a few beers. I drank iced tea. I'm in AA now."

"Did you drive back to Crystal's house later that night?"

"The neighbors left around midnight. Sis and I cleaned up the kitchen and then went to bed. I got up very early and drove back here."

Radhauser told him about the Medical Examiner's findings.

All the color drained out of Mitch's face.

"Did you kill your ex-wife?"

Mitch shook his head, then stared at his hands. "Once a con, always a con, right? It figures you'd think I had something to do with it."

"Did you?"

"No, sir."

"You understand if your alibi doesn't check out, I'll be back."

Mitch's gaze met Radhauser's and held as he recited his sister's name, address, and phone number from memory. "Please don't scare her. She's one of the few people who still believes in me."

Radhauser jotted down the information in his notebook. As he wrote, he realized he believed this man. It wasn't because he'd confirmed Mitch's alibi, found something else that exonerated him, or because some other person confessed to Crystal's murder. Mitch Reynolds exhibited that indescribable compassion only the innocent knew—the moral certainty he'd done nothing to harm Crystal written all over his face.

"Would you be willing to give me a DNA sample?"

Like an innocent man, Mitch Reynolds agreed with no argument. "It's hard to believe anyone would want to hurt Crystal. She was a fun-loving person. Real friendly. And smart, too. She was pissed off at me, but for good reasons. I behaved real stupid and irresponsible. I wasn't ready to be a husband and father at eighteen. I screwed around on her. Got myself in big trouble with the law. Her and my boy deserved better. Him and Crystal were real close. How's he doing?"

"About as well as anyone could be," Radhauser said. "I've met your son on several difficult occasions." His hand clamped onto his belt buckle. "Any man would be damn proud of him."

"And I am, sir, I swear to you. Crystal told me about his baseball scholarship. The University of Arizona." There was awe in his voice. "I never even graduated high school. That boy's not like me, thank God." He shook his head, as if it were too much for him to fathom and then started to cry, his arms stiff on his knees.

When Mitch settled down, Radhauser asked, "Did you ever know Crystal to cut her hair—whack it off in clumps with a razor blade or a pair of scissors?"

He stared at Radhauser for a moment. "Back when she was a ten-year-old kid, her stepfather sexually molested her. She told me she was ashamed, thought it must be her fault and that she wanted to be ugly." He smiled sadly. "Not that Crystal could be ugly if she tried."

As he left the halfway house, Radhauser wondered if Crystal had been ashamed of something Saturday night. Maybe it was the lie she'd told Loren Garrison about the paternity of the baby. Or maybe it was something else. Whatever the reason for her impulsive action, Radhauser was no closer to solving her murder. He sighed. But at least Travis still had a living parent who cared.

CHAPTER THIRTY-TWO

No one had been more surprised than Winston Radhauser to learn the search warrant for Loren Garrison's property had yielded a pair of bloody scissors that fit Crenshaw's description of the murder weapon. And the washcloth matched the one Travis had provided. Early analysis indicated the blood on the scissors was B negative—the same type as Crystal Reynolds.

He hadn't expected to find anything in the Lincoln. Garrison was too smart to leave bloody scissors there—but Radhauser had hoped the lab would come up with some trace evidence on the carpet, the driver's seat or in the trunk. Finding the scissors in a Saguaro cactus boot was a first, and he had to hand it to Columbo and Friday. Those dogs didn't miss much.

He checked out Mitch Reynolds' alibi with his sister and two neighbors. It matched perfectly with what Mitch had told him. Though it really wasn't pertinent to the case, Radhauser had spent the last hour on the phone with an old friend on the Phoenix force, tracking down Reynolds' history. He'd driven the getaway car in a series of convenience store robberies involving two other men. One of the robberies resulted in the death of an older man who worked behind the counter. Reynolds was convicted, along with the other two, of armed robbery and homicide. And although he was nowhere near the victim, he received only a slightly more lenient sentence. In a way, Radhauser felt sorry for him, hoped he'd stay out of trouble and find a way back to his son.

After a bad cup of coffee in the Sheriff's Station break room, Radhauser returned to his office, opened Crystal's file, and reviewed his evidence. He spread his crime scene photos on his desk and, once again, studied them. If Garrison had wrapped the scissors in one of the missing washcloths, he probably took the towels as well. Radhauser's search of Garrison's garbage cans, the garage, and the area surrounding the house had yielded nothing. He could have dropped the towels into a dumpster on his way back from Catalina. But if he'd done that, why had he kept the scissors and washcloth?

He shook his head. Garrison had no record, not so much as a traffic violation. The lab reported Luminol showed no trace evidence of blood in the Lincoln, not on the seats or in the trunk, not on the steering wheel or carpet. If he'd killed Crystal, Loren Garrison would have had blood on his clothing and shoes. With Crystal in the tub, there was no place for him to shower.

He could have used the towels to clean himself up and then put them in a plastic garbage bag before tossing them into his trunk. If he'd done that, surely a trace of blood would have remained and found its way into his car. Maybe Garrison had brought a change of clothing and shoes. But that would be premeditated, and he didn't seem the type to plan a murder. If only Radhauser could figure out what pushed Garrison over the edge.

In addition to Nate and Karina, Radhauser had interviewed some of Garrison's colleagues and neighbors. From all reports, he was not a violent man. Aside from arrogance, no one Radhauser interviewed said anything negative, not even his ex-wife. But cops don't question fate when it comes in the form of bloody scissors.

* * *

Matt parked high in the Saguaro-laden foothills, just beyond Gates Pass. Travis had been unusually quiet on the drive up the mountain, and in a way Matt was relieved. Today was the one-week anniversary of Crystal's death. Last Saturday night, she'd opened the sliding glass door and invited Matt inside. It was the biggest mistake of his life. If only he'd turned around and driven home.

He had no idea what to think about the scissors he'd found in his father's car. It could mean his father killed Crystal. Or someone else planted the scissors. But who would try to frame his father? And why?

Matt wanted to talk to Travis about it, but didn't know how to begin or how much to say. Travis knew Matt's father well, knew how particular he was about his car and he was too smart to leave a murder weapon in it for almost a week. Travis would never believe him capable of murder. Maybe Matt should tell him about the scissors. At the very least, he needed to tell Travis about the affair before he heard it on the news or read it in the newspaper.

Matt opened his Mustang's trunk and waited while Travis lifted the rectangular black box of ashes. It was made of particleboard and weighed much more than the seven pounds of ash a human body normally weighed. Six Phillips-head screws secured its top—an identification number stamped on the lid. Matt stared at it for a moment, hit hard by the realization Crystal, once so full of life, was now just a number on a fake wooden box. Matt grabbed a screwdriver from the toolbox in his trunk and slid it into his pocket.

He and Travis hiked through the desert to a high plateau overlooking the Tucson valley. It was silent except for the sounds of their footsteps, and some small lizards and ground squirrels scurrying along the dusty, rock-strewn path.

When they emerged into a clearing, Matt crouched with his back against a boulder. He breathed in the smell of the desert greasewood and creosote. Even if he were blind, Matt would still know the spring desert by the way that fragrance clung to the small hairs in his nostrils.

With all the beauty and solitude around him, his dark mood lifted. He and Travis had often watched the sun set from this location, the sky tangled with shades of peach and purple flames, while the Catalina Mountains tucked a rose-colored blanket over their rocky summits. It was a place where a poet could center himself. A place for belief in something larger.

"I never thanked you for trying to help me the night she died," Travis said. "You stuck around when others would have booked."

"I couldn't let you—"

"That's what I'm talking about, man."

Travis had a strange look on his face, and for a moment Matt wondered if he'd suspected at least a portion of the truth—Matt had known and tried to prevent him from seeing his mother in that bathtub.

After setting the box on the ground, Travis picked up a small, flat rock and rubbed it between his thumb and forefinger. He studied it for a moment, then tucked it into his pocket.

Matt took the screwdriver from his pants pocket. "Do you want me to open it?"

Travis shook his head. "I need to do it myself."

Matt handed him the screwdriver.

Travis's hands were shaking. The screwdriver skidded off the screw heads a couple times before he managed to remove the screws. He lifted the cover. Crystal's ashes were in a clear plastic bag, closed with a blue twist tie. Another tiny Ziploc bag that held the gold cross earrings was taped to the underside of the lid.

Travis stared at the earrings for a moment, then shoved the Ziploc deep into the pocket of his jeans. He untwisted the tie on the bag and opened it.

Matt had never seen human ashes before. He couldn't take his gaze off them. They were gray, nearly white, with visible fragments of bone. Crystal's bones. The hipbone he'd traced with his index finger. Her delicate wrist bones. He wrenched away from the box, made a choked noise that sounded much louder in the silence.

Travis didn't seem to notice as he knelt in front of the open bag.

Matt swallowed hard and joined him. Together they recited the Lord's Prayer.

When they were finished, Matt waited, wanting to give Travis time for whatever else he might need to think or say. He seemed to be content to look around him. Matt followed his friend's gaze out over rocky hills.

The Sonoran desert was a wild landscape, both secret and open, where wind circled the mountains and seemed to blow from every direction at once. In the valley below them, Palo Verde trees heedlessly spilled their last blossoms.

"Radhauser asked me if I knew she was pregnant," Travis said.

"I didn't. A little more than three months with a girl." He laughed, a torn sound, darker and far more complicated than humor. He rubbed the heel of his hand under his eyes. "Imagine. Me with a baby sister."

Before Matt had time to absorb the image, Travis stepped close to the edge of the canyon and quickly poured out his mother and the beginnings of his sister. A cloud of dusty ashes hung in the sky for a moment, then fell to the ground, covering the smaller cactus and sage bushes like snow. When all the ashes had settled, he stood and walked away.

Matt watched Travis's back for a moment as he walked farther out into the desert. If only Crystal had told Matt about the pregnancy, he might have understood why she couldn't handle anything else, why she couldn't bear to think about Travis knowing what they'd done. If Matt had known, he would have promised her his silence. It might not have changed the outcome for Crystal, but he would have felt better about himself. He hurried to catch up with Travis, who bent to pick a burr from his pant leg.

"I been thinking about a sermon Bryan gave." Travis rolled the burr between his thumb and forefinger. "He said wisdom grows out of disillusionment. We evolve from what hurts us, what happens in our own hearts as a result of that pain." He paused, then shook his head. "I sure as heck hope that's the truth and Travis Reynolds becomes one wise dude." He kicked a rock toward Matt as if it were a soccer ball.

Matt passed it back to him, waiting for an opportunity to tell Travis at least some of the truth.

"I wonder if she even knew she was pregnant," Travis said. "I keep thinking it might be a motive. But if she knew, why would she keep drinking? And if she didn't know, then no one else did, either."

Matt wanted to tell him she'd found out about the pregnancy on Friday morning, the day before she'd died, but stopped himself.

"Radhauser said there might be an article in tonight's newspaper and he didn't want me caught off-guard," Travis said, then told him Radhauser thought the razor blade was there because Crystal or the landlord had used it to clean paint off the tile.

Matt shuddered. Maybe his father killed Crystal and left the razor blade trying to make it look like suicide. He was a smart man, and he'd gone to great lengths to hide his affair with Crystal.

They wandered along a deep gully cut by spring rains as it wound through the Saguaros. In a way, Matt was relieved for the silence.

The desert was a land of thin air and illusion, where sand and perspectives shifted. Distance misled, and you could be deceived by both the closeness and the space between things. Just like with people, appearance and reality were frequently quite different.

"You sure everything's cool between us?" Travis finally asked. "You're closed up tighter than a bank vault. Did I do or say something to make you mad?"

Matt wiped his sweating hands on his pant legs. "You didn't do anything. It was me. I did something horrible and…" He trailed off.

Travis gave Matt a gauging look. "Do you know something about my mom's murder?"

Matt's throat felt dry. He'd always told Travis the truth. Always. Until now.

Travis kicked the dirt with the toe of his hiking boot. "I know it's only been a week, but things have been weird between us since Crystal died." His voice was gentle, but held something else, something that made the hairs prickle along the back of Matt's neck.

"I've been pissed off about other things," Matt said.

Travis shook his head. "Sometimes I don't get you. Your parents split, but at least they didn't disappear. And Nate's a good guy. I'd rather have three parents than none."

He was right. So many things about Matt's life had been easy. He wanted to start over. To rip everything that had gone wrong into shreds—pieces of scrap paper they could toss away. "I have to tell you some things," Matt said. "Before you read them in the newspaper."

On a boulder overlooking the Tucson Valley, Travis sat and

hugged his knees. "Go ahead."

Matt sat on the ground facing Travis, squared his shoulders and took two deep breaths. "My dad had an affair with your mother. It had been going on for about three years."

"No way."

"I know," Matt said. "It shocked the shit out of me, too. But my father admitted it. He says they kept it secret so we wouldn't have to choose between them and our friendship."

Travis stared at Matt, as if trying to see behind his eyes. Then he shook his head. "I came home from school early one day and your father was hanging a ceiling fan in our kitchen. There was something weird about the way they acted around each other. When I asked Crystal about it, she said the landlord hadn't gotten around to hanging the fan, so your dad volunteered to help."

"When Dad drove her home from work on Saturday, she told him about the pregnancy and claimed he was the father."

"Holy shit," Travis said. "That's too weird, man. Too weird." He kept shaking his head as if saying no, over and over. "Do you realize that would mean...the ashes...it was your sister, too."

Matt told Travis about the vasectomy, the way the neighbor had heard his dad and Crystal fighting about it in the driveway. "Your neighbor said he left around 7:00."

"What are you trying to say, man?"

"The police got a search warrant for the Lincoln. They didn't find anything. But that's because I found it first—a pair of scissors under the front seat with blood on them." He told Travis how they were wrapped in a green washcloth, like the one he gave Detective Radhauser, about the flat tire, and how he'd hid them in the desert before they got there with the search warrant. "Someone planted them in my father's car."

Travis's eyes were wider than Matt had ever seen them before. After a few moments, he slid off the boulder, stood and paced. "You're messin' around with a murder case to protect your father. That woman he screwed around with was my mom. She probably meant nothing to him. But he broke her heart." Travis's voice cracked.

"I'm sorry," Matt said.

"How could you—" Travis stopped, seemingly unable for a moment to continue. When he did, the first few words came out choked. "I should take those bloody scissors and cut off your old man's dick before I move up to his carotid. I should—"

"Please listen to me," Matt interrupted. "You know how my dad loves that Lincoln. We've helped him wash it lots of times. You could eat off the fenders and wheel rims. I've never seen so much as a gum wrapper in the ashtray or a cracker crumb on the carpet. He'd never hide bloody scissors under the front seat and leave them for the police to find. I agree with you, he's a jerk, but don't you see, he didn't kill Crystal."

"If you want the truth," Travis said. "What I see is an arrogant man who thinks he can take what he wants, no matter how much it hurts someone else."

Matt's jaw and neck muscles tightened. "I didn't want to be the one to tell you any of this. And there's still more."

"I don't want to hear anymore. I'm done with all of you, man. I moved out of Nate and Karina's house this morning."

The desert started to move underneath Matt. "Why?" he asked, his head spinning. "I thought you planned to stay until baseball camp starts."

"I could give you a lot of bull crap reasons, but the truth is I need to spend my time with other believers. Karina doesn't approve of my church. She doesn't say anything, but I can tell. I moved into an apartment with two church brothers. The church has to be the top priority in my life. And that means I have to end our friendship."

Matt sucked in a loud breath.

"You know what's weird, man? I didn't think I could go through with it." Travis shook his head. "But after what you just…" He stopped, started again. "It doesn't matter anymore."

Matt tried to swallow his hurt. The desert moved faster now, like a full-blown Spinning Tea Cup ride. "What about the plans you had for yourself? What about baseball and your scholarship?"

Travis looped his thumbs into the waistband of his jeans. "I can serve God on the baseball field. And Bryan wants me to start a chapter of Narrow Way on the University of Arizona campus."

When Matt finally stood, a drenching wooziness washed over him. Something had begun that he felt powerless to stop. "So now I'm a loser you're going to toss aside because I won't join your church."

"You'll never be a loser, Matt, at least not in the worldly way. But you were wearing my T-shirt, man."

"No...No...I wasn't. We have lots of black T-shirts that look alike."

"Don't bullshit me, Matt. You were there. You were at my house the night my mother died."

Matt didn't know what to say.

"I thought we were best friends. I thought we always told each other the truth."

Matt hung his head. Travis was the best friend he'd ever had and he wanted to tell him everything, but if he did he'd betray the promise he'd made to Crystal. He'd already let her down—let her die alone in that bathtub.

"It's not what you think," Matt finally said. "I came to your house to talk to you after I fucked-up my mother's wedding."

"You knew I was at the dance with Jennifer."

"I did," Matt said. "But I was so upset I forgot."

"I don't believe you." Travis gave him a disgusted look. "Be honest. Be a man."

"I screwed up, Travis."

"Yeah. You sure as hell did."

From his pants pocket, Travis pulled a pair of silver cufflinks with a raised black 'M' in the center and handed them to Matt.

"Where did you find them?" The words came out as if vines had strangled them.

Travis winced, and a tide of something sad and hopeless washed over his face. He stared at Matt for a long time. "I told Radhauser they belonged to my father. That my mother gave them to me to wear to the dance. I didn't know how to explain them being on the floor under the chair in her bedroom." He paused, started again. "I told Radhauser I was upset my mom had never showed them to me before, and threw the cufflinks against the wall. He believed me."

Travis's lie was a gift Matt shouldn't have accepted—undeserved and much too generous. "Why would you do that?"

"I don't know. What were you doing in my mother's bedroom?"

"I was changing my shirt," Matt said.

"Why not change in my room?"

"I'd been sleeping off my drunk in her room. She took my keys and wouldn't let me drive."

Travis stared at him for a moment, as if trying to ferret out the whole truth. "That was motherly of her."

"I don't know what happened to her, I swear to you. When I woke up and discovered her in the tub, I tried to help her, to check her pulse and see if she was still alive. My hands got so bloody, I freaked out and wiped them on my shirt. And then I got scared if anyone saw the blood, they'd think I hurt her."

Travis continued to search Matt's face, unasked and unanswered questions suspended in the air between them like particles of dust in sunlight. "You have to believe me," Matt said. "I loved Crystal."

Travis gave him a hard look. "Just drive me back to my car. I'm done talking to you."

"You need to let me explain." Matt scrambled to his feet, then stood still for a moment, trying to regain his equilibrium. "It's not what you think." No. The truth was much worse than anything Travis could imagine.

"I don't trust you anymore. And if you care even a little bit about me, you'll stop talking right now." Travis's voice was sharp, slicing the air like a razor.

Matt took a few deep breaths, then headed for his Mustang, Travis a few steps behind him. Just before they got to the car, Matt stopped walking and turned to face Travis. "Please," he said again. "You have to listen—"

"Shut up," Travis said. "Just shut the hell up, man."

Matt drove down the winding mountain road to the University Medical Center in silence. He brought his Mustang to a stop in the parking lot behind Crystal's Escort. "I can't believe you won't give me a chance to explain."

Travis got out of the car, hesitated for a moment, then closed the Mustang's door without saying a word.

CHAPTER THIRTY-THREE

Despite his reservations, Radhauser called Tim O'Donnell and arranged for them to meet at the Tucson Police Department in an hour.

"Jesus Christ. It's my day off. Can't it wait?"

"No," Radhauser said.

O'Donnell grumbled something Radhauser couldn't understand, but when he arrived at the TPD, Tim sat with a female officer at the front desk, eating a homemade blueberry muffin.

"We need to take a patrol car," Radhauser said.

O'Donnell grabbed his keys and started out the door. "What's so urgent?" he asked as he slid into the driver's seat, raking aside whatever notebooks and papers lay on the passenger seat like a foraging black bear. "You gonna tell me what this is all about?"

"I need someone with me when I arrest Garrison for the murder of Crystal Reynolds."

O'Donnell grinned. "My favorite part. Do I get to read his rights and clamp the handcuffs on the kid?"

"It's not Matt. It's his old man," Radhauser said. "Long story. I'll fill you in on the way."

Radhauser told O'Donnell about the ME's findings, Garrison's affair with the victim, Crystal's pregnancy by someone else, and the argument she'd had with Garrison in her driveway. He told him about the bloody scissors, a match for the victim's blood type, wrapped in a washcloth that belonged with the missing towels.

"Sounds like plenty of probable cause," Tim said. "But we both know the kid lied through his teeth. Those beer bottles had his fingerprints all over them. You think he was covering for his old man?"

"I don't know. Kids lie when they're scared. But Matt didn't kill her."

"How can you be so sure?" Tim snapped. "Maybe the kid hid the scissors. You said he was pretty pissed when he found out about his father's affair with the victim."

"I'm sure in the same way I knew Crystal Reynolds was murdered."

"Okay, so you were right. But that kid ain't no Huck Sawyer." Radhauser laughed.

"What's so funny?"

"You do much reading? It's Tom Sawyer and Huck Finn."

"Don't get all intellectual about it. You knew what I meant."

When they turned off Oracle Road onto Ina and then Paseo del Norte, O'Donnell flipped on the siren and lights.

Radhauser turned them off.

"You're no fun at all."

"You're a good cop, but you can be a real jerk. Do you know that?"

O'Donnell grinned. "I'm just messing with you."

The closer they got to the Garrison house, the smaller Radhauser's chest became, squeezing his lungs like the time he'd had pneumonia as a boy and been placed on oxygen. He took a deep breath and tried to relax, but something still didn't feel right. During his review of the evidence against Loren Garrison, the walls of his office had seemed to close in on him. If he'd really solved the case, then why did it seem harder and harder to breathe? Could O'Donnell be right? Should he check the Mustang for blood and take a closer look at Matt? Could the murder weapon be leading him away from the real killer?

Radhauser leaned forward in the passenger seat, sank his face into his hands, and reviewed everything again. Garrison had motive galore—a hell of a lot to lose if his reputation got called into question. It wasn't rare for a man to be enraged enough to kill his lover if he discovered her pregnant by someone else. But

Garrison had been with Crystal earlier in the evening. Why wait four hours to do it? Radhauser felt the slow, rolling pressure of doubt building inside him. It wouldn't let him go.

The scissors in the Saguaro would have been a clever, but relatively easy plant if someone were trying to frame Garrison. But why not put the scissors somewhere more incriminating, like the Lincoln?

Planting anything in Garrison's car wouldn't have been easy. He was meticulous about that vehicle, kept it locked when parked on campus. At home, he parked it in a secure garage. But Matt would have had access. If, like O'Donnell suggested, Matt tried to incriminate his father, why didn't he plant the scissors in the Lincoln? The kid might be pissed off with his old man right now, but he'd chosen to live with him after the divorce. No matter how hard Radhauser tried, he couldn't believe Matt capable of framing his own father.

Loren Garrison had plenty of opportunity—no alibi between 7:00 and 9:30, when Nate dropped off Sedona. The ME's estimated time of death could be off. Or Garrison could have driven back to Catalina after Sedona got home. The kid probably went straight to her room. Garrison said she doesn't talk to him.

Still, Radhauser wished he could be more certain, wished he had that gut feeling of being right. He didn't want to overlook some minor detail, like a loose thread in a sweater that could lead to a mass unraveling. Loren Garrison was a little too self-important, the kind of man cops liked to see brought down. But if he were innocent, Garrison would endure not only the grief of losing a woman he'd loved to a vicious murder, but the humiliation of being accused of it. Not even a pompous asshole deserved that.

When O'Donnell pulled into the circular driveway, Radhauser was happy to see the Mustang wasn't parked in front of the house. He knew Matt was taking Travis to Gates Pass to spread Crystal's ashes and was relieved they hadn't yet returned. Radhauser hated to arrest a man in front of his son.

* * *

Loren had showered and changed, and sat draped over his kitchen counter, drinking black coffee. Though he tried to put it out of his mind, Matt's question kept haunting him. No matter how hard he tried to push it down, it kept rising. *Who are you?*

It seemed ironic to him, after watching two police officers pull a pair of bloody scissors—presumably the weapon that had killed Crystal Reynolds—from a Saguaro cactus, that his thoughts were existential. People were born. They died. And in between those two events were pathetic and mostly-meaningless actions. Like the ones he'd taken that led to the demise of his family.

The internal wheels had been set in motion by his son's question, churning up things Loren hadn't thought about in years. As he stared at the ceiling, he kept asking himself the same question—a question that seemed to mock him. What happened to the ethical man he'd intended to become?

He leaned back against the barstool and tried to get the question out of his head. But it merely rephrased itself. Another variation. *Who the hell are you?* Maybe every man did this, pondered his identity alone at crisis-inducing moments. Times when your son stopped talking to you. Moments when someone you thought you knew was murdered and you feared your own son might be to blame.

Who the hell are you?

Still unable to answer, he employed the prompts he sometimes used with his students.

I'm the type of man or woman who—

He tried on various identities. *I'm an educator—the type of man who enjoys opening the minds of young people.*

No, the other voice inside him said. *You're the type of man who has affairs with his open-minded students—the type who cheats on his wife and lies to his children.* Though the voice of his conscience was loud and hard to ignore, he continued. *I'm the type of man who likes to ponder the big questions. A scholar.*

No, the other voice insisted. *You're the type of man who writes textbooks on morality and ethics, but has none. You're the type of man who uses women, and has an ex-wife and daughter who look right through to your shameful core. The kind of man who may have driven his son to a despicable act.*

239

He cried silently now, the tears leaking out, slipping down his temples. He was no closer to a definition than when the question first rose. If someone were to reach out and touch him, he felt as if he would shatter. He had to put those bloody scissors into some kind of perspective that didn't involve Matt.

The doorbell rang.

He wiped his face on a napkin and stepped into the entry and opened the door.

Detective Radhauser and a shorter, black police officer in uniform stood on the porch, a black and white Tucson Police car parked in front of the house.

"Are you Loren Garrison?" the black officer asked.

"Radhauser knows I am," Loren said. Holding the door open with his foot, he invited them inside. "What do you want this time? To search my underwear drawer? Or confiscate my silverware?"

In the entryway, the black officer stepped forward. "We have a warrant for your arrest for the murder of Crystal Reynolds and her unborn fetus. You have the right to remain silent and refuse to answer questions. Do you understand? Anything you do say can and may be held against you in a court of law. Do you understand?"

The officer stood in front of Loren, spouting off the entire paragraph as if it were one sentence.

Loren grabbed the warrant, read it, then handed it back to Radhauser. "Of course I understand. I'm not an imbecile. But this is ridiculous."

The officer had intense dark eyes that were impossible to read. His squared-off chin was clean-shaven, like his head. He looked directly at Loren and commanded, "Put your hands behind your back, sir."

Loren braced himself, planted his feet wide apart on the entryway tile and crossed his wrists behind his back. "Is this really necessary?"

As he heard the click of the cuffs, felt the pressure against his wrists, Loren stared at his cordovan wingtip shoes, so remote from the rest of his body. His legs were like rubber bands, his feet receding farther and farther away.

"I need to leave a note for my son," he said. "Matt will be worried."

The officer nudged Loren gently forward again, his big hand pressed into the small of Loren's back.

"I need to call my lawyer."

"There'll be a phone booth in the holding cell. You can call and leave messages for Matt and your attorney." Radhauser opened the back door of the patrol car. The officer protected Loren's head with his hand as he ducked into the back seat, then Radhauser reached down and fastened Loren's seat belt.

As they pulled out of the driveway, Loren's neighbor's bronze van glided down the cul-de-sac and into the driveway next door. When she craned her neck to see, Loren lowered his head.

CHAPTER THIRTY-FOUR

Saturday evening, long after the Catalina Sheriff's station had emptied of everyone except the weekend officer manning the front desk, Radhauser waited for Matt to confess what Radhauser already suspected. The kid had found Crystal dead and hurried out to Marana to intercept Travis. But who made the 911 call? None of the neighbors admitted to it. They'd traced the call to a phone booth outside a convenience store, five miles north of Crystal's house.

Radhauser studied his now completed notes on the case. Something bothered him but he couldn't nail it. He swigged the dregs of his coffee, then tossed the Styrofoam cup into his trashcan. His office smelled like the leftover pizza he'd found in the break room refrigerator and reheated for his lunch.

Through the open window behind his desk, the sunset disappeared, the sky darkening fast. Obsessing about the case had brought him nowhere. He closed his notebook, folded his arms on the desk, and lowered his head onto them.

Night was the worst time of day for him. That's why he played Laura's piano until he collapsed from exhaustion. He didn't want to get his wife and son out of his mind, but he knew it was time—knew he was headed for another breakdown if things didn't change. Before the accident, he'd had no idea grief was so ugly and isolating. And he wasn't the kind of man who shared it easily with others.

Ever since he'd questioned Matt and Travis, his internal wheels were set in motion, heaving up memories and dreams for his son he hadn't thought about in months. When his eyes blurred, he blinked back tears, furious at himself. He glanced at his watch. It was nearly 8pm, and it looked like Matt had lost his nerve and wasn't going to show.

Tonight, he'd bypass the piano, eat some real food, and get a good night's sleep. He packed his briefcase, turned off the light, and was headed out the door when his intercom beeped. He hurried back inside, flipped the switch for the overhead light and picked up the receiver.

"There's someone here to see you," the officer at the front desk said, a smile in his voice. "Claims she knows you. Her name is Millie Brooks and she's hell bent on seeing you and nobody else."

Before Radhauser had hung up the receiver, Millie sashayed into the office, a folded newspaper in her left hand. She wore her waitress outfit, including the red cowboy boots. "You look like a woman with a mission," Radhauser said.

"And you look like a man who needs some sleep." She flopped onto the chair in front of his desk, then opened the newspaper to the front page. "I know it's kind of late and I'm sorry to barge in on you, sugar, but is this for real?" She set the newspaper on his desk.

Radhauser scanned the headline. *Double Homicide in Catalina.*

He read on. *After an autopsy, Pima County Medical Examiner, Irvin Crenshaw, confirmed Detective Winston Radhauser's suspicions that Crystal Reynolds, the young waitress found dead in her bathtub, was the victim of a brutal murder.*

Nice of Crenshaw to give him a little credit.

The autopsy also revealed that Crystal Reynolds was pregnant, making this the first double homicide in the history of Catalina.

"I didn't write the article," he said, wishing the captain had held off a few more days before broadcasting Crenshaw's forensic brilliance to the media.

"You can tell me, sugar. Was she really pregnant? Or is this one of them tricks the police play to draw out the real killer?"

"We have a suspect in custody. Are you saying we don't have the right guy?"

She pressed her hand against her chest, as if too caught up

in her surprise to answer his question. "I'm sure you know what you're doing, sugar. I just need to know if they got the pregnancy part right."

Radhauser smiled. "If you read it in the newspaper, it must be true."

Millie flipped her hair back and tucked it behind her ears, then gave him a big smile. "I wasn't born yesterday. I tried to tell Bax it might be made up."

Radhauser told Millie that the ME had confirmed the pregnancy.

The clock on his desk ticked.

Millie crossed her legs, revealing a narrow edge of black lace. "Look, sugar. Baxter's in a bad way. Acting all weird and psycho about this. I need you to talk to him."

Radhauser briefly closed his eyes. He was so damn tired. "What do you mean psycho?"

"He's asking me and Gracie the same shit over and over, like some escapee from the loony bin."

Radhauser winced. "What's he asking?"

"If we knew how far along in the pregnancy Crystal was, and if she had one of them fancy new tests that told if the baby was a boy or girl. I said, 'Holy crap, Bax, I didn't even know she was pregnant.' Which ain't exactly true. I had my suspicions, but I tried to protect him."

Millie talked with her hands now, throwing them up in the air as if too exasperated to go on. "And Gracie's no help. She just clams up around Bax and won't say a word. If you ask me, she knows something. Her and Crystal was real tight."

Millie cocked her head. "Didn't I tell you he has this thing about his daughter coming back?"

"Yes, you did."

"And that Medical Examiner, he was positive?"

"Yes. I know I already talked with you and Gracie about this, but I want you to review it with me again. What time did Baxter leave the bar last Saturday?"

She told him the exact story she'd told before—maybe too

exact—that he'd left a little before 10pm, gone home and turned on the television, that she heard it when she'd emptied the trash around eleven. That there was a motion light over his garage door that stayed on for five minutes after the door closed.

"So, you're absolutely certain he never left the house that night."

"One hundred percent. I've known Bax a long time. We opened The Spur together." She stopped and looked at Radhauser.

He knew she wanted some acknowledgment. "Wow. You must have been a great help."

"Bax was in a snit that night. I fretted about him, so I watched him real close. You can't walk nowhere from The Spur."

She was right. Crystal's house was a good five miles from the restaurant. There was no way Baxter could have walked that distance in time to murder her. "Why were you so worried about him?"

"I could tell by his red face that his blood pressure was way up. Bax has some health issues."

"Do you know why he was upset?"

"No," she said. "But you can bet your boxer shorts it was about Crystal."

"Come on, I'll walk you out to your car."

Millie remained seated. "Will you talk to Bax? He's a good person and he's been through a lot. Just tell him the kid couldn't be his."

"I don't know that for sure."

"A little white lie," she said, turning her hands palm-side up. "What can it hurt?"

"It would be unethical," Radhauser said, while knowing he'd lied before and would do it again if it would help solve a case.

She lowered her head, directed her words at her lap. "You must think I'm plum pathetic, coming here like this. But please, could you just do one of them paternity tests? Give the poor man some peace of mind."

When he didn't respond, she lifted her face, her eyes wide enough for Radhauser to see her feelings for Thomas Baxter swimming inside them. If Gracie hadn't provided Millie with a solid alibi, Radhauser would consider her a suspect. "Where is Baxter now?" he asked.

"At home, moping around. I told him I'd work a double shift. But he called in a temp to cover the bar. I'm worried half to death and I had to talk to someone." She shook her head. "I didn't know where else to go." She stood and turned to leave the room.

Radhauser called after her. "I'm glad you came by, Millie. Baxter is real lucky to have you on his side."

She glanced back over her shoulder. "Yeah. Too bad he don't know it."

* * *

It was almost 9pm when Radhauser parked his car in The Silver Spur lot and walked around the brightly lit restaurant to Baxter's house. Through the front window, Radhauser saw a small lamp burning. He tapped on the door.

No one answered. Maybe Baxter had decided to work the bar after all.

Radhauser knocked louder.

Finally, Baxter opened the door. He wore a pair of sweat pants and a black T-shirt. "What do you want?"

Radhauser handed him the newspaper. "I wanted to give you a heads-up this article was about to appear, but I didn't get a chance. I'm sorry if it caught you off-guard."

He looked Radhauser up and down with weary, bloodshot eyes. "What makes you think I give a shit?"

"Nothing. Except you used to date Crystal and I got the feeling you cared, at least a little."

Baxter hesitated, his hand still on the doorknob. He stared at Radhauser's face as if searching for the man behind the one he projected—a deeper, more worthy and authentic man. "Are you married, Detective Radhauser?"

A dizzy, sick feeling built in his gut. He needed that real food. Now. He needed to get out of there. "Not any more."

"Kids?"

"A son."

"How old is he?"

246

Lucas' face swam into Radhauser's mind. Thirteen. A vulnerable age. Not a child, but not an adult either. Had he lived, Lucas would be bounding back and forth between the child he was and the man he would become. Radhauser puffed out his cheeks, let the air out slowly. "My son died."

Baxter nodded, as if everything was clear to him now. He pulled the door completely open and moved aside so Radhauser could enter. "I had a gut feeling about you."

Radhauser stepped inside. The house smelled different from the last time, like sandalwood and pine incense burning.

"Can I get you anything?" Baxter asked.

"I could really use a beer," Radhauser said, wanting Baxter to trust him enough to talk openly.

Radhauser took a seat on the sofa. A six-inch rectangular tray about an inch wide sat in the center of the coffee table, spirals of smoke curling up from the stick of incense it held. The stick was nearly burned out and a long, gray piece of ash dropped into the tray.

Baxter returned with two open bottles of Corona.

Radhauser took a long swig, then set the bottle on the coffee table.

Baxter's gaze flicked over to Radhauser's face, then instantly flicked away. "I'm cleaning the air of my anger," he said, nodding toward the tray. "I like to be calm when I'm working on Becka's dollhouse." Without drinking any of it, he set his own beer on the end table beside his recliner and dropped into the chair. He rubbed his hands over his face—pressing so hard Radhauser saw the flesh whiten on his stubby fingers.

"Why are you angry?" Radhauser asked.

"Is there any way the Medical Examiner could have made a mistake?"

"Doctor Crenshaw is good. And he says she was pregnant."

Baxter flinched, as if this confirmation had physically hurt him. And for a brief moment, Radhauser appreciated what little access we have to what's going on in another person's head.

When Baxter spoke again, it was as if he'd wiped his old voice away to let out a new, much higher, one. "She promised me we'd—" He stopped; started again. "She should have told me. I would have taken good care of her and the baby." He kept waving his hand back and forth as if shooing a mosquito away from him. His gaze darted around his living room for a moment before it came to rest on the photo of him pushing his daughter on the swing. It lingered there for an instant and then he shot Radhauser a panicked look. "Do you know if it was a boy or a girl?" Baxter's voice was tight, cautious, not the flippant man Radhauser had previously interviewed.

Something told Radhauser not to tell him it was a girl—at least not yet. Radhauser shook his head.

Baxter's shoulders slumped. After a moment, he picked up the newspaper again, folded it, then held it in his lap, rocking slowly from front to back. "I know it sounds crazy, but I need to know." Something flashed over Baxter's face, but it was gone before Radhauser could interpret it.

"I'll try to get that information for you," Radhauser said carefully.

"Thanks. Can you do a paternity test on me? I'm sure you of all people understand that it's important I know if the baby was mine."

"I'm sorry. The police department doesn't do paternity tests on demand."

On some level, Radhauser felt a little sorry for Baxter and hoped Crystal's baby belonged to Garrison or someone else.

"Do you know where I could get one?"

"Even if you found a place, you'd need tissue from the fetus for comparison."

"The Medical Examiner has that, doesn't he? I'll pay whatever you want," Baxter said. "Please."

Radhauser took another swig of his beer. He needed to play this carefully. "It sounds like you believe you could be the father. When was the last time you had sexual intercourse with Crystal?"

He blinked, then dropped his gaze. "We were together from Christmas through the end of February. We talked about having a child. I wasn't using protection. Then her hotshot boyfriend came back into her life." Baxter shook his head, his dark eyes glassy.

Radhauser had a perceptible feeling of something coiled up just beneath Baxter's skin, like a tension spring that couldn't be wound any tighter.

After finishing his beer, Radhauser stood. He opened his briefcase and pulled a swab from the box, swished it across the inside of Baxter's cheek, replaced the cap, then sealed it in a bag. "I'm writing you up as a suspect, so the captain doesn't question the expense," he said casually.

"I don't care about that. When will I know the results?"

"I'll try to put a rush on it," Radhauser said, knowing that even if the captain did authorize the test, it could be months before they got results.

Baxter stood, spun on the balls of his feet with the agility of a dancer and looked Radhauser straight in the eyes. "You know what I'm going through, don't you?"

Radhauser nodded.

"Will you call me as soon as you get the results?"

"Yes. And I'll do everything in my power to make it fast."

Just before Radhauser walked out the front door, he looked at Baxter again.

He stood very still, a foreboding expression on his face, like a doomed man about to be carted away to serve his time.

CHAPTER THIRTY-FIVE

It was one of those evenings when the moon came out early and looked as if its surface had been scarred with a black rash. Matt had spent too much time parked at the top of Campbell Avenue, trying to make sense of the things Travis had said after they'd scattered Crystal's ashes.

Headed home now, Matt turned on the radio, found a classical station. When Vivaldi's *Oboe Sonata* trilled through the speakers, Matt turned the radio off. Even music couldn't comfort him now. He drove in silence, unable to believe his twelve-year friendship with Travis had ended. He had to find a way to unravel all the complications, and make Travis understand. Matt had to forgive himself for having sex with Crystal. He had to purge the secrets and tell the truth. He glanced at his watch. Shit. It was after nine—too late to meet with Radhauser.

The sky had darkened and the stars seemed to come out all at once, a wide path of them spreading over Matt's head as he pulled into the driveway. He hit the remote on his visor and the garage door yawned open. The empty garage reminded Matt his father's Lincoln had been impounded.

He hurried through the dark house, flipping on the entry lights and looking for his dad, while at the same time hoping he wouldn't be home. Maybe he'd let his dad know he'd saved his ass by finding a perfect hiding place for the scissors. But if someone had planted them, his father would be unaware—might not believe Matt if he told him what he'd found and what he'd done with them.

Could he be wrong? Could his dad have killed Crystal and

been so careless as to leave the scissors under the car seat? It was odd how Matt could more easily believe his dad capable of murder than leaving a pair of bloody scissors in his precious car.

A light burned in the master bedroom. He thrust open the door. "Dad, are you in there?"

When he didn't answer, Matt entered. He checked the bathroom and his father's study. Above the roll-topped desk, the moon shone through the stained-glass sails of Matt's grandfather's boat on Lake Michigan. Mom had made the window as an anniversary gift, the year after the old man died. It captured one of the few childhood memories Matt's father had shared with them.

Matt rushed through the rest of the house, calling out his father's name. Maybe the police had found nothing and returned the Lincoln. Or maybe a colleague had picked his dad up and taken him out to dinner.

He hurried back into the kitchen. Then he noticed the red light on the answering machine blinking as steady as a heartbeat. He pushed the button and listened.

"Matt, it's Dad. The police have arrested me for Crystal's murder. They brought bloodhounds and found a pair of bloody scissors they believe to be the murder weapon on our property. My attorney is on his way. I'm sure this will all be cleared up soon. In the meantime, lock up the house. I want you to stay with your mother. I'll call you when it's over. Hopefully I'll be home by Monday. I know you may not believe me anymore, but I'm really sorry, son. Maybe I deserve this humiliation. But you don't."

Matt hit the replay button and listened a second time. There was humility and fear in his father's voice. Matt felt as if someone had dropped a huge boulder on his shoulders, the weight of all the grief he'd caused. *This belongs to you and you must carry it now.*

The old terrors rose. He couldn't shut them out, and he raced around the house in a panic, not knowing what to do or where to turn. He checked all the doors and windows. Mom and Nate probably didn't know what had happened. Matt couldn't think straight. He should have told Radhauser everything. And now it was too late. They'd think he was lying to protect his father.

If Matt hadn't tampered with the scissors, it would be obvious to the police someone had planted them. Radhauser would never believe Loren Garrison stupid enough to leave a bloody pair of scissors under his seat. And even if his dad was guilty, it was still Matt's fault. The only way his dad could have killed Crystal would be if he were enraged, out of his head, because he'd found his son in her bed.

He needed to talk to someone. He thought about Nate, the things Jennifer had said about the way he could be trusted to keep a confidence.

It was dark when Matt pulled into his mother's driveway. The garage door was up. He parked behind her Honda Prelude—a wedding gift from Nate—and stared at the taillights for a moment, unable to take his gaze away from them. "Oh please, God, no," he whispered.

After the wedding reception, his mother had called Danni, looking for him. When he wasn't there, she'd assume he'd be with Travis. With all the hoopla surrounding the wedding, she wouldn't remember Jennifer's spring dance. His mother's next logical move would be to drive to Catalina. It was her new Prelude, with its long rectangular taillights, he'd seen leave at 10:30.

Radhauser had arrested the wrong parent.

Matt's hands gripped the steering wheel so hard his knuckles turned white. His disbelief was so total he didn't know what to say or do. How could he choose? Dozens of thoughts wove through his mind, but he couldn't untangle them. He was a grown-up—a man who'd soon be leaving for college. His father, whom Matt had judged without mercy, was sitting in jail accused of a murder he hadn't committed. Matt couldn't let him spend the rest of his life in prison. But what would happen to his little sister without their mother?

He didn't know how long he sat there, unable to move. It felt like an hour, but it was probably only a minute. This was a big decision and he wasn't sure he was man enough to make it. Who was he kidding? He wasn't a man. Matthew Garrison was a stupid kid, not ready for anything, only afraid.

A wire snapped. He needed to get away, to go as far as his Mustang and the MasterCard would take him.

Without packing anything, he started driving. He was halfway to Phoenix before he realized where he was headed. Then it all made sense. Of course—where else would he go? He felt a giddy happiness. It would all be over soon.

It was after midnight when he hit Flagstaff. He stopped for the night in a rest area off Interstate 40. Matt parked under a clump of huge conifers, pushed his seat back, and drifted off to sleep, the air smelling of pine and rain—the San Francisco Peaks black against the moonlit sky.

At ten on Sunday morning, Matt filled his Mustang with gas. He drove through a McDonald's window and bought two egg McMuffins and a cup of hot coffee. Just outside Flagstaff, he picked up Highway 89. Less than an hour later, he crossed the Navajo Indian Reservation on his way to Page, Arizona.

He'd been twelve the last time he'd been here, and either hadn't noticed or had forgotten the stark beauty of the reservation colors—brown, mauve, and turquoise hills. Pink-bottomed clouds left shadows on the cliffs, darkening their surfaces like spirits moving. He thought about Justin dying in this beautiful part of the country and wondered if his spirit was among the Indian ones whose presence Matt felt as he drove.

Hogans dotted the hillsides—their doorways pointed eastward into the rising sun. There were small square houses and lean-tos covered with pine branches. Along the roadside, crude stands where Navajos sold their jewelry and rugs.

Matt stopped his Mustang while a herd of sheep crossed the road—red paint marking their coats. A little boy, barefoot and brown, ran after them, trying to nudge them back inside the wire fence from which they'd recently escaped.

At last, he spotted the sign. *Welcome to Wahweap. Boat Rentals.*

He parked the car and hurried into the office. A Navajo man wearing blue denim coveralls worked behind the counter.

"I'd like to rent a speedboat," Matt said.

"How many days?"

"Just for today."

"Skis?"

"No, sir."

The man looked at his watch. "Special off-season rate. You bring back by nine, cost forty-five dollars. Gas tank full. You refill before returning boat."

Matt gave him his license and his credit card. "Can you give me directions to Mountain Goat Cove?"

The man got out a map and marked it.

The summer season hadn't yet begun and the lake was relatively empty on a Sunday afternoon. Matt drove the boat at full throttle for about an hour when he began to recognize some landmarks, like Padre Bay and Gregory's Butte. A few houseboats scattered along the shoreline. An occasional larger speedboat passed Matt and he rocked gently in its wake. He found the spot easily, cut the motor, and drifted silently into the half-moon shaped cove.

There were no other boats inside Mountain Goat Cove. He smiled. About thirty feet from shore, he dropped anchor, took off his shoes and socks, rolled up his pant legs and jumped into cold water that came up to his shoulders—so much for rolling up his pants. His family had rented the houseboat in July and the water had been shallower and much warmer then.

"Hello," he yelled as he walked toward the shore. His voice seemed to flow away and then return to him from somewhere above, bouncing off the cliffs. *Hello. Hello.* It was the same echo he'd heard last time, but nestled inside it rang another voice not quite Matt's own—feathery and alive, like a whisper, or someone nearby breathing.

"Justin," he said, and a moment later the name came back. *Justin. Justin. Justin.*

In the weeks and months after Justin died, Matt had pretended his cousin was still alive. He talked to him in his mind—carried on conversations about baseball, school, and Sandra Beasley, the girl who'd sat behind Matt in sixth grade. He'd tried to make his counselor understand that Justin had been everywhere. Matt couldn't even close his eyes because Justin was inside them, too.

Now, as he got closer to shore, Matt shivered. He climbed to the same ledge from which he'd pushed Justin six years ago. The sun had warmed the rocks and Matt lay on his back, pulling the late afternoon warmth around him like a blanket. A few moments later, he fell asleep.

Matt had often dreamed of Justin dead beneath the surface of the lake, his foot caught between two boulders, eyes open but unseeing, his hair floating above his scalp like black seaweed. But today, for the first time, he saw Justin struggling to release his foot, saw the frantic look in his dark eyes, the scraped skin on his ankle, the way the blood curled out, thin as smoke in the water.

When Matt awakened, the sky was dark and the moon had risen over the lake, trailing behind it a luminous path of silver. For a moment, he didn't remember where he was—enveloped by a profound stillness that threw whatever else was in motion into exaggerated clarity. He heard the slap of the waves as they hit the side of the boat he'd rented. Though he could see no other boats, there was the sound of a motor in the distance. Laughter from a moored houseboat. An animal scurrying on the rocks.

He felt gripped by sadness for the absence of Justin, Crystal, and now Travis from his life, his fear for his parents, and the pain of leaving Danni. The feeling began to expand into an icy loneliness that was attached to this place. Grief suffocated all other emotions. He lay back down, pressed his hands to his temples.

He studied the Big Dipper—a string of stars that some long ago astrologer had connected. Like everything else, it was all so random. What if the ancient Greeks had failed to name it and some modern astrologer called it a backhoe instead?

He thought over the old ground again. What if he and Justin had stayed with their family on the houseboat instead of taking the dinghy into Mountain Goat Cove? What if Matt hadn't needed to show off his courage? What if he had taken Justin's hand and led him down the pathway from the ledge, instead of pushing him to his death?

What if his dad hadn't had an affair? If his parents were together, there would have been no chance Matt would have slept with

Crystal and betrayed his best friend. And his mother would never have found him there. If he could cry he would, but he couldn't anymore and the "what ifs" kept coming.

He sat up and looked over the ledge. Beneath him, the water was black and the brighter stars' reflections appeared to sink deeper into the lake, while the more distant stars and the moon, about three-quarters full, seemed to float on the still surface of the water. It gave the illusion of a world turned upside down—as if the sky and the earth had changed places. The gentle movement of the waters made the reflections quiver and dance like diamonds.

Matt dropped his head onto his knees and stayed that way for a long time. How could he make a choice between his parents? He would like to say he prayed for guidance, but he didn't. He was so filled with grief for Crystal, for his devastated mother and his father, a proud and honored philosopher now in prison for a murder he didn't commit. There was no room for prayer inside him.

If he hadn't made a scene at his mother's wedding, if he hadn't gotten drunk and slept with Crystal, she'd still be alive. His redemption seemed unimaginable. His mind felt blank and he tried to keep it that way.

Dazed and tottering, he clambered to his feet and stood, poised on the lip of the cliff, darkness surrounding him. He felt no fear. "You were right, Nana. Grief is the price we pay for love." Without a moment of hesitation, Matt stepped over the edge and dropped into the quivering water below.

CHAPTER THIRTY-SIX

His mother always told him everything had a nature and truth had the nature of rising. When Matt resurfaced, lake water dripping from his hair, the night had grown woundingly cold with a breeze whistling down the cliffs. A transcendence took place inside him, so light he could not imagine what to call it. He was alive and uninjured and something had changed. The boy he was when he left his mother's house was not the boy he was now. He didn't feel like a boy at all anymore. Rumi said, *There is a voice that doesn't use words. Listen.*

He sucked in breaths, closed his eyes for a moment against the feelings overpowering him, the unexpected joy. He had given up all hope of redemption, and yet there it was—sparkling on the star-strewn lake, the same lake that had taken Justin had spared Matt. And Matt listened to the voice that didn't use words. He knew he must tell the truth, free his father, even if it meant his mother would go to jail.

He was drenched and shivering, but more hopeful than he'd been in years. He'd seen Justin. It didn't matter that no one would believe him. Justin, still twelve years old with his shock of dark hair and his bright eyes had met Matt's gaze, levelly and fiercely, and told him to go back. And in that moment, as his feet grazed the same rocks that had held tight to Justin, Matt saw himself in perfect focus—saw that he was forgiven.

He swam over to the speedboat and hoisted himself into it.

By the time he got back to the marina an hour later, his fingers and toes were numb from the cold. He felt as if icicles were dangling from his hair. He slipped into his shoes and socks, the

257

only dry clothing he still had, tied up the boat, filled it with gas and hurried inside, just before closing.

At the marina store, he retrieved his credit card, paid for the boat rental and gas, then charged new clothes. A pair of khaki pants, pleated in the front like Dockers, a red shirt, a yellow jacket with *Lake Powell* embroidered over the breast pocket. He changed in the fitting room, his hands tingling and red. He dropped his still-damp clothes, black and smelling of lake water, into the trashcan on his way out.

* * *

Nine hours later, after stopping for a nap just outside of Lake Montezuma, Matt took the steps to his mom's back porch two at a time. Through the window, he saw his stepfather sitting at the kitchen table, a stack of standardized aptitude tests in front of him. He seemed lost in thought.

Matt rapped on the back door.

A smile blew wide across Nate's face as he leapt up from the table and answered. "You're up early."

Matt paused, tried to regulate his shaky breathing. "It's really important. Are Mom and Sedona still sleeping?"

Nate nodded.

Matt's stomach tightened with the faint beginnings of fear. He had to get the words out before he lost his nerve. "My father's been arrested for Crystal's murder. And I have to tell someone the whole truth," he said, his breath coming way too fast.

Nate grabbed Matt's arm and pulled him into the kitchen. It smelled like last night's spaghetti sauce and freshly-brewed coffee.

Without letting go, Nate led him through to the living room. "You need to sit down," he said as he gently lowered Matt onto one of the loveseats. "Deep breaths. Let them out slowly."

Nate left the room for a moment, then returned with a glass of water and handed it to Matt. "Drink," Nate said and sat on the facing loveseat.

Matt drank.

"I read the article in tonight's paper," Nate said. "But it made no mention of having your father or anyone else in custody."

Matt set the glass on the coffee table. "The police found a pair of bloody scissors I'd hidden in a Saguaro behind our house." He explained how he'd found them beneath the driver's seat in the Lincoln and had wanted to protect his father.

"Oh, Matt. That's not good."

"He didn't do it," Matt said.

"I know how much you love your father, but how can you be so sure?"

Matt told his stepfather about the taillights he'd seen leaving Crystal's house, the way they matched his mother's Prelude.

Nate smiled sadly. "Oh, Matt. Your mother was looking for you. She told me she couldn't go to Aruba with so much turmoil between you. I drove her out to Catalina around 10:30. When she saw your car in the carport, she figured you were spending the night with Travis. She must have forgotten about his dance. Once she knew you were okay, we drove back to the Hacienda del Sol."

Matt's tears rose. His mother had already known he'd been at Crystal's house. No wonder she'd questioned him about the bloody shirt.

"Someone is trying to frame my dad." He gawked at his hands, still wrapped around the water glass, while the facts ricocheted through him one more time. "It's my fault they arrested him. If I'd just told…" Matt's throat tightened. After all the nice things Nate had said about him when he'd offered tuition money for Iowa, Matt wasn't sure he had the courage to tell him about his drunken sex with Crystal. "Jennifer said the students at Marana really trust you and that you keep their confidences like a priest."

Nate gave him a closed-mouth smile. "I try. I know you don't like me very much. But you *can* trust me."

Matt shifted in his seat. "It's not that I don't like you," he said, realizing it was true. "But, please, I need you to promise you won't tell Mom or Sedona."

"Listen to me. This is a murder investigation. What I will promise is we'll work together to figure out what needs to be said to others."

"I didn't tell the police the truth about the night Crystal died."

Blood rushed to Matt's head, an ocean between his ears. He told Nate he'd driven out to Catalina, and Crystal had invited him inside. "We drank a lot of beer."

Nate listened intently, watching Matt without a flinch of judgment. He said nothing until Matt finished. Then Nate stared at him, his head cocked slightly. "Why was it your fault? Did you have an argument with Crystal? Were you angry over her affair with your father?"

He told Nate the truth—he was mostly sad about Danni and angry with himself for the way he'd behaved at the wedding, how he hadn't yet known about his dad and Crystal.

Nate studied him for a moment in which Matt felt naked, like his stepfather could see right through his clothes and into his core. "Is there something else you're not telling me?"

Matt saw the opening. It was like being lost in the darkest part of a cave and seeing a flash of light that gave him hope for a way out.

"You can trust me, Matt. I'll help you if I can. I know you're scared. Anyone would be." Nate's tone was soft, almost sad.

"Why would you want to help me when I've been nothing but a jerk to you?"

Nate smiled. "Sometimes we have to bend the bitterness to get ourselves straight again."

"I lied to the police. I lied to everyone." Matt kept looking at Nate, trying to see inside him, trying to determine if he really could trust this man his mom had married, this man he'd once thought of as his enemy. "Crystal lit some candles and we started dancing. I didn't mean for it to happen."

"For what to happen?"

"I didn't mean for us to do it. To have sex."

When Nate continued to look sympathetic, Matt's tears fell for the first time since Crystal died. He didn't deserve understanding or anything else from this man.

Nate reached across the coffee table and covered Matt's hand. "You may have used poor judgment, but it's not the worst thing that's ever happened." He stood, found a box of tissues on the end table and handed them to Matt.

"She's dead," Matt said. "And now my father is in jail."

He blew his nose, then told Nate about Crystal's anger when he'd mentioned telling Travis, about her wanting him to sleep off the beer. How he'd awakened because he heard a car out front. "At first, I was afraid Travis had come home. I checked the clock. It said 10:38pm."

"That would have been your mother and me."

"I fell back to sleep and when I woke up the second time, I heard the front door open and close, then a car door slam." He explained how he'd run to the window to make sure it wasn't Travis, then into the bathroom to throw up and that's when he saw Crystal in the tub. He told Nate the reasons why he didn't call 911.

"Did you see the second car? Did you recognize it?"

"No. But it couldn't have been a Lincoln. The taillights were round, not the four stacked rectangular lights on Dad's car. And it turned north on Oracle. My dad would have headed south to go home. He was there at 9:30 when you dropped off Sedona. And I don't think he would have left her alone."

Nate's face changed and in it, Matt saw a little fear. "Why did you clean everything up?"

"I was scared. I didn't want Travis to know I'd been there. I wanted to drive home, but I had to stop Travis. I couldn't let him see—"

"I can understand that," Nate said. "I might have done the same thing if it were my friend."

"I don't know what to do now."

"Come with me." Nate led him back into the kitchen, then handed him a yellow lined tablet and a pen. He pulled out a chair at the oak table. "Write down exactly what happened, just like you were writing a school essay. I play racket ball at the club with a criminal defense lawyer. I'll call him, ask him to come by and look over what you've written."

Nate grabbed the phonebook from the kitchen drawer and thumbed through it. "After that, we'll call Detective Radhauser and set up an appointment."

Matt knew his stepfather was right. Sometimes you get a glimpse of something and then you realize you've known it all along. There was no other way—he had to tell Radhauser the whole truth. Every single bit of it.

While Nate called his lawyer friend, Matt wrote out everything he could remember about that night.

An hour later, Nate's friend read it over. "I'd be happy to go with you to see Detective Radhauser," he said to Matt. "It would be best if you had an attorney present."

"I don't want to do that." Matt feared it would make him look guiltier than he already was.

"Are you sure?" Nate asked. "It's for your own protection."

"I'm positive."

Nate looked at his friend and shrugged. "He's eighteen. It's his decision."

Ten minutes later, with his stepfather's hand firmly planted on his shoulder, he phoned Radhauser.

"You're doing the right thing," Nate said. "Our best defense is the truth."

CHAPTER THIRTY-SEVEN

When Radhauser arrived at the Catalina Station on Monday morning, Matt Garrison and his stepfather sat in the waiting area. The kid's hands were tucked, palms together between his knees. His hair was disheveled—a little too much white in his eyes. He looked like he feared being tortured and strung up by his heels.

Figuring Matt had come to plead his father's innocence, Radhauser took off his Stetson, nodded to the overweight sergeant behind the desk, then turned to Matt and Nate. "You're early. Are you that eager to see me?"

Neither of them spoke. Just before he hung his head, Matt's gaze flitted to the left, where his stepfather sat.

Nate cleared his throat. "Matt has some things he needs to tell you."

Radhauser beckoned them both to follow him. He pulled a chair from the break room and dragged it down the narrow hallway. It made a harsh, rasping sound as it slid over the vinyl tiles. He led them into the same interrogation room where he'd first questioned Matt. Radhauser closed the door. He arranged the third chair for Nate, then sat across from them at the table. "Can I get either of you anything?"

"No thanks." Nate answered for both of them.

For a moment, Matt seemed absorbed in adjusting the sleeves of his jacket.

Radhauser set up the tape recorder.

Matt got a panicked look on his face. "Does that have to be on? Can't we just talk in private?"

Radhauser flipped it off and waited. He knew a lot about Matthew David Garrison from the interviews he'd conducted. Knew he'd been a normal, happy kid, until his cousin drowned. Radhauser had researched the newspaper archives and found the story. Matt had been the only witness.

When he'd interviewed Matt's sixth grade teacher, Radhauser learned about Matt's behavior right after the drowning. About his quitting baseball the same year he'd been voted most valuable player on the team that had taken the state and regional championships and was headed for the Little League World Series.

At Canyon del Oro High School, Radhauser read a copy of the essay Matt had written on the place where the dead wait—the place Matt most wanted to visit. For reasons no one had been able to shed light on, Matt punished himself. And it had been going on for years.

Matt handed Radhauser the yellow sheets with his account of the night Crystal died.

Radhauser took them and set them face down on the tabletop. "What did you do that night at Crystal Reynolds' house that has you feeling so guilty?"

The kid's face was red and blotchy. Radhauser could see the words forming, almost hear them rising in Matt's throat. But whatever he'd wanted to say stayed caught there. Even the silence knotted.

"Answer the question, please."

Matt stared at him for a long moment.

Nate stood behind Matt now, with both hands clamped on the boy's trembling shoulders, protecting him. He glared at Radhauser. "What's the matter with you? This is hard. Give him a chance."

"It's okay," Matt said. "He's given me several chances."

In the distance, Radhauser heard the sound of tires humming along Oracle Road, the lonely howl of a coyote in the desert behind them.

Matt was frozen to his chair, his eyes wide and unblinking.

Radhauser knew he had to orchestrate this carefully. "There's something I want to tell you, Matt, and it's really important."

He waited until the kid's breathing had grown more regular and he felt it was safe to go on. "There can be no redemption without telling the truth."

For a few seconds, Matt stared at him.

Radhauser could almost see the kid's mind working, comprehension washing over his face.

"I know that now," Matt said. "It's why I'm here."

"I want you to tell me, in your own words, what happened the night Crystal died."

"I already wrote everything out for you. They are my words."

"It's important that you speak them," Radhauser said.

Nate squeezed Matt's shoulder, then sat back down beside him. "Just tell Detective Radhauser what you told me."

Matt fumbled for a moment, then started to talk. He didn't stop until he'd told everything.

As he listened, Radhauser's mind worked overtime and it was all he could do to contain his excitement. He'd just gotten the missing piece. The context. A new slant on Loren Garrison's motivation. Radhauser's anxiety over arresting the wrong man lifted, then disappeared completely as he closed his eyes and let the scene play out with lightning speed in his mind.

Garrison had driven back to Catalina that night. Maybe he'd gone with good intentions, wanted to apologize for the way he'd behaved earlier. Maybe he'd wanted to tell Crystal it didn't matter whose baby it was, that they'd get married and raise it together. Or maybe he wanted to volunteer to go with her for the abortion, hold her hand through the procedure. But when he got to her house in Catalina, he'd found his son's car parked in the carport. Loren knew Travis was at the dance and his curiosity got the best of him. The house was unlocked. He walked inside, just like he'd done dozens of times before. Loren Garrison hadn't planned to murder Crystal. He'd merely wanted to talk to her.

When he found no one in the kitchen, only empty beer bottles, he wandered into the living room, found the candles still burning. Feeling confused now, he tiptoed down the hallway, saw the short denim skirt, her white low-cut blouse, her bra and panties strewn on the hallway floor. Crystal's door was closed, but not latched. Loren Garrison had eased it open.

And when he did, he saw his son in his lover's bed. Garrison was enraged. What man wouldn't be? It was one thing to know your lover had slept with someone else. But this was too much. The thought that the baby Crystal carried might belong to his son—to Matt—must have lingered in his mind for a moment. A moment in which he saw Matt's dreams for college and his future disappear. The bathroom light was on. He'd show that bitch. He picked up the scissors she'd used to cut her hair. Crystal had drunk too much and dozed in the tub. What could be easier?

"Detective Radhauser, are you listening to him?"

Snapped back into the present by Nate's voice, Radhauser opened his eyes.

Nate stood behind Matt again, both hands on the boy's shoulders.

Radhauser stood. "Thank you for coming in, Matt. I know it took courage to tell me all of that."

"Aren't you going to arrest me?"

"No. The evidence supports your story. Your fingerprints were on the beer bottles. The tire tracks in the carport matched your Mustang. And I found evidence of vomit on the toilet seat— which I now know was yours."

"If you already knew all of that, why didn't you call me in? Put me in jail for perjury or something?"

Radhauser knew he'd bent the rules in ways he never would have predicted. But Matt was only a kid, scared out of his wits. "I wanted to give you a chance to come forward on your own."

"So, you'll let my father go now."

"I'm afraid not. We're holding him over for arraignment. It's scheduled for today at 10am."

Matt leapt to his feet. "But I told you, he didn't do it." With a little help from Nate, Matt sat back down. "Weren't you listening to me? I was there." Matt repeated what he'd already told Radhauser about the sounds he'd heard, the water running into the tub, the car he'd heard at 10:38, which turned out to be his mother and

Nate. And then he'd awakened again around 11:20 and heard the front door open and close. How he'd gone to the window and looked out, heard a car door slam across the street, the engine turn over as the car started and drove away.

"Did you see the car?"

"It was dark."

"So, you didn't see it?"

Matt grimaced and swatted at Radhauser's words as if they were flies. "But it couldn't have been my father's car. The taillights were all wrong. And he was home at 9:30 when Nate dropped off Sedona."

"That's right," Nate said.

"You love your father, don't you, Matt?"

"I guess so."

"Someone killed Crystal Reynolds. Your father had motive, means, and opportunity."

"I'm sure other people had motive, too. How about her boss? Travis said he was really pissed off at Crystal for missing so much work. Or the man who impregnated her? It wasn't my father."

"Thomas Baxter can account for his time. And he has a witness willing to swear he never left the premises. There's a motion light over his garage. It comes on whenever the garage door opens."

"Witnesses can lie," Matt said. "And those scissors I found in Dad's car were bogus. Someone planted them."

"Your father parks in a closed garage. By his own admission, he never leaves the car unlocked on campus or in a shopping center. We found no evidence that a lock had been tampered with. The only other person who has access to that car is you. And you didn't plant the scissors, did you?"

Matt sat up straighter in his chair. He shook his head. "No way. But somebody did."

Radhauser watched the boy struggle to compose himself.

"The morning after Crystal died, my dad swam laps in the pool like he always does on Sunday." Matt told him about the repairman, how Sedona said he claimed he'd gotten a call about a garage door malfunctioning, insisted he was in the neighborhood, why not let him check it out. "The truck said Anderson's Garage Doors. We do it up and down."

"And I suppose she let him in?"

"She opened the garage door for him. I was eating cereal at the kitchen counter. When I looked again, the door was closed and he was gone. My dad got the car greased at the Chevron Station last Tuesday. Don't you see? Opportunities existed. Someone could have planted the scissors."

"What did the garage door man look like?"

"I didn't see him. But Sedona might remember."

"You have a good imagination, don't you, Matt?"

"I'm telling the truth now. I'm not imagining anything. Haven't you ever arrested someone who turned out to be innocent?"

"Yes. And some of them were exonerated when new information came into light."

"That's what I'm trying to tell you." There was frustration and urgency in the kid's voice. "I'm giving you that new information."

"Humor me for a minute," Radhauser said. "Just close your eyes and imagine your father returning to Catalina to talk with Crystal, his lover. The woman who'd just accused him of fathering her child." Radhauser lowered his voice, the way a person does when he hopes his capacity for cruelty will be forgiven. "Now imagine how he might have felt when he found his son in her bed. Imagine the thoughts that may have gone through his mind."

"That's enough," Nate said. "I'm taking him home now."

As soon as Nate touched his arm, Matt's mouth dropped open as if he were about to say something more, but no noise came out. Instead, his face crumpled and his eyes filled with something that to Radhauser looked a lot like doubt.

* * *

At 10am, Karina slipped into the first row of benches, closest to the empty jury box, to await Loren's arraignment. The courtroom smelled like cedar, leather, and old books.

She wore a dark blue skirt with a matching jacket, a tailored white silk blouse, and a pair of sensible navy pumps. When she'd talked with Loren on the phone this morning, after Nate and

Matt left to meet with Radhauser, she had tried to reassure him that new information was still being uncovered.

Even though she believed Loren would be released on his own recognizance, Karina had spoken to a bail bondsman and had come prepared to post up to $300,000 bail. This was a terrible mistake, one she hoped Nate and Matt would help to remedy. Her job for this morning was to do whatever it took to bring Loren home.

As she sat waiting, moments in her life with him came together in a swirl of scenes that moved back and forth through time—scenes sometimes filled with happiness, and just as often tinged with sadness. She tightened her grip on her own arm. This was the man who'd held her hand through the births of both their children. The first man she'd ever loved. The man who'd had an affair with her friend. The man who'd betrayed and humiliated her.

She looked at the prosecution table where a vaguely familiar-looking man reviewed the contents of a manila folder. The man frowned until his eyebrows met over the bridge of his nose. A moment later, he shook his bald head, closed the file, folded his hands on the table in front of him and smiled, as if pleased by what he'd read. He was in his late forties, with broad shoulders and dark, pitiless eyes. She recognized him from photographs she'd seen in the *Arizona Daily Star*. Richard Summerfield, the District Attorney.

The side door opened and the bailiff ordered everyone to rise.

Summerfield stood, adjusted his tie, buttoned his suit jacket, a charcoal gray pinstripe, perfectly tailored—square across the shoulders and curved inward at his waist. He tucked his right hand into the pocket of his trousers—striking the pose Karina had seen attorneys strike on television.

Judge Thornton McGuire entered and took his place behind the bench. "Call the case," he said, nodding to Summerfield, then sank back in his high leather chair.

Everyone except the District Attorney sat.

Summerfield smiled. "The People v. Loren Paul Garrison."

Judge McGuire turned to the bailiff. "Bring in the defendant."

Karina held her breath. She kept pleating and unpleating her skirt.

Loren, dressed in baggy blue cotton pants and shirt that looked like surgical scrubs, was escorted into the courtroom. His long legs were shackled together at the ankles with an eight-inch chain that rattled with each step. He looked as if he'd aged ten years in the three days since she'd seen him, his eyes and cheeks sunken.

A lump rose in her throat, but she swallowed to force it down.

She struggled to get her mind around the realization that Loren was in real trouble. No matter how invincible she had always believed him to be, he was now a defendant in a first-degree murder case. Why had she expected that Loren would be treated differently from anyone else charged with so serious a crime?

She tried to catch his eye, but he kept his gaze straight ahead, shuffling up to the defense table and taking his place beside his attorney, Victor Conrad.

Judge McGuire waited until Loren stopped behind the defense table and turned to face him. "Are you Loren Paul Garrison?"

Loren stood, erect as a soldier. "I am, your honor."

Summerfield stared at Loren for what seemed to Karina a moment longer than he needed to. His eyes narrowed slightly. "Let the record reflect that I am handing the defendant's counsel a certified copy of the information charging Loren Paul Garrison with the crime of murder in the first degree in the slaying of Crystal Louise Reynolds and her unborn child."

Karina cringed, her gaze riveted on the judge.

Summerfield crossed the courtroom and handed a single sheet of paper to Conrad, then returned to his seat.

Without glancing at the document, Conrad laid it face down on the table.

The judge looked directly at Loren as he read the charges against him. "How do you plead?"

Loren took an audible breath. "I plead guilty, your honor."

Karina heard the slap of her own palms against her cheeks. She held her head in her hands. "No," she whispered. "No."

A buzz came from the reporters at the back of the courtroom. Judge McGuire slammed his gavel and demanded order.

The courtroom silenced.

Victor Conrad shook his head hard, as if trying to wake himself up from a nightmare. "I'd like a recess, your honor. To confer with my client."

"In my chambers," McGuire said. "Now."

As Loren followed his attorney out of the courtroom, he turned and looked at Karina. When she met his gaze, he gave her a sad smile.

Something pinged inside her mind. A piece of puzzle she hadn't been able to make fit, snapped into place. Realization trickled over her like ice water. Everything she thought she knew about her ex-husband flew out the window. He hadn't killed Crystal. He had just lied, risking everything, to protect their son.

CHAPTER THIRTY-EIGHT

In his mom's kitchen, Matt thumbed through the Yellow Pages, looking for garage door repairmen. Anderson's Garage Doors was the first listing. He called the number, expecting to get an answering service. Instead, a woman answered. "Hello."

For a moment, Matt thought he'd dialed the wrong number. "I'm sorry. I tried to call Anderson Garage Doors – We do it up and down."

She laughed. "We do indeed. Five days a week. But never on Sunday or Monday."

"Could you check your records and see if one of your trucks made a service call at 6762 North Harelson Road? It would have been about ten o'clock last Sunday morning."

Again, she laughed. "It's a one-truck, one-man business. Just my husband. And, like I told you, Charlie doesn't make calls on Sunday or Monday."

"Are you sure? Could he have made an exception last week?"

"Do you have a complaint about your service?"

"No. Not at all. The service was great. I'm only trying to find the person my dad called so I can thank him. You see, I'm the one who messed up the garage door."

"I'm sorry to disappoint you. But my husband spends every Sunday and Monday, maintaining the grounds at The Silver Spur Steak House out in Catalina."

Matt tightened his hand around the receiver. He felt a surge of energy, as if he needed to run. This had to be more than a coincidence. He was on to something. "Sorry to bother you."

"I hope you find who you're looking for," she said. "It's nice to get a compliment instead of complaints."

Matt checked his watch. Close to noon. Mom had gone to his father's arraignment and his sister had stayed home from school with a sore throat. He sprinted down the hallway to her bedroom, tapped on the door and opened it without being invited. All the tall windows were open and the bedroom was full of sunlight.

Sedona's face was puffy, her eyes red. But she smiled when she saw him. "What's with the red shirt? Does it mean we can finally uncover the mirrors?" Her voice was hoarse, either from the sore throat or from crying. "I'll need them someday. Mom says when I'm fifteen I can wear a little makeup to school. Not that I'll ever want to show my face there again. Did you hear the shit they're saying about Dad on the news? *Ethics Professor Arrested for Double Murder in Catalina.*" Her gaze landed on the Lake Powell logo above his pocket. "You sure you're okay?"

It was strange and unexplainable—their father was in jail and being slandered by the press, but Matt couldn't think of another time since Justin died when he'd been as hopeful as now. "Someone is trying to frame him. And I think I know who."

She flinched. Her eyes went wide and he saw the swift tears fill them. But she held firm while he confided everything except the fact that he'd had sex with Crystal. He had wanted to protect her, but time was running out and he needed her help.

She turned away for a moment and when she looked at him again, her face filled with fear. "Is Dad going to jail?"

"He's already there," Matt said. "Even though you're pissed off at him, you know he could never kill anyone. And with some help from you, I intend to prove it."

"Really? You want me to help you."

He nodded. "If you feel up to it."

"I'm not really sick." She leaped out of bed and pulled on a pair of overalls under her nightgown. "I couldn't face the kids at school."

Matt looked at her again, intensely focused on her eyes. "Tell me what that guy who showed up to fix the garage door last Sunday looked like."

"Why?"

"Think about it. The door worked fine when I used it on Saturday night. So why would Dad call for a repair? Who makes service calls on Sunday, then just takes off without even leaving a bill? That man must have planted the scissors in Dad's car."

She tugged a yellow sweater over her head, then maneuvered out of her nightgown. It puddled on the floor at her feet. She kicked it into the closet. "Why would he do that?"

"I don't know," Matt said. "But it can't be a coincidence this garage door guy works as a groundskeeper at The Silver Spur. Maybe he was the one who killed Crystal. Maybe he used to be her boyfriend. Maybe he's the father of her baby." He paused for a moment. "Maybe the garage door man saw Dad with Crystal. Maybe he knew about their affair and wanted to blame Dad for her murder."

Sedona looked terrified. The red kept rising on her cheeks, like mercury climbing. "Kind of nerdy. Short and stocky. He wore a black baseball cap, but the hair that stuck out from its edges was dark. He had on black-rimmed glasses that made his eyes look gigantic. His white coveralls were way too long for him. He had the legs rolled up like a real dork."

"Excellent," Matt said, impressed by her powers of observation.

"Sometimes I wish we could rewind Dad. And know him from the beginning."

At moments like this, she was not the little girl he'd helped up the steps to their tree house, the girl who'd stolen his Halloween candy, and left her dance leotards on the bathroom floor, or the one who had to be bribed to stand still for her vaccinations. She was insightful, forgiving, and brilliant.

"Finish getting dressed and I'll drive you out to The Silver Spur. We'll see if you recognize their gardener."

CHAPTER THIRTY-NINE

Even though Loren Garrison had pleaded guilty, Radhauser kept working the case. No one ever pleaded guilty to a first-degree murder charge unless they'd struck some kind of deal with the District Attorney. Something didn't feel right.

He called ahead to make sure Gracie worked the lunch shift. He hadn't been able to stop thinking about the garage door repairman Matt had mentioned, the strangeness of his showing up without having been called, and the opportunity he'd had to plant the scissors.

When he'd called Anderson's Garage Doors, trying to get an emergency service call, the man's wife said she wished people would stop phoning. Radhauser pushed her, said he'd pay triple the going rate. Then she told him to call The Silver Spur Steak House out in Catalina. Now that was one big coincidence. And sure enough, the van Matt had described was parked in the lot when Radhauser arrived.

He pulled into an empty spot and parked his Bronco. Waves of heat rose from the asphalt. When he pulled open the double doors into The Silver Spur, Gracie was on the phone behind the podium, jotting a reservation into the book. She smiled when she spotted him. "If you came back for the pineapple upside-down cake, you're a little bit early. Baxter hasn't baked them yet."

He tipped his Stetson for a second before taking it off. "I'm here to see you. But I'd love a big glass of iced tea."

She smiled uncertainly at her boots, then slid a glance toward the bar where a bartender Radhauser had never seen before served beer to what looked like the same men who'd been here the last time he'd talked to Gracie. She ordered his iced tea and waited for it to be poured.

"Your usual corner table by the window?"

"Why not? Can you spare me a few minutes?"

She nodded and led him around the bar. It smelled like fried onions and beer. They both slid into the booth. "How are your classes going?" Radhauser asked.

"I'm in the middle of final exams. Memorizing all the bones in the body for anatomy. Did you know the foot has twenty-six? Twenty-eight, if you count the sesamoid bones at the base of the big toe. But you didn't come here to quiz me." She paused and smiled. "At least, not on anatomy."

"What can you tell me about that Anderson Garage Doors panel truck in the parking lot?" Radhauser took a swig of his tea.

"That belongs to Charlie," she said, then confirmed what the man's wife had told him, that Anderson did the landscaping work on Sunday and Monday mornings. "Baxter pays him in free beer and all the food he can eat. Are you having problems with your garage door?"

"Yes. And when I saw his truck, I thought this might be my lucky day."

"He's cutting Baxter's grass. But he'll be at the bar soon."

"I need you to do something for me, Gracie."

"What?"

"Go back to the night Crystal told you she was pregnant."

Gracie looked away, then back at him again, her dark eyes wet and accusing. "How do you know she told me that?"

"Because she was happy, and you were her best friend and she wanted to share that good news with you."

Gracie smiled sadly. "She couldn't wait to tell her boyfriend. She was already planning a May wedding in the courtyard at the Arizona Inn. She said she wanted me to be her bridesmaid." Her eyes filled with tears.

"Did she mention how far along she was in the pregnancy?"

"About a month. She'd taken a home pregnancy test."

Radhauser nodded. So, Crystal had lied to Gracie.

"This is really important. Did Baxter know?"

"I didn't mention the pregnancy," she said. "Bax was disgruntled over Crystal not showing up when he'd expected her to work the bar. I tried to explain how excited she was about planning a wedding."

"How did Baxter take the news?"

"He started pacing, and muttering to himself about what an idiot he'd been. At first, I couldn't make sense out of it. Apparently, he'd had some papers drawn up making Crystal a co-owner of The Spur. He said they'd planned to have a baby together. Maybe even get married."

"Did you have any idea he and Crystal were romantically involved?"

"There were some rumors. But Crystal never confirmed any of them. And she bitched about him as much as the rest of us." Gracie gave him a sad smile. "Crystal wasn't a bad person. She just wanted to be loved. And she was an expert at getting men to fall for her. Now that I think about it, it's probably why Millie didn't like Crystal very much." Gracie's eyes lit with mischief for an instant. And in that moment, Radhauser could see what she must have looked like as a little girl.

For the first time since his wife and son died, Radhauser felt the stirrings of tenderness for another woman. Gracie was at least a decade younger, but she understood both the folly and the burden of being human.

Maybe after all this was over, he'd call her, see if she'd like to have dinner or take a picnic lunch up to Mt. Lemmon. He shook his head, an attempt to get a grip on his emotions. He was in the middle of a murder investigation. And, despite Garrison's confession, it was beginning to look as if he'd arrested the wrong man. He didn't have time for distractions. "Did Baxter eventually calm down that night?"

"At first his voice was quiet and really sad. Then he went ballistic, called her a lying bitch." Gracie stared at Radhauser for a moment, her eyes wide. "But we all knew it was his grief talking."

"What happened next?"

"He stormed out of the bar, left it for Millie and me to handle. We heard his front door slam. I wanted to warn Crystal. But Millie said she'd go over and talk to him. And if Baxter left, she'd call Crystal. Baxter didn't go anywhere."

"How about Millie? Did she leave the premises before midnight?"

Gracie shook her head. "She went over to talk to Baxter, but she didn't leave the premises. Most of my tables look out on the parking lot, and her car was there until she went home around one. Baxter said she had a headache, that he'd told her to lie down for a while. She did. But the headache didn't go away. Bax behaved real nice and helped me close up."

Something cracked and a new possibility seeped in, further diluting Radhauser's conviction that Garrison killed Crystal.

CHAPTER FORTY

When Matt heard the sounds of a lawnmower behind the house, he and Sedona inched around the side of the garage and into the backyard. All around them, the air smelled like freshly cut grass. The garage had another electric door on the back and a driveway that led to an alley. Matt looked up—examined both sides of the back door. There were no motion lights. He thought about the alibi Radhauser had told him about. No one inside the restaurant could have seen Baxter leave from the rear of the garage.

A tall man, wearing a pair of white coveralls, pushed the lawnmower. He had his back to them. "Is that the man?" Matt asked.

"No," Sedona said. "Too tall and not fat enough. But the coveralls are right."

A moment later, another man stepped out the sliding glass door and handed the tall man a bottle of beer. He wore white pants, a long-sleeved chef shirt, and a pair of white oxfords. It was Thomas Baxter, the man he'd met at Crystal's memorial service. The man Travis called Barcode.

Sedona tugged Matt's arm. "That's him," she whispered. "He's not wearing glasses or the baseball cap this time. But it's the same man. I'm positive."

Matt sensed the danger, felt a blush of fear rise on his neck. He grabbed Sedona's arm and tugged her around the corner of the garage and out of sight. "You go sit in the Mustang and lock the doors while I talk to him."

Her expression turned instantly grave. "No way. I'm better at this than you are."

"It's too dangerous. We should go see Radhauser, tell him what we found out."

"I can do this," she insisted. "I know I can."

He practically dragged her back to his Mustang. He buckled his seatbelt and started the car, but before he could put it in gear, she opened her door, slipped out, and ran towards Baxter's house.

By the time Matt caught up, she'd rung the doorbell and Baxter stood in front of them. "What can I do for you?"

Sedona gave him her most brilliant smile. "Good morning. I'm taking orders for glazed donuts. You're not going to believe this, but my school band got invited to the Tournament of Roses parade. It's quite an honor. We're going to represent the whole state of Arizona. But we have to raise a hundred thousand dollars."

"Good luck, kid."

She used her foot to stop the door from closing. "Please, Mr. Baxter," she said, flashing another smile. "You could sell them in your restaurant for twice what you pay for them. People love to help kids. I play the clarinet," she added. "And I'll put your name on a little sign and wave it in front of the television cameras in Pasadena. You'll be proud, I promise."

He turned to Matt, who stood with his legs wide and his arms folded across his chest. "You're Travis's friend, aren't you?" Baxter asked.

"Yes, but he's also my bodyguard," Sedona said, her eyes sparkling. "My mom is overprotective. And Cassius Clay had another gig."

Baxter laughed and invited them inside. He wasn't all that large, but the room seemed to shrink when he entered it. "Give me a minute. I was in the middle of something."

Sedona pulled a small spiral notepad from her purse. It was hot pink. "Can I sign you up for three dozen glazed?"

He leaned against his kitchen counter, gluing a tiny doorknob on an elaborate dollhouse, when he stopped and looked at Sedona again. "Don't I know you from somewhere?"

"I've never seen you before in my life," she said. "But you probably saw one of my on-stage performances. I'm a member of the Tom Thumb Players."

Again, he laughed. "Do I look like the kind of man who goes to the theater?" He squinted and stared at her hard. "What do you really want?"

Knowing he'd recognized her, Matt grabbed Sedona's arm. "We need to go and leave this poor man alone. He doesn't want any donuts and you've bothered him long enough."

"He asked me a question." Sedona jerked away, ignored Matt, and looked up at Baxter. "I want lot of things. But right now, I want you to buy my donuts. When I'm older, I want to be an actress. And this trip to Pasadena could be my big chance to get discovered."

Matt stepped closer. His fists were cold and knotted shut. He looked around. Through an open doorway, he saw a pink bedroom, a canopy bed. A bookcase painted white with pink rosebuds. The long, windowless wall held a hand-painted mural of a castle and a horse-drawn carriage with a dark-haired princess inside.

"If it were your little girl," Sedona said, shooting a glance at one of the photographs on his wall, "with a chance like this, wouldn't you want people to help her reach her dreams?" Sedona's gaze locked with Baxter's.

He grinned. "You're something else, kid. Put me down for three dozen. And then get out of here. I've got work to do."

Sedona smiled. "Thank you. And we'll leave as soon as you tell me why you masqueraded as a garage door repairman last Sunday morning."

Matt felt something like ice-cold electricity shoot through him. He reached for her arm and pulled her close to him.

Baxter laughed. "You've mistaken me for someone else. I was right here last Sunday morning. Making pineapple upside-down cake, like I always do. Go over to the restaurant and have a piece. Tell the pretty, dark-haired waitress, her name is Gracie, that it's on me."

Baxter followed them to the doorway. His shoelaces were too long and the tips made a clicking sound against the hardwood floor.

Once they were outside, Baxter closed the door behind them.

CHAPTER FORTY-ONE

Radhauser was nearly finished with Gracie and about to head over to talk to Charlie Anderson when Baxter entered the restaurant, dressed as a chef. He looked around, spotted Radhauser talking with Gracie, and a big smile crossed his face.

Gracie slipped from the booth and leapt to her feet. "I gotta go," she said, and was halfway to the bar before Radhauser had a chance to respond.

Baxter whispered something to Gracie and she hurried over to a table where two middle-aged men sat studying their menus.

Radhauser motioned Baxter over to the booth. He didn't make a habit of lying to suspects, and lying to Baxter about his DNA was the most gratuitous kind of cruelty, but Radhauser believed he had no other choice. "I didn't know you were a cook, too."

"I hired someone a few years ago. But I still work the kitchen a couple days a week. And I bake pineapple upside-down cakes almost every morning. What brings you all the way out here again? You got a crush on Gracie?" Baxter worked a toothpick into the gap between his front teeth.

"I came to talk to you."

Baxter laughed, a dull clattering sound. "I already told you everything I know." Sunlight shone through the window and particles of dust hung in the air above the table.

"Sit down for a moment. I talked to the ME last night. He put a rush on your DNA and I have some paternity results for you."

Baxter slipped into the booth and stared at Radhauser.

"Crystal was three and a half months pregnant with a girl."

Baxter passed a shaking hand over his eyes. "A girl? Are you one hundred percent—" He stopped abruptly. "Do you know if she was mine?" Baxter's voice wobbled like a tightrope walker without a net, who'd made the mistake of looking down.

"Do you want to go someplace more private?"

"No. Just tell me."

Radhauser set his glass down too hard and his iced tea sloshed over the side. He took a deep breath and lied. "The DNA matched. No doubt. I'm really sorry, Mr. Baxter. But that baby girl belonged to you."

There was an awful pause. The air in the room had a tightly packed feel, dense and brittle. Radhauser kept staring into Baxter's eyes, locking on, and in the moment it took for Baxter to change his expression, to force the truth from his face, Radhauser caught him.

Baxter's gaze shifted toward the window.

Radhauser felt the warm current in his blood. Baxter had either killed Crystal or knew who did. The kid was right. Loren Garrison had been framed.

And now Radhauser had to be very careful. "I need to get going. In case you haven't heard it on the news, we've arrested a suspect in Crystal's murder." He wanted to put Baxter's mind at ease until Radhauser had time to get the proof he needed. He slipped out of the booth. If Baxter noticed, he gave no sign.

At the register, Radhauser got out his wallet to pay for the tea, glanced at the photograph of Laura and Lucas he'd recently placed in the compartment where he'd once carried his driver's license. To his surprise, a feeling of profound belonging washed over him. They'd been a family. And in some ways, they always would be, but it was time for him to move on.

"Is that your wife and son?" Gracie asked.

"Yes." Radhauser had finally figured out what mattered most was giving yourself over to the people you loved.

"They're beautiful," she said.

"Yes. They were."

He gave Gracie a five-dollar tip, then looked back at the booth where Baxter still sat with his head in his hands.

When he heard the sound of a lawnmower, he followed it around the garage and into the yard behind Baxter's house. He made a note of the second garage door, realizing in a flash that Baxter had it installed because of his phobia about backing up. *So, that's how he managed to get his vehicle out of the garage without activating the motion light.*

Radhauser walked along the concrete driveway to the alley where Baxter could have easily driven around to the windowless side of the restaurant and gotten out onto Oracle Road.

When the man cutting the grass spotted Radhauser, he stopped the mower and turned off the engine. His face was red and his forehead covered in sweat. He wiped it with the back of his hand.

Radhauser hurried over to him. "I'm Winston Radhauser. Are you Charlie Anderson?"

"Yeah. How'd you know?"

"Your wife told me I'd find you here. I've got a garage door that won't open. I saw your vehicle last Sunday around Oracle and Ina."

"That wasn't me," he said. "Bax borrowed my van to pick up crepe myrtle at that nursery down on Oracle and Orange Grove." He nodded toward three five-gallon pots on the back patio. "Call my wife back. She can set you up with an appointment for Tuesday." He walked over to a picnic table on the deck and picked up a bottle of beer, took a long swig, and then placed it back on the table.

Radhauser headed for his car to radio for backup. Halfway across the parking lot, he spotted Matt's Mustang, parked beside the Anderson's Garage Door van. Both Matt and Sedona stood beside it. While he had to hand it to the kid for his clever piece of detective work, he hoped Matt hadn't done anything stupid.

Matt smiled when he spotted Radhauser. "Sedona recognized Baxter as the guy who posed as the garage door repairman. Do you believe me now?"

Radhauser tipped his Stetson. "Any time you want a job working for me, you're on, kid. We could use another pitbull. But right now, I want you to go home and wait. I'm going to radio for backup. And then I have another lead to follow. But I'm arresting Thomas Baxter for evidence tampering. I know he planted the scissors in your father's car. And if he didn't kill Crystal, he knows who did. One way or another, your father is coming home."

Sedona gave him one of her dazzling smiles. "You sure you don't need any more help?"

Radhauser laughed. "You've done quite enough, thank you very much."

"May I go with you when you tell my dad?" Matt asked.

Radhauser nodded, a sense of pride welling inside him. So, this was what it felt like to watch a boy turn into a man. He dropped his arm across Matt's shoulders. "I'm sure your dad would like that. I'll call you when the paperwork is done."

"I want to go, too," Sedona said. "I can't wait to see his face when I tell him how we solved the case." She bowed from the waist.

Matt clubbed her gently across the back of her head as she climbed into the Mustang. He closed her door and walked around to the driver's side. There he paused, grinned, and tipped an imaginary Stetson at Radhauser, then got into the car.

Radhauser stood for a moment, watching the Mustang turn out of the parking lot and head towards Oracle Road. Then he called for backup, took the handcuffs from his car, slipped his revolver from his holster, and hurried back inside for Baxter.

* * *

Millie lived in a small cottage-like bungalow on Sparrow Wood Lane, about four miles north of The Silver Spur. The house was painted yellow and had blue shutters with hearts cut out of their centers. A lavender-colored picket fence surrounded the front yard. The house had no garage, and the white Chevy Beretta GTU with the spoiler and red racing stripes in the driveway made Radhauser smile, despite the gravity of his mission, and it told him Millie was home. He opened the gate and walked up the poppy-bordered sidewalk. The property surprised him in that it was perfectly maintained—the small yard landscaped with rocks and drought-friendly plants. A place Millie obviously loved.

He tapped on the door.

She opened it, wearing a pair of white shorts and a blue and white sleeveless sailor shirt cropped just above the waist—an outfit that might be appropriate for Sedona. "Hey, sugar. It's about time you asked me out on a date."

Radhauser tipped his Stetson. "May I come in?"

She nodded, gave him a big smile and stepped aside. "I reckon there's never been a time I wouldn't invite a handsome cowboy into my house. Can I get you something?" She cocked her head. "Coffee, iced tea, or me?"

He laughed. "I'll take the tea."

"Too bad. I'm much sweeter." She poured two glasses of sun tea and handed him one.

He took it, along with the napkin she offered, and sat down at her kitchen table beside a bay window overlooking the backyard. He removed his Stetson and set it next to his iced tea. There was a bowl of fresh fruit on the table—apples, oranges, bananas, grapes, and Bing cherries. The mingling smells made his stomach churn. Or was it the task in front of him?

Millie sat across the table, her gaze fixed on his. "Did you have that talk with Baxter?"

Radhauser had already lied about this once, and rationalized another wouldn't matter. "I put a rush on the DNA. Turns out the baby was his."

Her face, partially hidden behind her hair, grew very still. "I thought those tests took a long time?"

"They do," he said, and then lied again. "Unless they're ordered by the Medical Examiner."

"Does Bax know?"

Radhauser nodded.

She grimaced. "How'd he take it?"

"Not well." Radhauser kept his gaze firmly on her face, wanting to see even the slightest reaction to what he was about to say. "I had to arrest him for impersonating a garage door repairman and planting the murder weapon in Doctor Garrison's car."

She shuddered as if a small bolt of electricity had hit her. "Trust me, Baxter ain't got it in him to kill no one, especially Crystal." She picked three cherries from the fruit bowl, removed their stems and lined them up in a row on the table. She glanced at him quickly, as if checking for a reaction to what she'd said.

Radhauser remained silent. He'd thought he solved the case, had enough circumstantial evidence for a good prosecutor to send Loren Garrison away for life. And that realization frightened him more than anything. He needed to tread carefully. He couldn't afford any more mistakes.

Millie seemed like a straight-shooter, someone who'd tell the truth, especially if she thought Baxter would be in trouble if she didn't.

"Planting those scissors makes Baxter look pretty guilty. Based on that and the fact he was the baby's father, I suspect a jury will convict him." He paused for a moment, giving her enough time to absorb his words. "But we both know who did kill her, don't we, Millie?" he finally said.

She gave him a sad and closed-mouth smile before she nodded.

"Do you want to tell me about it?"

"Did Bax give me up?"

"No."

She gave him a real smile this time, then popped one of the cherries into her mouth, reached across the table and squeezed his hand. Her eyes puddled with tears. It took her a moment to form her question. "So, how did you know?"

Radhauser took a drink of tea, then set the glass down. "Solving a murder is like putting a jigsaw puzzle together. Sometimes you need a missing piece and once you've got it, the rest is easy."

"Am I the missing piece?"

He nodded. "You're in love with him, aren't you?"

She stared into his eyes for a moment, but said nothing.

"I need you to tell me what happened that night."

Millie sighed, a bottomless sound. "Gracie tried to make excuses for Crystal missing work again. Thought she could make it better by telling Bax how excited Crystal was about getting married. But it didn't work. Bax got all riled up. He stormed out of the restaurant. I heard his front door slam from inside The Spur. When the bar crowd thinned out, I rushed on over to check on him."

"What was he doing when you got there?"

"Pacing. When he saw me, he started talking about how him and Crystal planned to have a baby together. How he'd had paperwork drawn up to make her co-owner of The Spur. That really got to me. It was our dream. Not much more than a hamburger shack when Bax and me first started. We go way back to high school together." Millie stopped and stared at her hands. "He called me his partner. I guess he only meant it in the business sense. I…well, I took it to mean life."

Radhauser waited a moment, then prompted her to go on.

"I'd heard Crystal puking her guts out in the bathroom back in late January. So, I figured she was pregnant. I thought maybe I'd go talk to her, tell her how much Baxter would love the baby. And if she and her boyfriend didn't want it, then maybe Bax and me…" She lifted her shoulders, a trace of lost hope for a life with the man she loved still visible on her face. "We could raise it up together."

"Gracie said your car was in the parking lot all evening."

"I used Baxter's car. But I swear to God, I didn't go there to kill Crystal."

"If not, why didn't you take your own car?"

"When I said I wanted to talk some sense into her, Baxter tossed me his keys. I think I mentioned his fetish thing. Backing up got so hard that he had another door put on his garage. I wasn't trying to hide anything. His car was already pointed toward the back."

"What happened when you got there?"

"Crystal's front door was unlocked. I knocked, but not real loud. I knew Travis took her car to the dance, but I saw another car in the carport. The house was dark except for the kitchen and them candles she'd left burning on the coffee table." Millie rolled her eyes, as if she couldn't imagine anything more stupid. "It was real quiet. I tiptoed down the hallway. A light was shining from under the bathroom door. Crystal's bedroom door was almost closed. I inched it open and saw someone in her bed. I swear to God he looked like a kid about Travis's age. It made me damn mad. I opened the bathroom door to confront Crystal and there she was passed out in the tub. So drunk she'd whacked all her hair off. And that was her best feature, too."

Millie kept shaking her head, as if she still couldn't believe what she'd seen in Crystal's bed. "I could tell by the swell of her belly that I'd been right. She was at least three months. When I seen that empty vodka bottle, I thought about Bax's baby and how Crystal's drinking could damage it. What's that thing they're always warning pregnant women about? Fecal alcohol something." She paused and looked at Radhauser again.

He wished he could laugh, but humor had deserted him. "Fetal alcohol syndrome," he said.

"Yeah. That's the one. I went into the kitchen to make some coffee so I could sober her up, talk some sense into her. But when I opened the drawer looking for the filters, I seen all them steak knives Crystal had stolen from Bax. At least a dozen."

Millie started crying, big copious tears dripping from her cheeks.

Radhauser looked around for a box of tissues, then settled for his napkin. He handed it to her.

She blew her nose, patted the bags under her eyes.

A few quiet moments passed.

"What happened next, Millie?"

"It's weird, I know. But I kept staring at that drawer full of knives, thinking about Bax giving her half The Spur, and her stealing from him like that. It made me madder than a hornet. Even madder than when I caught Harold— he was my first husband—in our bed with his secretary."

Radhauser had seen enough murders to know the way rage could build up like a pyramid of sticks laid out for a fire. And when the match was struck, rage could take a person inside it and use them in ways they'd never thought possible.

Millie blew her nose again. "I guess I must have gone back into the bathroom and picked up them scissors, because the next thing I knew, I stood in the middle of her bathroom with blood all over me." She tried to drink some of her iced tea, but her hands shook so hard the ice cubes rattled in the glass.

Radhauser gave her a moment. "Then what did you do?"

"I stood there, I don't know how long. Crystal stared right at me, but her eyes had gone blank, like on them deer heads hunters hang over their fireplaces. I grabbed the towels from the racks and wiped off as much blood as I could. I took off my cowboy boots and carried them, along with the towels and the scissors out the front door. I even remembered to wipe off my prints. Then I crossed the street, got into Baxter's car, and drove to his house. I knew Bax would be a suspect and I didn't want Gracie to see the motion light and think he'd gone out, so I drove through the alley and used the back entrance."

"What did Baxter say when he saw you?"

"At first, he didn't say anything. He just stared at me. Then he told me, real gentle like, to take a shower. He gave me some of his ex-wife's sweats and a pair of his socks to put on, and said he'd burn the towels, my bloody uniform, and boots. And then he gave me money to buy new ones. I didn't want to take it because I already had some spare uniforms and a pair of new boots. But Bax insisted. He said not to worry, that it would be okay. He walked me to my car, gave me a hug. He told me to go home and get some sleep, that he'd help Gracie close up The Spur."

Radhauser didn't have another set of handcuffs with him, and he wasn't sure he'd use them if he did. He stood and helped Millie up. "I'm sorry," he said, and meant it. "But I have to arrest you for the murder of Crystal Reynolds."

When he finished reciting her rights, he gave her time to close up her house, call a lawyer, and her sister in Bisbee.

Her brown eyes lifted up toward him. "Don't feel bad, sugar. I figured you'd be coming for me. But I do need a big favor."

Radhauser nodded for her to go on.

"I want you to see to it that Travis gets my Beretta. It's sporty and perfect for a college boy. I'll sign over the title. It's all paid for and still smells brand smacking new. I never let no one smoke in it. Not even me."

Radhauser told her he'd talk to Travis about the car, then took her arm as if escorting her to a dance, and led her to his car.

CHAPTER FORTY-TWO

In early August, just two weeks before Matt was scheduled to leave for the University of Iowa, Travis phoned. "Hey, man, what's up?"

Matt clamped his fingers down on the phone. His hand started to tremble. He held the receiver tight against his ear in an attempt to stabilize it and stop his shaking.

"I get it you're surprised to hear from me, but I didn't expect speechless. I'd really like to talk before you leave."

Matt's eyes filled with tears. "You name the place and time and I'll be there."

Travis remained quiet for a moment. "Thanks, man. I'm in Patagonia with the baseball team. Think you could drive down on Saturday and meet me at the lake? I finish up with practice around 7pm. I could be there at 7:30. By the pier where my mom took us fishing with Justin."

* * *

Matt parted the reeds at the entrance to the old wooden fishing pier where Crystal had once helped them load worms onto their hooks. He could still see her in a pair of blue shorts and a bright green T-shirt, laughing at three ten-year-old boys afraid of nothing except those slimy, squirming bloodworms they had to feed onto fishhooks. He smiled at the memory and then looked for Travis.

He sat at the end of the pier, tossing a navel orange into the air as if it were a baseball and staring out at the water, his feet dangling over the edge.

When Matt sat next to him, he smelled the tangy orange, the slight pine scent of Travis's shampoo, and the dust and sweat on his baseball jersey—that familiar Travis odor.

"Thanks for calling."

Travis said nothing. He peeled the orange, dropped the peelings into the water, then handed half of it to Matt. The two of them sat quietly for a few moments, eating orange slices and watching the twilight, as the sun's final shadows grew longer. Just before the light disappeared, Travis turned to Matt. "What's up with the blue shirt, dude? Did the stores run out of black T-shirts?"

Matt didn't know how to explain, how to tell Travis the way the spring and summer had changed him. "I confronted my demons and now I'm expanding my wardrobe and all my other horizons."

"That's good," Travis said. "Me, too."

For a moment, Matt was uncertain what Travis meant. Was he expanding his horizons to include Matt again? Had he found a way to incorporate their friendship into the rules of The Narrow Way?

"I've decided to leave the church," Travis said, as if he'd read Matt's thoughts. "And I've been seeing my father."

Matt cocked his head and stared at Travis, unable to believe what he'd just said. Travis told Matt about the letters Radhauser had found, and the way he'd honored Crystal's wishes by giving them to Travis on his birthday. About the note Crystal had written explaining what she'd done and why. "Detective Radhauser had already talked to my dad and he had a phone number. I called him right away." Travis grinned. "He has that same gene you got, dude. He bawled when I told him who I was."

Matt was too shocked to form any words.

"Dad came down last weekend to watch me practice." Travis told him how great it had felt to finally have a dad cheering on the sidelines. "I got him a University of Arizona baseball cap." Travis looked happy, as if there was a big window full of sunlight in his eyes. "I've been reading a lot, man. And I've concluded that God lives inside all of us. Love doesn't need any church to exist. The funny thing is, it was inside me when I walked away from Bryan and The Narrow Way. Imperfect love is still love, don't you think?"

Matt thought about his dad and Crystal. He didn't know if she'd loved his father, but he was certain she'd loved Travis. "I submitted my questions to Iowa and they sent me a summer reading list. Joseph Campbell said the greatest hell is being separated from yourself."

"That's good, man. It's the right school for you."

Matt swallowed. "I've missed you." He took a chance Travis would understand everything those three words implied.

"Radhauser told me how Columbo Matt and his dramatic sidekick, Sedona, led him to Baxter and Millie." He shook his head. "I would never have believed they could do something like that. Just goes to show you, man. Never trust a guy with a comb-over."

Matt laughed.

"I'm sorry I doubted your father."

"I doubted him, too," Matt said. "But something good did happen. Sedona is spending every other weekend with Dad, so I won't have to worry so much about him while I'm in Iowa."

"I'll pick up some of the slack, man, and get him and Sedona tickets to a couple of my home games. Nate and Karina, too."

The night sky over the water grew black, and away from the glare of street lamps the moon rose, speeding toward the lake, leaving behind it a trail of shimmering sequins. The air cooled quickly and smelled like the trout lakeside campers pan-fried over their fires.

It was hard for Matt to remember that sense of falseness in so many things he'd done, the hovering grief over Justin. This night he was pure awareness. There was a huge, spacious quality to his existence as the waves lapped the shore, as regular as a heartbeat, while the reeds under the pier brushed their own rhythms against the bottom of the splintered boards.

"I know you tried to protect me from having to see my mother in that bathtub the way you did."

Matt no longer needed to confess he'd had sex with Crystal. It would only hurt Travis further. And he understood the impulse to remain quiet was the same one Matt's parents and Crystal had for keeping their affair a secret.

Travis soft punched Matt in the shoulder. "I'd like to have my brother back, dude. Even if he's a clueless geek." His gaze met Matt's and held.

Matt believed they were looking right into each other's souls, as though there was no air or wood or flesh between them. As if they both understood and always had, exactly who they were and why they had to do the things they did, unquestionably, with love and without accusation.

For a moment, Matt didn't speak, didn't want to break the spell. "I'm here," he finally whispered. "I never left."

The lake was a sheet of black glass beneath them. And the moon and stars were mirrored there, silver and bright.

Matt didn't know how it was that he and Travis had drifted so far from that innocent and wise place in the desert where their friendship had first begun. In truth, he didn't know how any of us lost ourselves, or how we were rediscovered. He didn't know what mysteries eventually sustained us through life. But he did know that he and Travis would discover their separate visions, and help each other in the quest to find that inward light where miracles of love and compassion could leap out of the most ordinary hearts.

Into our dreams.

And into our waking.

ABOUT SUSAN CLAYTON-GOLDNER

Susan Clayton-Goldner was born in New Castle, Delaware and grew up with four brothers along the banks of the Delaware River. She is a graduate of the University of Arizona's Creative Writing Program and has been writing most of her life. Her novels have been finalists for The Hemingway Award, the Heeken Foundation Fellowship, the Writers Foundation and the Publishing On-line Contest. Susan won the National Writers' Association Novel Award twice for unpublished novels and her poetry was nominated for a Pushcart Prize.

Her work has appeared in numerous literary journals and anthologies, including Animals as Teachers and Healers, published by Ballantine Books, Our Mothers/Ourselves, by the Greenwood Publishing Group, The Hawaii Pacific Review-Best of a Decade, and New Millennium Writings. A collection of her poems, A Question of Mortality was released in 2014 by Wellstone Press. Prior to writing full time, Susan worked as the Director of Corporate Relations for University Medical Center in Tucson, Arizona.

Susan shares a life in Grants Pass, Oregon with her husband, Andreas, her fictional characters, and more books than one person could count.

FIND SUSAN ONLINE:

Website
www.susanclaytongoldner.com

Facebook
www.facebook.com/susan.claytongoldner

Twitter
twitter.com/SusanCGoldner

Blog
susanclaytongoldner.com/my-blog---writing-the-life.html

Tirgearr Publishing
www.tirgearrpublishing.com/authors/ClaytonGoldner_Susan

BOOKS BY SUSAN CLAYTON-GOLDNER

A BEND IN THE WILLOW

Released: January 2017
ISBN: 9781370816842

In 1965, Robin Lee Carter sets a fire that kills her rapist, then disappears, reinventing herself as Catherine Henry. In 1985, when her 5-year-old son, Michael, is diagnosed with a chemotherapy-resistant leukemia, she must return to Willowood and seek out the now 19-year-old son she gave up for adoption. Is she willing to risk everything, including her life, to save her dying son?